May All Of You And God Forgive Me

An Unsolved Murder
Mystery

Enjoy

[signature]

BY HANS M. BRODER, JR.

BOOKLOGIX˙

Alpharetta, GA

First edition August 2021

ISBN: 978-1-6653-0325-5 - Softcover
ISBN: 978-1-6653-0324-8 - Hardcover
eISBN: 978-1-6653-0326-2 - eBook

Book design and cover by Mia Broder
Illustrations by Waymon Michael McCormick, pages: iii, 4, 14, 25, 43, 46, 82, 83, 168, 218, 273, 319, 332
Illustrations by Michael F. Broder, pages: iii, 5, 340 Illustration by Mia Broder, page: 184
Photography by Mia Broder, pages: 9, 349

www.hansbroder.com

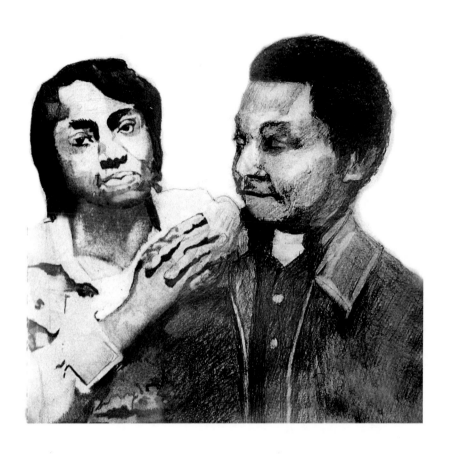

In memory of Virginia and Jerry Banks

Table of Contents

Part II: Trials, Old Jail, and Sheriff

Part III: Prison, Defense Team, and Appeals

Acknowledgments

I owe special thanks to all the individuals who provided information about events that occurred nearly fifty years ago. I was able to interview members of the King and Banks families, former detectives, lawyers, jurors, judges, and witnesses who were involved or had knowledge of the facts.

I visited The University of Georgia Library and poured through its archived *Clayton County News-Daily* and *Henry and Clayton Sun* newspapers. There were archived newspaper articles from *The Atlanta Journal and Constitution* that were extremely helpful. Thanks to Rita Camp who gave me access to all the old newspaper publications of *The Henry County Weekly-Advertiser* and *Henry County Herald*.

I read two books that provided insight into the history of Henry County: *Henry County Georgia: The Mother of Counties* by Vessie Thrasher Rainer and *True Southerners, A Pictorial History of Henry County, Georgia* by Gene Morris, Jr., County Historian. Two other books provided details of the murders and subsequent arrest and incarceration of Jerry Banks: *Sins of Henry County* by Charles L. Sargent and *In Spite of Innocence* by Michael L. Radelet, Hugo Adam Bedau and Constance E. Putnam. I perused a periodical, *Perversion of Justice: A Double Murder in Henry County Re-examined*, by Donald E. Wilkes.

I also relied on resource materials obtained from Wikipedia, Murderpedia and various news articles found on the Internet. I was able to view Henry County Superior Court transcripts of the Jerry Banks' trials obtained from court archives.

I owe thanks to Sharon Graham and family members who assisted in the editing of the manuscript; my daughter, Mia Broder, who provided the design; and Waymon McCormick and Michael Broder, who provided the illustrations for the book. And finally, the publication would not have been possible without the assistance of my writing consultant, Susan Soper.

Preface

My mother told me that I was going to be blessed with success and happiness because I was born on Sunday. In many ways her prediction came true. I would have a meaningful career and a happy marriage in comfortable surroundings. As a member of a large family, I had a wholesome upbringing. I was raised on a dairy farm where my parents instilled the European values of hard work. I was able to spend the majority of my life in Stockbridge, a rural community in middle Georgia. During my time as a local banker, I was able to keep abreast of the community events through well connected individuals who had a part in the shaping of Henry County's history.

In 1974, Henry County experienced one of the most puzzling and bizarre murders of its time. Who killed the well-known high school music director and a college student and left their mutilated bodies in the thicket? The high-profile murder case stunned the citizens of the community. For forty-seven years, no one had stepped forward to confess or produce any evidence that could lead to the identity of the assailant. On two occasions law enforcement was certain that it had the killer behind bars, but evidence later proved otherwise.

This writing, based on true events, is considered literary nonfiction. While the names and events surrounding the murders are factually true, some of the subplots are fiction and some others do not follow in chronological order. It is not to say that they did not occur, because they could have. The story follows familiar themes: a murder, an investigation, an arrest, a trial and a conviction. The outcome, however, is far more complicated and takes several twists and turns before an injustice is undone.

Several well-publicized murders occurring during the period that have a connection to the story are also mentioned. However, there are many other incidents of note that occurred during the twelve-year period. The sequence of events weaves through a memorable time frame of the local county's history between 1970 and 1982. The characters mentioned are everyday people who reflect the culture, attitudes, opinions and ways of life during the period.

In the late 1960s Henry was considered a large county by area, but its population only supported two high schools, one for all Black students and one for all White. The residents in and around the small towns where this story unfolds are down-to-earth, God-fearing, conservative folks. All persons are honest, treating one another with respect and Southern hospitality. Historical information is liberally described throughout the book.

To borrow a title from an old Western movie, the story features the Good, the Bad and the Ugly. *The "Good" is the main character accused of committing two vicious murders based on circumstantial evidence. The "Bad" is the law enforcement and the legal system that arrested, prosecuted and the sentenced him to death. The "Ugly" is the loss of life and the human suffering that resulted. The subject matter and the portrayal of the characters in the story are not intended to criticize or lay blame. Looking back, it is easy to second guess the actions of law enforcement, the prosecution, defense attorneys and the judges. The goal of this writing is to tell the story close to the way it happened. One must remember this occurred in the 1970s, a different era. History is a great teacher and much has changed since then. There are lessons to be learned from the tragedies. To paraphrase an often-used quotation: "Those who refuse to recognize the mistakes of the past are bound to make them again."*

Part 1

Murder and Investigation

CHAPTER 1 | Marvin King's and
Melanie Hartsfield's Last Day

Marvin King, born in 1938, was raised in Brunswick, Georgia and was one of seven children. His father made a living as a roofing contractor. While in school, Marvin was given the opportunity to play the trumpet in the school band. He soon excelled in playing the instrument and was selected for the All-State Band. He graduated from the University of Georgia, received a master's degree from Auburn University and later completed his six-year teacher certification at Auburn. In the late 1960s he accepted the music director position at Jonesboro High School in Jonesboro, Georgia. As a teacher and a mentor to the music students, he was popular and had a positive impact on many students.

To support his family, Mr. King also played professionally to supplement his teacher's income. His career introduced him to several well-known musicians, most notable Doc Severinsen, the former band leader for *The Tonight Show Starring Johnny Carson*, and trumpet-playing legend, Harry James. Mr. King was also a member of a local band named "The Mark Five" which played Motown and popular dance music.

Eighteen-year-old Melanie Ann Hartsfield resided on Mt Zion Road in Morrow. She graduated from Jonesboro High in 1973. She had played in school bands throughout her junior high and senior high years. An above average student, she served as band

Melanie Ann Hartsfield

officer for one year and was one of the better clarinet players in the concert band. Melanie was a full-time student at Clayton Junior College in Morrow, majoring in secretarial studies. Music, however, was her primary interest and she was Clayton Junior College's student representative to the Atlanta Symphony Orchestra. Her grade point average allowed her to be a member of the Phi Beta Lambda Business Club.

***

On November 7, 1974, Marvin King arrives at Jonesboro High School at his usual time, around 7:30 a.m. He goes to the teachers' lounge and pours his morning cup of coffee, two creams, but no sugar. He reads the Thursday's *News-Daily* that is delivered to the school. He enjoys the peace and quiet as he catches up on all the local news before the other teachers arrive. The lounge gives the teachers the opportunity to talk about certain students and gossip about the goings-on in the front office. Mr. King has no interest in the idle chatter which has become commonplace in the lounge. He focuses on the sports section that discusses the upcoming football game with LaGrange High School Saturday night. LaGrange has a powerhouse football team with a perfect 7-0 record. They appear to be destined to make the state playoffs for the third straight year. Jonesboro has a competitive team, but it will be no match against LaGrange, even though Jonesboro has home field advantage. Mr. King is more interested in his Cardinal marching band outperforming its counterpart, which is usually the case.

When the homeroom bell rings, Mr. King makes his way to the

band room. It will be a busy day for him as his first class is the concert band, which is preparing for state competition. Later in the morning he travels to Kilpatrick Elementary School on Tara Road to witness a beginner band's performance. From there a stop at the Jonesboro Library on Smith Street and then he plans to return to the high school. The marching band will have its final walk-through for the upcoming game after classes end at 3:30 p.m.

Because the Jonesboro Cardinal marching band has approx-imately one hundred members, the school system has hired an assistant band director. Terry Blaylock is just out of college and is a former student and band member at Jonesboro High. Three des-ignated seniors act as assistants. It takes everyone's full attention to coach and teach this year's group of disorganized musicians. The marching band includes all the senior high music students in grades 9 through 12. Those who have difficulty with the routine, especially the freshman, are encouraged to concentrate on staying in step with the band member directly in front of them and not to worry about playing their instruments. In fact, sophomore John Henry, who excels in class, finds marching and playing his trom-bone at the same time a challenge. He misses so many notes that Mr. King instructs him just to finger the notes and refrain from blowing into the mouthpiece.

Since the songs and marching routine have not changed from the previous week, the band director plans to skip the eve-ning's marching practice and leaves the duties to Mr. Blay-lock.

Mr. King's responsibilities also include supervising the music and band directors at the nearby elementary, middle, and junior high schools. Band par-ticipation has become a priori-ty among the parents in Clay-ton County. Students consider

Marvin Lee King

it "cool" to be in the band. Because of his many duties, Mr. King is granted a day off from time to time. One of these off days is the upcoming Friday. He has planned to use his free day to go deer hunting with Mark Foster, one of his Mark Five band members. Even though he prefers the time spent at the lodge swapping stories rather than sitting in a tree stand waiting to ambush a helpless deer, he welcomes the time off.

Mr. King makes a telephone call to principal Fred Smith. "Fred, I have some personal business I need to take care of after lunch. I have informed Terry what sheet music the students should practice. I will be back before 3:30 p.m."

Mr. King hurriedly walks to the school's parking lot, gets into his red Opel wagon and leaves the campus.

***

At 7:30 a.m. Melanie Hartsfield grabs her McGraw Hill textbook and her Cardinal school jacket with the four band emblems sown on the large letter "J." Her drive west on Mt. Zion Road and north on Highway 54 to Clayton State Junior College takes only fifteen minutes if there are no traffic issues along the way. This quarter her secretarial studies classes are in the morning—second and third periods. Fall quarter is moving along quickly with only six weeks remaining before final exams. She likes her instructors, especially Mrs. Jackson who teaches Advanced Typing. Her years of playing the clarinet give her tremendous finger dexterity which enhances her typing skills. Melanie was already a good typist, but she decides to take the course to improve her accuracy. She normally out-types the others in the class on the five-minute speed tests. But, since typos and spacing errors reduce the final per minute word count, she is not satisfied with her past performance.

Her second class is Beginning Stenography. As an aspiring secretary, she knows that she needs to be proficient at shorthand. She feels that she is making progress and is on track to make an A in the course.

Melanie has a part-time job at Riverdale Junior High coaching the school's chorus. She is scheduled to be there at 1:30 p.m. But first she must meet with Mr. King to discuss some rumors that she has heard and seeks his advice. Mr. King is known to be a sympathetic and caring teacher who frequently offers counsel to students. He promises to meet her at the convenience store at the corner of Highways 138 and 42 in Stockbridge after the completion of her classes that morning.

While she is in her car waiting for Mr. King, a black sedan pulls into the convenience store parking lot. Neither the driver nor the passenger gets out of the vehicle. At approximately 12:45 p.m. Mr. King arrives. Melanie grabs her pocketbook, locks her car and hops into Mr. King's car. They drive off. Within a few seconds the dark sedan exits the parking lot. Who are those people in that car and are they following the Opel?

CHAPTER 2 | The Narrator

I am Hans Broder, a country banker and long-time Henry Countian. I am the narrator of this story. As best as my memory will allow, I will attempt to guide you through Jerry's strange, sad and tragic journey through the legal system. I am not a lawyer or affiliated with law enforcement, but some of my friends are. They would provide me with details that were not readily available to the general public. Numerous persons familiar with the Jerry Banks saga shared their individual accounts with me. I am relying on the assimilation of these interviews, news reports, trial transcripts and prevailing rumors to tell this sad tale. I kept up with most of the Banks who I grew up with and resided with in the immediate area surrounding the farm. However, I knew little of what became of Jerry Banks beyond childhood. People outside of Henry County had never heard of him. That would soon change.

My employer is a small community bank located on Highway 42 in Stockbridge. The First State Bank's staff consists of two loan officers, two customer service representatives, three part-time and full-time tellers and three clerks and bookkeeping personnel. I am the CEO. The bank is considered small in asset size but is known to have a big heart when it comes to helping its customers.

My name should tell you that my family roots did not originate in Georgia. In 1951, the Broder family relocated to an area in north Henry County known as unincorporated Stockbridge and became residents of the Banks community.

Horseshoe Farm

At the conclusion of World War II, my father, Hans Broder, completed his military service in the Swiss Army. As a result, he was able to complete his university studies. With a degree in engineering agronomy, he found a teaching position at a local Swiss agricultural college. He was soon approached by two businessmen who were considering the purchase of farmland in America. The investors needed someone knowledgeable in agriculture to start up a dairy farm. It was an opportunity too good to pass up. Thinking it would be only a short-term assignment, he accepted the challenge. Margrit, his wife, and the three children were able to stay in the home of Margrit's parents in Switzerland. Hans took a train to La Havre, France, boarded the ocean liner, U.S. America and headed for New York. His eventual destination was Stockbridge, Georgia.

Hans left behind a large family in a small community in north-eastern Switzerland. Located in the Rhine Valley, the town of Sargans lies between two majestic Alps. In the visible distance is the small principality of Liechtenstein and neighboring Austria. Hans Broder gave up his Swiss roots, which included eating the best chocolates and his favorite Emmentaler cheeses. There would be no more alpine hiking in the summer or skiing in the winter.

My dad soon realized that the job was taking longer than he expected and planned for his family to join him. I remember the voyage on the SS Ile de France *across the Atlantic, the flight from New York and the drive that ended at the farm eight days later, May 22, 1951. Little did we know that Stockbridge would become our permanent home. My parents eventually purchased the farm*

and became U.S. citizens. They would have five more children—
we totaled six boys and two girls.

Even though no cowboys or horses would be utilized at the
dairy, the original Swiss owners called their purchase, Horseshoe Farm because the name had an American West connota-
tion—ranches are large and owners revered. The 430-acre farm
was situated on both sides of Buster Lewis Road, three miles from
downtown Stockbridge. Most rural roads in Henry County were
unpaved and the areas along the roads were sparsely populat-
ed. The farmland contained several small streams and rich bottom lands that made the area very conducive for dairy farming.
Horseshoe Farm was surrounded by the Thames dairy to the west
on Red Oak Road, the Bailey and Jarrett dairies to the south on
Hudson Bridge Road and the Clark and Raleigh Henry dairies
to the east on Rock Quarry Road. A portion of Horseshoe Farm
on the east side of Buster Lewis Road adjoined Henry and Ethel
Banks' homesite.

Life on the farm was difficult at times. Initially, Hans and
Margrit were not familiar with the culture and spoke little English. Nevertheless, they were industrious, hardworking and determined to persevere. In addition to the Holstein milk cows, they
raised hogs and chickens for eggs and meat. They had a boun-
tiful garden and a small orchard that provided vegetables and
fruits for their sauerkraut and apple strudel. Hans insisted that
all his children contribute to the operation of the dairy, whether milking the cows, feeding the livestock, gathering up the hay
or taking care of the day-to-day general maintenance. While the
other smaller surrounding dairies discontinued operation for one
reason or another, Horseshoe Farm survived and thrived.

The Broders were looked upon with curiosity by the neighboring Banks families. They were White, spoke a strange language,
were staunch Catholics and had never tasted southern fried foods.
Their attitude toward Black people was unlike what was commonly expected from Whites in the deep South. Until the Broders
arrived in America, they had never met a Black. There were dark
skinned people from the Mediterranean regions that could be seen
traveling through Switzerland, but there were none who resided

in the German-speaking Rhine Valley where they grew up. So, the Banks appeared just as strange to the Broders, as the Broders appeared to the Banks. Despite the differences, a trust and respect quickly developed between the Broders and the Banks. They became particularly good neighbors. Many of the young Banks men and their neighboring friends worked on the farm, especially when it came time to load hay or haul silage.

CHAPTER **3** | Involuntary Manslaughter

On June 11, 1970, 19-year-old Jerry Banks is attending a family birthday cookout in McDonough. His siblings and various family members are present. Through the course of the evening an altercation between his older brother Ludie Banks, Jr. and his cousin Robert Walker erupts. When Walker approaches Ludie Banks, Jr. with a knife, Jerry intervenes holding a handgun. Walker disregards Jerry's warnings to stop and continues to wield a knife in a threatening manner. Jerry fires his gun twice into the air in an attempt to stop his advances. Walker continues to come toward Jerry. The third shot strikes Walker. Jerry is subsequently arrested and charged with murder.

Henry County Police Officer Babb answers a call early Sunday morning at a Highway 155 address and discovers a wounded Robert Lee Walker. The 22-year-old Black male is rushed to Grady Hospital in Atlanta. He is pronounced dead a few hours later that morning from a single gunshot; the bullet had struck him just below the heart on his left side.

Without money, Banks cannot afford an attorney. The judge selects an attorney from a small pool of young lawyers who have agreed to do public defender work. The successful, seasoned lawyers seldom volunteer to do court-appointed work. The court's pay for the service is less than the usual hourly fee obtained from regular clients. In the Flint Circuit the Court pays lawyers $150 per case which is to include their expenses.

The Hon. Hugh Dorsey Sosebee assigns A. J. (Buddy) Welch, Jr., as the appointed public defender. Welch graduated from the University of Georgia in 1966 and the Walter F. George School of Law at Mercer University in 1969. After receiving his juris doctorate degree, he returns to McDonough to join Earnest Smith's law firm. Attorney Smith, who has a successful law practice, promises Buddy a partnership.

Henry County is in the Flint Judicial Circuit which also includes Butts, Lamar and Monroe counties. The circuit has only one Superior Court Judge and one Solicitor. Criminal cases in these counties are heard by Judge Sosebee and prosecuted by Edward McGarity.

Judge Sosebee was born in 1916. He graduated from the University of Georgia in 1938 and earned his law degree from the Walter F. George School of Law at Mercer University. He lives in Forsyth and had served as the city's attorney and represented Monroe County. He was elected as solicitor for the Flint Judicial Circuit in 1954. In 1964, Mr. Sosebee was appointed Superior Court Judge of the Flint Judicial Circuit by Gov. Carl Sanders. He is a 32nd Degree Mason, member of the Strict Observance Lodge No.18 of Forsyth, and a devout Christian. His courtroom decisions closely follow his conservative and religious values.

Judge Sosebee regularly travels from one county courthouse to the next, hearing cases in his jurisdiction. A strict Judge, Sosebee knows all the facets of the law. He seldom must rely on a law clerk to look up case law for him to render a legal opinion. Having been a former district attorney, he is not easily influenced by loquacious lawyers with their courtroom antics. He carefully deliberates on every motion before handing down an impartial decision. Judge Sosebee has no use for lawyers who have not properly prepared for trial. A continuance motion is hard to come by in his court. If a jury finds an accused guilty and the evidence is overwhelming, he passes down a stiff sentence. If an accused has a prior conviction in his court and is found guilty again, the defendant could expect to receive the maximum sentence.

Edward E. McGarity prosecutes all felony cases that originate in unincorporated Henry County, as well as in the four cities of McDonough, Stockbridge, Hampton and Locust Grove. Mr. McGarity was sworn in as solicitor for Flint Judicial Circuit in 1964 to fill the unexpired term vacated by the now Judge Sosebee. Mr. McGarity was later re-elected. The title of solicitor was changed to district attorney; however, the duties remained the same.

District Attorney
Edward E. McGarity

Mr. McGarity was born in McDonough on November 30, 1919. His father was a businessman engaged as a cotton merchant and farmer. He graduated from Crichton's Business College. He is an active member of the First Baptist Church of McDonough, the Elks and is a World War II veteran. Mr. McGarity is active in politics having served in the Georgia House of Representatives and the Georgia State Senate.

Mr. McGarity is a member of a long-standing Henry County family. They own sizable amounts of farmland, rental property and other real estate. They own the local feed and seed store and have financial interests in several small businesses. There are very few people in Henry County who have not heard of the McGaritys. Likewise, there are few people born and raised in Henry County Mr. McGarity does not know. With such local knowledge, District Attorney McGarity has a "home-field advantage" when it comes to picking jury members. He is an excellent trial lawyer and an effective District Attorney (D.A.). He has lost very few cases and would be a formidable opponent for a young public defender.

Since twenty or so guests at the McDonough cookout witnessed the shooting, mounting a reasonable defense is a challenge. In lieu of a trial, Welch suggests that Jerry consider negotiating for a lesser sentence. It is a common strategy in capital offenses where there are mitigating circumstances for the district attorney to offer a plea deal. If the defendant agrees to plead guilty to a lesser charge, the district attorney would recommend to the judge that he hand down a lighter sentence. The plea bargain removes the case from the court calendar and lightens the judge's workload. Judges seldom deny such motions from opposing attorneys. The district attorney is satisfied because he gets another conviction on his resume. The county taxpayers benefit from the cost saving of not having a trial.

Mr. Welch proposes a plea bargain to District Attorney McGarity believing Banks acted in self-defense and any reasonable jury will find him innocent. "The young man does not need to rot in jail! But I believe I can get him to agree to a manslaughter charge if he can be assured of a probated sentence," Mr. Welch tells Mr. McGarity.

Mr. McGarity responds that he is not sure that Banks is innocent. "He came to the cookout with a loaded gun. He, like the victim, had too much to drink. I believe he went there looking for trouble. Why would anyone who attends a family gathering need a gun, unless he intends to use it?"

Jerry tells police that his brother, Ludie, had mentioned that he was going to have it out with his cousin the next time he saw him. Ludie swore that he was going to stop Robert from messing around with his wife. Jerry brought along the gun in case he needed to intervene as peacemaker.

The police report states that Banks' brother had gotten into an altercation with Walker, his cousin. As tempers flared, Walker threatened to cut him. Banks fired warning shots, but that did not stop Walker. Several witnesses said he had a knife. The detectives looked, but never found a knife anywhere at the crime scene.

Welch says, "Banks has no record of any past run-ins with the law. This was his first offense. I believe the jury will view Banks as a victim of circumstance rather than a vicious killer. He may be a brash young man who made a poor decision, but he has a job and deserves to be home with his family."

McGarity replies, "The jury may see Banks as a school dropout with no ambition and a nuisance to Henry County. If he killed his blood relative, what will he do the next time he loses his temper?"

Mr. McGarity reminds Buddy Welch he is a young lawyer who has not tried many capital-murder cases. Jurors in Henry County, both Black and White, do not like murderers walking the streets regardless of the circumstance. "You have the chance to get Banks out of jail in a few years. You will be risking a life sentence without parole or maybe the death penalty for your client. Think about it. Think about it long and hard. I will give you twenty-four hours to make up your mind, that's all."

Buddy Welch goes to bed that night pondering what to do. The case is already on the calendar and scheduled for trial in three weeks, so there is not a lot of time. He thinks he has a plausible defense, but he knows that all his witnesses are Black, the victim is Black, and Banks is Black. Many deep-rooted Southerners do not trust Black people. Whether they speak the truth or not, it does not matter.

It is a sleepless night. As a lawyer, he has yet to make such a difficult decision. Banks' life is in his hands. He does not like playing God.

First thing in the morning, Welch calls Banks' wife, Virginia, to ask her if she wants to participate in his meeting with Jerry. He tells her about the discussions he had with the D.A. the day before. She is anxious to come. She has not seen Jerry for two weeks and misses him. She has a lot to tell him about their mischievous little two-year-old. Little Jerry is getting into everything and has many new words that he is trying to say. Welch picks up Virginia and they drive to the jail to meet with Jerry. Once in the meeting room, Buddy addresses the couple.

He tells them that the D.A. is willing to drop the first-degree murder charge with a guilty plea to second-degree murder. Judge Sosebee will probably hand down a sentence of ten years in prison, but with good behavior, parole is just a couple of years away.

Virginia exclaims, "Ten years, oh my God!"

Banks cries out, "The man was coming at me with a knife. He would have killed me and other people if I hadn't shot him. I shouldn't have to go to jail for that!"

Mr. Welch says, "If you go to trial and are found guilty, you could get the death penalty. Since the police did not find a knife at the scene, the D.A. will convince the jury that you attended the cookout with the intent to shoot Walker. If Mr. McGarity is successful, the jury will find you guilty."

"Oh my God! Jerry, what, have you done?" Virginia blurts out.

Mr. Welch continues, "I know you will miss Virginia and little Jerry, but the years will go by quickly. You will be here in the Henry County Jail and your wife will have visiting privileges. It is your decision, Jerry. If you are found guilty, you will probably be sent to the prison in Reidsville. "I will appeal your sentence. We should be able find witnesses or some evidence that can be used to get the sentence overturned."

Virginia spends another twenty minutes with Jerry before the guard signals that time is up. Uncertain of what to do, she goes to see her uncle, J.W. Lemon, the owner of the Lemon's Funeral Home, and her pastor at Mt. Olive Baptist Church to discuss and pray over their decision. Aunt Opal advises her to tell Jerry not to take the D.A.'s offer and the others agree. The next day Virginia tells Jerry to go to trial and take his chances with the jury. Aunt Opal and Uncle J.W. promise her that they will help her with the babysitting and offer to give her money to pay expenses if she is left without Jerry for a while.

Jerry is adamant that he shot Walker in self-defense and had no intention of killing him. He wants to have his day in court. Mr. Welch informs Mr. McGarity of Jerry's decision. Unfortunately for Jerry the jury does not buy Jerry's account of what happened. Too many witnesses testified that Banks acted in a fit of anger and challenged Walker to a fight. The police were not able to find Walker's "alleged" knife. He is found guilty. Judge Sosebee subsequently sentences Banks to life imprisonment.

***

Young Jerry Banks gets a taste of prison life as he is introduced to the Henry County Jail. The Henry County Work Camp, which at one time housed the County's less violent criminals, was closed in 1965. As depicted in the movie, *Cool Hand Luke*, starring Paul Newman, the inmates are allowed outside the camp to maintain county roads and buildings. Without the work camp, prisoners are sent to the Henry County Jail that has a "bull pen." The name originated from the notorious Andersonville prison where inmates were kept in close confinement. Prisoners were herded into the facility like cattle. Conditions in modern "bull pens" certainly do not compare to those of years past, but it is not a place for claustrophobic inmates. At a complete maximum, the fifty by fifty-foot building could house up to thirty prisoners. Bunk beds are stacked closely together. There are no desks, but two card tables, three sinks and three open toilets shared by the inmates with no privacy. Prisoners are allowed to shower three times a week in a separate bathhouse. Escorted in pairs, prisoners are given fifteen minutes to wash and shave. Exercise is limited to one hour a day which includes loitering around the small fenced-in yard beside the jail. Food is limited to cereal for breakfast, sandwiches for lunch and a full meal with meat and vegetables for dinner.

Jerry Banks' good behavior allows him to become a trustee. Instead of being confined strictly to the bull pen, he is allowed to work outside during the day with the other trustees. He is also promised one of the few private cells when one becomes available. The guards who supervise the work detail do not consider Banks dangerous or a flight risk. He spends the next nineteen months in the Henry County Jail.

Public defender Buddy Welch files an appeal to the Georgia Court of Appeals. Welch is able to produce the knife that Walker had allegedly used in his confrontation with Banks. He produces witnesses who heard the warning shots. With the knife, new witnesses and the re-evaluation of the testimony presented at trial, the justices deem Banks' action not to have been pre-mediated. The Georgia Appeals Court determines that under the circumstances the penalty was too harsh. The justices rule that Banks is entitled to a new trial.

Rather than retry Banks, District Attorney McGarity, with the concurrence of Judge Sosebee, offers Banks a plea deal. Jerry Banks is released for time served and receives a one-year probation, in exchange for a guilty plea of manslaughter. With Jerry's consent, Welch enters a plea of guilty to involuntary manslaughter.

Jerry Banks is released from the Henry County Jail in January 1972. He is twenty years old, a free man and has a wife and an infant son who need him.

CHAPTER 4 | Henry County, My Home

There is little one can tell you about Henry County that would interest a non-resident. Its early history has produced few local distinguished patriots or noteworthy statesmen. As a result, the county is named after a Revolutionary hero, Patrick Henry, who lived and died in Virginia. The City of McDonough, the county seat, is named after Commander Thomas McDonough, who is recognized for his heroics at Lake Champlain during the War of 1812. Neither patriot was ever known to have set foot in Georgia. At least the City of Stockbridge, the northernmost town, can recognize a local citizen. Dr. Levi Stockbridge was a respected and long-standing teacher who made invaluable contributions to the youth of Henry County. Later, the county produced local Confederate soldiers who distinguished themselves during the Civil War. A relative of the Crumbley family, Charles T. Zachry, is honored on a monument erected in the McDonough City Square.

Henry County, twenty miles south of the state capitol, is one of 159 Georgia counties. It was created in 1821 by the Georgia State Legislature from land acquired from the Creek Indian Nation. In the beginning, Henry County was an undisturbed wilderness with very few permanent residents. As a defensive measure, the State of Georgia encouraged settlers to populate the region to create a buffer to fend off unwanted military forces who wished to lay a claim on the land. As an incentive, the Georgia Legislature estab-lished a land lottery. For a nominal fee, interested individuals and families could register to draw for one of the available surveyed tracts. Those with past military service and/or other pre-deter-mined qualifications were given a free draw in appreciation for past service. Each participant was awarded a tract that consisted of approximately 200 acres. Settlers soon arrived to claim their chosen parcel and began clearing the land. Some of the earli-est arrivals were the Crumbley, Kelley, Hinton, Lewis and Childs families. The abundance of timber provided lumber for homes as well as firewood for cooking and heat. The cleared land was cul-tivated into pastures for livestock. Settlers relied on their gardens to produce vegetables and fruits for the dinner table.

Small settlements containing farms, homes, schools, churches and stores began to appear throughout. Those along the streams began to thrive. Roads to connect these settlements soon led to the establishment of towns. The cities of McDonough in 1823, Stock-bridge in 1829, Hampton 1873 and Locust Grove in 1893 became business hubs. The agrarian way of life shaped the culture of its citizens and was the driving force behind the local economy. Re-covery from the Civil War brought cotton to the forefront as the cash crop of choice in the region. Eli Whitney's cotton gin re-moved the hulls surrounding the cotton balls and seeds embedded in the fiber, thus giving textile mills clean fiber to weave. The cat-alyst for growth, however, was the completion of the two railroads that crisscrossed Henry County in the 1890s. The railroads put the county on the map. Placards at the depots identify the partic-ular stops: Stockbridge, Flippen, McDonough, Locust Grove and Hampton, names of cities and towns travelers never knew existed.

The invasion of the Boll Weevil in 1919 virtually wiped out the promising cotton crop and sent the rural economy into a tailspin. Production was already on the decline as the soils were depleted from overplanting as farmers were unaware of proper fertiliza-tion and crop rotation methods. The Great Depression made rural living more difficult. There was little opportunity to earn money. Subsistence depended solely on what one could grow on the farm and trade for needed goods and services.

Unemployment, bank failures, foreclosures and bankrupt-cies were common. Those who were fortunate to find work in the City of Atlanta left the county. Those who remained on the farm were beset with prolonged poverty. For the uneducated and poor, sharecropping had become the primary means of subsistence.

The post-World War II period brought some improvement to the local standard of living. Economic stimulus came from Washington in the form of Social Security Benefits. Georgia Senator Richard Russell sponsored the School Lunch Program and the Food Stamp Program. These programs uplifted the living conditions for the rural families. President Eisenhower's Federal Aid Highway Act provided the funding of interstate highways and the eventual construction of Interstate 75 through Henry County. By 1950 Henry County was on the road to recovery. The humble population of 15,857 increased exponentially in the coming years. Henry County had finally become an attractive place to live. Since Henry County is within easy driving distance of Atlanta, the residents have the best of both worlds: they could live in the country and enjoy city wages.

In the 1960s the Vietnam War was causing a great turmoil and unrest throughout the nation, especially for those who were eligible for the military draft. All males above the age of eighteen who did not have health issues or legitimate deferments were subject to be called. Eleven Henry Countians died while on duty in the Vietnam conflict, the only war America has ever lost.

While as a community we mourned those who died serving our country, we applauded the moon landings. We were disappointed by the resignations (under fire) of President Nixon and Vice President Agnew and we wondered if the computer was more than a passing fad. Locally, Hartsfield Airport became a regional hub, and Interstate 75 dissects the county enhancing travel to and from Henry County. Stockbridge would get a new 100-bed hospital, Atlanta International Raceway in Hampton draws thousands to watch NASCAR races and, today, McDonough Power and Equipment employs 1,100 to build the Snapper Lawn mowers.

I am excited and look forward to the 1970s. I have graduated from college, gotten married, left my high school teaching post and settled into my banking position. Henry County is my home. I know of no other place where I would rather live.

CHAPTER **5** | About Jerry Banks

Jerry Banks was born on January 18, 1951, in the unincorporated part of Henry County. Kelleytown was named after one of the early settler families attracted to the area because of the abundance of good farmland. He had brothers, Ludie and Perry, the oldest being Ludie, and a sister, Mary Jo. For the most part the four were raised by their mother, Nannie Dodson.

Jerry Banks grew up in the South at a time when it seemed that television aired only news, wrestling, New York Yankee baseball games and nothing else of interest. For young Blacks whose households owned a television set, there were *Superman*, *Lone Ranger*, *Lassie*, and the *Amos 'n Andy* shows.

The center of the Kelleytown community is located at the intersection of Kelleytown and Airline Roads, where the focal points of interest are the grocery store and the gas station with its two gas pumps. When motorists drive over the hose that rings the bell, the attendant rushes out to fill the tank and cleans the windshield. Regular gas was twenty-five cents a gallon. Like every small community Kelleytown has a ball field situated in a former cotton field. The priorities of a country boy in order of importance are playing ball, hunting and fishing, church, school and, last of all, the chores. Mama Dodson has a different mindset of what is important: church and school.

The remnants of the cotton era left many landowner's tenant houses still occupied by those who had once tended to the fields and harvested the crops. The houses are now being rented to the less fortunate and uneducated Blacks and Whites in the area. Jerry Banks was raised in such a house. The small clapboard house has two bedrooms, a kitchen and a living room. The outdoor toi-

Jerry Banks

let, known as the "outhouse," fortunately has been replaced with limited indoor plumbing facilities. The front yard contained two large oaks trees that insured that no grass would grow. The red clay ground underneath needed to be raked or swept, not mowed, on a regular basis. Tied to one of the trees by a thirty-foot chain was a yard dog that served as a lookout to alert occupants whenever a stranger set foot on the property.

Jerry Banks knew that he was poor but so were his White friends. He, however, had never experienced real hunger. Blacks and Whites played together in rural areas. But in public bathrooms, restaurants, schools, and churches, Blacks and Whites were segregated. In Jerry Banks' mind, it mattered not which faith you worship: Those White church-goers follow the same Bible teachings and abide by the same Ten Commandments as do the members of his segregated Black church. The mentality that the Blacks are an inferior race for many has not changed since the pre-Civil War days. As a young man Banks never understood the reasons for discrimination nor did he like it. But he accepted it. It was the way of life in the rural South. The treatment of Blacks influenced his attitude, and resentment would surface as he grew older.

Jerry Banks attended Smith Barnes School which replaced Stockbridge Rosenwald School. Still standing across the street but unoccupied, Stockbridge Rosenwald School was one of many schools built in the rural South in the early part of the twentieth century to educate young Blacks. The school was built and funded by the Rosenwald Foundation, established by the president of Sears & Roebuck. Henry County Public Schools were fully integrated in 1966; Jerry Banks attended the newly built Stockbridge Senior High School. Approaching his sixteenth birthday, he decided he was content to go through life with just an eighth-grade education.

***

Jerry Banks, like many young adults, made decisions they later regretted. Without a father to set him straight on the importance of getting an education, it was easier to drop out than sit bored in a classroom. He told his mother: "Why am I wasting my time listening to language and math teachers? I can already speak English and I know how to add, subtract, divide and multiply. That's all I need. What good does this extra learning do for a Black man? I need to be out there making money."

So Jerry Banks finds a job as a part-time employee, driving a truck hauling rock and asphalt for Riverdale Paving Company. He is a young man trying to make a living to provide for his family. Work had been slow. Coupled with the uncooperative weather, the asphalt plant is closed for the week. With no asphalt, there is no hauling to be done; consequently, he uses the time to help his neighbors. With his free time, he likes to hunt.

CHAPTER **6** | About Virginia Lemon

Virginia was born in 1954. She was soft-spoken, reasonably attractive and was considered a compassionate person. Virginia was
one of several children born to Louise and Frank Elbert Lemon. When her parents separated, Frank's sister, Opal Lee Phelps,
agreed to raise Virginia and her younger sister, Gloria. Opal had
four children of her own, so Virginia became a member of a large
household. Her uncles, Willie Lemon and Bobby Lemon, were
prominent Henry Countians. Willie is the owner of Henry County's only funeral home that served the Black community.

Virginia Lemon and Jerry Banks met while attending junior
high school. Jerry lived in Kelleytown and Virginia in Stockbridge. Although they lived eight miles apart, they were in the
same school district. He was two years older, but her sweet demeanor and his boyish charm created a mutual attraction. Both
were raised by a single parent and shared their households with
several siblings. Jerry had no interest in school, but Virginia did
her homework and made good grades. Her Aunt Opal would have
it no other way.

After Jerry dropped out of school, he found part-time work. He
now had a little money, a driver's license and from time to time
could borrow Ludie's or his mother's car. He had the opportunity
to pursue his romance with Virginia.

Jerry loved music even though he could not play an instrument and was never invited to sing in the church choir. There was a Motown song he dedicated to Virginia: The Temptation's "My Girl." He had written down the words and hummed to her when no one was around, so as not to embarrass her.

I don't need no money, fortune, or fame
I've got all the riches baby, one man can claim
Well, I guess you'd say
What can make me feel this way?
My girl, my girl, Virginia

Jerry had made up his mind. Attending school was not for him. Sitting in English class and daydreaming about Virginia he composed a poem.

When the school bell rings
My joyful heart sings
The day shall not pass
While we are sharing a class
Now to say thanks to God above
For sending me my one true love

Later Etta James' recording of "At Last" provided the lyrics that expressed Virginia's feelings for him.

At last, my love has come along
My lonely days are over and life is like a song,
At last the skies above are blue
My heart was wrapped in clover the night I looked at you, Jerry

At seventeen-years of age Virginia dropped out of high school because she was pregnant, and they married. Aunt Opal Phelps offered the couple a small rental house on Red Oak Road. Being next door, she was readily available to help the young mother. She had a knack for raising children. She had four of her own and from time to time she would take in a stray child to allow time for the distressed parents to resolve their financial difficulties or marital problems. She had the energy and patience to cope with a house full of noisy children. She loved to cook and care for their every need. When playtime was over and it was time for bed, she tolerated no foolishness and expected them to behave. She read bedtime stories to the little ones while making sure the older ones finished their homework. Good behavior, good manners and good study habits were required while under her care.

Aunt Opal thought that Virginia was too young to have a baby. She told her that she was going to teach her how to care for the newborn. A few weeks before the expected delivery date she took Virginia to the store and told her: "Now honey child this is what you are going to need. You buy a supply of cloth diapers, Johnson's baby powder, petroleum jelly and other baby stuff." Aunt Opal's sister, Doris Lemon, no longer had a need for the crib and playpen she used to raise her children. The last daughter, Christine, had outgrown her infant clothes. These were gladly given to Virginia. Aunt Opal bought a pail with a lid to store the dirty diapers until they could be washed. She suggested that Virginia pick out a cute little blue blanket for the baby.

Virginia delivered the six-pound eleven-ounce boy at home. It was an easy delivery, and the baby, Jerry and Virginia were doing fine. Aunt Opal wasted no time in showing Virginia how to breast feed, change diapers, bathe and later, how to prepare the formula.

Had Virginia finished high school, she would have considered nursing school. She liked taking care of people. At the encouragement of her younger sister, Gloria, Virginia began part-time, in-house care of an elderly neighbor. She enjoyed the work and later got employment at Lake City Nursing Home.

Two more children, Elbert and Felicia, followed.

CHAPTER 7 | The Banks Family

When the Boll Weevil crisis eventually subsided, the cotton growers were unable to find enough laborers to pick the cotton crop. As a result, the larger landowners began downsizing their operations by selling their land. Some of the buyers were the very sharecroppers who had worked the land. Knowing the sharecroppers did not have the wherewithal to pay for the land, they were allowed to pay for their purchase from the annual sale of their crops. One such former sharecropper was Henry Banks.

Robert Banks, one of Henry Banks' children and Jerry's cousin, lives on the old home place on Buster Lewis Road. He married his neighbor Christine Lemon, daughter of Andrew and Doris Lemon and Virginia's cousin. Robert and Christine shared their family history with me.

***

In 1947 Henry Banks purchased a hundred acres on Buster Lewis Road, a rural farm road that served as a connecting route from Highway 42 in the City of Stockbridge to the unincorporated town of Flippen. The road is named for one of the early landowners and farmers. The most noted descendant of the Lewis family is Hattie Lewis Goodhue. Mrs. Goodhue built and operated with her husband, Marshall, a small country store on their family property. The small store was located at the intersection of Buster Lewis Road and old Highway 351. (Later Highway 351 was renamed Jodeco Road. Buster Lewis Road was paved in 1956 and is now Flippen Road.)

Henry was married to Ethel who provided him with nine children. Raising such a large family was an overwhelming task for Ethel and a financial challenge for Henry. The Banks relied on the farm to feed their family. To make ends meet, Henry sold cotton and a variety of vegetables including corn, sweet potatoes, beans, peas, etc. He had a regular produce route to stores, restaurants and individuals who wanted or needed fresh vegetables. The farm always yielded an abundant watermelon crop. Mr. Banks did not have to worry about poachers because his melons were large and too heavy to tote away.

Unbeknownst to many, Mr. Banks' cash crop was of an illegal nature. He had a very productive moonshine still hidden in a secret room inside an old barn on his property. The beverage was convenient to the local drinkers as the nearest liquor store was twenty miles away. Even Sheriff Cook was known to comment, "The Banks' thirst quencher is the smoothest in Henry County."

Henry subsequently sold portions of his farm to other Banks family members which included A.B., William, and James Banks. As their children grew up and married, many remained in the area including Robert Banks, James Banks Jr., Evelyn Banks Studstill, Clarence Banks, and Myra McDaniel. A.B. Banks' wife Mattie Banks opened and operated Banks Community Store until it closed in the 1960s. Joe Simmons built and operated Simmons Country Club, where alcohol was served. The facility was a popular night spot that regularly featured weekend entertainment and dancing. Troublemakers were not welcome. (The facility closed in 1980 to the disappointment of many.) The neighborhood had a baseball diamond and fielded its own Little League baseball team. There was something for everyone.

Although those with larger tracts of land did some farming and had gardens, most had full-time jobs in and around Atlanta. Many of the young men worked at the nearby dairy farms during their summer breaks. There they hauled hay, fixed the fences, and tended to the cattle. The young women were able to find domestic work in the area.

Besides teaching their children to work, the parents stressed the importance of education. Some students attended the small Red Oak Elementary School located on a narrow dirt road. The road was later paved and renamed Walt Stephens Road. Other students attended Rosenwald School located on Tye Street, which later was replaced by Smith Barnes Elementary. The Banks along with other families regularly attended Mt Olive Baptist, Red Oak United Methodist, Trinity United Methodist, or Floyd Chapel Baptist churches in the Stockbridge area.

For a short time, a tenant house on the McCain farm which was situated across from the Red Oak United Methodist Church was the home of the King family. Martin Luther King, Sr., known as "Daddy King," lived on Red Oak Road while ministering to churches in Henry County. It was at the Floyd Chapel Baptist where his son was said to have preached his first sermon while still a teenager. The most renowned civil rights activist, Martin Luther King, Jr. had his humble beginning in Stockbridge near the Banks community.

Over the years the Banks' neighborhood expanded from Buster Lewis to include Tye Street and Red Oak Road and merged with the Black-populated section in the City of Stockbridge. By the 1970s the mostly Black residents had grown to a neighborhood of hardworking homeowners. They were devout Christians, paid their taxes, and were an asset to Henry County. The community could attribute its existence to Henry and Ethel Banks, who as former sharecroppers purchased a farm on Buster Lewis Road. With all the family members working the land, they were able to pay off the note holder in just ten years. For their contributions to the community, Banks Drive and Banks Road were subsequently named for them.

Jerry and his new wife, Virginia, were welcomed to the Banks community. Their new home was located on Red Oak Road a short distance from Virginia's Aunt Doris and Uncle Andrew.

CHAPTER 8 | Hunting Trips

Jerry Banks loved to hunt. His uncle Roy had taken time with the fatherless youngster and taught him the art of hunting. At family get-togethers or when talking with friends, Jerry always wanted to share his latest hunting story. People who heard them claimed that they were not sure if the stories were always true.

Saturday, October 26, 1974, begins the first week of deer hunting season. It is a cool morning with sunny skies, the type of day that Jerry Banks hopes for. He and his brother Perry are going hunting. Jerry does not have a shotgun, but Perry is bringing his 12-gauge with cartridges and promises to let Jerry use the gun. Jerry also invites his cousin, Mamian Webster, to come along. It is the week-end and nobody must work.

Jerry tells his cousin that he had promised to help his neighbors, the Slaughters. Gracie wanted him to rake up some leaves and fix something at her house. He would be done by lunch time and could hunt in the afternoon.

Mamian asks, "You know a good place where we can go?"

"I know there is deer in the bottoms along the creek. That would be the best place to start," Jerry responds.

After Virginia prepares lunch for the family and the always-hungry Mamian Webster and Perry, the boys set off for the woods behind the house on Red Oak Road accompanied by Jerry's dog.

The puppy has no name and it would be the dog's first hunting adventure with Jerry. It is about 1:30 p.m. a perfect day for deer hunting or anything that they can shoot. The 12-gauge shotgun is a family hand-me-down, but it still has plenty of shots left, even with the electrical tape that is holding together the cracked gun stock. Mamian brings his old 16-gauge shotgun. Jerry wears an old hunting jacket that has several pockets. He has cartridges and hunting knives in two of the pockets. In another pocket he has a can opener that can be used to open cans of pork-n-beans, peaches, beer bottles or the like, in case somebody brings something that needs to be opened.

Mamian is always bragging that his gun is better for killing rabbits which is what he's after. It has smaller pellets and won't blow the rabbit to smithereens like the 12-gauge. Jerry does not care about rabbits. The 12-gauge would bring down his deer in one shot. They all agree to make a bet. The winner is the one who kills the first animal. The two losers must skin and dress the kill.

They begin scouting the land south of Red Oak Road. The logging trail leads to a wooded area filled with scrubby pines and sweetgum trees. From there the trail opens into a meadow. Leaving the meadow, crossing a small creek they reach the Broder bottom. The field is bordered on the south by Rum Creek. Early farmers used the bottoms to grow sorghum crops. They squeezed the sorghum stalks and used the sap to produce molasses. Some distilled the molasses into rum, thus the name Rum Creek.

***

Curious, Mamian asks, "Where did you find the dog?"

"He takes up around here and stays when little Jerry Jr. started feeding the mutt. Someone must have dumped him out onto the road, and he wandered over to our house. The young'uns grew fond of the dog, and I didn't have the heart to get rid of him. Besides, he would make me a good hunting dog," answers Jerry.

Mamian jokingly says, "So far all I have seen from him is a lot of sniffing, barking and running around. He hasn't found any rabbits nor flushed out any birds. Those animals that are there, he scared off with his barking. I don't think he can find his tail if it wasn't attached."

"He's a smart dog! You can tell by looking at him, those sharp pointed ears and that wagging tail. Watch this: 'Here, Dog. Here, Dog!' See how those ears perk up. 'Fetch! Fetch! get us something to eat.' See how he wags his tail, as if he understands everything I say. Sometimes he crawls on his belly as if he is about to sneak upon some unsuspecting critter. He's going to be a smart hunting dog," counters Jerry.

Mamian replies, "You are right, you are always right."

Bang…Bang…Bang…Bang

"Did you hear those shots, Mamian?" asks Jerry.

Mamian responds, "Yea, sounds like that there is someone else hunting in these woods."

"They must have missed. I betcha that deer are still out there for us to get," Jerry says.

The boys have no luck as they wander around trying to spook a rabbit or deer out of the brush. The only excitement is when the dog races to a thicket and begins barking. As the boys approach, all they find is matted down grass, where a deer had slept, and the hoof prints indicate that it is long gone.

A murder of crows sitting in a tall nearby pine tree observes the goings on and begins cawing. To Mamian the incessant cawing sounds as if the birds were teasing the hunters. Already frustrated at not finding any rabbits or deer, Mamian fires a shot in the direction of the crows. The birds scatter and fly off. He is pleased that the cawing stops.

Jerry says, "I can't understand it. This bottom has always had something to hunt."

This day, however, nothing can be found. They decide to venture to the other side of the creek. Since the creek is too deep to cross, especially for the dog which has never been swimming, they climb upon the shoulder of Rock Quarry Road and walk over to the other side.

Rock Quarry Road is the north-south route from Highway 42 to Hudson Bridge Road. It is the shortest distance to the Interstate 75 intersection for Stockbridge folks wishing to go south. At the time the Interstate opened for travel in October 1969, Hudson Bridge Road is unpaved. The interchange has the distinction of being the only ramp off Interstate 75 that exits onto a dirt road. Consequently, the interchange has seen little commercial development. Aside from the Matador Inn, there is no reason for a traveling motorist to exit at the interchange.

The road is named after the granite quarry that is located near the Southern Railroad tracks and its intersection with State Route Highway 42. Before Rock Quarry is paved around 1972, it is a small winding dirt road with two rickety wooden bridges that cross over Rum and Reeves Creeks. The new road is straightened, and the wooden bridges replaced with concrete culverts. Shortly after leaving Hudson Bridge Road, the old unpaved road features a westerly arcing bend before it reaches the banks of Rum Creek. That section of the old road was left intact, so the property owners could have access to their land. Over time, the secluded dead-end dirt road becomes a favorite parking site for teenagers on a date and a convenient place for people to dump trash. For the most part, only the local residents are aware of the existence of the old-abandoned road.

The trio starts up the old-abandoned Rock Quarry Road that begins with a barrier of rock and debris that acts as a warning to motorist: This is a dead-end road. Beyond this point you will end up in the creek. Beware!

After a short walk, the dog runs ahead and races toward a thicket of briars and bushes. As the dog enters the thicket Mamian starts hollering, "I think I see a deer in there." Perry is in possession of the 12-gauge at the time. He immediately points the shotgun in the direction of the thicket, where the dog had come to a stop and is barking.

Mamian shouts, "I know there's a deer in there!"

"Please, Perry, don't shoot my dog," begs Jerry.

Perry yells, "I not interested in your scrawny dog. I am going to get me a deer! You and Mamian are gonna have to skin it." He shoots once, removes the shell, throws it over his shoulder into the bush, reloads and shoots again. But now the dog, frightened by the pellets peppering the bushes in front of him, scampers away.

The excited Perry shoots again just in case he missed the deer with his first two shots. Perry runs to the spot where he thinks he will find his fallen deer. Curious as ever, Jerry and Mamian follow right behind. When they reach the thicket all they find is nothing but a pile of rocks that farmers had gathered over the years from the surrounding fields and piled up. Being near the rock quarry, all the fields had an abundance of granite stones that were hard on plows. The pile is partially covered with brown leaves and moss. From a distance it resembles a silhouette of a deer; at least it did to the desperate deer hunters. The boys spend another hour looking for the elusive deer. They know if there is a deer around, it has been scared off.

Jerry kids Perry about his poor marksmanship. "Perry, you are the worst shot I have ever seen."

"There wasn't a deer in there, just a pile of rocks. You all just brought me bad luck today," bemoans Perry.

It was a fun day. They joke with one another as they walk back to Red Oak Road and home. They cannot stop laughing at Mamian for shooting at the crows, Jerry at trying to train his no-account dog, and Perry for shooting at shadows. Jerry tells himself that the next time he will get that deer.

***

The next time would come in two weeks, Thursday November 7th. The day begins like many other days as of late. Jerry gets up early because he has a busy schedule planned. He says goodbye to Virginia and the children. Aunt Opal is taking them grocery shopping. Jerry downs a second cup of Maxwell House coffee. After hunting with his cousin, Mamian Webster, and brother, Perry Banks, two weeks earlier, Jerry is excited about going back to those same areas as before. He misses their company, but he expects to have more success by hunting alone. Perry has let him keep the family 12-gauge shotgun, but only for a little while. Jerry does not want to waste the opportunity and intends on using it. He figures that he would go back to the creek bottoms where the deer most likely are bedded down for the day. If the deer are there his experienced dog would certainly find them.

When Jerry is not working for the paving company, he is doing odd jobs for Gracie and Judge Slaughter, who live three houses down on Red Oak Road. Today he helps Judge strip down an old clunker. The engine, transmission and all reusable parts had already been salvaged. Jerry's job is to remove the remaining non-salvageable parts and then crush the metal. He could do the work with a screwdriver, crowbar and a sledgehammer. Once Jerry fills Judge's F-350 truck with crushed metal, Judge will sell the load to a recycling plant in Forest Park. He rushes so that he can finish and free up his afternoon.

Jerry lives in a transitional area that is changing from rural to urban, where clusters of homes are separated by farmland and woods. It is an ideal location for a hunter. A short walk out the back door is prime shooting for rabbit, deer, turkey, quail, dove, or whatever is in season. No need to fear trespassing or disturbing the peace and quiet of the neighborhood. November is hunting season and there are plenty of deer along creeks and surrounding bottoms just outside his door. Jerry prefers to hunt late in the afternoon.

What Jerry Banks discovers on his hunting trips this day will change his life forever.

Jerry and his dog, chained to a pine tree behind the house, are eager to go. The hunting trip gets off to a slow start. He has no luck finding game in the nearby woods or the bottoms. He decides that the deer must be on the other side of the creek and heads south on Rock Quarry Road. Once he crosses over Rum Creek, he climbs down the bank on the west side where the abandoned road dead ends as it nears the new paved road. When he reaches the location where Perry had shot at the pile of rocks, the dog runs ahead. The dog stops and begins to paw the ground next to what turns out to be two pools of fresh blood. Jerry assumes that the blood probably belonged to a deer that had been recently killed and field dressed by a hunter. He had seen such sites on previous hunting trips and does not pay the blood stains much attention. He only wishes that he had been the one who shot the deer and that Perry and Mamian were with him to see it. From the size of the stain, the deer would have been too big for him to carry. He knows that Virginia and Aunt Opal will be glad. They usually do not want any part of butchering a deer.

Well, it was not to be this day. Jerry has not gotten to shoot the shotgun all day, not even once.

Jerry had not noticed the drag marks that led from the blood stains to a thicket of bushes about hundred feet away. He is too busy maneuvering through brush and briars to follow his dog. From the barking and the dog's agitated behavior he suspects that there is something hidden in the bushes.

Immediately in front of the now quiet and sniffing dog is a body partially covered with a blanket. As Jerry gets closer it appears that there are two bodies underneath. As he peels back the blanket, he sees two people lying face down and covered with blood.

Jerry mumbles under his breath, "Oh, my God!" Jerry rests his shotgun against a tree. As he folds back the blanket a little further, he can tell with certainty that they are dead. With all that blood it appears that a shotgun probably killed them. The sight takes his breath away. Staring at the two lifeless people, he wonders who they are and what are they doing out here? He looks around. He sees no other person or car within sight. He realizes that someone must have shot these two on the abandoned road and then dragged them into these bushes. It is a secluded place, where no one would think to look. If it were not for the dog, it could have been days, weeks, or months before anyone found the bodies.

Meanwhile, his dog resumes barking up a storm. It takes a while for Jerry to calm himself and settle down his dog. The pair of bodies are lying face down. The backs of their clothes are covered with blood. Jerry spots a man's wallet lying next to one of the bodies.

"I got to know who these White folks are," thinks Jerry. The wallet has a lot of stuff in it, credit cards, a picture, but no money.

Jerry is frightened and does not know what to do. He wishes the others were with him so they could give him advice. At first, his thoughts are just to get the hell out of there. As he slowly walks back to where the blood stains are, he decides that he needs to tell someone what he has discovered. But, first, he thinks he should throw the wallet away. People might think he stole the man's money. Accompanied by his dog and still carrying his shotgun, he heads to the paved Rock Quarry Road to flag down someone who can call the police.

Rock Quarry is not a heavily traveled road. This is before the rumored hospital and the housing developments would be built. It is approximately 5 p.m. when Jerry is able to stop the first motorist and explain that he had come across two dead bodies in the woods. Somewhat apprehensively, the driver in a pickup stops, rolls down his window and listens to Banks' incredible story. He chooses not to get involved and drives off. The next motorist, Andy Eberhardt, sees Jerry waving his arms while holding a shotgun, and slows down but does not stop. As he drives away, he thinks that there may be a possible hunting accident, so he stops and backs up. He listens to Jerry's story and promises to call the police department.

Andy Eberhardt, who lives only a few miles away on Jodeco Road elects to call the Henry County Sheriff's Department from home. Later, he decides to return to Rock Quarry Road with his son, Lake, to inform Banks that he made the call and to offer whatever assistance he could.

At the police station, the day shift is preparing to leave for home. Those plans give way as the call alerts Det. Dick Barnes and Det. C. H. (Charlie) Tomlinson, who immediately leave to investigate. Ofc. Johnny Glover, who is in his patrol car, rendezvous with the other officers on Rock Quarry Road. Jerry shows the officers the locations of the blood-stained roadbed and the bodies lying under a red blanket. At first, they have difficulty recognizing the gender of the bodies, the detectives first assume that both are female, since both are disheveled, scraped, bloodied and have long-hair. After further examination, they realize otherwise. Both are fully clothed, she in a blouse, pants and red sweater and he in short sleeve shirt, tie and dress slacks.

The stunned Barnes reports the discovery to police headquarters in McDonough. A swarm of law enforcement personnel from Henry County and surrounding areas soon arrive and line Rock

Quarry Road with their vehicles, some with their emergency lights flashing. It is now approximately 6:30 p.m. and darkness is quickly approaching. Detectives using flashlights and lanterns search for clues and try to make sense out of the baffling murders.

CHAPTER 9 | Jimmy Glass

Since the 1850s the Democratic Party has ruled the State of Georgia. I supported and voted for Democratic candidate Jimmy Glass when he first ran for a Henry County School Board seat. I had just turned eighteen that July and it was the first election in which I was eligible to vote. I have watched him rise to power. Jimmy Glass, raised on a farm in unincorporated Flippen, Georgia, later got into the insurance business. He married Martha Hall.

Jimmy Hasting Glass' introduction to public service began with his election to the Henry County School Board in 1966. In the general election in 1970, Candidate Glass was re-elected. That year Henry County voted across Democratic lines and all Democrats were victorious. Presidential candidate, Jimmy Carter, and Georgia gubernatorial candidate, Lester Maddox, won easily.

In many rural Georgia counties such as Henry, law enforcement is carried out by the sheriff. The sheriff is elected by popular vote and must run for office every four years. Under his authority, the police chief and chief detective oversee law enforcement, while the deputies are responsible for running the county jail and serving warrants for the courts. All these personnel are hired and fired by the sheriff.

In mid-1972, Jimmy Glass is appointed to fill the unexpired term of Sheriff Hiram Cook, who vacates for health reasons, and he becomes Henry County's twenty-sixth Sheriff. Later that year, he successfully runs for re-election. He is a well-liked sheriff who attends every funeral and takes care of his friends and supporters. His popularity gives Sheriff Glass a lot of latitude in how he runs his office. The inherent duties accompanying the position of a Henry County Sheriff make Jimmy Glass the most powerful public official in the County.

Sheriff Jimmy Glass

Sheriff Jimmy Glass arrives at the murder scene shortly after he is informed of the murders.

The investigation is underway.

CHAPTER **10** | The Murder Investigation

Charlie Tomlinson, who I knew before he joined the police department, reports for duty thinking it is going to be another typical Thursday night shift. Not much happens during a weekday night. Fridays are payday for most of the blue-collar workers who seldom lay out on Fridays for that reason. So, they remain at home on Thursdays and stay out of trouble. Charlie assumes with only a few incoming calls he can spend his time at the station and catch up with his routine paperwork. It would be a different story if it were Saturday night when the partying, drinking troublemakers are on the prowl. But this is Thursday night. As it turns out, it would be one of the longest nights for Officer Tomlinson in recent memory. Charlie shared his experience and events of that evening with me.

***

On the evening of November 7th, the detectives face the challenge of solving a brutal double homicide. The victims are killed near where their bodies are found. There is no vehicle, no murder weapon and no signs of a struggle. There is no identification except for rings on their fingers. The engraved Jonesboro High School class ring worn by the female victim belongs to Melanie

Ann Hartsfield. The Clayton County Police Department earlier in the day received a missing person's report for Melanie. The male victim wears a University of Georgia class ring and a wedding band, but the fingers are too swollen to remove at the scene. The Clayton County authorities are notified by the Henry County Sheriff Department that the female victim could be their missing person. They immediately respond to the call.

They join the contingent of Henry County detectives and police officers who have already gathered at the site. Capt. P.S. "Sugg" Howard oversees the investigation and is aided by Det. Dick Barnes, Det. Bobby Lemon, Det. Billy Payne and Det. Paul Robbins. Det. Tommy Floyd is on his way.

Sheriff Glass arrives on the scene shortly before nightfall.

Sheriff Glass begins, "Detective, I see you have everything under control."

"Yes, sir," says Det. Barnes. "Charlie and I were the first to arrive. Capt. Howard has assigned two patrolmen to guard the murder scene. No unauthorized persons are allowed to come up here. Several detectives have talked to the witness. Det. Tomlinson is here and has helped me sort things out."

Sheriff Glass asks, "Who is the witness?"

"It's a young Black man named Jerry Banks. He is standing over there. He lives nearby on Red Oak Road. I got his phone number and address. I will take you over to him," answers Det. Barnes.

Sheriff Glass turns to Banks, "What can you tell me, Son?"

"I was hunting when my dog followed a scent to this patch of bushes and trees. I found the two bodies in there," replies Banks.

Sheriff Glass asks, "Did you see who did this?"

"No, sir," answers Banks.

Capt. Howard describes to Sheriff Glass what Jerry Banks had discovered: "We have a young White female 5-foot-4 to 5-foot-5 tall, weighing about 130 pounds. A White male with medium long hair, middle-aged, 5-foot-8 to 5-foot-9 in height and weighing 165 to 170 pounds. We know the victims were shot in the lower back and in the back of the head at close range. It appears to be an execution style slaying. Two blood stains found on the dirt road indicate where the victims were shot and then dragged up here. Both are fully clothed and neatly dressed. We searched everywhere for anything that would give us a clue."

Sheriff Glass says, "Do we know who they are?"

"Det. Payne removed the class ring from the female victim. From the inscription inside, the female is identified as Melanie Hartsfield. We are not

From left to right: Det. Barnes, Det. Lemon,
Cap. Howard and Det. Payne at the murder scene

sure who the male victim is. He is wearing two rings. We should find out when the coroner removes the rings during the autopsy," answers Capt. Howard.

Sheriff Glass shaking his head continues, "That's awful. Have you found any evidence?"

"No wallet, pocketbook or useful evidence have been found so far. It's getting too dark to look. How the victims got to the dirt road remains a mystery as no vehicle is found. Capt. Berry from the Clayton County Police Department has arranged for a generator and lights to be delivered later this evening," replies Capt. Howard.

Eberhardt speaks as he approaches the Sheriff, "Excuse me, Mr. Glass, I am Andy Eberhardt. I am the one who called the police. This young man flagged me down and told me about the bodies he found in the woods."

"That's fine. Pardon me, Brother, I'm late for a meeting," Sheriff Glass says.

Det. Barnes tells the group standing around the bodies that Ronnie Stewart, the coroner, is on his way.

***

The detectives are not allowed to move the bodies or disturb the crime scene. Once the coroner finishes examining the deceased victims, Capt. Howard instructs Det. Billy Payne to take his final photos. The late-arriving Det. Payne had taken numerous pictures of the bodies and the crime scene with the department's new Polaroid camera. Det. Glover is stationed on Rock Quarry Road with instructions not to allow anyone who is not directly involved in the investigation to have access to the site.

At approximately 9 p.m. Mr. Stewart places the victims in separate black body bags and transports them to Carmichael's Funeral Home. Dr. Howard from the Georgia Bureau of Investigation, (G.B.I.) laboratory is called and will conduct an autopsy when he arrives.

Rather than wait until the next morning, Sheriff Glass orders Det. Payne to bring Banks, who had already returned home, to the police station for his official statement. He is considered an important witness since he is the one who found the bodies. He may provide some clues.

***

Det. Payne goes to Red Oak Road to summon Jerry Banks. It is near midnight, and he finds Jerry in his night clothes sitting in the living room watching television. He is unable to get his horrible discovery out of his head. Virginia and the kids are in their bedrooms. Jerry Banks is apprehensive and tells Det. Payne that he is tired and asked if could wait until morning.

"No, it's important. Every available detective in the department is working on the murder case. We need to gather all the facts we can as soon as possible so we can catch this killer. We need your statement," stresses Det. Payne.

It is near midnight when Jerry arrives at the detectives' office. Located behind the Henry County Courthouse the detective's offices are housed in a trailer comprised of a waiting room and three offices. Since most of the detectives are still at the scene or running down leads, Jerry is asked to wait until the assigned detective returns to the trailer. Finally, at 2:30 a.m., Det. Hart takes Jerry's statement. Most of the questions are routine. Jerry repeats the story he told numerous times to the detectives at the murder scene earlier. It has been a long day for everyone involved, especially Jerry, who is returned to his home in the early hours of the morning.

Early Friday, November 8th, Capt. Howard and Det. Ted Ray return to the crime scene. They relieve the personnel who had the unfortunate duty of working the site during the night. Shortly after their arrival, Capt. Howard finds a spent shell casing around 9 a.m. and minutes later Det. Ted Ray locates a second shell. Since the shells are found near the bodies, they assume they were ejected from the killer's murder weapon. Both shells are Winchester Western 00 buckshot that came from a 12-gauge shotgun.

Other detectives arrive later and begin to scour the wooded area west of Rock Quarry Road in hopes of finding useful evidence and clues that had been overlooked the night before. The skies are clear, and the temperature is below normal, but still comfortable for a late autumn day. The stones placed by Det. Floyd the night before mark the location of the shooting and are a gruesome reminder of the discoveries. There are also footprints, tire tracks and pieces of a broken taillight on the dirt road near the bloodstains. Nothing of consequence is found between the dirt road and where the bodies were found.

On November 10th Sgt. Tommy Floyd and Det. Paul Robbins make an official visit to Banks' home to inform him that a shotgun was used in the murders. Sgt. Floyd begins, "Mr. Banks, since you were seen with a shotgun at the scene, we need to conduct a ballistic test. Sheriff Glass requested that all guns belonging to hunters who hunt at that area be confiscated and sent to the G.B.I. lab for ballistic testing."

Local, state and national news media have zeroed in on Henry County. Such a crime story is a boost to their readership and makes interesting viewing for their television audiences. Everyone is starving for details. Sheriff Glass relishes the opportunity to speak to the reporters. He gets a kick out of seeing his picture in the newspapers. When he is asked to do an interview with Ray Moore from *Channel 2 News*, he is anxious to make a good impression. He has his uniform dry-cleaned and pressed with extra starch. He insists that his barber open the shop early to give him the movie-star haircut. The ten-minute airtime on channel 2 makes Sheriff Glass a local celebrity.

For days following the murders, the waiting room in front of Sheriff Glass' office is filled with members of the press. Joined by Capt. Howard they speak to the various reporters. Such interviews are duplicated on numerous occasions.

Sheriff Glass begins, "We have a particular suspect in mind that we consider as suspicious. The possible suspect is a Clayton County resident. Henry County Sheriff's Department is pursuing leads with the help of the Clayton County Police. Two shotgun shells were found near the scene. Both shells are Winchester Western 00 buckshot. Clayton County authorities said they are the same as those used in the slaying of College Park Police Ofc. Eugene Barge, Thursday morning. The shells are 12-gauge magnum. We are checking out a possible connection between the two slayings."

"What could be the motive?" asks a reporter.

Sheriff Glass responds, "We don't know if it's jealousy or a bad grade in school or what. There is the possibility that more than one suspect is involved. It could be a male and female. Our initial assumption is that robbery was the probable motive."

"What makes you think that, Sheriff Glass?" asks another reporter.

Sheriff Glass continues, "Both bodies had been stripped of their valuables and identification except for their rings. Mr. King's wallet was not on his person, nor did we find Miss Hartsfield's purse."

Capt. Howard adds, "Mr. King's car was later found about half a mile from the murder scene. My detectives believe that the car may have been at the scene and moved after the slayings."

"What makes you think that?" asks the inquisitive reporter.

Capt. Howard says "We are examining some evidence found on the old Rock Quarry Road that will place the Opel at the murder scene. If true, it explains how the bodies got there. There were plastic shards found near the bloodstains. The shards found on the ground probably resulted from a pellet striking the taillight."

"We hear that you also found Miss Hartsfield's car," says the reporter.

Capt. Howard continues, "Miss Hartfield's car was located about four miles away in the North Stockbridge area. Miss Hartsfield's pocketbook was found in Mr. King's car. Her coin purse however was not in the car. Supposedly, the purse along with Mr. King's wallet were taken by the assailant."

"Any thoughts on what the two were doing together on a lonely dirt road," the reporter asks.

Sheriff Glass interrupts, "None. I will let you draw your own conclusions."

Capt. Howard adds, "For those of you who are curious, they were fully clothed and there were no findings of hanky-panky."

Sheriff Glass says, "The department has nearly every detective working on the case trying to construct a timeline between when Mr. King and Miss Hartsfield were last seen, and when their bodies were discovered. The detectives have a lot of leg work to do."

"The sheriff's office and Henry County Detectives are still digging for clues and interviewing possible witnesses. We continue to receive an assortment of anonymous tips," Capt. Howard says as the interview concludes.

***

In an interview with a reporter from *The Weekly Advertiser*, former Sheriff Hiram Cook recounted his fifteen years of service as Henry County's Sheriff by elaborating on his most memorable moments while in office. Because of the recent King and Hartsfield murders, he enumerated several cases that occurred in the vicinity of Nan Morris Mountain and Hudson Bridge Road. Sheriff Cook knows the location well. The area is near his home on Highway 351.

Sheriff Cook begins telling his story. "At one time, Nan Morris was the owner of much of the land in the area. The mountain is no more than a hill, but it is one of the higher elevations in Henry

County. While I was a rookie deputy working for then Sheriff Henry Amis, I had the occasion to view the crime scene of a double slaying of Benton Ford and Sarah Rawls in March 1940. I was horrified to see the battered bodies that were bludgeoned to death. The murders caused a tremendous stir at the time, and the killer was never found, or a plausible motive determined. The murders occurred off of Hudson Bridge Road. I can tell you that case and the thought of seeing those poor mutilated people made a lasting impression on this young deputy."

Former Sheriff Cook recalls another murder in 1946. "A local resident, Julia Norris, was found murdered near the railroad tracks in the same general vicinity. She was last seen walking west on Hudson Bridge Road. Ms. Norris was robbed, raped and tied to a tree, where she died from her wounds.

"Then just recently, another victim named Raymond Davenport was found. A farmer discovered the body in dense underbrush. Davenport, a mechanic, had been shot twice. The former Hampton resident was missing after he went to a convenience store in East Point. His body was apparently dumped off Rock Quarry Road."

The three murder cases parallel in many ways to King and Hartfield killings. All the bodies were discovered in close proximity to where King and Hartsfield were found. All the victims were brutally murdered.

Former Sheriff Cook said that he came to the same conclusion as did Sheriff Glass when he was quoted, "The Hudson Bridge area is a murder dumping ground. Not only does the police department recover numerous stolen vehicles there, but they also find bodies from time to time. Hudson Bridge and Rock Quarry Roads are remote areas that are interstate accessible. The trees, shrubs and isolation make it an ideal place to hide a body."

***

One of my duties as a teacher at Stockbridge High School was coaching Boys' B-team basketball. Late to a 5 p.m. game, I hurriedly parked my car behind the gym and rushed inside leaving my keys in the ignition. The boys played well but lost. I stayed for the girls' and boys' varsity games. Upon leaving I discovered that my car was gone. Two days later the police located the car on the seldom traveled dirt Hudson Bridge Road. Fortunately, it was undamaged but out of gas. It was one of the stolen cars Sheriff Glass referred to in his interview with a reporter—my red Capri.

***

The investigators learn that there was no connection between the King and Hartsfield murders and murder of the College Park policeman, as the alleged killer was captured and confessed. After intense questioning, the detectives determine that the suspects were nowhere near Stockbridge at the time of the murders. The mysterious hunters that were in the area on the day of murders voluntarily give statements to the police. It was determined that the two owned different gauged shotguns from the one that killed Hartsfield and King. The investigation hits a dead end. There are no promising suspects.

On December 5th, Det. Floyd and Det. Robbins return to Banks' home to pick up the shotgun for the second time. Jerry says that he has returned the gun to Perry.

Det. Floyd suggests, "Let's go to your brother's house and pick up the shotgun. We also need to ask you a few more questions. We need to do this at headquarters."

"That's all right. I don't have nothin' to hide," replies Jerry.

From there Jerry is taken to police headquarters, where he is questioned further about his possible involvement in the crime. Det. Robbins suspects that Banks has not come clean about his part in the discovery of the bodies. Tommy Floyd, who is later promoted to Sergeant, does the questioning.

Det. Floyd asks, "Jerry, on the day you found the bodies, did you fire your shotgun and throw the hulls into the bushes? Did you do this anytime from when you left your home, until you found the bodies?"

"No, sir," replies Banks.

Det. Floyd continues, "Do you know of anyone who had?"

"No, sir," replies Banks.

Det. Floyd continues, "The day following the shootings, detectives found two fired shells near where the pools of blood were located. We assume the discharged shells came from the killer's gun. We had the crime lab test-fire your shotgun. The crime lab reports those two shells were fired from your gun."

"Wait a minute! Somebody made some type of mistake! I did not shoot the gun," Banks angrily responds."

CHAPTER 11 | The Funerals

On Friday morning, November 8, principal Fred Smith assembled his staff and available teachers in the teachers' lounge for an emergency meeting. He told his faculty that he had some tragic news: "Our beloved teacher, Mr. King, is dead." He wanted his teachers to be aware of his death and answer what few questions he could before he made an announcement to the student body. Immediately, a hush engulfed the room as those present in the meeting went into total shock.

***

Finally, Mrs. Hudson, the senior English teacher who began her tenure at Jonesboro High School at the same time as Marvin, asked, "Was he in a car accident? Did he have a heart attack? What happened to him?"

"The police think that he was murdered in Henry County along with a former student, Melanie Hartsfield," says principal Smith.

Mrs. Patterson, weeping, "Oh, how awful! Who would do something like that?"

"I just got a call from the Clayton County Sheriff who gave me the bad news. He did not offer any details. He said there was so much conflicting information and confusion at the present time that he would have to get back to me later," explained Smith.

The principal then makes the announcement to the students over the intercom, who like the teachers, are in disbelief.

When the marching band reports to practice after 6th period, Fred Smith and first-year teacher, Terry Blaylock, meet with band students in the endzone of the football field.

Terry chokes on his words as he speaks, "This is the worst day of my life. I genuinely loved and respected Mr. King. I cannot believe that he is no longer with us. I do know that if Mr. King were here, he would want us to carry on."

Robert, the drum major, who had spoken with some senior band members after he heard the earlier announcement, said, "I believe I can speak on behalf of the band members. We want and must carry on in the tradition that Mr. King had instilled."

Principal Smith having learned more details of the murders, tells the where and how the deaths occurred but is unable to offer any explanation as to the why and who did it. As he recounts the event, those in attendance are stunned and many are in tears.

Jonesboro students and faculty mourn the deaths as the flag at Jonesboro High School is flown at half-staff. The pep rally scheduled for later that day at the school is cancelled. The band members elect to perform at Saturday night's football game against LaGrange. The expressions of grief over the loss of the well-respected band director surface at the halftime as band members weep during their performance. One of the majorettes carries a single black flag in honor of Mr. King. The crowd remains standing well after Mr. Smith had asked the crowd to stand in silent prayer for Mr. King and Miss Hartsfield.

The outcome of the game really did not matter.

***

Obituaries for both victims were published in the newspapers. Bobby King, the widow, is so distraught that she cannot not bring herself to handle the planning of the service or making the burial arrangements without the aid of family members. Charles and Evelyn Hartsfield, Melanie's parents, make the arrangements for their daughter. There would be two separate services and burials.

Abe Dickson, owner of Dickson Funeral Home in Jonesboro, is responsible for preparing the bodies for burial. After one quick look under the sheets, he knows that he could not restore the shot-gunned victims to a presentable state. The blasts to the back of each head left both victims with disfigured faces requiring closed-casket funerals. The mourners had to rely on past memories, rather than visually seeing their loved ones for the final time.

At 2 p.m. the following Saturday, friends and family gather at the Mt. Zion Baptist Church on Mt. Zion Road to pay their final respects to Melanie Hartsfield. Miss Hartsfield is described by church members as a "good Christian young woman, who would do anything for anybody." The church is packed. Even the extra folding chairs the ushers have placed down the aisles and foyer are taken. Latecomers are forced to stand in the rear of the church. The grief is intense, as Melanie's parents, siblings and friends are in disbelief that their beloved Melanie has been taken away from them. Most of the regular congregation is present. They have watched Melanie grow up in the church. She had been a member of the children's choir and later the adult choir. She was a member of the stage band that performed each year at the church's December musical that depicted the Christmas story.

Rev. Clint Rogers says, "Melanie loved her God and for that she is assured of a place in heaven." Since there are those in attendance who did not know her as well, he enumerates her many accomplishments during her brief time on earth. "Melanie Hartsfield had been one of Mr. King's prized students and was an excellent clarinetist. In addition to being a member of the Jonesboro Senior High, she was remarkably close to the King family. She often babysat for the family and was good friends with the oldest daughter, Teri. Although Teri King was a freshman at the University of Georgia, they kept in contact with one another. They were classmates at Jonesboro High and fellow band members since junior high school," he adds.

After Rev. Rogers sums up his remarks and recites "The Lord is My Shepherd" psalm, he introduces Rev. Paul Camp who eloquently finishes the tributes to Melanie. The members of the Riverdale Junior High choir join the Mt. Zion Baptist choir in song. Kleenexes and handkerchiefs are seen *en masse* as the choirs sing a beautiful rendition of "Amazing Grace." The classic gospel song had been one of Melanie's favorites.

Many who attend the memorial service for Miss Hartsfield also attend Mr. King's tribute later that day at 4:30 p.m. Students, parents and friends of the popular band director jam the Phillips Drive Chapel in Morrow. Two buses packed with band members arrive early and are escorted to the chapel through the parking lot that is already overflowing with cars. Two off-duty policemen are forced to rope off the entrance and exit and stop further parking on the lawn and the neatly landscaped grounds. The Jonesboro High School band, dressed in black-and-red marching uniforms, serves as honorary escorts during the funeral services. They form two columns on each side of the walkway leading up to the chapel.

In addition to the usual family and friends, local politicians, newspaper reporters and curiosity-seekers are among the attendees. School buses and vans transport students from the high school. Four other Clayton County policemen are directing traffic on Morrow Road and Phillips Drive, encouraging late comers to park on neighboring streets. Mourners and onlookers fill the seats, stand in the lobby and gather outside the chapel in order to pay their final tributes to Mr. King.

The Kings are active members of Jonesboro First Methodist Church. Rev. Philo McKinnon begins his remarks by giving some background information. "Marvin King was born and raised in Brunswick, Georgia," he says. "He moved his family, which includes his wife Bobby, also a former Brunswick native, and his children Teri, Lee, Hal and Todd to Jonesboro. He and Bobby have provided a wholesome environment for raising their family. Although the close-knit family is unprepared for the sudden loss of their husband and father, I pray that God will provide all of them a source of strength and guidance."

Rev. McKinnon offers a few complementary remarks. "Marvin, while growing up in a large family in Brunswick, had a humble beginning. His father made a living as a roofing contractor. He realized at a young age that his calling was not the roofing business.

Marvin was blessed to have a unique talent to read music and play the trumpet well. His musical skills earned him scholarships and eventually brought him to our community and our church."

Jonesboro High Principal Fred Smith speaks next. "In the late 1960s Marvin accepted the music director position at Jonesboro High School. Mr. King also taught music at elementary schools throughout the county. As a teacher and a mentor to the music students, he was a popular teacher and had a positive impact on many students. Those who knew him considered Marvin to be an excellent band director who was liked and respected by the students."

Mr. Smith lauds Mr. King for twenty minutes as he continues. "In 1967 Mr. King was chosen by one of his students as STAR Teacher from his high school. Sponsored by the Clayton County Chamber of Commerce, the award recognized the teacher that had the most influence in the student's scholastic achievement. The following year, King was named as the Outstanding Educator by the Morrow Jaycees. His bands were always rated as 'superior' at the annual competitive music festivals. Later the Clayton County Chamber of Commerce also recognized Marvin as Citizen of the Year in the field of the arts."

Mrs. King sits motionless absorbed in memories of Marvin. Their first date, the birth of their first child, moving into their dream home at Lake Spivey and the Cardinal band performing at Marvin's first home football game. She asks herself, "Oh, why did this have to happen?"

Mark Foster, a member of the Mark Five band tells the mourners, "Marvin was a tremendous talent as a musician. His skill as a trumpet player was unmatched in the Atlanta area. Marvin had played the National Anthem before the Atlanta Braves game. Most recently he and the band had played at Gov. Busbee's election celebration party." It was the last time Marvin King performed with his band.

Foster tells some of the light-hearted stories that Marvin and his Mark Five band members experienced while performing their Motown music in various clubs in and around Atlanta. Everyone is respectfully amused. Bobby could not hold back her tears throughout the entire service. She just wants it to be over. She knows the tributes and accolades are well-meant, but she would rather have Marvin back by her side. Although she is in a church setting, she cannot comprehend how she can ever forgive those who had committed this terrible act.

During the highly emotional service the family members and students weep and console one another. Later the family makes the three-hour trip to Brunswick for the burial at Memorial Park. The graveside service is at 2 p.m. on Monday, November 18, where Marvin King is laid to rest.

CHAPTER **12** | November 9th:
First Detective Meeting

Friday evening, Sheriff Glass instructs Capt. Howard to contact his detectives for a mandatory meeting Saturday morning at 8:30 a.m. in the conference room at the detectives' trailer. Trustee Charles Holloman nicknamed "Washpot," brings the sausage and biscuits and prepares a pot of coffee. When Trustee Washpot, is not attending to kitchen duties, he spends his free time drawing buildings located around the McDonough Square as well as sketches of the deputies and inmates. One of the guards commented, "When Holloman gets released and if he stays out of trouble, he could probably make a living as an artist."

Several of the Sheriff's deputies are also present. It is the first of several meetings dedicated to the discussion of the King and Hartsfield murders.

Sheriff Glass says, "The press is hounding Sugg and I for answers about the murders. I have asked you here today to see what progress you have made in finding any clues. Gentlemen, do we have any new information?"

"We know that Miss Hartsfield is last seen leaving Clayton Junior College shortly after noon. When the junior high secretary calls her mother to inquire if Melanie is ill, Mrs. Hartsfield begins to get concerned. She has never been late. Melanie is expected at the Riverdale Junior High School at 1:30 p.m. for her part-time job tutoring the choir. The call worries Mrs. Hartsfield to the point that she notifies the Clayton County Police Department about Melanie's disappearance.

Capt. Howard adds, "Jonesboro High Principal, Mr. Smith, told police that Mr. King signed out shortly before noon. We received a call from a witness who saw Mr. King leaving the Jonesboro Library around 12:30 p.m. After that time, we could find no other witnesses who could recall seeing either one alive."

Sheriff Glass asks, "Do we know how the two got to Rock Quarry Road?"

Capt. Howard responds, "Yes, I am getting to that. We located King's Opel wagon yesterday afternoon. It was spotted by a patrolman parked in a field off Tye Street. No keys, but Hartsfield's pocketbook was found in the Opel. Her money purse is missing. We are having the car towed in and will dust for prints. Later Miss Hartsfield's locked 1964, four-door, blue-and-white Ford Galaxy 500 was found parked in front of a convenience store at Mays Corner Shopping Center. There were no personal belongings other than her school stuff in the car,"

Sheriff Glass continues, "If we put all of our minds together maybe we can solve this puzzling crime. Sugg, I want to appoint four teams of two detectives each. I want you to work day and night until you find this killer. I want Bill Hart to assist lead investigator Shug Howard. Tommy Floyd and Paul Robbins are to handle the field investigation. The other team of Billy Payne and Dick Barnes can run down leads. Charlie Tomlinson and Bobby Lemon will be the fourth team for now. Charlie and Bobby will canvas the neighborhood to see if anybody saw or heard anything suspicious that day. My staff and I will assign whatever tips come through my office to one of the teams."

"Sir, I think the killer must have had an accomplice," Det. Barnes explains. "It would have taken two people to drag and conceal the bodies into the woods. If the victims were followed to Rock Quarry Road, who drove their car away from the murder scene? If they were abducted and driven to Rock Quarry Road, the killer needed someone to hold his passengers at bay, while he or one of the victims drove. Since there was no sign of a struggle, the victims must have known the killers."

Det. Robbins adds, "Since Melanie's purse was found in Marvin's wagon, they were abducted after leaving together from Mays Corner."

Sheriff Glass has more questions. "What have we learned about the murder weapon?"

"We know it was a shotgun that was used to kill the victims," replies Capt. Howard. "The shells we found were manufactured by Winchester. I plan to send the casings to the crime lab. It would help if we could send the shotgun as well. The lab could positively match the spent shells with the hunter's gun. We should confiscate shotguns from all the hunters known to hunt in the area. There are tire tracks and footprints that we need to run down. We think the taillight or turn signal cover was broken by a stray pellet fired by the shooter. The shards of glass we found belong to a vehicle that was at the scene. That's all the physical evidence we found."

Det. Floyd says, "I spoke with Mrs. King. She is very distraught and says she has no clue as to what her husband was doing with Melanie that Thursday. Melanie is a family friend and has babysat their youngest child, Todd, on numerous occasions. She is also a high school friend to King's oldest daughter, Teri."

***

On Wednesday, the 11th of November, Veterans Day, Sheriff Glass, wearing a patriotic red poppy next to his shiny badge, tells the *Clayton County News Daily*, "Detectives are hoping to question two persons who have information about the killings."

Capt. Howard adds, "The identities of the two men are known, but we cannot disclose their identities at this time. They are between the ages of eighteen and twenty-three and may have been hunting off of Rock Quarry Road. We have been informed that they live in Henry County. That's all I can tell you."

The King and Hartsfield murders catch the attention of the governor's office. Gov. Jimmy Carter signs an executive order offering a $1,000 reward for information leading to the arrest and conviction of the person or persons involved in the murders.

CHAPTER 13 | Autopsies

The coroner's responsibility is to certify the cause of death, identify the body and issue a death certificate. He is a public official who is elected to a four-year term. Ronnie Stewart and his fraternal twin brother, Donnie, were my high school classmates. Following graduation, he went to work at Carmichael's and eventually became its funeral director. There he gained the experience and knowledge needed to run for and get elected coroner. Stewart, above average around the waist, was described as having a demeanor like a gruffy old bear but was a teddy bear inside. While performing his duties as coroner, he had seen few such horrific homicides.

Henry County Coroner Ronnie Stewart helps load the stretchers into the ambulance. He enters the rear of the ambulance, stations himself between the two stretchers and gives the all clear to the driver. With lights flashing and siren blasting, the trip from the old Rock Quarry Road to Carmichael's Funeral Home in McDonough takes less than fifteen minutes.

The funeral home resembles an early 1900s Southern home, full of happiness and life, not sadness and death. The town's busy funeral home is located on Hampton Street just off the square and within shouting distance of the jail and courthouse. A local doctor, G.R. Foster, is informed of the murdered bodies' arrival and is summoned. The time, circumstance, and cause of death require certification by a physician. It is obvious to Coroner Ronnie Stewart that these are not routine homicides. He quickly rules out murder-suicide as a possible motive. The victims were not killed elsewhere and then dumped in the woods. They were murdered near where their bodies were found. Coroner Stewart and Capt. Howard agree that the crime lab folks should be contacted to participate in the autopsy of both victims.

Henry County Det. Tommy Floyd and Det. Robbins leave the crime scene and head to the funeral home. They are followed by Capt. Billy Berry, the chief detective from the Clayton County Police Department. He wants positively to identify the male victim. Learning that the female victim was the missing student from Morrow makes it a priority case for his department. Capt. Berry had spent his entire day investigating the pre-dawn shooting in College Park of one of his officers, Eugene Barge. He was also killed by a shotgun. His department needs to know if there is a connection between the two shootings.

While waiting for the autopsies to begin, Det. Robbins and Capt. Berry strike up a conversation. Capt. Berry says, "My men and I have been really busy. It seems the drug problems in the South Metro area are on the rise. We are having an increase in overdose deaths reported to the department by Clayton General Hospital and are experiencing more drug related arrests. Many of these are young adults and minors. I think we have some 'big-time' drug dealers who have infiltrated our area. I am concerned that the situation may get worse."

Det. Robbins replies, "I hope these dealers don't start doing business in Henry County."

Mr. Stewart finally reaches Dr. Larry Howard, who has already left his office. Dr. Howard is proud of his nineteen years of service to the State of Georgia and the busy Georgia Crime Laboratory. He is currently the state's top authority in forensic crime investigations. He has completed approximately 4,000 autopsies in Georgia. He arrives at the funeral home at approximately 9:30 p.m.

Capt. Berry receives a call from one of his detectives who informs him that the Clayton Police Department had received an anonymous tip and thinks they know who is responsible for the shooting of Ofc. Barge.

***

Dr. Foster, a long time McDonough family physician and my family doctor, arrives to examine the bodies. Dr. Foster is also a member of Board of Directors of my bank, so in essence he is my boss. He tells me of his call from Carmichael's Funeral Home. He and Dr. Howard are old acquaintances and perform the autopsies together.

Dr. Foster had the opportunity to examine the bodies before Dr. Howard arrived. He tells Dr. Howard that it appears that the gun shots are the causes of death. From the amount of *rigor mortis*, he estimates the deaths occurred earlier in the day, sometime after lunch.

Dr. Howard confirms, "Yes, I would say around mid-afternoon. It is rather late, but would you care to assist me in performing the autopsies?"

Det. Floyd says, "We have identified the female from the inscription in her class ring. She is Melanie Hartsfield. We were unable to remove the University of Georgia class ring from the male victim. His fingers are swollen."

"A little petroleum jelly should do the trick," Dr. Howard says as he lubricates the fingers. "Here, detective. I will let you read the inscription."

Looking at the inscription Capt. Berry remarks, "Marvin King. Yes, it is the Jonesboro High School band director!"

"Now that we know who the two victims are, Dr. Foster and I have a lot of work to do. Would you gentleman please excuse us. I do not want to treat any injured fainters," Dr. Howard says with a broad smile.

Det. Robbins answers, "Don't worry, Doc. You don't have to ask me twice."

Capt. Berry apologizes, "It's been a long day for me. I am headed home."

Dr. Howard turns on the tape recorder and begins to dictate.

"The male victim identified as Marvin King shows the presence of two shotgun wounds. One shotgun wound entered the upper arm just above the left elbow, measured approximately one and a half inches in diameter, passed through the elbow and then re-entered the left side, passed in the back of the main body cavity, sectioned the spinal column and spinal cord in the lower back area. One shot exited from the right side of his spinal column approximately four inches to the right side of the spinal column.

"I am removing from the path of the shot, a pellet that appears by its size and shape to be a 00 buckshot near the entry area of the right arm.

"Mr. King has a second wound entry in the center of the back of the head at the base of the skull. This charge exited from just to the left of the midline in the forehead. The body also showed extensive drag marks on the front of the body evidenced by abrasion marks over the ribs and chest area."

Dr. Foster asks, "Does the double 00 buckshot come from a 12-gauge shotgun?"

"As far as I know, that's the only cartridge that can be fired from a 12-gauge barrel," responds Dr. Howard.

Dr. Howard continues to record as he moves to the second examining table. "The female victim identified as Melanie Hartsfield reveals injury caused by two shotgun wounds, one of which is in the right side of the neck and exited through the top of the head just left of center. There is another shotgun wound of entry in the left side of the back which passed through the abdominal aorta. Three large pellets exited from the right front evidenced by the associated pellets marks in the abdominal area. This charge lacerated the liver and sectioned the abdominal aorta. This body also has drag marks that includes the breast and chest area indicating she had been dragged on her stomach feet first over a considerable distance. I am removing wadding that was discharged from the shotgun."

Dr. Foster says, "I believe we can conclude that neither victim would have survived the first or second shot."

"It's nearly midnight and I am tired," Dr. Howard says. "It's nice to have some company when dissecting a body. I often find myself talking to the deceased. I ask them who did this to you. I have yet to get a reply."

Dr. Foster, chuckling, says, "When they do, it's time to find another line of work."

"Bob, it's good to see you again. Unfortunately, this time it was under rather tragic circumstances," Dr. Howard says as he shakes Dr. Foster's hand. I will take my photos, the pellets, and wadding back to the lab for further examination. I will take blood and swab samples from the two victims and run the routine tests in the morning. I will let you review a copy of my report, before I send it to the detectives."

CHAPTER 14 | November 15th:
Second Detective Meeting

Like many southern towns, the City of McDonough has a town square. To the north is the courthouse and jail. On the southside of the square are various business, all connected but with different facades. Walking from east to west on the corner is the First National Bank, followed by John Frank Ward's Drug Store and Jessie Gasses Clothing Store. On the opposite corner is Hubbard's Barber Shop. Clarence Hubbard has operated the business since the 1950s. In the front portion of the building are four barber chairs. In the back portion is one snooker table and four pool tables. If one is looking for entertainment in the City of McDonough, there are two choices: the movie theater on the eastside of the square, catty-corner from the Henry County Jail, and Hubbard's poolhall. Both do a brisk business.

A regular pool game costs a nickel per player. Snooker is a dime. Grady, a middle-aged Black man, collects the money and racks the pool balls. Rotation, nine ball, and eight ball are the most popular games. The house rules suggest that the loser of a particular game pay for the other players. Grady also cleans and polishes shoes for customers who request a shine while getting their haircut.

I played my share of pool while I was in high school but have not touched a cue stick since. I admit that I was not a good pool shooter. There was one important lesson I learned from playing pool: "Don't bet a fellow who brings his own pool cue to the hall." He is most likely a better pool player than you are. It can be an expensive lesson.

Today I am here to get a haircut and pickup whatever informa- tion is circulating in McDonough. Mr. Hubbard is a short, thin- haired polite fellow. He has been my barber from time to time since I was a boy. These days, when I am in the barber's chair, we usually trade stories and share our thoughts on politics and current events. The information I can gather is often more current and factual than what I read in the newspapers. Over the clacking noise of the cue ball striking the balls and the chatter around the billiard tables, he tells me that the major topic is the King and Hartfield murders. His customers are disappointed that Sheriff Glass and his detectives have not been able to make any headway in solving the case. If there are suspects, the Sheriff is being very secretive about who they are.

***

Reporters from the media are persistent in seeking informa- tion about the murders. Capt. Howard, a large intimidating figure wearing his usual leather jacket, reports to the press. "The autop- sies determined the time of death was between 2:30 p.m. and 3 p.m. last Thursday. I cannot comment on the motive for the slay- ing, but a full investigation is underway by the sheriff's office and Henry County detectives." Sheriff Glass adds, "We have a few leads, and I am confident we will solve this case soon."

Sheriff Glass has become frustrated with the lack of progress in solving the most baffling murder case in Henry County's his- tory. The crime has occurred during his watch, and it is his re- sponsibility to deliver a suspect. There are doubters who begin to question whether he can oversee such a complicated police inves- tigation. Sheriff Glass has no law enforcement experience prior to being elected Sheriff. His only meaningful credential is that he is related to a former Henry County Sheriff, Newton Glass. Newton was Henry County's 19th sheriff and served from 1885 to 1901.

Jimmy Glass had been an insurance adjuster for seventeen years before running for office. He does not want his failure in solving this case to impact his popularity or jeopardize his re-election bid.

Although not a member of one of the investigation squads, he is devoting most of his time keeping abreast of the detectives' activities and speaking to the press. All the time, he assures the public that his department is hot on the trail of a suspect, but in actuality there is little hard evidence and only speculation as to what happened. The detectives are no closer in finding their man, than they were a week ago.

During this period, Sheriff Glass neglects his usual administrative duties. His wife, Martha, sees little of him. For criminals it is a good time to commit a crime in Henry County. There are too few police personnel available to give chase or arrest lawbreakers. Most law enforcement personnel are tied up in some form or fashion with the King and Hartsfield murder case.

***

It is November 15th and Sheriff Glass assembles three of the investigative teams in his office. Officers Tomlinson and Lemon have been assigned back to their normal police duties.

Sheriff Glass begins, "Gentlemen, you fellows are working hard but it is not enough. The trail is getting cold. We should have solved this case by now. We need to show some progress, the public demands it! I am considering bringing in some new detectives. Don't be surprised if some of you are reassigned or dismissed. The department does not have enough patrol cars to assign all of you to traffic duty."

The detectives, especially Capt. Howard, are taken aback by Sheriff Glass' disparaging remarks. Capt. Howard responds, "We visited every household within two miles of the murders trying to find an eyewitness. My men have interviewed more than seventy persons. They have talked with Miss Hartsfield's parents and friends. None of them are aware of a secretive relationship between her and Mr. King. If there was, she never talked about it to anyone. She has no boyfriends that we can determine. Det. Floyd and Det. Robbins went to the school and spoke with teachers and several people who knew Mr. King.

"Mr. King's situation is a little more intriguing. As a band director and teacher, we can find no 'dirt'. He did not do drugs nor was he involved in the selling of drugs. The principal rates his job performance as superior. He was a hard worker and was seldom absent from work. We focused on his moonlighting activities. His band was extremely popular and performed on most week-ends, more often during the summer months and holidays. The band performed at many country clubs and local events. Gigs at private parties seldom ended before midnight. There was always an abundance of alcohol present. Heavy drinking and occasional pot smoking were not uncommon. Who knows? There may have been hard drug activity in the back rooms as well?

"We spoke with the members of the band. Mark Foster said that there was no drug use by the band members. We do not know if he was telling the truth. But this is the 1970s. Everybody is getting high. Most musicians need the stuff to perform. In this type of environment where drugs are prevalent, something illegal may have occurred. Maybe it was something that they saw or knew that got them killed. Mr. Foster also confirmed that he and Marvin were good friends and had planned to meet that evening."

Det. Robbins speaks up. "I think we ought to look seriously at the Banks boy. Since he is the informer and remained at the scene, most folks do not consider him a likely suspect, but I do. He may be trying to outsmart us. I believe he tried to rob the couple when he spotted them parked on the dirt road. When they refused, he shot them. To make sure they would not survive to identify him, he then shot them again. He dragged their bodies to where they could not be easily found. He covered them with a blanket to keep away animals. Buzzards flying above would alert searchers of the location of something or someone that has recently died. He moved the car just far enough away to where he could walk back, flag down a motorist and pretend to be innocent. All the while, removing any suspicion from himself. It was a great plan of deception."

Sheriff Glass says, "Let's concentrate on Banks."

"I will take care of it," promises Capt. Howard.

After the meeting Sheriff Glass asks Sugg his opinion of Banks as a possible suspect. He reminds the Sheriff that Banks has a previous arrest record. He pleaded guilty to an involuntary murder charge and served time in the Henry County Jail.

Capt. Howard answers, "I believe there are those who hunt for food. There are those who hunt for sport. And there are those who hunt to kill. Sheriff, behind that innocent face is a killer. He has no regard for life nor remorse for his prey, be it a deer or a human being."

CHAPTER 15 | Murder Weapon

I am told that a good detective in a murder investigation seeks out a suspect who has a motive, the opportunity and no verifiable alibi. These are only subjective assumptions. But, when the investigator can tie a weapon to a particular suspect, then he has conclusive evidence. Handguns have serial numbers and possession requires a license. Hunting firearms such as shotguns do not. The use of a paraffin test to determine if a suspect had recently fired a gun is not reliable. A discharged bullet from the bore of a particular rifle or pistol; however, will leave a distinctive marking. A microscopic comparative analysis can match a firearm to a discharged bullet. The spent shell casing fired from a shotgun will also possess unique markings. Such evidence is difficult for the defense to refute. However, there is no scientific means to match a discharged pellet load to a particular shotgun. Thus, connecting a shotgun to a shooter is not a simple task.

A ballistic expert at the G.B.I. crime lab determines that the spent shells found at the murder scene were fired from Banks' shotgun. This type of firearm and the cartridges used are not unique and can be purchased at any retailer that sells hunting supplies. The shotgun and the spent shells become the key evidence in the investigation of the Marvin King and Melanie Hartsfield murders.

*Sgt. Floyd examines
the Stevens Arms shotgun*

***

Stevens Arms was founded by Joshua Stevens in Chicopee Falls, Massachusetts, in 1864. The company was purchased by the Savage Arms Company on April 1, 1920. Stevens Arms continued to operate as a subsidiary. The merger made Savage the largest producer of arms in the United States at the time. From 1927 until 1955, Stevens began producing a single-barrel shotgun like the one Banks was carrying on the day of the murders.

The shotgun belonged to his father. After his death in 1946, it remained in the Banks family. The shotgun is used periodically for hunting by the Banks brothers and is kept at the family home on Highway 155. Perry, living at home, becomes the custodian of the shotgun. Jerry has been an avid hunter since his youth. Over the years Jerry learns everything there is to know about handling a firearm.

In the 1960s the Rock Quarry and Hudson Bridge Road areas were the locations of several dairy farms. The King and Hartsfield murders occurred on land that was once a part of Raleigh Henry's dairy farm. Although most of these dairies are no longer in business, there remain remnants of cultivated tracts that were once cropland or pasture. Over time the farmlands quickly converted back to underbrush and pine trees. The presence of cattle is replaced by deer, rabbits, turkeys and other wild game. Consequently, Rock Quarry Road becomes a popular hunting location, so much so, that the landowners post "No Hunting" signs along the old, abandoned dirt road. However, hunters take little notice of the signs and hunt anyway. In the process discarded shotgun shells casing are often left behind.

The spent shells or casings, or hulls as they are called, found near the murder scene were fired from a 12-gauge shotgun; more specifically identified as Winchester Western XX-Super X 00 Buckshot Mark V cartridges. Each cartridge contains nine to twelve pellets weighing approximately three and half grams. The ammunition was probably purchased from Stockbridge Western Auto managed by James Love. Since the shot is accurate from thirty to fifty yards, it is commonly used by deer hunters. The 00 buckshot is unique to the 12-gauge shotgun.

On one of the victims' wadding remnants were discovered. The type of wadding used in shotgun shells differs from one manufacturer to another. One manufacturer does not pack wadding in its cartridges. When a Winchester Western is fired from close range, it will leave particles of polyethylene granules on and around the entry hole. These are unique to the Winchester Western.

CHAPTER 16 | Serial Killer,
John Paul Knowles

Today is the eleventh day after the horrific murders of Marvin King and Melanie Hartsfield. At the conclusion of Sunday morning Mass and lunch, our Broder clan heads to the Stockbridge Elementary School to play basketball. The asphalt court is a big improvement over the dirt court at the farm. My sister, Angela, aspiring to make the high school team wanted to show off her new jump shot.

Later Sunday afternoon I would be looking forward to watching the Atlanta Falcons game against the Baltimore Colts on television. Coach Norm Van Brocklin was recently fired after the Miami Dolphins beat the Falcons 42 to 7. Defensive coordinator Marion Campbell has taken over as the new head coach. The Falcons are a bad team. Because of the promotion of former Georgia Bulldog Campbell, I have a renewed interest in the Falcons who are headed for another miserable season. I had to be in front of the television by game time, 4 p.m.

It was a fun afternoon. We invited a couple of other players who were there to join us in a full-court game. We were puzzled by the blaring sirens and the number of emergency and police vehicles heard racing down Highway 42. There were also helicopters flying overhead. The immediate thought was that an airplane had crashed.

After a week, countless rumors surface each day as the murders are still the topic of discussion at grocery stores, beauty shops, churches or wherever two or more locals are gathered. Newspapers that publish stories about possible suspects only create more speculation. Some are sure it is the unfriendly neighbor down the street or blame an evil demon sent from hell. Random calls to the police "tip line" often provide names of individuals who the tipsters think deserve to be in prison, even if they had nothing to do with the killings. There are many differences of opinion about all aspects of the crime. Everyone, however, agrees that it was a senseless act.

On the day of the Hartsfield and King murders in Stockbridge, there was also a double murder in Milledgeville, Georgia. Both incidents are equally puzzling and were committed by heartless and vicious killer or killers. The two homicides, occurring within an hour's drive from one another, may be connected.

***

The Clerk of Henry County Superior Court is a refined and highly respected woman named Sara Taylor, who has held the position since 1969. Mrs. Taylor's daughter, Elyse, was a high school classmate and former 4H-er. We always spoke to one another whenever I was in the courthouse.

This day she sees me coming and steps out of her office to greet me. She is craving details about the manhunt that occurred in north Henry County yesterday. I proceed to tell her what I knew of the events.

Apparently, the Georgia Bureau of Investigation (G.B.I.) was tracking a suspected felon from Florida northward through the backwoods of Georgia. Law enforcement knew he had made eating and refueling stops in Brunswick and Abbeville. The G.B.I. had a description of the vehicle and a license plate number of the stolen car. The bureau had asked all police jurisdictions in Georgia to be on the lookout for the suspect. The request came with a warning. "He is armed and very dangerous."

The team of law enforcement agents was closing in on the suspect. They speculated that he is the dangerous escaped fugitive who is linked to several recent unsolved murders the same one who is on everyone's "most wanted" list. Every policeman with a car radio was aware of the search and was on constant look out for anyone who vaguely fitted the description. Every police department had been sent a photo of the suspect. Strategic roadblocks were stopping motorists and searching vehicles. From the stolen credit cards, he was using, the agencies knew where he had been and where he might be headed. They knew the make and model of the stolen vehicle he was supposedly driving. However, law enforcement had not been able to pinpoint his exact whereabouts. They surmised he had left Florida and was driving north through rural Georgia probably headed toward Atlanta. Then, they got a break.

A G.B.I. spokesman reported that a service station attendant in Lakeland, Georgia near Valdosta, told authorities that he spotted a 1974 blue Ford Torino on Saturday. He said that he noticed two persons in the back seat and the driver alone in the front. The driver had stopped to buy a pack of cigarettes. When shown the F.B.I. photograph of the suspect, the attendant acknowledged, "That's him. That's the man I saw driving the car." From the license plate number, authorities learned that the vehicle was a rental car leased from Hertz in Tallahassee. The driver of the Torino is an employee of Cottrell Inc. named James Meyers. He had rented a motel room in Perry, Florida, a small town just south of Tallahassee. The twenty-nine-year-old businessman from Delaware frequently traveled to Florida to visit clients. When Florida authorities searched Meyers' motel room, they found all his belongings intact. However, Meyers and his vehicle were nowhere to be found.

A passing motorist reported to the Florida State Patrol that he witnessed a trooper being held at gun point while parked and standing beside his patrol car. The thirty-five-year-old Trooper Charles Campbell had stopped a vehicle that fit the description of a stolen vehicle belonging to a Florida woman. Apparently, the driver of the stolen car overpowered the trooper and abducted him. A massive manhunt ensued in north Florida and South Georgia to locate Trooper Campbell.

***

In Henry County, Sundays are generally quiet and uneventful periods for law enforcement. Businesses are closed and citizens attend church. Travelers who make overnight stops at motels choose to sleep in before they resume their journeys. Senior patrolmen and deputies usually have the day off, consequently the department has limited number of patrol cars on duty.

The detective teams have accumulated a great deal of overtime as they followed up leads. Those who are off duty Sunday are expecting a quiet restful afternoon. The weather is sunny and warm, a gorgeous afternoon. The sense of urgency to resolve the King and Hartsfield murders has subdued somewhat.

Ofc. Hancock radios in. "Dispatch, I am parked at McDonough Kiwanis Pool observing traffic on Highway 42. I have spotted a car that matches the description of a vehicle that the G.B.I. has reported as stolen. It is a blue Ford Torino, Florida tag, serial number, ENC 583."

"Yes, the car is stolen!" replies dispatch without delay.

Ofc. Hancock says, "I will give chase."

"All units, Ofc. Hancock is in pursuit of a suspect in a stolen car. He is just exiting the McDonough City limits and is traveling north on Highway 42 toward Stockbridge," dispatch announces.

***

Jerry Key's family operated a plumbing business and lived on a small farm on Mays Road in Stockbridge. They were frequent visitors to our farm, either to do a plumbing repair job or purchase a bull calf. While in college Jerry and I worked together during a summer break. We had the dubious job of packaging and shipping bra orders to retail stores for the Lovable Company in Atlanta. Jerry was not interested in joining the family business.

Instead, he chose to pursue a career in law enforcement.

Ofc. Key, patrolling the Stockbridge area, is the nearest unit that can offer backup. He races the Crown Victoria with lights flashing, siren blasting, to the Hudson Bridge Road intersection where he sets up a roadblock.

The intersection is within a few hundred feet south of what locals know as Hudson's Bridge. The original winding, narrow dirt road contained a wooden plank bridge which crossed over Rum Creek before intersecting Highway 42. In the 1960s the road was paved and its intersection with Highway 42 moved to the south. The old bridge no longer exists, but the name, Hudson Bridge Road, survives.

Ofc. Key chooses a location where metal guard rails line the shoulders along Highway 42. The Georgia Department of Transportation placed the barriers to prevent unsuspecting motorists from plunging down the steep embankment. The guard rails narrow the overall width of the two-lane roadway and its grassy shoulders. A single police car strategically parked on the road can block an oncoming vehicle from getting through. The eluding driver will have few options to circumvent the roadblock.

Ofc. Key reaches his destination in the nick of time. The driver of the stolen car traveling north on Highway 42 has topped the hill and is bearing down on the roadblock. Ofc. Key's police car with flashing blue lights is now in clear view to the approaching driver in the stolen car. He realizes that he has been spotted and the roadblock is meant for him. The driver has a dilemma. He hears the siren. He looks in his rearview window and sees the pursuing police car gaining on him. It is too late to turn around. He is trapped. To evade capture there is only one logical course of action.

Ofc. Key expects the driver to stop. Instead of slowing and surrendering, the driver speeds up and crashes into the front end of the patrol car which sits in the middle of the road perpendicular to the guard rails. The driver reckons that with enough speed the impact would shove the police car off to one side and the create an opening lane for his getaway.

Ofc. Key stands behind the patrol car leaning over the hood with his cocked gun in hand. When he hears the driver gunning the engine and notices the approaching vehicle picking up speed, he backs away from the patrol car. As the Torino rams into the patrol car, the impact of the collision knocks the retreating Ofc. Key backwards. The two vehicles are demolished. Ofc. Key is lying some ten feet from where the approaching vehicle came to an abrupt stop. Luckily, he lands on the grassy shoulder inches from the unforgiving concrete. His injuries are minor. The driver on the other hand, is bleeding profusely, as his head had struck the windshield.

The pursuing Ofc. Hancock hears the thunderous impact and rushes to the site of the collision. Figuring the driver is badly hurt, he is surprised to see the suspect trying to exit the vehicle. The Torino driver's side door is too mangled to open, but he is able to squeeze through the passenger's side door and crawl to safety. The dazed and injured driver opts to make a run for it. With a pistol in hand, he heads for the bushy area along the eastside of the road and southside of the creek. He runs in the direction of the reservoir to the east. Before he can reach the dense underbrush, Ofc. Hancock fires and strikes the fleeing driver in the right leg. He grabs the bleeding calf as the pain shoots up his leg. He is limping noticeably as he reaches the thick underbrush and escapes.

Capt. Howard, in an unmarked police car, arrives shortly thereafter followed by other units from Henry County and the City of Stockbridge. Capt. Howard assigns one of the officers to take Ofc. Key to the local doctor to treat his non-life threatening injures. He immediately makes an area-wide appeal for help. His calls are answered by over one hundred metro units, plus all available Georgia State Highway Patrolman, G.B.I. and F.B.I. agents. The final count exceeds two hundred who participate in the massive manhunt. Helicopters, blood hounds and an army of men are in pursuit. It is probably Georgia's largest and most intensive manhunt ever concentrated in one area. Those who are not scouring the woods searching for the suspect, have situated themselves on the surrounding roads forming barriers of patrol cars, emergency vehicles and unmarked police cars. These are reinforced by locals with rifles and shotguns who want to help. A perimeter that includes sections of Highway 42, Highway 138, Crumbley Road and all roads in between is blocked off and manned by law enforcement to thwart any possible escape. Homeowners who are in the quarantined areas are told to lock all doors and be on alert. The scene is akin to a military operation where everyone is in readiness for anticipated enemy attack. They soon learn that the threat is from only one person, but he is the "most wanted" fugitive who has ever set foot in Georgia.

Twenty-eight-year-old John Kenneth Knowles, aka John Paul Knowles, is an escaped fugitive who has allegedly left a trail of murder victims across the U.S. One newspaper accuses him of using stolen credit cards taken from victims in thirty-seven states. In a four-month period it is estimated that Knowles could be a suspect in as many as thirty-five homicides, rapes, burglaries and thefts. Knowles is described as six-foot-tall with reddish hair and well mannered. With his good looks and glowing personality, he can easily outwit unsuspecting victims who have taken him into their confidence. A petty criminal from Florida, Knowles had been in and out of jail, since the age of nineteen. Arrested July 1974 in Jacksonville, he manages to escape from a work camp. He flees to San Francisco, where he supposedly begins his murder spree.

Terry Clark

At 4:30 p.m. November 17, 1974, law enforcement officers, tracking dogs and circling helicopters have been searching for Knowles for four hours and have managed to tighten the dragnet around the perimeter. Terry Clark had returned home from a deer hunting trip earlier in the day. He lives alone in a small quaint white house with blue trim on Crumbley Road. The twenty-seven-year-old Clark is a Grady Hospital maintenance worker and Vietnam war veteran. He hears over the radio that a manhunt in the area is underway. As a precaution, he keeps his loaded shotgun by his side and vigilantly looks out his living room window for any suspicious activity. Suddenly, he notices a stranger trying to steal his pickup truck. He reacts quickly. He grabs his shotgun and runs outside to protect his property.

Clark yells, "Hey you, get away from my truck. Drop that shotgun or I will blow your head off!"

"Don't shoot! I am hurt and I need help," answers Knowles.

Clark replies, "I don't have a phone. So, let's walk toward those houses across street, where I can get someone to help you."

Clifton Brewton, Pastor of Salem Baptist Church, with his family and guests inside sees the two walking toward his house. Clark, clutching his shotgun, follows closely behind Knowles and is not immediately recognized by Brewton. Consequently, he ushers everyone into a locked back room. Armed with only a butcher knife, he is prepared to protect his family. He intentionally ignores Clark's knock on the door. Clark motions with shotgun for Knowles to walk to the neighboring Stonecypher house. Meanwhile, Mr. Brewton alerts the authorities and then calls his neighbor Stonecypher. One of the children is heard hollering in background, "He is out there! It's him! He's carrying a gun! He is going to kill us!"

The intruder Knowles is easy to identify. He is holding a makeshift bandage covered with blood against his forehead. He is limping badly. Knowles is carrying a shotgun that he managed to find and steal from an unoccupied house. By now however, the injured Knowles is exhausted and the adrenaline rush that provided him the impetus and energy to flee has worn off. He is in pain and too weak to put up resistance. Calmly, Terry Clark single-handedly captures Knowles.

Paul Robbins escorts fugitive John Paul Knowles after capture

Terry Clark was one of my boyhood pals in grade school. I often spent the day with Terry when he visited his uncle C.C. Clark. His dairy adjoined the Broder farm cornfield that fronts on Rock Quarry Road. I recall several exploring forays into surrounding woods we made. It is the same site where the King and Hartsfield bodies were found.

At the Stonecypher house they are able to hold their hostage until help arrives. It is only a few minutes. But, to Brewton, Stonecypher and Clark, the arrival of the police cannot come soon enough. Knowles is quickly surrounded by armed agents and police who handcuff him. To the delight of the captors, neighbors and law enforcement, the manhunt is a success. Everyone is out of harm's way and there are no further injuries reported.

With the drama over, hundreds of police and neighbors converge onto the Stonecypher property. Loud cheers can be heard coming from all directions. There is a huge sigh of relief by the panic-stricken Crumbley Road community. Law enforcement in Henry County and throughout the South rejoice upon hearing the news of the capture. Soon, newspaper and television reporters arrive *en masse*. They begin interviewing anyone who wants to talk. TV cameras film the hordes of onlookers trying to get a glimpse of the suspect as he sits motionless in the heavily guarded police car. A local doctor is summoned to examine Knowles. Unaccustomed to all the attention, Clark quietly retreats to his bungalow where he speaks only to the detectives in charge.

A G.B.I. agent proclaims, "Clark, you are a hero. What you accomplished here today in fifteen minutes, the G.B.I. and F.B.I. had not been able to do in four months—capture this madman. How do you feel? Were you afraid?"

"No, this was nothing compared to what I experienced in 'Nam," answers Clark.

***

My friend and at times, my personal physician, Dr. Joe A. Blissit, gets a call to tend to a captured fugitive, John Paul Knowles. He was injured in the car crash at the roadblock and received a superficial gunshot wound as he fled. Lying on Stonecypher's kitchen table, closely guarded by Det. Paul Robbins, Det. Billy Payne and Coroner Ronnie Stewart, Knowles is fortunate on two counts; first, not to have died in the collision at the road block and second, to have a medical doctor available when captured.

After Dr. Blissit dresses Knowles' wounds, he is taken to the Henry County Jail. Captive Knowles is placed in a special cell under the watchful eyes of Henry County Deputies. The Henry County Jail has the dubious honor of holding two notorious prisoners. Both are suspects in the King and Hartsfield murders. Detectives, however, have no proof that Knowles committed the murders. As a result, Knowles' stay in Henry County is short-lived. Bibb and Baldwin County police have convincing evidence that implicates Knowles for murders he allegedly committed there.

News accounts report that witnesses have identified Knowles from a photograph that shows him using one of the victim's credit cards. The same card was used to purchase gas in Abbeville, Georgia and later, to rent a motel room and to buy new clothes in Macon. To answer for those crimes Knowles is transferred to a maximum-security facility in Bibb County. He is assigned a public defender, who advises him to remain silent. On the advice of his attorney, Knowles is uncooperative and offers little additional information that would aid agents in resolving several other pending murder cases.

The crowd slowly disbands. It has been a long day. One that they will never forget.

When Henry County Police search the wrecked Torino, abandoned by the fleeing Knowles, they find Trooper Campbell's hat and gun belt. Meyers and Campbell, the two individuals the Lakeland service station attendant identified as being in the vehicle with Knowles, remain missing. Their whereabouts must be somewhere between Valdosta and Stockbridge. Hopefully, the abductees are still alive.

CHAPTER 17 | November 20th:
Third Detective Meeting

I had the occasion to catch Det. Robbins in the bank one after-
noon while he was standing in line. He mentioned that he had
been to the crime lab to deliver some evidence and was headed
back to McDonough. I took the opportunity to inquire about his
progress in the King and Hartsfield murder investigation.

He said that he would come to my office after he cashed his
check. He began the conversation by saying that he could not dis-
cuss the case. So, I changed the subject. We talked about the fun
we had in high school and what disappointed seasons our football
team, the Golden Tornadoes, had. Paul then volunteered to talk
about the detectives' meetings and all the work he and Tommy
were doing in trying to please Capt. Howard and Sheriff Glass.
There was frustration in the department over not finding an imme-
diate suspect. Paul probably told me more than he should have.
The enlightening discussion ended with Paul saying that he knew
who the killer was and that he was certain he was their man. He
speculated that an arrest would be made soon.

***

Wednesday the 20th of November, three days after the capture
of Knowles, Capt. Howard, at the direction of Sheriff Glass, calls

for a meeting of the investigative teams. The early afternoon time frame works well for both the day and night shift officers and detectives. All present expect to hear good news, perhaps a possible suspect in the Stockbridge murders.

Sheriff Glass addresses the group. "I want to thank all you men who sacrificed your Sunday afternoon and took time away from your families to search for and capture Knowles. As it turns out, he was wanted in several jurisdictions. He had been eluding the G.B.I. and F.B.I. for months, until we caught him on Crumbley Road. He is a sleazy character, all right. Not only did he total the blue Torino he stole from one of his victims, but also one of our practically new police cars. For those of you who have not heard, Ofc. Key, who was nearly run over at the roadblock, is recovering. He is going to be fine.

"In the meantime, Capt. Howard and the G.B.I. have questioned Knowles about his possible involvement in the King and Hartsfield murders. It has been reported that he was seen in the Henry County area on the 7th of November. But so far, he won't admit to any murders in Henry County or elsewhere for that matter. Agents are convinced that he is a suspect in several murders. As you know, he did not stay in our jail very long. The G.B.I. sent him to a more secure facility in Macon. Until he confesses or we find some evidence that ties him to the King and Hartsfield murders, we will continue to search for other suspects. With that I will turn it over to Capt. Howard."

Capt. Howard is next to speak. "We have asked all of you to meet today to discuss the progress of the investigation. I am hoping that you have uncovered some positive leads," he says. "As the chief detective of the field investigation, Tommy, I will start with you."

Det. Floyd picks up here. "Mr. Fite at the crime lab called me last week and confirmed that the shell casings found at the scene came from a 12-gauge shotgun. The blanket used to cover the bodies belonged to Mr. King. I know this because I saw a similar blanket at the King residence. Mrs. King also confirmed that her husband had a matching blanket."

Capt. Howard asks, "Do you have any theories about who the

killer might be?"

"I am of the opinion that this crime has the appearance of a planned murder," responds Det. Floyd. I think this for several reasons. It is an execution style shooting. The killer or killers took the time to conceal the bodies in some underbrush so that they would not be quickly discovered. An amateur would have gotten anxious and left the scene as quickly as possible."

Det. Robbins asks, "Tommy, why do you say killers? Do you think there is more than one person involved?"

Det. Floyd answers, "We know that King's car is at the murder scene at the time of the shooting. Someone had to drive his Opel to the second location where someone else, a second person, could pick him up. The bodies could have been dragged by one strong person. Two could have disposed of the bodies quicker. I imagine the killers did not linger very long after the shooting."

Det. Robbins asks, "If there are two killers at the scene, wouldn't they have carried the victims, instead of dragging them and leaving a trail?"

Then Det. Barnes also asks, "Any significance in covering the female and not the male?"

"That's a good question," Det. Floyd responds. "I am not sure. Banks could have rearranged the blanket when he viewed the bodies. As to the question of premediated murder, the killers moved King's car to a second secluded area in hopes that it will not be immediately located. The driver of the vehicle wiped down the steering wheel, dashboard and doorknobs. The only prints remaining in the car belonged to King and Hartsfield. No, gentlemen, this was not a random shooting. The persons knew what they were doing. They were careful to leave no clues."

Capt. Howard adds, "We know that there is only one set of tire thread at the scene. Those belong to King's Opel. That means that King, Hartsfield and the killer probably arrived at the same time and in the same car. Or, if the killer followed them to the old, abandoned road, he would have left his vehicle someplace else and out of sight. From there he walked to where the Opel was parked. The killer probably surprised the pair and forced them out of the car. As they were walking around to the rear of the car, they were shot."

Det. Barnes says, "Whoever drove the car to the Rock Quarry Road location is familiar with the area. They must have been there before or scouted the location at an earlier time."

Det. Ray adds, "It is possible that the victims knew the killer since neither one had been tied or gagged. It appears that the victims did not resist."

Det. Floyd mentions, "Only local people know about these secluded spots. These victims were not chosen by chance."

"I guess whoever moved the car and why it ended up a mile away from the murder scene remains a mystery," adds Capt. Howard.

Det. Hart says, "If your theory about an execution is correct, then I must ask this question: 'Why would anyone want to kill a teacher and a student? What would be the motive?'"

"Somebody wanted them dead. They saw something, knew something or did something that was a threat to someone. That's all I know," replies Det. Floyd.

CHAPTER **18** | The Swimming Hole

The nearest public pool to Stockbridge is in McDonough run by the Kiwanis Club next to the Little League Baseball fields. Recreational facilities such as swimming pools are segregated. "Jim Crow laws" which call for "separate but equal" treatment of Blacks has been around for nearly a hundred years. Rural farm boys, both Black and White, must rely on creeks and ponds for their water recreation.

Growing up on the family farm, I spent many summer days, either fishing or swimming in Rum Creek. It was on one of these occasions that I first met Jerry Banks. He was among a group of neighborhood boys with whom I was acquainted. It was during the summer of 1960. Jerry was around nine years old and visiting his cousin, Clarence Banks, who lives on Buster Lewis Road. I remember the encounter as if it occurred yesterday. It was in the middle of the "dog days" of August when the heat and humidity made it difficult to enjoy the outdoors. Clarence said that on hot days an afternoon at the swimming hole would be the perfect place to be. That day Clarence calls a couple of the neighborhood friends and suggests that they walk down to the creek and go swimming.

All farms in the South need a source of water for the livestock to have something to drink. At a minimum, a small running stream or a spring-fed pond will do. The more fortunate farmers have flowing creeks suitable for irrigation and offer some recreational opportunities for the farm boys. Broder's farm has Rum Creek bisecting its bottoms. A creek that never runs dry, even during record droughts. Rum Creek had been dredged by President Roosevelts' Works Progress Administration (WPA) in the 1930s, so it has some steep banks. Over time the creek had eroded the shoulders, but in areas where big trees have footholds along the banks, the creek retained its narrow shape.

Upstream from the trees were pockets of deeper water known as fishing holes that were perfect places for brim and catfish to hide. Fishing was always the priority and the primary excuse given to parents to visit the creek. The promise to bring home the catch always gets a "Well, all right, go ahead." The Broder fishing hole was the most popular. On this hot summer day, the fish would not be biting, but the cool flowing water was too hard to resist.

As an additional treat, nearby trees were filled with wild muscadine vines. By the middle of August, the purple muscadines were ripe and ready for picking. One could fill a belly with the sweet Georgia muscadines.

***

Clarence and Jerry are joined by the Slaughter brothers, the Merrick twins and a kid everyone called 'Lip' as they head down Buster Lewis Road toward the creek. First, they make a stop at the Banks Community Store. Located in a small block building, the neighborhood store is owned and operated by A.B. and Mattie Banks. With a few quarters Clarence buys RC Colas and sugar cookies. They pass the Johnson and the Lemon houses. Doris and Andrew Lemon are outside watering their flowers. When they reach Henry Banks' place, Oliver, the youngest in the family, asks to come with them. On the shoulders of the road are ripening maypops (passion fruit), the size of hen eggs. Instead of stomping them and creating a loud popping sound, the boys start throwing the soft-shelled maypops at each other.

In those days, farm boys wore the same trousers, known as

overalls, for the whole week. Mama only washed clothes once a week and that was on sunny days, mostly on Saturdays. It was not uncommon for boys not to wear anything under their overalls. So, swimming had to be done in the nude. As long as the snapping turtles were not hungry, there was little danger in swimming that way! That day, we all went swimming in our underwear.

The swimming hole is in a section of the creek that had two large water oak trees on opposite sides of the banks that act as dam that created a perfect swimming hole. The trees also created approximately four feet of sandy beach along the bank directly upstream from the tree. The pool of water is approximately nine feet from the top of the bank. The distance from one side to the other is about thirty-five feet. One of the larger limbs from the oak tree extended out over the center of the creek. Earlier that summer I had climbed up the tree and fastened a rope around one of the higher limbs. The swing was made up of old hay ropes and thrown-away baler twine knotted together. Like Tarzan, one could swing over the creek from one side to the other. There was a large knot at end of rope so one could get a good grip.

My brother, Joe, and I were already at the swimming hole taking turns swinging on the rope when the group arrived. We would take a running start, grab the rope and swing across the creek and land on the bank on the other side. When we did not make it, we let go of the rope and jumped into the water. I decided that I would show off my diving skills. I jumped off the bank and did a swan dive into the swimming hole. I made sure I jumped far enough to clear the sandy beach and shallow enough not to scrape my stomach on the creek bottom. It looked dangerous, but if one was careful and hit the four feet water just right, it was an easy dive. The whole time this fellow who they nicknamed 'Lip' was constantly talking and bragging about something. Not only did he have a protruding lower lip, but he could not stop using it.

I remember Clarence teasing, "Lip, that dive looks pretty easy" If that Broder boy can do it, show them what you can do."

Lip exclaims, "Why there isn't nothin' to it. I have jumped from higher and scarier places than this."

"Then show us Lip," Clarence said. "I think you're afraid."

Lip proceeded to take off his shoes, shirt and overalls. He was down to his raggedy under-shorts. And after staring at the water below which to him looked higher than it actually was for the longest time, and receiving more smart-alecky remarks from those gathered around, one of which was Jerry, Lip finally jumped from the bank. He had miscalculated his dive. Half of him landed in the water and the other half landed on the sandy beach. From the waist up he did a beautiful belly flop into the creek and from the waist down he landed abruptly onto the beach. There, at the same time we heard a thump, a splash and a groan. A few seconds later, when it appeared that Lip survived the dive, everybody burst into laughter.

Lip was helped up the bank where he recovered. The swimming, diving and swinging on the rope continued to everyone's delight for the remainder of the afternoon. Each of us had our fill of muscadines. No one remembers seeing Lip at the swimming hole the rest of the summer. Everyone laughed when Clarence called the dive, "Lip's Leap into Creek."

CHAPTER **19** | December 9th:
Fourth Detective Meeting

It's been a month and two days since the infamous murders. The families of the victims are still grieving and searching for explanations as to why their loved ones had to die so tragically. They must be asking, why does it take so long to find the killers? Another meeting of the detectives provides the answer. Capt. Howard, Sheriff Glass, and Det. Floyd, Det. Robbins and Det. Barnes are in attendance in the detectives' meeting room at the trailer.

Capt. Howard begins the discussion. "As some of you have heard, Kelly Fite completed his test on the third shell casing we found the other day. He is reasonably sure that the spent shell could have been fired from the same shotgun as were the first two that we found earlier. He is also certain that all three match those spent shells from the cartridges that I fired behind our building here. It is the same old Stevens shotgun that Jerry Banks had in his possession the afternoon of the murders."

"I believe that wraps up the case. We have our killer. Let's pick him up," proclaims Sheriff Glass.

Det. Robbins, who is certain Banks is guilty says, "Tommy, that does away with your theory. We can stop looking for a hit-man."

"Yes, this was a crime of opportunity. Banks saw the couple parked on the secluded abandoned road. With his gun in hand, he decided to rob them. The teacher probably resisted and tried to persuade Banks to leave them alone. A heated argument followed with Banks shooting them. We have the evidence to prove that Banks did it," concludes Capt. Howard.

Det. Robbins adds, "Banks lied about the wallet and tried to blame the shooting on someone else. An innocent person doesn't have to lie."

"I remember Banks from the days when he was a trustee. I never had him figured as a cold-blooded killer," Det. Floyd says. "I find it hard to believe that he would shoot two people over their money. So far, we found the pocketbook but not King's wallet. He then dragged the lifeless bodies into a thicket, returned to fetch a blanket to cover the female victim, and threw the spent shell cartridge into the bushes. He then drove King's Opel to another secluded spot about a mile away, walked back to the scene to flag down a motorist, and reported the location of the bodies. All the while, he had the murder weapon on his person while he spoke with the police officers."

Capt. Howard says, "Tommy, I don't need to remind you that he pleaded guilty to killing his cousin."

"Yes, I know," Det. Floyd agrees. "But he was an eighteen-year-old kid then with no prior arrests. A crime that was committed at a party, where alcohol was consumed, and a fight ensued. After serving time, why would he risk going back to jail? By all accounts he was an ideal prisoner and was not a threat to anyone. He was allowed to do repair work and lawn maintenance in and around the City of McDonough and all the while requiring very little supervision. It just doesn't fit. If Banks had not taken the time to report the crime, it would have taken a while for someone to find the bodies. He may never have been implicated in the crime."

Sheriff Glass states, "If all that is true, then we will find out for sure, when we take him into custody."

Part II

Trials, Old Jail, and Sheriff

CHAPTER **20** | Banks is Arrested
and Charged

With the matching shell casings as evidence, Sheriff Glass is convinced it is time to make an arrest. He instructs newly promoted Sgt. Tommy Floyd to see Johnny Bond and get a warrant.

Johnny Bond was appointed by the Grand Jury in 1958 to handle the Henry County's Justice of the Peace duties and has held the position ever since. Like a magistrate judge, one of his responsibilities is writing warrants. Since Judge Sosebee resides in Forsyth and is not readily available, it is easier and quicker for law enforcement and others to obtain warrants from the local justice of the peace.

Sgt. Floyd finds Mr. Bond at his business. Mr. Bond's full-time job is operating his service station, but his justice of the peace position is taking more and more of his time. His station on Atlanta Highway is within convenient walking distance to the Henry County Courthouse. He handles approximately seventy to one hundred criminal cases and thirty to forty civil cases each quarter. The cases vary from bad checks and family disputes to murder. Mr. Bond has completed all correspondence courses and periodic seminars offered by the United Justices of the Peace of Georgia. He is fully knowledgeable of the duties and responsibilities of the job. Mr. Bond is respected by Sheriff Glass, Superior Court Clerk, Sara Taylor and all the lawyers.

Sgt. Floyd says, "We got confirmation from the G.B.I. lab that ammo from the hunter's shotgun matches the shell castings found in the vicinity of where the murders took place. Sheriff Glass thinks that there is enough evidence to pick up a Black man named Jerry Banks."

Judge Bond, "It sounds like you have probable cause to arrest Banks. I will issue the arrest warrant."

Sgt. Floyd asks, "While you are at it, could I have a search warrant as well? We think that there may be stolen items taken from the victims at his house."

"Sure, be glad to," responds Judge Bond.

***

On December 11th Sgt. Floyd and Det. Robbins knock on Jerry Banks' front door. Virginia is working at the nursing home and the children are at Aunt Opal's house. When Jerry answers the door, he sees through the tattered screen door, Sgt. Floyd holding up a white legal document.

Sgt. Floyd tells Jerry Banks, "We are here to place you under arrest. May we come in?"

"I can't believe this! For what?" the shocked Banks answers back.

Sgt. Floyd looking directly into his eyes says, "For the murder of Marvin King and Melanie Hartsfield."

With his right hand on the butt of the pistol, still in its holster, Det. Robbins pushes open the screen door and enters the living room. With his left hand he grasps the handcuffs hanging on his belt."

Sgt. Floyd instructs Banks to come along peacefully. Jerry does not resist. He lowers his head in disbelief as Det. Robbins applies the handcuffs. "This is a mistake, a bad mistake," he says.

Sgt. Floyd reads him his Miranda Rights. "You have the right to remain silent. Anything you say can be used against you in court. You have the right to talk to a lawyer for advice before we ask you any questions. You have the right to have a lawyer with you during questioning. If you cannot afford a lawyer, one will be appointed for you before any questioning, if you wish. If you decide to answer questions now without a lawyer present, you have the right to stop answering at any time. Do you understand?"

Overwhelmed, nodding and speechless, Banks is escorted to the back seat of the patrol car for the ten-mile ride to the Henry County Jail.

***

The discovery of the third red shotgun shell near the murder site on December 13th, reinforces the case against Banks and brings the investigation to a conclusion. The red spent shell found by Det. Hart is taken to the G.B.I. crime lab on Confederate Avenue in Atlanta, where the technician confirms that it also is a likely match to the shotgun casings previously sent to them by Capt. Howard. All were apparently fired from Banks' gun.

After suspect Banks is officially booked and placed behind bars in the bull pen, Sgt. Floyd questions Banks again. "Before I take you to the interview room, Jerry, tell me what you know about Mr. King's wallet. When the detectives searched the bodies, they did not find a wallet or a pocketbook."

"I picked up the wallet. I can't remember if it was near the bodies or along the way where they were drug. I looked inside to see if there was any money. There wasn't any, so I threw the wallet in the bushes," says Banks.

Sgt. Floyd asks, "If there was no cash, why didn't you take the credit cards. Didn't you see the expensive watch and rings on them?"

Banks: "I didn't want any of it. Besides what would I do with them? Mr. Floyd, instead of talking to me, you should be talking to the Black dude I loaned the shotgun to. He goes by the name Robert George."

***

Sgt. Floyd then escorts Jerry Banks to one of the detective offices which is used from time to time as an interview room. The small drab office in the trailer that faces away from the jail has no windows and contains just a small desk surrounded by four chairs. Waiting there are Sheriff Glass and Capt. Howard. The room is already filled with cigarette smoke as they have been there over a half an hour impatiently waiting for their suspect. They know they have their man. The interrogation should just be an academic exercise. A confession would wrap up this case. It will console the grieving families and bring relief to the nervous citizens. Everyone can rest easy as the whereabouts of the killer is no longer a concern. He sits in jail. A guilty plea would be a feather in the caps for the Sheriff Glass and the detective team members, who solved one of the most publicized murder cases in the history of Henry County.

Sheriff Glass tells the deputy to remove the handcuffs, but not the ankle cuffs. "Please bring Banks a cup of water," he says.

Sheriff Glass begins, "I am Sheriff Glass, and this is Capt. Howard. We have a few questions for you. Do you know why you are here?"

"Yes, sir, but I didn't do it!" Banks replies angrily.

Sheriff Glass says, "Don't raise your voice. It was your shotgun that killed the two people. How do explain that?"

"I don't know, all I know is that I didn't do it," says Banks, emphatically.

Sheriff Glass continues, "Was anyone else hunting with you that day?"

"No, sir, I was by myself. Just me and my dog," responds Banks.

Capt. Howard then says, "Tell me about your shotgun. What kind is it and what type of shells does it use?"

"It is a 12-gauge. I borrowed it, the shotgun, from my brother Perry and he gave me the shells. I don't know any more about the gun or the shells than that," answers Banks.

Capt. Howard continues the questioning. "Did you fire your gun the day of the murders?"

"No, sir, I did not see any deer to shoot," Banks responds.

Capt. Howard says, "Det. Robbins tells us that you picked up the man's wallet. We could not find it at the crime scene. Where is the wallet?"

Banks: "I threw the wallet into the bushes. It had no money or driver's license in it," answers Banks.

Capt. Howard asks, "Why didn't you put the wallet back where you found it?"

"I didn't want to have anything do with the wallet. It's bad luck to take anything from a dead man! I threw it down as I walked out of the woods," replies the frustrated Banks.

Sheriff Glass continues to grill Banks with rapid questions. "What were those people doing when you first spotted them? Were they sitting in their car? Were they talking?"

"No! They were dead under the blanket!" Banks repeats.

Sheriff Glass asks, "Banks, have you ever killed anyone?"

"Yes, sir. I shot my cousin in self-defense. He came at me with a knife," explains Banks.

Sheriff Glass says, "Banks, isn't it so that you tried to rob them and when they refused to hand over the wallet and walked away from you, you shot them in the back. Since they were still alive, you knew you had to make sure they were dead and shot them again."

"No! That ain't so!" responds Banks.

Capt. Howard accuses Banks: "You, Banks, stood over the life-less, bloody bodies and went through their pockets. No innocent man would do that."

"The wallet was laying on the ground. Yes, I just picked it up. Wouldn't anyone?" replies Banks.

Sheriff Glass raises his voice. "We don't believe you. If you confess now, I will see that the judge goes light on you. You won't have to go the electric chair and with good behavior you might get out and see your family again in a few years."

"No! I'm not guilty and I have nothin' to confess!" agitated Banks replies.

Sheriff Glass tells the deputy to take Banks back to the jail.

***

The Henry County Jail sits on the outer perimeter of the City of McDonough Square. The square is created by the convergence of several two-lane roads. If one travels from Stockbridge to Jackson, Decatur to Griffin or Covington to Hampton, one drives through the City of McDonough and passes the jail. In 1888, Henry County government officials approved the construction of a new jail. The lot was purchased for $50. The attractive brick structure was small, but modern for its time. It was built at a cost of $5,000. A fence encircling the building was added later. Jerry's temporary home has remained virtually unchanged for eighty-five years.

The following day, Sgt. Floyd visits Jerry at the Henry County Jail.

Sgt. Floyd tells Banks that they went to Moseley Road and took Mr. George into custody. He denied that he borrowed your gun. I think he is telling the truth. Jerry, why did you lie about loaning the gun and accusing George of the murders?

Jerry confesses, "I admit that I had lied about the loaning the gun. I said that in anger to get the police off my back."

***

Later that day, Sheriff Glass and Capt. Howard hold an informal news conference with the local press.

Sheriff Glass begins. "We have arrested Jerry Banks, a Black man who lives in Stockbridge, and charged him with the murders of Marvin King and Melanie Hartsfield. We kept interviewing Banks and found his stories just didn't add up. We used the ballistic tests to match his shotgun to the shell casings found at scene. With that evidence we are charging him with the murders. He said he was hunting alone and does not have a reliable alibi about his whereabouts at the time of the murders."

Capt. Howard adds, "From our investigation of King and Hartsfield murders we have gathered enough evidence and expert witnesses to ascertain that Jerry Banks is the sole perpetrator of the crime. We contend that robbery was the motive. The accused admits handling and discarding the man's wallet. The accused, Banks, is seen by several witnesses in possession of a shotgun shortly after the time of murders. We have a ballistics expert who will confirm that his shotgun was used in the commission of the crime."

CHAPTER 21 | Arraignment and
Grand Jury Hearing

I have always been intrigued by courtroom drama and challenges faced by defense lawyers. The black and white Perry Mason television shows are some of my favorites. Each week a murder is committed. Lt. Tragg is called to investigate the homicide and subsequently makes an arrest. District Attorney Hamilton Burger has a motive and compelling evidence from which to seek an indictment at the upcoming arraignment hearing. He is certain the prosecution has an air-tight case as all the evidence incriminates the accused. The alleged murderer, however, claims his or her innocence and engages Perry Mason as defense counsel. Paul Drake, the clever private detective, searches for evidence that he hopes will contradict the district attorney's charges. Meanwhile, Perry Mason and his attractive secretary, Della Street, interview would-be witnesses who could testify for the defense. Each week Perry Mason manages to outwit Lt. Tragg and Hamilton Burger as they uncover new evidence and sometimes a surprise witness. The viewing audience knows Mr. Mason will eventually win the case, but they are always in a quandary as to how he is able to determine that his client is not guilty and then correctly identifies the real murderer. The drama climaxes during the final minutes of the one-hour show. Perry Mason, using his courtroom skills, manages to coerce a confession from an unlikely suspect. The rightful killer who is often sitting in the courtroom is immediately taken into custody. Perry Mason's client is released from jail and thus avoids a future jury trial.

Jerry Banks, now under arrest and accused of a double homicide faces a similar challenge. He has the opportunity to show that he is unjustly accused at the upcoming arraignment hearing. Jerry Banks will enter a plea of "not guilty." He contends that the sheriff's department has arrested the wrong man. Unless I am mistaken, it is doubtful that Jerry Banks can expect a Perry Mason-like miracle at his hearing.

***

Judge Bond is conscientious about giving the accused his day in court within the three required days after arrest. Jerry Banks' hearing is held in the courtroom located in the basement of the courthouse. Judge Bond's court is very informal. On Thursday the 12th of December, the arraignment hearing for Banks begins in Henry County Justice of Peace Court. Banks is escorted by two deputies from the bull pen to the courtroom. Wearing an orange jumpsuit, he is handcuffed and shackled. Since he is accused of murder, the deputies take all the necessary precautions. There are always angry friends and family members of the victims, who might resort to violence, if given the opportunity. When the hearing begins, present are Capt. Howard, Sheriff Glass and Sgt. Floyd along with Jerry Banks and his attorney.

District Attorney Edward McGarity questions several detectives who investigated the case and one expert witness from the G.B.I. crime lab. The most damaging evidence is the testimony from Kelly Fife, who states that the shogun inflicting the fatal wounds is similar to the gun that was in Jerry Banks' possession.

Jerry is advised not to speak. Instead, his newly engaged attorney enters a plea of not guilty on his behalf.

My officer friend tells me that Nannie Dodson, Jerry's mother, had visited Jerry Banks at the Henry County Jail a week earlier. She was accompanied by a young well-dressed Black man, John Hudson Myers, Jerry's new attorney. Myers was overheard tell-

ing Mrs. Dodson and Jerry that the state had a weak case. From past experience his law firm had observed, local police from rural counties make a mess out of such investigations," he said. "It was often easy to get their clients acquitted." Myers agreed to represent Jerry for a small retainer.

Myers says, "I am here to get your side of the story. Mrs. Dodson tells me that you are innocent, but I want to hear it from you. Did you kill those people?"

"No, sir! I just found the bodies," repeats Banks.

Myers says, "What we need to do is to find you a foolproof alibi. Somebody, who can acknowledge that you were someplace else, when the murders took place that afternoon."

"I was helping my neighbors with some work around their house, Banks says. Mrs. Slaughter and her husband are getting up in years. Due to his disability, he can no longer do much outside work. With the three kids, I know I need the extra money. I was there until about 3:30 p.m. I went to my house ate some lunch and then headed out."

Myers instructs Banks to tell him about the shotgun.

Banks responds, "I borrowed the gun from my brother Perry. He also gave me some shells. He told me he had some business to take care of and that he couldn't go with me."

Myers tells Banks that they have two weeks to get ready for the trial and to come up with a defense strategy. "I will speak with your brother and the neighbor. We will talk again before the trial."

***

Judge Bond: "Mr. Banks, these are damaging accusations. What do you say to these charges?"

Myers: "My client tells me that this is some kind of a mistake. He did not kill those people."

Judge Bond: "Well, Mr. Banks, do you know who did?"

Banks: "No, sir."

Judge Bond addressing Mr. Myers and Jerry Banks: "I believe there is enough evidence here to keep you in jail without bail until the Grand Jury can hear your case. You are hereby bound over to the Grand Jury who will determine if there is sufficient evidence to indict you."

***

In Georgia, law enforcement does the investigation, collects the evidence and makes the arrest. The Grand Jury reviews just the facts that resulted in the arrest and Grand Juries consider the evidence presented to determine whether there is enough probable cause to indict an individual of the charged crime. Once indicted by the Grand Jury, the regular jury composed of twelve men and women decide the guilt or innocence. From the evidence presented, the system allows one's peers to decide who should face a trial or be released. If tried and found guilty the same peers determine the punishment. Grand Jurors are selected from the same pool of citizens as are the regular jurors.

During a typical day, Grand Juries will hear different types of criminal cases from prosecutors. Usually, these cases are felonies. Judges, court officers, Grand Jury clerks or a juror selected by the members of the Grand Jury can preside. Prosecutors will come in, present evidence in the form of witnesses, documents, photos and video/audio. This is done often over the course of a day, a week or longer. In most cases, the accused has an opportunity, but by law is not required, to testify. If the accused testifies, he or she can only be questioned by the prosecutor. The defense attorney cannot question the witness; however, the individual jurors can submit questions to the prosecutor. At the close of presentment of the evidence, the prosecutor reads legal instructions and the law to the jurors. The Grand Jury may then vote an indictment, also known as a "true bill." To vote an indictment it only requires a quorum.

Grand Juries are also the investigative arm for the citizens of Henry County. The Grand Jury is empowered by law to make statutory inspections of governmental departments, agencies and facilities. The condition of the Henry County Jail has been a favorite issue of late. The entire body of Grand Jurors would visit a particular department. From their findings and interviews with the personnel in charge, a report is prepared. The presentments with its recommendations are given to the Superior Court Judge for filing. The recommendations are not binding or self-executing. The information, however, becomes a matter of public record and serves as a guide to the elected officials in determining Henry County's needs and future expenditures.

***

The Grand Jury convenes the week of January 13, 1975, in the basement of the Henry County Courthouse with the legitimacy of 110 warrants to consider. There are twenty-four Grand Jurors present. Several traffic offenders come ahead of Jerry Banks' case. The newly installed radar equipment in patrol cars gives the speeders on Interstate 75 little chance of escaping a fine. Each is fined, lectured by the judge and sent home a few dollars poorer.

On Friday the 17th, Jerry Banks' case is presented. District Attorney Ed McGarity introduces the facts of the case, various pictures taken from the crime scene and other evidence including the weapon and spent shells. He introduces the same witnesses who testified earlier at the arraignment hearing. In short order, the Grand Jury members unanimously vote a true bill. Jerry Banks must stand trial for the murders of Marvin King and Melanie Hartsfield.

The January term of Henry Superior Court had begun with criminal court starting on Monday the 5th. The all-important *Georgia v. Banks* follows several other trials that were already on the calendar. Jerry Banks' jury trial is scheduled for the last week of the month.

CHAPTER 22 | Knowles' Murder
Spree Ends

In early December 1974, John Paul Knowles is transferred to the Douglas County Jail in Douglasville, Georgia. There he is questioned intensely by agents of the G.B.I. to no avail. Special Agent Ronnie Angel, assigned to the case, eventually convinces Knowles to cooperate by appealing to his ego. He tells of blank tapes he bought at the Zayre department store and recorded what he could remember about his murders. He gave the tapes to this attorney with instructions not to make them available to the public until after his death. He was hoping to find a writer and a publisher that would tell his story posthumously.

Agent Angel tells Knowles that his name is in the newspapers every day. "I guess you may hold the record for the number of killings committed in different states in the shortest period. Don't you want the public to know what you've done while you are still here and can read about it?"

Knowles replies, "I have always outsmarted the cops. I should have been wiser and not gotten arrested in July. The fight I had with the loudmouth bartender in Jacksonville was stupid. I should have waited until the bar closed and then taken care of him some other place."

"You stabbed the guy!" declares Angel.

Knowles smugly retorts "So, he deserved it. It didn't much

matter. One night a few days later, I had no trouble breaking out of the rinky-dink place when the guard fell asleep. I just picked the cell door lock and walked out the front door as if I was invisible. Y'all were lucky to catch me in Stockbridge. I should have ditched the Ford earlier and found another car. That was my mistake.

"Yes, I also told this lady reporter, who I met at a bar, that I had a run in with the law. She was visiting from England and took an interest in me. She said that she would write a book about me one day. She sure will be surprised when she learns the whole story."

Agent Angel says, "I can make you famous. But you must tell me who you killed and where you hid the bodies. Let's start in Georgia. Just tell me about what you did in South Georgia."

Knowles brags, "I guess I must have killed a bunch of people. Many of them nobody knows about. And they will never find the bodies. I can't even remember where I left them."

"Do you remember August 23rd? That's the day you were in Musella, Georgia. What can you tell me about a twenty-two-year-old Kathy Pierce in Musella?" asks Angel.

Knowles reveals a detailed account: "I was just about to get on Highway 42 and noticed this little house. I was getting hungry and kind of tired of driving. So, I stopped and rang the doorbell. A pretty young girl came to the door. I told her that I needed to use her phone. She let me into the house without the slightest hesitation. When I was pretending to talk on the phone, she started acting really nervous. I was afraid she might have recognized me or something. So, I took the telephone cord and strangled her. She had a young boy playing in the living room. I didn't want to hurt the boy. She didn't have much money, but I took what I could find and some food. I left and headed north.

"I ended up in Ohio. I killed a man there. I took his car and headed to California. From there I decided to go back to Florida. I had lived in Florida all my life. On the way I killed a few more people so I decided I had better keep on the move to avoid getting caught."

Angel says, "Authorities received a missing person report in November on Edward Hilliard and a Debbie Griffin. They were last seen in Commerce, Georgia and were heading to Florida. What did you do to them?"

Knowles says, "I was going through Macon, I picked up these two hitchhikers who were on the side of the road trying to hitch a ride, I stopped. We rode a bit. I was getting horny. The girl got prettier by the mile. So, I decided that I needed some sex. But I had to get rid of the man. I had my knife. So, we stopped near some woods around Milledgeville so I could pee. I made them get out. I stabbed the man and promised the terrified female if she would give me sex, I would let her go. She did, but I killed her anyway. I enjoyed watching her die more than the sex. From there, I decided to go back to Florida."

Agent Angel leaves the interrogation room and enters the adjoining observation room where two other detectives are watching and listening. The room is soundproof and has a one-way window. Agent Angel announces to his colleagues, "What do think? Isn't that one evil bastard! I believe I have him in my confidence. He's telling me everything."

The supervisor instructs Angel to ask Knowles if he would show him where he hid the remains of the people who he allegedly killed.

Agent Angel returns to the interrogation room.

Knowles continues, "Thanks for the Coca-Cola. I always liked Coke especially when it's mixed with Wild Turkey bourbon. Well, I made it all the way to West Palm Beach, where I stole this car from this lady and took her hostage. She said she was a publisher. I needed her to stay alive to help with my memoir, so I didn't kill her. I let her go the next day in North Florida. A couple of days later, after passing through Fort Pierce, a Florida a patrolman pulled me over. He told me that the car I was driving had been reported as stolen. He ordered me to get out of the car. When I got out, I tackled him to ground and wrestled away his gun. He didn't know what hit him.

"I made him put his hands behind his back and I put his handcuffs on him. I put him in the backseat of the police car, the same place he wanted to put me. It was a thrill driving that Florida State Patrol car with my confused and dazed prisoner in the back seat. I took his hat, his extra set of handcuffs and badge. The shoe was on the other foot. Now, I was Trooper Campbell, a Florida State Patrolman, and I didn't even have to graduate from the police academy."

Knowles pauses a moment. "By the way, where are you from? How did you get a name like Angel?"

Agent Angel hesitates. "My first name is Ronnie. My father changed his name at Ellis Island when he and my mother came to America from Italy. His real name was Ronaldo Angelo. My mother told my father that it was an Angel of God that helped bring them to America. So, he changed his last name to Angel."

Knowles tells Agent Angel the events leading up to more deaths. "When I came upon this blue Ford Torino, I turned on the police lights and siren and pulled the car over. The man inside was shocked when I pulled out my gun and told him to get out. I handcuffed him and ordered him to get into backseat of his Torino. He was even more surprised, when I got the handcuffed trooper out of the patrol car and also threw him into the backseat of the Torino. Now I had two prisoners. I hid the police car in the woods and drove the Ford for a while. As I passed through Hawkinsville, I decided I didn't need to be hauling these fellows around in a stolen car. I suspected when the trooper didn't report in, every cop from Florida and Georgia would be on the lookout for him.

"As I approached Warner Robins, I saw a secluded area on the side of the road. I made them get out of the car and we walked into the woods. I told them I would handcuff them to a tree. Not to worry, because I would call somebody to leave directions to where I left them. I was thinking that I just needed enough time to get away. They did not give me any trouble. As I was walking back to the car. I reasoned that they would be better off dead, rather than to be allowed to freeze to death or be eaten by a wild hog or something. So, I went back and shot them."

Annoyed, Agent Angel says, "Hunters later found the bodies of the Florida State Patrolman and the driver of the rental car who was a salesman from Delaware named James Meyers. He left behind a beautiful wife and one-year-old girl. Trooper Campbell had been with the patrol for twelve years. He will be missed by his wife and three young boys. One of his sons played on the little league team he coached."

Knowles continues, " I have saved the best part for last. At another time while at a restaurant bar, I am having an after-dinner drink. I am talking to this fellow. I tell him that I am traveling by myself and come from out of town. My car broke down and it will be a day or two before the garage can get parts to fix it. I tell him that once I pay the repair bill, I won't have any money left to get home. This man, Carr, invites me over to his house near Milledgeville to spend the night. Mr. Carr has a nice house, a brand-new Chevrolet and expensive whiskey. I ask where his wife is? He tells me that she is a nightshift nurse and will not be back until morning. We get to drinking and telling stories. I decide that it is probably time for me to go. I go into the kitchen and find a pair of scissors in the drawer next to the bread box. I walk back into the den where he is sitting and sneak up from behind and stab him. When his daughter hears his groaning and comes a running, I have to get rid of her, so I choke her to death."

Agent Angel is angry. "You stabbed Mr. Carr more than twenty times and strangled poor little Mandy with a silk stocking. What made you decide to kill these people?"

Knowles goes on, "Well, the man looked rich and had stuff I wanted. I knew he had a new car, but the man also had a closet-full of clothes and shoes, that fit me. So, I took some of the sport jackets, slacks and what not. His wallet was full of money and credit cards. I took all that and his brief case and jumped into his Impala. I headed up Highway 42 to have some fun in Atlanta."

Angel slyly suggests, "If you want to get credit for all the murders you are bragging about, we are going to need proof that you did it. We need to find the bodies and the murder weapons, etc. We can put you in a police car and drive you to the places where you say you committed the crimes and hid the bodies. Would you agree to show us where they are?"

Knowles smiles and raises his eyebrows. "Yes, sir. I will. I killed thirty-five people and I want to enjoy my fame. You know the papers call me the 'Casanova Killer'. I am a real lady's man."

Angel continues to encourage Knowles. "To start with, we need to find the trooper's gun. You had it with you when you tried to run the roadblock in Stockbridge, but you didn't have it when you were arrested. The G.B.I. and the local police went back and searched the area. Scuba-divers dove into the lake and found nothing."

Knowles tells Angel that he knows about where he threw the gun. "It is in bushes not far from where he wrecked the Ford. I can show you."

Angel says, "That's great. I will make the arrangements."

***

State, federal and local law enforcement agents from various jurisdictions take turns questioning Knowles to find answers to their unsolved murder cases. Because he is allowed to read the newspaper clippings, he begins to relish the notoriety. Knowles cannot stop bragging. Authorities need bodies and evidence. Knowles agrees to take authorities to the various locations to provide onsite details of the crimes. The highest priority is the murder of one of their own, Florida Trooper Campbell. Knowles tells the agents that he discarded the weapon while eluding the police following the roadblock collision on Highway 42. The ballistics tests of the gun would offer convincing proof that Knowles pulled the trigger. G.B.I agents and local authorities have searched the area and are unable to find the weapon.

On December 18, 1974, Agent Angel and Douglas County Sheriff Earl Lee load Knowles into the back of a patrol car and head toward Henry County. The Sheriff is behind the wheel. They leave the Douglas County Jail traveling east on Interstate 20 with Knowles handcuffed in the back seat. Agent Angel, sitting on the passenger side, is not aware that Knowles has a hidden paper clip in his back pocket. From the numerous times he has been in handcuffs as a juvenile, he had become a master at picking locks.

As they approach the Lee Road exit on Interstate 20 in Lithia Springs, Knowles manages to unlock the handcuffs. Suddenly, Knowles lunges forward, grabs Sheriff Lee's handgun while still in the holster and discharges a shot through the dashboard. Sheriff Lee immediately clamps down on Knowles' hand before he can pull the gun from the holster. At the same time, he attempts to steer the swerving patrol car with his left hand. The patrol car is still traveling at a high rate of speed as it oscillates between the grassy shoulder and edge of the Interstate 20's concrete surface. Instinctively, Agent Angel is able to retrieve his weapon, turn and fire three shots into Knowles' chest. Sheriff Lee is able to gain control and maneuver the vehicle to a safe stop. Knowles slumps over motionless. The harrowing experience is over in a matter of seconds. John Paul Knowles, born April 17, 1946, died December 18, 1974.

***

Before Knowles' death other agents had taken turns questioning him. Knowles volunteered additional details that confirmed what the agencies already suspected: he was a serial killer. However, Knowles' confessions did not include the murders of Marvin King and Melanie Hartsfield. Investigators determine that Knowles could not be the killer because he had used a stolen credit card in Macon around 3:30 p.m. that day. According to Capt. Howard, "It is unlikely that Knowles killed King and Hartsfield, hid their bodies, moved King's car and got to Macon by 3:30 p.m. The timeline just doesn't work."

I was disappointed to learn that Capt. Howard and the detectives now disregard Knowles as a possible suspect. I believe that Knowles certainly fits the profile and given the opportunity he was certainly capable of committing such gruesome murders. Persons within the police department say that the likely killer is probably someone local. Someone who has knowledge of the abandoned Rock Quarry Road. It has been eight days after the arrest of Jerry Banks and the subsequent death of John Paul Knowles. Jerry Banks looks more and more like the guilty party.

***

While traveling through Florida, Knowles met with his former attorney, Sheldon Yavitz, who had defended him as a juvenile. He informed the lawyer that he was the serial killer the authorities were looking for. After the encounter, Knowles described the murders, he had committed and sent his taped confessions to his attorney. He gave specific instructions to Yavitz to withhold the information until after his death. The tapes were subsequently turned over to the Bibb County Court. The transcript of the conversation found on the Knowles' confession tapes did not include all the unbelievable murders Knowles had professed committing. It is possible that Knowles committed more murders after he submitted the tape recording to Yavitz or had just forgotten to include them all. Thus, the total number and the details will never be known.

The details from the transcript of the tapes allowed law enforcement to confirm a list of homicides. Knowles provided information that authorities either did not know or had merely speculated about. Referring to the transcripts, several news resources described the gruesome trail of murders left behind by Knowles, including many he had not previously divulged to Agent Ronnie Angel.

- On August 1, 1974, Knowles picked up a thirteen-year-old hitchhiker, Ima Jean Sanders, in Warner Robins. He raped and strangled her. He, then dumped her body in a wooded area in Macon.
- On September 3, 1974, Knowles met businessman William Bates at a tavern in Lima, Ohio. After sharing a few drinks with Knowles, Bates was strangled dumped in some nearby woods. Knowles took Bates' car, money and credit cards and headed to California.
- On the way, he murdered Emmett and Lois Johnson, who were camping in Ely, Nevada.
- The next victim was 65-year-old Alice Curtis, who was bound and gagged, while Knowles ransacked her home and stole her Dodge Dart. Mrs. Curtis, who wore dentures, choked to death on her gag.
- Later, he felt compelled to kidnap and strangle Lillian and Myette Anderson, ages seven and eleven, who witnessed him abandoning Mrs. Curtis' stolen car. He buried their bodies in a swamp.
- Next, he entered the home of Marjorie Howe in Atlantic Beach. After he strangled her with a nylon stocking, he stole

her television set.

- On October 19, 1974, Knowles entered the home of 53-year-old Doris Hovey in Woodford, Virginia, and shot her with her husband's rifle.
- October 22, Ben Sherrod was discovered in Brewton, Alabama, handcuffed to a chair and shot to death. Evidence suggested Knowles was the killer.

Only eighteen murders were officially confirmed. Had Knowles lived he might have been able to provide proof of the other seventeen. A detective who handled the investigation in Milledgeville was quoted in the local paper, "I am glad he is dead."

***

According to what I have read, Knowles was a mentally unstable man with a violent temper. He was one of seven children and grew up in a poverty-stricken environment. He was always in trouble and resented authority. His parents abused him and sent him to the Dozier School for Boys in Marianna, Florida hoping to correct his deviant behavior. While institutionalized, he was further abused. Instead of being reformed, he became an incorrigible juvenile delinquent destined to become a hardened criminal. Later he was in and out of jail and associated himself with evil people. I understand that while in the Florida State Prison, he developed a pen pal relationship with Angela Covic, a recently divorced cocktail waitress from San Francisco. Knowles had a charismatic way and was able to convince Ms. Covic to help him. She paid a lawyer to obtain his early parole. Knowles was so overwhelmed with her kindness that he asked her to marry him, which she agreed. He had never known anyone who showed him such genuine affection. Upon release, he traveled to California in hopes of starting a new life with his new bride. Unfortunately for Knowles, Ms. Covic had a change of heart. Consulting a psychic, she was warned of impending danger if she continued her relationship with Knowles. So, she called off the wedding. That rejection, I think, triggered his violent behavior and the ensuing murders.

***

A short time after the shooting of John Paul Knowles, news accounts reported his whereabouts at the approximate time of King and Hartsfield murders. On November 8th, the day after their murders, Knowles checked into a Holiday Inn in Atlanta. There he met British journalist Sandy Fawkes in the hotel bar. Impersonating Carswell Carr, a victim from two days earlier, he impressed her with his dress and apparent wealth. He agreed to accompany her to Miami where they spent three days together. During the encounter he told her that he did not have long to live, because he would soon be killed for something he had done. The bizarre relationship ended with Knowles not harming her.

Should Ms. Fawkes write her book I would be interested in how she describes her escapades with Knowles, a serial killer who the press identified as the "Casanova Killer." Ms. Fawkes should title her book "A Date with the Devil." A quote from a local author, Sharon Graham, described John Paul Knowles this way: "Like a dark, malevolent tornado, Knowles ripped through Florida and Georgia leaving a path of destruction. He did it to become famous. By some strange grace, he is not."

CHAPTER 23 | The Banks Family Christmas

Jerry Banks is arrested shortly before Christmas in 1974 and held without bail. His trial is scheduled for January. For Virginia and the children, it is a family Christmas without their father. There is hope that he would be acquitted and allowed to return home after the conclusion of the trial. Virginia considers having a belated Christmas whereby the family could also celebrate Jerry's release. But a guilty verdict would mean Jerry would not be coming home, thus denying the family a happy Christmas.

Mount Olive Baptist Church in Stockbridge, whose origin dates to 1870, is Aunt Opal's and Virginia's church. Certain members of Mount Olive foresee an unhappy and gloomy Christmas at the Banks household unless something is done. The preacher and the "Welcoming Committee" plan a surprise for their beloved Sister Virginia.

Pastor Jester's wife, Estoria, and the ladies of the committee arrange a Christmas dinner: each guest is to bring either a vegetable dish, salad, dessert, rolls or a beverage. Pastor Jester and Estoria are to prepare the turkey and dressing. Not to forget the children, the men are responsible for the Christmas gifts. Aunt Opal co-ordinates the affair at her house and informs Virginia of the time the guests might be arriving. Aunt Opal and Virginia's sister, Gloria, set up the folding chairs they had borrowed from the church. Opal is thankful that everyone also helped in arranging the house for company. She would be terribly embarrassed if the church members came to a messy house.

The Pastor has taken up a special collection for Jerry's family during last Sunday's church service. The generous congregation donates enough to buy the kids gifts and give Virginia a check for her household and living expenses.

Virginia decides to forgo the usual Christmas morning festivities with the children. Instead, she opts to celebrate Christmas with the expectant dinner guests. Virginia's spirits are lifted when she and little Jerry Jr. decorate a small Christmas tree that Opal bought at Yule Forest, a local Christmas tree farm on Highway 155. The tree variety Opal selects is appropriately named Virginia Pine. It grows locally and closely resembles the more popular and more expensive North Carolina Frazer Fir. It fits perfectly by the window in the living room and compliments the makeshift manger situated on the small coffee table. Donned with colored lights and icicles, the Christmas tree creates a perfect setting for a memorable Christmas despite the circumstances.

Virginia manages to buy a few clothes for the children at a clothing outlet in Griffin. She neatly folds each child's present and places them in some old boxes she had saved. The presents are wrapped in the colorful red paper that glimmer under the tree's few bright decorative lights. Without a father around, Virginia uses the gifts as an enticement for the children to be on good behavior during the holidays.

Little Jerry Jr. is now five years old, Eddie is two years old, and Felicia recently passed her first birthday. The young children have seen little of their father but Jerry Jr. looks forward to having him back home. Their lawyer had guaranteed Virginia and the children that their father would be home by Christmas. But it was not to be.

The Christmas guests arrive just before noon. Pastor Jester is the last to arrive. First, he has two important stops to make in the morning visiting elderly bedridden church members. Opal had hoped on having dinner first while the food was still warm, but the little ones, especially Jerry Jr., had anxiously waited all morning to see what Santa has brought them. They are so full of excitement and curiosity that any delay in allowing them to unwrap the presents would be cruel. Right now, eating is the last thing on their minds.

Virginia relents and says, "OK, you can go ahead and open your presents while I set the table but hurry up. Everyone is hungry and we don't want the food to get cold. The turkey smells so good!"

"Thanks, Mommy and thanks to everybody," Jerry Jr. says.

Virginia's new clothes receive lukewarm attention. But the new Schwinn bike and tricycle the church purchased and assembled, are a big hit. Santa has made Jerry Jr. and Eddie incredibly happy. Felicia loves her Mattel Drowsy Doll dressed in pink with white polka-dots. The most appreciated gift is the $500 check that Pastor Jester gives Virginia.

Virginia is overwhelmed and in tears. "Pastor, I don't know what to say. Please thank everyone at Mount Olive Church. They are all so kind," she says as she hugs the pastor.

The house is too small for a room full of guests with little boys trying to ride their bikes. Virginia tells the boys, "Children you have to go outside but first you must eat your dinners." Pastor Jester says an inspirational blessing and asks God to help all those who have suffered. He prays for Jerry and his family and blames the devil for all the evil in the world.

The delicious meal, fellowship and joy of watching the kids play overshadow the uncertainty of the family's future. Virginia wonders, "God knows! What is going to become of us if Jerry is found guilty? I am twenty-four-years-old and face raising three children alone."

CHAPTER 24 | First Trial:
January 29, 1975

All attention is directed toward the City of McDonough, the location of the upcoming Georgia v. Banks *trial. The trial brings the City of McDonough and Henry County notoriety. Since many out-of-towners who come to the trial are not familiar with Henry County nor its Courthouse, it is appropriate that I share a brief history.*

The history begins when early Georgia law required courthouses to be located within one day's horse and buggy ride from its furthest point within the county. McDonough being in the geographic center met the requirement and became the county seat and houses the County's government. To accommodate the growing Henry County, a new courthouse was constructed in 1887 to replace the original, built in 1824, and is relocated to a site just north of the public square. A two-story annex was recently added in July 1970.

With its steeple, the new courthouse was the tallest building in Henry County. Inside the steeple was the traditional clock tower. The clock was installed and became operational in July of 1897. Originally, the mechanism that operated the clock's movement was similar to a Swiss cuckoo clock. Weights wound around the internal gears, powered the clock's movement. The gravitational pull of the weights caused the gears to turn. The clock had two weights, one was for the time mechanism and the other activated the striker. For the clock to keep accurate time the weights had to be calibrated correctly. The courthouse with its clock became the center of attention and could be heard by travelers before approaching the city. Locals did not need a pocket watch; they relied on the courthouse clock for telling time.

On June 9, 1952, the courthouse was damaged when the weight that provided the movement to the clock's hourly chimes, fell through the ceiling and landed on the courtroom floor. Among the scattered contents of the broken wooden box were heavy pieces of scrap-iron. After seeing the mess, the Henry County Clerk of Superior Court, Mrs. Fouche, was said to have remarked, "It is amazing that this old clock has kept time with nothing but a bunch of rusted bolts and metal."

Fortunately, no one was in the courthouse at the time. The historic clock was patched together, but by 1967 it was in dire need of reconditioning and repainting. The old wooden hands were replaced as were all the inner workings. The clock now operates by electricity and keeps perfect time except during power failures and lightning strikes. Nesting pigeons are a problem from time to time. To the delight of those in and around the McDonough City Square, the clock chimes were also restored.

***

Eighty-five Henry County citizens are sent jury duty summons and are ordered to report to the courthouse jury room on Monday January 27, 1975, for the January term of superior court. Sixteen are excused for one reason or another. The remaining sixty-nine are divided into panels from which jurors will be selected for the various cases slated to be heard during the term. The jury pool is mostly White, as more than eighty percent of the County's population is White. The Henry County Board of Commissioners annually appoints a jury commission to qualify the candidates for the jury pools. These candidates had been selected and compiled by the Henry County Registrar. Individuals are selected from the Henry County voter registration list who are known not to have age, medical or professional conflicts. If so, such candidates would automatically be excused.

Media attention is centered around the Jerry Banks murder trial which is scheduled to begin Wednesday the 29th of January. Traveling from Forsyth, Judge Sosebee arrives early in preparation for the long day, overcast and cold. Defense Attorney John Hudson Myers is already in the courtroom when District Attorney Edward McGarity and his assistant Kenneth Waldrep arrive. They greet one another and shake hands. Myers promises a strong defense for his client, Banks. With a cunning grin McGarity responds, "You're going to need one. Good luck!" McGarity has not forgotten Banks from his earlier arrest and conviction.

Buddy Welch, who had represented Jerry Banks in the previous manslaughter case, is again appointed his defense attorney. Banks is considered a pauper in the eyes of the law and is entitled to free legal representation. His family, however, chooses to replace Welch with an Atlanta attorney. John Hudson Myers, originally from Alabama, is a partner in Myers and Mull law firm. He attended Georgia Military Institute and graduated from Emory Law School. He was admitted to the Georgia Bar after passing the exam on his first attempt, as do eighty-five percent of the Emory Law School graduates.

Myers, whose office is in the Candler Building on Peachtree Street in Atlanta, has planned to meet with Banks before the trial. A wreck on Interstate 75 creates a traffic jam and delays his arrival to McDonough. The last-minute meeting does not take place.

Myers is short in stature, bespectacled, smartly dressed and with a short afro. The friends who recommended Myers to the Banks family consider him to be well-spoken and ambitious. They reckoned that a Black criminal attorney from the city would be better qualified to represent Jerry Banks than a young White lawyer from the country. Myers is an active member of the NAACP, and his older brother had participated in the 1965 Selma March. After a meeting with Myers, the family pools together enough cash to convince him to represent Banks at the pre-trial hearings and subsequent jury trial if necessary.

***

As deputies open the courtroom doors, all the available seats are quickly filled. The bailiff announces, "Take your seats." The hands on the courthouse clock point to 9 a.m. The bailiff asks all in attendance to rise. "Hear-ye, hear-ye, this Court is now in session. The Honorable Judge Hugh Sosebee presiding. Please be seated."

Judge Sosebee, donned in his black robe, enters from his chambers located on the front right of the courtroom. That section of the courtroom is elevated and overlooks the attorney tables and seating area. The Judge's desk, referred to as the "bench," is situated on an elevated platform which is enclosed on three sides by an ornate paneled wall. Behind his desk and centered between the beautiful carved molding is a framed copy of The U.S. Constitution. At the right front corner are the American and Georgia flags, hanging motionless from the two gold-colored vertical rods anchored in a stand. Attached atop of the rods are decoratively perched golden eagles.

Court reporter Dianne Buttrill is already seated in her enclosed box, at the front and to the right of the Judge's bench. She will type the transcript of the trial and accept exhibits from the lawyers. The elevated and enclosed witness stand is to the immediate left of the Judge's bench and awaits its first prosecution witness. At a table to the left of the witness stand sits Sara Taylor, Clerk of Superior Court. She serves as the custodian of the jury list and protects legal documents and evidence accumulated during the trial. Tables for the opposing attorneys and defendant are situated directly in front of thirty-inch railing separating the court participants from the visitors and press.

Resting against the right wall inside the railing is a tall gentleman in a deputy's uniform named Maj. Hulon Bowen of the Henry County Sheriff's department. He steadfastly observes the activity in the courtroom. For security purposes he and the deputies stand in the rear of the courtroom and are on constant alert. In such an emotional trial they keep a special eye on the defendant and victim's families and friends. Everyone who has entered the courtroom has been checked for weapons. Nevertheless, verbal outbursts and fist fights have been known to occur in these situations.

While surveying the packed courtroom, Judge Sosebee announces, "The case today is the State of Georgia versus Jerry Banks." At the table to the right is District Attorney Edward McGarity who represents the State of Georgia. He is attired in a light blue, striped seersucker sports coat, blue pants and a matching blue and white-striped tie. His Southern dress accents his gentlemanly nature. He is flanked by his assistant Kenneth Waldrep, wearing a gray sports jacket with checkered-patterned slacks and matching extra-wide tie. To the left at a table facing the bench is John Hudson Myers, the defense attorney. An aisle in the center of the courtroom leads to a gate that serves as entry for witnesses called to the stand and other authorized persons. Only Judge Sosebee has a private entrance directly from the judge's chamber.

In the courtroom, seated on the back row, is Charles Hartsfield, Melanie's father. He is prepared to remain for the duration of the trial and not leave until a verdict is reached. He has a determined look on his face and is counting on the prosecution to do its job in convicting Melanie's killer. He feels somewhat confident that it will after Det. Robbins called him shortly after Jerry Banks' arrest. "Mr. Hartsfield, we have arrested the fellow that killed your daughter and Mr. King. There is no doubt about it." Mrs. King elects not to attend but members of the King family are expected to arrive later in the day.

Judge Sosebee clears his throat and says, "We are ready to proceed? Deputies bring in the accused."

Jerry Banks, a five-foot ten inch, slim built, one hundred sixty-five-pound, light skinned young Black man, enters the courtroom from the rear. He is expressionless and stands next to Mr. Myers, who points to the chair where he is be seated for the duration of the trial. Jerry is clean shaven and nicely dressed in a white sports jacket, long-sleeved white shirt and black pants. His appearance, suitable for Sunday morning church service, gives Jerry a look of innocence. Virginia is allowed to sit at the defense table, but she chooses to join Jerry's brother, Perry, on the first row directly behind her husband. Aunt Opal is at home watching the children. Many in the courtroom wonder and ask themselves, "How could this quiet, unassuming young man have committed such an evil and senseless act?"

Judge Sosebee says that the first order of business is the selection of the jury. Forty-eight from the jury pool make up the four panels of potential jurors. Each juror is assigned a number and will be seated in numerical order in the courtroom.

At the preliminary meeting of jurors on Monday, each person filled out a questionnaire. The information was given to the lawyers in advance to limit the number of questions the jurors would be expected to answer. With the jurors seated in the courtroom, their names are called again, and each gives his or her occupation and that of his or her husband or wife, if married. The opposing attorneys are already sizing up the candidates. A name gets a check mark if it is perceived the juror's background and occupation would potentially favor their side.

Judge Sosebee addresses the jury. "Let me say this, ladies and gentlemen, under the law, every person is presumed innocent and is not presumed to be guilty. Each defendant is entitled to a fair and impartial trial whose guilt or innocence is to be decided by members of his peers. The Sixth Amendment guarantees the accused the right to a speedy and public trial by an impartial jury. A jury of one's peers does not mean a Black defendant must be tried by an all-Black jury or that a male defendant must be tried by an all-male panel.

"You will be asked questions by the lawyers on each side that are designed to find out something about you. Your answers will determine which of you will be called to hear this case. Do not take offense if you are excused. It's nothing personal, it's just how the system works. The law requires that if you are selected to serve you must have an open mind about the case. After all the evidence has been presented, the witnesses examined and cross-examined, and each side has made their arguments, I will read you the law that is applicable to the charge that you will be called upon to decide. You will then retire to the jury room to deliberate and to reach a verdict. Do you have any questions?"

None of the jurors have any questions. Judge Sosebee continues, "Now, there are certain questions that the State is required to ask in a felony case. I'm going to let the District Attorney McGarity ask those questions to you as a body and then after those questions are asked, I will let the clerk, Mrs. Taylor, call twelve of you into the box, where you will be questioned individually. I suggest that those who are not called, listen so you understand the procedure. Your turn will come soon enough. Mr. McGarity will now swear you in."

McGarity walks over to jury box and begins, "I'll ask all the jurors to stand and please, raise your right hand. Do you solemnly swear you shall make true answers to such questions as may be asked you by the Court or its authority touching your qualifications to serve as a juror in this case, so help you God?"

Jurors all respond, "I do."

McGarity continues, "Ladies and gentlemen, this is the case of the State of Georgia versus Jerry Banks, who is charged that on the 7th day of November 1974, he did with malice and aforethought kill one Marvin King, by shooting the said Marvin King with a certain shotgun. He is further charged that he did kill one Melanie Ann Hartsfield with a certain shotgun.

"Have you, from having seen the crime committed or having heard any of the testimony, delivered on oath, formed and expressed any opinion in regard to the guilt or the innocence of the prisoner? If you have, indicate by the uplifted hand."

No one raised his or her hand.

Judge Sosebee: "Mr. McGarity, you may proceed with the general questioning."

McGarity: "Are any of you related to Jerry Banks by blood or marriage?"

None indicate such a relationship.

McGarity: "Is anyone acquainted or related in any way with the attorneys John Hudson Myers or me, I am Edward McGarity."

Judge Sosebee: "I think everybody here knows who Ed McGarity is. I see two raised hands. What is your connection with the attorneys?"

Juror: "We both frequent the same church as Mr. McGarity."

Judge Sosebee: "You two candidates are excused from serving as jurors on this case."

McGarity: "How many of you have read about Jerry Banks in the newspaper or heard about him on television."

Judge Sosebee: "Since all but one of you have raised his or her hand, I ask you if anyone has already formed an opinion as to the defendant's guilt or innocence?"

Juror: "Yes, I am a woman and a mother of a college student. I cannot be impartial in this case involving the murder of a young student."

Judge Sosebee: "If that's how you feel, you are also excused from serving."

Judge Sosebee looks in the direction of the Clerk of Superior Court, Sara Taylor. "Let's proceed to the individual questions. Ms. Taylor, please ask the first panel of juror candidates to enter the jury box." The twelve jurors enter the jury box in single file and remain standing in front of their seats. First Mrs. Taylor calls the names, followed by Deputy Bowen, who gives the numeric count. After hearing his or her name and assigned a number, each juror, one by one, takes a seat.

The jury box is situated on the left side of courtroom. It consists of two rows of comfortable leather armchairs, seven in front and five on the second row. The floor is elevated, and the chairs spaced so that every juror can make visual contact with the witness, judge and the occupants seated at the attorney tables.

The attorneys are then allowed to ask each candidate questions. First to answer is a woman of Dutch heritage, wife of the manager of a geranium plant nursery. Following is a woman employed by an insurance company, a housewife married to a train engineer, men employed by Southern States, Carolina Freight Carrier, American Can, John Harland and a data processing supply equipment company. One housewife is married to a fireman.

Twelve more prospective jurors are called to the box and the procedure repeats. Among them is the wife of a grocery store owner, a woman cashier for Dairy Queen, a male civil service employee, a bearded Georgia Power employee, a Holiday Inn waitress, a female C&S Bank teller and men employed by the Hampton

Police Department, Carter Trucking and Vulcan Materials.

McGarity questions the first juror, "Has anyone in your family or friend been a victim of a violent crime?" The juror answers, "No, sir." Myers follows, "Are you or anyone in your family related to an officer of the law or a judge?" Each attorney jots down each candidate's answers. The process continues until each candidate in the panel is questioned.

At the end of the questioning, a short recess is called by Judge Sosebee. All the smokers congregate in the smoking area and light up. When court reconvenes, Mrs. Taylor reads the candidates' names in numerical order. Each attorney is allowed a certain number of "peremptory strikes" without giving a reason and an unlimited number of "strikes for cause" in selecting candidates to serve on the jury. The selection process ends when fourteen candidates survive the strikes. Twelve become the jurors and two are the alternates. The final count is a jury composed of seven men and five women, two of whom are Black, as are the two alternates.

One of the prospective jurors was irritated at Mr. McGarity for a particular question he asked about her recent divorce. Afterwards, she is heard mumbling under her breath that she would not vote for him at the next election. Disappointed by not being selected, another young woman tells her friend who was chosen: "I wish I had been picked." The friend responds, "You are the lucky one! I dread hearing all the horrible details and looking at those gruesome photographs of the murdered victims."

Judge Sosebee in his usual remarks addresses those in attendance, "As I look at the ladies and gentlemen in the jury box, I believe we are complying with the spirit of the Sixth Amendment. I want to thank you jurors for your willingness to serve. I know that fulfilling your patriotic duty is more important than the $10 a day that you are getting paid. I want to admonish you not to discuss the case with anyone. Don't allow it to be discussed in your presence. If anyone tries to approach you about it, report it to the bench."

Judge Sosebee, referring to his notes continues, "I ask you spectators to remain orderly and refrain from talking during the trial. If the urge to use the restroom arises, I suggest you wait until there is a break in the action. If a juror needs a glass of water or a restroom break, ask the bailiff and he will alert me. We can adjourn for a short break. At the noon hour we will adjourn for lunch. Deputies will bus you jurors to Jackson's Restaurant on Macon Street for lunch."

When court reconvenes, Judge Sosebee gently strikes his gravel. When all are quiet, he asks if the prosecution and defense are ready to proceed.

CHAPTER 25 | Prosecution
Witness Testimony

One of my friends who was a member of the security detail at the trial provided me with the details of what transpired in Judge Sosebee's third-floor courtroom. He said twenty minutes before the trial was to start, the courtroom was already packed, and others were standing in the hall hoping to get a seat whenever someone left. Due to the shortage of space, witnesses who were not allowed in the courtroom were told to find seating downstairs. The Grand Jury room was vacant and made available for their use. Deputies acted as runners to summon witnesses as they were called to the stand. The jurors and alternates were milling around the jury room waiting to be called to the jury box. It will be up to them with their varied backgrounds and experiences to make the final decision, at least at this judicial level, in this controversial case.

***

The trial transcript provides a glimpse of the proceedings and testimony. After Mr. McGarity and Mr. Myers make their opening remarks, the first State prosecution witness, Charles Richard Barnes, is called. Det. Barnes, a thin man with a receding hairline and Beatle-style haircut, has been with Henry County Sheriff's Department for approximately one year. Det. Barnes was one of the first to arrive at the scene after the department received a call of a possible homicide in Stockbridge. He is sworn in by Mr. McGarity.

McGarity: "Now, I'll ask you whether or not you or the sheriff's office received a call to investigate an alleged shooting up around Stockbridge, Georgia?"

Det. Barnes: "Yes, sir. I was told on the phone that there would be a Black male, a young Black male, standing on the side of Rock Quarry Road. He would be there waiting. He had found two bodies in the woods."

McGarity: "All right, who did you find when you arrived at the scene?"

Det. Barnes: "The defendant, Jerry Banks."

McGarity: "I'll ask you whether or not that he had anything with him, or on his person?"

Det. Barnes: "Yes, sir, he did. He was in possession of a single barrel, 12-gauge shotgun."

McGarity: "All right, sir, now what did you find when you arrived at the scene, besides Mr. Banks?"

Det. Barnes: "Approximately, I would say, a hundred and fifty feet from the road were two pools of blood that appeared to be relatively fresh. Then he took me to a path leading off to the right approximately a hundred and ten feet into the woods and there the two bodies were."

McGarity: "Do you know how long he had been at the scene at the time you arrived?"

Det. Barnes: "No, sir, I do not. He stated that he was hunting and walked down into the woods and saw the puddles of blood. He said he followed his dog as he ran off into the woods and found the bodies. They were partially covered by a red blanket."

McGarity: "Did you know who the victims were?"

Det. Barnes: "No, sir, not at that time."

McGarity: "And then did you do anything else, Mr. Barnes, with reference to the investigation of this alleged shooting?"

Det. Barnes: "The following Sunday, I went to the defendant's house and picked up his gun for the purpose of test-firing it for comparison with shells that were found at the scene. I brought it back to the detectives' office. I was present while Capt. Howard test-fired the gun. Then later, after the gun was picked up the second time, I carried the gun to the State of Georgia Crime Lab. I turned it over to Kelly Fite for ballistics comparison with shells Capt. Howard test-fired from the gun and compared them with the shells that were previously found at the scene."

McGarity: "He's all yours, Mr. Myers."

Mr. Myers cross-examines Det. Barnes, "Did you check the weapon when you arrived on the scene?"

Det. Barnes: "No, sir."

Myers: "Did you smell the barrel to see if it had been fired?"

Det. Barnes: "No, sir."

Myers: "Did you check his pockets for live rounds or spent rounds?"

Det. Barnes: "No, sir."

Myers: "So, you don't know whether or not he fired the gun."

Det. Barnes: "No, sir."

Myers: "Did you ask Jerry Banks why he had that weapon?"

Det. Barnes: "I assume he was hunting. I believe there's a good bit of hunting that goes on in that area."

Myers: "You told us that you had located two pools of blood approximately a hundred and ten feet from where the bodies were actually found. How do you suppose they got there?"

Det. Barnes: "Yes, sir. They appeared to have been drug into the woods. There were what appeared to be drag marks leading from the pools of blood down a small path into the woods. From the number of abrasions and pine needles and stuff, which were on the clothing also gave the appearance of someone having been drug."

Myers: "Arms first or feet first?"

Det. Barnes: "They were drug feet first, facedown."

Myers: "Did you have occasion later to talk to Mr. Banks?"

Det. Barnes: "The following Sunday, the 10th, around three o'clock at his home."

Myers: "Why did you go there?"

Det. Barnes: "We were going to eliminate his shotgun as the murder weapon by conducting a ballistics test on shell casings found at the scene."

***

Direct examination continues as Assistant District Attorney Waldrep calls T.K. Floyd to the stand. Tommy Floyd is a detective with the Henry County Sheriff's Department and was born and raised in McDonough. Sheriff Glass had taken a special liking to Tommy. He promoted him to Sergeant and assigned him to conduct the field investigation of the King and Hartsfield murders.

Waldrep: "Were there any identifying characteristics about the gun that you can remember?"

Sgt. Floyd: "Yes, sir. The shotgun had a black electrical tape on the fore piece."

Waldrep: "Mr. Floyd, were you able to determine the identity of either one of these bodies at the time you were on the scene?"

Sgt. Floyd: "Yes. We determined that the identity of the female as Melanie Hartsfield."

Waldrep: "How was that determined?"

Sgt. Floyd: "At the scene, a class ring was observed on the White female's finger. We removed the ring and inside was inscribed the name, Melanie Hartsfield. We then went to Det. Robbins' automobile and placed a request to our dispatcher to check surrounding counties for missing person's reports on Melanie Hartsfield."

Waldrep: "What about the other victim?"

Sgt. Floyd: "The White male was wearing a University of Georgia ring and also a wedding band. We were unable to get his class ring off at that time, but it was removed later prior to the autopsy."

Mr. Waldrep: "And was there an inscription inside this ring?"

Sgt. Floyd: "Yes, sir. Inscribed inside this class ring was M.W. King."

Waldrep: "How long were you at the scene and what did you find during your search?"

Sgt. Floyd: "It was dark and getting chilly. I was there until about 9:30 p.m. From there, I went to Carmichael's Funeral Home where Dr. Howard was prepping for the autopsy. With what little light we had, we searched around where the pools of blood were. I was present when the paper wadding from the shotgun, a piece of skull and a piece of plastic from a tag light were found."

Waldrep: "I understand that the search continued well into night till the early morning. What was found in the morning?"

Sgt. Floyd: "Two spent shotgun shells were found."

Waldrep: "What can you tell the Court as to the significance of the shells?"

Sgt. Floyd: "I received a call from Kelly Fite of the Georgia State Crime Lab on November 10th. He said the type of shotgun we should be looking for is a 12-gauge. I received another call from Mr. Fite on December 4th. He stated that the shell casings that were found at the scene and the shell casing fired from Banks' shotgun by Capt. Howard appeared to be a perfect match."

Waldrep: "What did you do in response to the report?"

Sgt. Floyd: "Det. Robbins and I went to Jerry Banks' house and requested that he accompany us back to the sheriff's department and bring his gun along. We wanted to ask him some more questions. He agreed to come, but his gun was at his brother's house. We drove to Highway 155 near the Ozias Church and retrieved the shotgun from Perry. Det. Robbins delivered the weapon to Mr. Fite at the Georgia Crime lab. He wanted to test-fire some additional shots to confirm his initial findings."

Waldrep: "All right, sir, did you subsequentially receive a report confirming the match from Mr. Fite?"

Sgt. Floyd: "Yes, sir. I told Capt. Howard of the report and he in turn told Sheriff Glass. Sheriff Glass then instructed me to arrest Banks. He said that there was enough conclusive evidence to get a conviction. So, on December 11th, I obtained warrants from Justice of the Peace Johnny Bond to arrest Mr. Banks and do a complete search of his residence."

Waldrep: "After the arrest did you have an occasion to question Jerry Banks further?"

Sgt. Floyd: "On December 12th, I met with Det. Robbins, who had Mr. Banks in his automobile at the scene of the homicide. Banks showed us the approximate vicinity of the discarded King wallet. A quick search didn't turn up anything. We returned the next day with a team of detectives and members from the crime lab to continue the search. Det. Hart found the wallet."

Waldrep: "Did you uncover any other evidence that day?"

Sgt. Floyd: "The team was equipped with axes, machetes and metal detectors. We searched in the general area where the first two shell casings were found. Det. Hart found another red Winchester Western spent shotgun shell."

Waldrep: "Do you know what was done with the shells that were found at the scene? I believe there were two at one time, and one later."

Sgt. Floyd: "Right, the first two that were found at the scene were stored in Capt. Howard's office until they were taken to the Georgia Crime Lab. The third shell was taken by a member of the crime lab, who turned it over to Mr. Fite."

Myers: "Did you locate the vehicles belonging to the victims?"

Sgt. Floyd: "We first found the automobile belonging to Melanie Hartsfield in the Food Giant parking lot in the shopping center known as Mays Corner. Mr. King's red Opel wagon was located off Rock Quarry Road."

Myers: "Were the vehicles dusted for prints?"

Sgt. Floyd: "The Clayton County I.D. Unit dusted the vehicles inside and out. I was told that there were several readable prints. Those in the 65 Ford all belonged to Miss Hartsfield. Several prints were found in the Opel. Those prints belonged to both Miss Hartsfield and Mr. King." A clean print of Miss Hartsfield was found on the rearview mirror."

Judge Sosebee: "What about on the steering wheel?"

Sgt. Floyd: "No, sir, none were on the steering wheel."

Judge Sosebee: "No readable prints on the steering wheel?"

Sgt. Floyd: "No readable prints; no, sir, Your Honor."

Myers: "So, in fact they were traveling together."

Sgt. Floyd: "Based on the fingerprints, they were together at some time."

Myers: "As to the shell casings did you find any prints on the shells?"

Sgt. Floyd: "No, sir."

Myers: "While Mr. King's automobile was processed for evidence did you find any unusual contents?"

Sgt. Floyd: "I am not sure I know what you mean."

Myers: "Did you find any beggar lice, cockle burrs, briars or any other plant residue in the vehicle. Some clues that indicate a hunter may have driven the automobile?"

Sgt. Floyd: "Not that I recall."

Myers: "Okay, Tommy, let me ask you this question. What other valuables were found on the bodies of the victims when you found them?"

Sgt. Floyd: "A ring and wristwatch were found on the body of Melanie Hartfield. A class ring, a wedding ring and wristwatch were found on the body of Marvin King."

Judge Sosebee: "Do you know the brand of the wristwatch?"

Sgt. Floyd: "I was told his watch is a Gruen. Both watches were running when they were removed from the victims."

Myers: "Were there items of value found in King's vehicle?"

Sgt. Floyd: "There were numerous tapes in the car, eight track tapes, a green army blanket, also a rubber mat, an air mattress, and in an area where the spare tire is stored were his briefcase and her pocketbook. In the glove compartment was a loaded pistol."

Myers: "Had the pistol been fired?"

Sgt. Floyd: "No, it had not."

Judge Sosebee: "Did you inventory the pocketbook?"

Sgt. Floyd: "Basically, in the pocketbook was a comb, a brush, a wallet with some change. A written inventory was not taken."

Myers: "Were the keys to the Opel found?"

Sgt. Floyd: "A search was made around the car and no keys were found."

Myers: "Now Mr. Floyd, tell the jury what Jerry told you about the fellow to whom he said he had loaned the shotgun."

Sgt. Floyd: "He told me that he was lying about Robert George, that he did not loan Robert George the gun, and that he had done this in order to get us off his back. Those were the words he used."

Myers: "Jerry turned over his weapon to you knowing full well why you wanted the weapon, is that correct?"

Sgt. Floyd: "Yes, that's correct."

Myers: "Suffice to say, knowing what the purpose was for taking this weapon, he gives it to you on one occasion, and another occasion, he takes you to his brother, Perry, to retrieve the shotgun. What did Banks say to you about the shells?"

Sgt. Floyd: "He said there was no way that they could match."

Myers: "When you executed your search warrant at his house on December 11th, what were you looking for?"

Sgt. Floyd: "I was looking for the missing wallet, any identification of Marvin King or Melanie Hartsfield and any valuables that may have been taken from those people."

Myers: "Did you find anything?"

Sgt. Floyd: "No, sir, I did not."

Myers: "You then took him into custody, and what did you do after you brought him back to the police station?"

Sgt. Floyd: "I'll have to refer back to my notes."

Myers: "Okay, all right, at least we need the truth."

McGarity: "Your Honor, I object to counsel making such remarks in front of the jury."

Judge Sosebee: "Well, I will sustain the District Attorney McGarity's objection to any remarks that are not pertinent to the examination of the witness."

Myers: "Now, after the arraignment hearing did you continue your investigation, if so, why?"

Sgt. Floyd: "To satisfy my curiosity, I suppose. I could not think of a motive. That's what I was looking for."

Myers: "Did you eventually find a motive. Are you satisfied with the investigation?"

McGarity: "I object, Your Honor. It calls for an opinion?"

Judge Sosebee: "What is it you are dissatisfied about? What questions do you want answered by Mr. Floyd about this case?"

Sgt. Floyd: "Well that's basically it, just a motive for the killing."

Myers: "Let me ask you one other thing. After you arrested Jerry Banks what was the next step of the investigation?"

Sgt. Floyd: "On December 12th, he was taken to the Georgia Department of Public Safety for a polygraph examination."

Myers: "Mr. Floyd, I understand that he was also given a lie detector test in Clayton County?"

McGarity: "Your Honor, I know where this is going. I object

to this line of questioning. Any results from a polygraph test are inadmissible in court."

Myers: "The defense would like to see a copy of these reports."

Judge Sosebee: "Before I rule on the objection, I would like to excuse the jury."

Myers: "I understand that polygraph reports can be admissible if both sides agree."

Judge Sosebee: "I see Mr. McGarity is shaking his head. I will sustain the motive when the jury returns. Neither the State nor the defense can use the results of the polygraph tests."

***

I can only speculate that Jerry failed parts of the polygraph test. Sgt. Floyd was told that the machine indicated that Banks was untruthful when asked about the wallet and the loaning of the gun to someone else. When Sgt. Tommy Floyd confronted Jerry Banks about picking up the wallet and lending the gun, he admitted that he had lied. How did Jerry Banks fair with the most important question, "Did you kill Marvin King and Melanie Hartsfield?" Since Mr. McGarity objected to having the polygraph test results admitted as evidence, leads me to believe that perhaps he was truthful with that answer. I guess as of now we do not know for certain.

It has been proven multiple times that lie detector tests are highly inaccurate. In fact, they are somewhat biased against innocent persons. Test subjects, who are not criminals, tend to get nervous, their pulse rate rise, they perspire heavily, thus causing the machine to register a false reading. Test subjects who are experienced liars can outsmart the machine. Polygraphs or lie detector tests are useful to law enforcement during interrogations but are disallowed as admissible evidence.

***

Waldrep redirects the examination of Sgt. Floyd, "Tommy did you do any testing of defendant's shotgun?"

Sgt. Floyd: "We wanted to see how long it took to fire four shots from Banks' gun. I did two tests behind the detectives' office. At the first firing, I fired the weapon, I ejected the spent cartridge, I reached into my coat pocket for another cartridge, reloaded, cocked the gun and fired it again in six seconds. I did it once again, and it was five seconds. I repeated the first procedure, and it was five seconds."

Waldrep: "How were you timed on this occasion?"

Sgt. Floyd: "Capt. Howard was holding a stopwatch on me."

Myers cross-examines Mr. Floyd: "Mr. Floyd, I ask you, are you familiar with firing a single barrel shotgun, such as this?"

Sgt. Floyd: "Yes, sir, I have been known to go hunting for fun."

McGarity: "All right, you may step down."

***

After a lengthy examination of Sgt. Floyd, the State of Georgia calls and swears in its next witness, Det. Bill Hart. Mr. Hart has been employed as a detective for the Henry County Sheriff's Department since March of this year.

McGarity: "I'll ask you if you had an occasion to go to the alleged murder scene of Marvin King and Melanie Ann Hartsfield on December 13th?"

Det. Hart: "Yes, sir, I did."

McGarity: "I present you with this particular State exhibit and ask you to identify it."

Det. Hart: "It is a Western Super X 00 Buck, Mark V shotgun shell that had been fired. I found the shell fifty-one feet and four inches from the blood stain identified as Mr. King's."

McGarity: "All right, what did you do with the shell?"

Det. Hart: "After I had picked it up, I marked it and turned it over to the representative from the Georgia Crime Lab, who was there at the scene."

McGarity: "I present you with another State exhibit and ask you to identify the contents."

Det. Hart: "It's the billfold that has the initials M.K. on one side of it and University of Georgia on the other, with the personal effects of Mr. King's on the inside. I found it approximately 120 feet from the blood stains on the dirt road."

Myers cross-examines Det. Hart, "Were you involved in the search for evidence on December 13th?"

Det. Hart: "I was a part of a team that was trying to locate the other two shells that we felt were missing at that time and to conduct a search for the billfold. Jerry Banks had told us the general area where he had thrown it."

Myers: "Did you find any other unusual things in the area?"

Det. Hart: "There were animal bones; I don't know whether it was a cow, a horse or what."

Myers: "Hopefully not human bones; Wouldn't you say that these were probably the remains of a kill left by a hunter. The area must be a popular hunting area?"

Det. Hart: "I would suppose so."

Myers: "And over a month from the date that was determined to be the date of the shooting, you found a shell, is that correct?"

Det. Hart: "Yes, sir."

Myers: "And the area was not roped off in any way?"

Det. Hart: "No, sir."

Myers: "So the area was open to people who may have traveled the area."

Det. Hart: "Yes, sir."

Myers: "That's all I have Your Honor."

Judge Sosebee: "Were you ever present, Det. Hart, when this gun, that's on the table there, was test-fired?"

Det. Hart: "No, Your Honor, I was not."

McGarity: "You may step down."

***

Everyone present in the courtroom became intrigued when Mr. Myers questioned Det. Hart about the bones that were found. Could this secluded and accessible to the Interstate place be a dumping ground for bodies? Is there a serial killer who had used Rock Quarry Road to dispose of victims? Det. Hart, however, testified that upon further examination, the bones were not human but those of deceased animals. Speaking from personal experience, when farm animals died, the carcasses were usually dragged into the woods rather than buried. Every farmer has an animal graveyard in a secluded-wooded area somewhere on his farm. It is ironic that King's and Hartsfield's bodies were found amid what could have been a former burial ground.

The Court recesses for the evening at 6:45 p.m. and resumes the next day at 9 a.m. January 30, 1975.

Kelly Fite is sworn in and examined by Assistant District Attorney Kenneth Waldrep. Mr. Fite has been employed as an microanalyst with the Georgia State Crime Laboratory in Atlanta. He has a Bachelor of Science degrees in chemistry and mathematics. His specialty is firearm identification. He would be asked to identify State exhibits that included a shotgun and spent cartridge casings.

Fite: "On the 9th of November, two cartridge casings were brought to me. Yes, I examined them and determined from my studies under the comparison microscope that both were fired by the same weapon, probably a break-type weapon such as a single or double-barrel shotgun. Later Paul Robbins of the Henry County Sheriff's Office brought to the Georgia Crime Lab on December 2nd three 12-gauge cartridges and requested that I compare these cartridges to the two given to me on November 9th."

Waldrep: "What did your comparison show?"

Fite: "It showed that all these cartridge casings contain identical firing pin impressions and breach-face markings. In my opinion all five cartridge casings were fired from the same weapon."

Waldrep: "I show you this weapon and ask you if you can identify it?"

Fite: "Yes, sir, I can. It's a twelve-gauge shotgun that was brought to the Georgia Crime Laboratory on December 6, 1974, by C.R. Barnes of the Henry Sheriff's Department. He requested that I test-fire it and compare my test cartridge casings to the others."

Judge Sosebee: "Did you do that?"

Fite: "Yes, sir, I did. The test cartridge casings fired from the shotgun show identical breach face markings and firing pin impressions as the other cartridges."

Waldrep: "I show you this shell, wadding and red sweater and ask you if you can identify them?"

Fite: "Yes, I can. It's one Winchester Western 12-gauge 00 Buck cartridge casing, and it was the last casing given to me by a colleague on December 13th. I compared the casing to the other shells and found similar markings and impressions. This is shotgun wadding which was brought to me at the Georgia Crime Laboratory on December 2nd by Paul Robbins. This wadding is identical to 12-gauge Winchester Western wadding that the manufacturer places in their buckshot loads. This red sweater which was removed from one of the victims and brought to me on November 8th by Dr. Howard. He asked me to examine the gunshot hole in the back of the sweater and determine from what range the gun was fired. He also asked me to examine the area of the wound for gunpowder or any type of trace evidence."

Waldrep: "Did you do so?"

Fite: "Yes, I did. I found numerous particles of a white powder, which microscopically are identical to the polyethylene packing found in Winchester Western buckshot loads. It is used as a cushion for the buckshot. The shell shot into this sweater was a Winchester Western Buckshot shell."

Waldrep: "From your tests that you might have run on the weapon were you able to determine from what range these shots were fired?"

Fite: "From the fire test the pellet patterns taken at varying distances, the test shots at five feet most closely duplicate the holes shown in this red sweater."

Waldrep: "I show you this pill box containing five 00 buckshot which Dr. Howard brought into the lab and ask if you can identify them?"

Fite: "These are lead pellets taken from Mr. King's shirt and Miss Hartsfield's sweater. Their characteristics are of a 00 buckshot."

***

Mr. Myers cross-examines Mr. Fite, "Other than what the detectives told you, of your own knowledge, for a fact, do you know where these shells came from?"

Fite: "No, sir, I don't."

Myers: "How and when was the shotgun brought to you?"

Fite: "The shotgun was brought to me by Det. Barnes on December 6th and was returned to Paul Robbins on the 11th of December."

Myers: "Other than what Mr. Robbins and these other gentlemen told you, do you know for a fact, of your own knowledge, where this wadding came from? Furthermore, do you know for a fact, of your knowledge, where the shotgun, clothing, and pellets came from."

Fite: "No, sir, I don't."

Myers: "Let me ask you this. Is there any way, medically or scientifically, that one could determine the age of a shotgun casing or how long a shotgun casing has been laying on the ground?"

Fite: "No, sir."

Myers: "In your opinion as an expert, that you could tell whether the pellets found in a wound, could be traced to any particular shotgun if that person was wounded with a such a weapon?"

Fite: "There's no way."

Myers: "There's no way. If I were shot with this shotgun or any shotgun, and you didn't see the shotgun being shot into my person, would there be any way for you to determine which shotgun did it?"

Fite: "No, sir, not which shotgun fired the pellets."

Myers: "You can match a shell by its impression to a particular gun, but there's no way you can determine from which weapon or where the shot ended up."

Fite: "That's true, sir."

Mr. Waldrep redirects examination of Mr. Fite, "Mr. Fite, all shotgun shells, have wadding and pellets that are different from other type shotgun shells. Would you say that the particular wadding and pellets are consistent with those found in a Winchester Western 12-gauge 00 Buck cartridge casings as found at the murder scene?"

Fite: "Yes, sir."

Mr. Myers re-cross examines Mr. Fite, "Kelly, I just have one question, and that question is, from all your findings, test patterns, and so forth, muzzle to target tests, et cetera, all the technical language that we've talked about and tried to explain, is there any way, medically or scientifically you have determined, for this jury, that this shotgun, Jerry Banks' shotgun, killed anybody:"

Fite: "No, sir, I can't."

McGarity: "All right, you can step down."

***

Mr. Waldrep calls the next witness, Paul Robbins, and swears him in. Mr. Robbins is employed by the Henry County Sheriff's Department as a detective. He was raised in Henry County and has been with the department for two years,

Waldrep: "Can you identify this particular exhibit?"

Det. Robbins: "It's shotgun wadding that I found on the dirt road near one of the pools of blood."

Judge Sosebee: "Would you step down and go to the blackboard. Please show the jury the location of the pools of blood, where bodies were found and where you found the wadding."

Waldrep: "Can you describe for the Court and jury what you saw at the scene."

Det. Robbins: "Approximately 120 feet from the roadbed down a path, there were two bodies lying there. One was the body of a White female, who appeared between eighteen and twenty years old. She had on a red turtle-neck sweater, black pants and brown shoes. Lying next to her, was a White male victim. He had on a blue shirt, a dark blue tie, and blue checked pants and black patent leather shoes."

Waldrep: "How long did you stay on the scene that night?"

Det. Robbins: "I stayed on the scene approximately two-and-a-half to three hours before I left and went to the preparation room of Carmichael's Funeral Home."

Waldrep: "When the bodies arrived at the funeral home were you able to identify the bodies?"

Det. Robbins: "When I arrived, Dr. Howard was getting ready to do the autopsies. At that time, he removed the 1959 Class of Georgia ring from the finger of the male victim. When he took it off, he handed it to me, and I read the name out loud. Capt. Berry with the Clayton Count Police Department knew the victim right off."

Mr. Waldrep continued examination of Det. Robbins. He confirmed the testimony given by the previous witnesses, Det. Barnes and Sgt. Floyd. Det. Robbins acknowledged that he was present when two shotgun shells were found and pointed to the "Xs" on a blackboard where they were found. He told the jury that on November 9th and December 2nd he took shotgun shells to the Georgia Crime Lab. He described the trips to Banks' house and Perry's house to pick the 12-gauge shotgun.

Judge Sosebee: "Det. Robbins let me ask you this. When you met with Banks, did you ask him whether or not the shotgun was fired that day?"

Det. Robbins: "He said he hadn't fired that gun in that area, within a mile of the area, and I even asked if he had any empty shell casings in his pocket, and his answer was 'no'."

Waldrep: "Did Mr. Banks make any statement to you about the billfold?"

Det. Robbins: "He stated that he had picked up the billfold from the ground. Saw that there was no money in it and threw it away about thirty steps from the body."

Waldrep: "Did you search for King's billfold on that day?"

Det. Robbins: "Yes, sir. But I had my suit on and I didn't want to get into the briars and thick stuff. We decided to go back the next day. In about thirty minutes the following day Det. Hart found the billfold."

Myers cross-examines Det. Robbins: "Paul, tell us again now, when did you arrive on the scene and who was there?"

Det. Robbins: "November 7th, approximately 6:15 p.m. I saw Sgt. Floyd. He was just arriving as I was getting there. I saw Sgt. Payne, Det. Barnes, Sgt. Tomlinson, Sgt. Glover and Jerry Banks."

Myers: "Did you speak with Mr. Banks?"

Det. Robbins: "No, sir."

Myers: "Did you or to your knowledge did any of the detectives who were there, ask Banks why he was holding a weapon?"

Det. Robbins: "No, sir."

Myers: "Did you search the bodies?"

Det. Robbins: "As I began searching, Mr. Tomlinson handed me a ring from the White female, a 1974 Jonesboro class ring."

Myers: "Did you personally search the female victim?"

Det. Robbins: "She didn't have anything to search for."

Myers: "About the wallet, did you ask him if he found the wallet prior to finding the bodies?"

Det. Robbins: "I asked him did he take it from the body."

Myers: "My question was, Paul, did you ask him if he found the wallet prior to finding the bodies?"

Det. Robbins: "No."

Myers: "Where was the wallet found?"

Det. Robbins: "About 300 feet from the blood stains."

Myers: "It was approximately 300 feet from the blood stains. But you don't know whether or not Jerry found this wallet prior to finding the bodies?"

Det. Robbins: "No, sir."

Myers: "You are familiar with the area. Have you ever seen anyone hunting there?"

Det. Robbins: "I have seen people hunting on the other side of the road."

Myers: "Would you say the secluded area around the scene with its thick undergrowth would be where game can be found?"

Det. Robbins: "I suppose so."

Myers: "Would one expect hunters to go in the brush after game?"

Det. Robbins: "Not in that thick brush."

Myers: "When you were hunting, Paul, where did you hunt?"

Det. Robbins: "I hunted where there weren't too many briars."

Myers: "That's all."

McGarity: "Step down."

***

From the transcript Defense Attorney Myers asked each detective who was at the murder scene that evening whether they saw Jerry Banks in possession of a shotgun. All testified that they had. In all the commotion, Jerry Banks made no effort to conceal his shotgun. No one asked if it had been fired or if it was even loaded? I would have thought one of the police officers might have suggested to Banks to put the gun away. Since Banks said he was a hunter, you could assume that there would have been some discussion about hunting. Did you see any game today? Were you looking for rabbits or deer? Is this a good place to hunt? After the initial encounter with Patrolman Tomlinson, Jerry Banks' presence was for the most part ignored. Banks remained at the scene until way after dark at which time he and his dog supposedly walked home.

There was another puzzling aspect of the shotgun that was only lightly touched upon on by the defense. It is a common fact that even a less than an intelligent criminal would immediately dispose of the weapon used to perpetrate a crime. It makes little sense that Banks would intentionally flaunt the murder weapon under the noses of the investigators that evening. The shotgun could have been buried or hidden in a secure place, perhaps with the mindset to retrieve later. On the other hand, if Jerry Banks had not possessed a firearm that evening, it would have been difficult for him to explain what he was doing there. A hunter in the woods without a gun would certainly have created suspicion. I wonder in what direction the investigation would have gone had the shotgun not been in Banks' possession that evening.

***

Mr. McGarity calls his next witness, Dr. Larry Howard, and swears him in. "Please tell the Court your line of work and your educational background."

Dr. Howard: "I am the director of the Georgia Crime Lab and I oversee all of medical legal pathology. I hold a bachelor's degree in Chemistry and Bacteriology from the University of Montana, a Doctor's Degree from University of Minnesota and have completed post-doctorate work in pathology at Emory University."

McGarity: "Well, Dr. Howard, I'll ask you whether or not that you had any occasion to come to Henry County, Georgia on or about November 7th, 1974?"

Dr. Howard: "My purpose of coming was to do an autopsy on bodies later identified to me as Marvin King and Melanie Ann Hartsfield."

Dr. Howard describes the condition of the bodies and the entry and exit wounds. Each had been shot twice from the rear. The discharged pellets penetrated King's elbow and back severing the spinal column. He found Miss Hartsfield's wounds on the right side of the neck, on left side of the back and right side of the abdomen. From the angle of the wounds to their bodies, the second shots occurred when they were down on the ground.

McGarity: "Now, I ask you, after making your examination and autopsy of Marvin King and Melanie Ann Hartsfield, if you have a determination as to the cause of their deaths?"

Dr. Howard: "Yes, sir. Dr. Foster and I determined that Mr. King and Miss Hartsfield died as a result of shotgun wounds to the back of heads."

McGarity: "I'll ask you, Dr. Howard, do these exhibits represent buckshot taken from the back of King's body and the wadding and shots found in the body cavity of Melanie Ann Hartsfield?"

Dr. Howard: "Yes, sir."

McGarity: "What did you do after you removed them from the body?"

Dr. Howard: "I gave them to Mr. Fite for examination."

Judge Sosebee: "Did you find any other wounds on the body of either person?"

Dr. Howard: "None other than the postmortem scratches. Each had drag marks over the interior, which were particularly pronounced over the front of the ribs."

McGarity: "Dr. Howard, did you have occasion to make a determination as to the approximate time of death?"

Dr. Howard: "Yes, approximately two-thirty in the afternoon

of the day I did the autopsy, November 7th."

McGarity: "I ask you, Dr. Howard, whether or not that you did a pelvic examination of the Hartsfield girl?"

Dr. Howard: "Yes, sir. I was looking specifically for evidence of seminal fluid. There was none, meaning that no sex relationship had been culminated."

McGarity: "That's all I have. I turn the witness over to you, Mr. Myers."

Myers cross-examines Dr. Howard, "Now, Dr. Howard did you find any bruises that would indicate if the hands, feet, neck or something had been bound?"

Dr. Howard: "I cannot say that, because if they were bound by something that was smooth, it would not have left any marks. The only thing I can say, there wasn't any evidence of the marks."

Myers: "One other thing, Dr. Howard, and I'll let you go. Are you familiar with an execution-style killing and is that what we have here?"

Dr. Howard: "From the pictures that were taken of the bodies that I viewed today; I would determine that the deaths could be considered as execution-style."

***

Mr. McGarity calls his next witness, Phillip Stuart Howard, known to his friends as "Sugg." Capt. Howard is Chief of the Henry County Detectives and reports directly to Sheriff Jimmy Glass. He is sworn in to testify for the State.

McGarity: "Did you return to the scene the next morning to search for evidence?"

Capt. Howard: "The purpose of the search was to find anything that might have a bearing or might tend to be evidence in this case. I found one Winchester Western shell 00 Buck Mark V. It was found in the wooded area, approximately thirty-seven feet from the blood stains. Mr. Ray found the other shell approximately, I'd say, five or six minutes after I found mine. He and I got together and wrapped a piece of tape around them. They were then brought to my office, locked in my desk. From there they were turned over to Sgt. Floyd and Det. Robbins and transported to the Georgia Crime Lab."

McGarity: "All right, sir. Now, I'll ask you, Mr. Howard, whether or not you made any kind of test with defendant's shotgun?"

Capt. Howard: "I fired three shots at the rear of the courthouse in front of the detective division. The three shells I fired on November 10th came from the shotgun Det. Dick Barnes brought to me. He had obtained the shotgun from the subject, Banks. I turned them over to Det. Robbins. On December 6th he transported these to the Georgia Crime Lab."

Myers: "Do you remember speaking to the press on December 13th?"

Capt. Howard: "Yes, I reported that the department did not have motive for the homicides at that time."

Myers: "Of your own knowledge do you know whether or not the police or the detectives have been able to establish such?"

Capt. Howard: "At this time, no, sir."

Myers: "That's all I have."

McGarity: "The State of Georgia rests."

The Court adjourns for the lunch recess.

***

Having served on a jury in Judge Sosebee's Court, I can attest to those who participate in a criminal jury trial for the first time, that they will be surprised with the amount of time spent waiting. The accused, held without bond, is sitting and waiting in jail. The attorneys and the victims wait for their case to be placed on the crowded calendar. The jurors report to the jury room on Monday of the trial week and wait until they are selected to serve on a particular jury. The witnesses who arrive on the day of the trial wait outside of the courtroom until they are called to testify. And then, while the jury deliberates on the charges, everyone waits on the verdict. Time passes at a snail's pace.

Jury duty requires patience. It helps to have a good book or crossword puzzle to keep one entertained during the delays. The waiting enhances the anxiety and nervousness as there is uncertainty to what lies ahead. It is an emotional period for families. The outcome could be a joyous occasion following a not guilty verdict. The handcuffs and shackles are not required as the defendant goes home. All the waiting endured during the trial process is soon forgotten. But, if the jury renders a guilty verdict, the waiting for the convicted may last a lifetime.

CHAPTER **26** | Defense
Witness Testimony

A week before the scheduled trial, John Hudson Myers meets with Jerry Banks at the Henry County Jail. He tells Jerry that he has spoken with Virginia, Gracie Slaughter and Perry Banks about possibly testifying. In Georgia, a wife cannot be made to testify against her husband. Virginia could vouch for Jerry's activity the day of the murders, which included helping the Slaughters and the afternoon deer hunt. Her testimony about Jerry's caring nature toward the children and their need for a father figure would tug on the heart strings of the female jurors. Her testimony, however, may get discounted by the other jurors. Myers feels comfortable with his two defense witnesses. The rotund Mrs. Gracie should come across as a loving grandma type. A member of the AME Church next door, she is a devout Christian, a person of moral values, and one who would not tell a lie. Perry is a little rough around the edges and says what is on his mind, but his testimony should help convince the jury that it was his shell casings that the detectives found, not Jerry's.

***

Myers tells the deputy at the jail, "I am here to see Jerry Banks."
"I will let you in, but you will have to talk to him through the

bars. We do not have an empty cell that I can put you two in," replies the deputy.

Myers asks, "Jerry, how are these people treating you?"

"The meals are good, but I want to get out of here in the worst way," says Jerry.

Myers promises Jerry, "If all goes well with the trial, you will be out of here in no time flat. I had good meetings with your brother and your neighbor. Their testimony should convince the jury that you didn't commit the murders."

Jerry asks, "Is Virginia gonna to testify?"

Myers replies, "By Georgia law a wife doesn't have to testify for or against her spouse. She is nervous about it. She is willing if it will get you out of prison. The problem with Virginia testifying is that jurors feel sorry for her as a mother, but they may not believe her as a witness. Jurors suspect that a wife will say whatever it takes, even lie, to help a husband. I don't think putting her on the stand is a good idea."

Jerry then asks, "Are you gonna let me tell the jury that I am no murderer?"

Myers is emphatic. "The burden of proof rests with the prosecutors. The district attorney must prove that you had the opportunity and reason to harm those people and that you are the one who pulled the trigger. He has no eyewitnesses and no motive. Besides, you are the one who reported the crime."

Jerry replies, "I think, if I tell them my side of the story, they will believe me."

Myers interrupts, "Wait a minute, Jerry. If I let you testify and you slip up, the jury will show you no mercy. Remember Jerry you are a convicted felon, charged with murder of all things. Cross-examination by Mr. McGarity or Mr. Waldrep could be brutal. They will try to confuse you and try to get you mad. If they succeed and you display even the slightest bit of anger in front of the jury, you are done for. I will think about it, but more than likely you don't need to take the stand."

***

Mr. Myers' first witness for the defense is Mrs. Grace Mae Slaughter. Her friends call her Gracie. She lives on Red Oak Road in Stockbridge and has lived there for seventeen years. She has been Jerry Banks' neighbor since he and Virginia moved into Opal Phelps' rental house. Only three houses separate them. She is sworn in and is examined by Mr. Myers.

Myers: "Do you recall the events of November 7, 1974?"

Mrs. Slaughter: "Yes, I do."

Myers: "What time, Mrs. Slaughter, did Jerry come to your home that day?"

Mrs. Slaughter: "Around nine, nine-thirty or ten o'clock in the morning."

Myers: "Is Jerry in the habit of coming to your home?"

Mrs. Slaughter: "Yes, he is. He's there almost every day."

Myers: "And why is he coming down to your home every day?"

Mrs. Slaughter: "Because of my husband, James, they call him Judge. He's too disabled to work much. He comes down and helps him."

Myers: "What sort of work does Jerry do at your home each day?"

Mrs. Slaughter: "He do a little of everything, what he does is feed hogs, shuck corn, helping tear up cars for junk, pick up trash, tote in wood, keep fires."

Myers: "On the morning of November 7, 1974, you said Jerry came down about nine-thirty or so. What time did Jerry leave your home that day?"

Mrs. Slaughter: "It would have to be after looking at TV."

Myers: "Well, what was on the TV?"

Mrs. Slaughter: "*Another World*. He stops work so he can keep up with *Another World*."

Myers: "What time does *Another World* come on?"

Mrs. Slaughter: "Three-o'clock on Channel 2."

Myers: "Do you know what happened after that point?"

Mrs. Slaughter: "Well, I was churning after they went out. When I was taking up butter, I saw him come through the gate to go home. He said he was going hunting."

Myers: "Do you know what time it was then?"

Mrs. Slaughter: "It was later in the afternoon."

Mr. McGarity cross-examines Mrs. Slaughter, "And you say he comes there every day?"

Mrs. Slaughter: "Every day."

McGarity: "Every day. All right, what time did he get there on November 8th?"

Mrs. Slaughter: "It was between nine-thirty and ten o'clock."

McGarity: "How do know that?"

Mrs. Slaughter: "Because I do, that's the time he gets there every day."

McGarity: "And what time did he leave?"

Mrs. Slaughter: "He left that day around five, six o'clock, that's the time he leaves every day."

McGarity: "Now, you said something about that you came to know him when he was a 'trustee'. What do you mean by that?"

Mrs. Slaughter: "That's what I took him to be, a trustee. He was walking around McDonough in prison clothes."

Myers: "I object to that."

Judge Sosebee: "I will sustain the objection."

McGarity: "Did you say that you and Mr. Banks watched *As the World Turns* on the day of the murders?"

Mrs. Slaughter: "No. We were watching *Another World*. It came on at three o'clock in the afternoon."

McGarity: "Back around November, do you know if he hunted at night?"

Mrs. Slaughter: "I don't know, I am not with him."

McGarity: "You don't know whether he went hunting or not, do you?"

Mrs. Slaughter: "No, I don't know whether he went or not."

McGarity: "Did you take a look at your watch and put down the time that he left?"

Mrs. Slaughter: "No, I didn't have any reason to."

McGarity: "But yet and still you're telling this Court and jury that he didn't leave there until five or five-thirty?"

Mrs. Slaughter: "That's the truth."

***

Mr. Myers calls Perry Banks, Jerry's brother, to the stand. He is sworn in and testifies for the defense. Perry is Jerry's younger brother and lives with his mother on Highway 155 in Stockbridge.

Myers: "Perry, do you recall the conversation that you and Det. Tommy Floyd had last Wednesday at your house?"

Perry Banks: "Yes, he talked to me about Jerry."

Myers: "What did he tell you, or ask you, if anything, about this case?"

Perry Banks: "He said that he wanted to talk to me, and he asked me did I know anything about Jerry's case? I said, 'No'. He asked me did I, do it? I looked at him and said that I didn't do it, either."

Myers: "Do it. Do what?"

Perry Banks: "Kill those two people. And I looked at him in the eye, smiled and said, No! He said that he didn't want to see Jerry railroaded any more than I did. Then he gave me a card and said, 'If you change your mind about talking to me, call.' And that was it."

Myers: "Are you sure he used the word, 'railroaded', Perry?"

Perry Banks: "Those are the exact words."

Myers: "Can you tell the Court about that gun?"

Perry Banks: "It's mine. It's a family gun that my brother, Ludie, gave me about three years ago, I believe."

Myers: "Where did he get the shotgun?"

Perry Banks: "Our father gave it."

Myers: "How long has your family owned this shotgun?"

Perry Banks: "Probably about forty years, I imagine."

Myers: "Now, Perry, have you ever been hunting in the woods around Rock Quarry Road and used the shotgun?"

Perry Banks: "Yes, sir."

Myers: "Have you had occasion to fire this weapon while hunting off of old Rock Quarry Road, or in that area?"

Perry Banks: "Yes."

Myers: "If you're hunting large game, say, deer, what kind of shells do you use?"

Perry Banks: "Slug or double 00 buckshot."

Myers: "When you fired this weapon off of old Rock Quarry Road, what did you do with the shell casings?"

Perry Banks: "When I shoot, I just let them jump out and fall on the ground."

Myers: "When you hunt off of old Rock Quarry Road with this weapon, or in that area, are you in the bush, are you walking down the road, or just where are you?"

Perry Banks: "I'm in the bush."

Myers: "Explain, why you do that?"

Perry Banks: "Well, that's where you hunt cause that's where the deer are."

Myers: "When was the last time you were hunting off of old Rock Quarry Road?"

Perry Banks: "I went deer hunting over there about two weeks before Jerry went hunting."

Mr. McGarity cross-examines Perry Banks, "What kind of shells did you use when you went hunting over on old Rock Quarry Road?"

Perry Banks: "I think I got two 00 buckshot shells from a cousin of mine."

McGarity: "What brand?"

Perry Banks: "A Winchester Western Auto."

McGarity: "Do you know what color they were?"

Perry Banks: "They were green."

McGarity: "So then you never hunted on old Rock Quarry Road with any red shells then, did you?"

Perry Banks: "Before then, I had been hunting over there for the last couple of years. I used all kind of shells."

McGarity: "What did you shoot at?"

Perry Banks: "Deer."

McGarity: "Perry how old are you?"

Perry Banks: "I am nineteen."

McGarity: "Are you employed?"

Perry Banks: "No."

McGarity: "How do you make a living?"

Myers: "Excuse me, Your Honor. I would object to that on the grounds of materiality. It doesn't have any bearing on the case."

Judge Sosebee: "Well, it might, or it might not. It goes to the credibility of the witness. The Court will overrule the objection."

McGarity: "All right, answer the question. Tell the Court how you make a living."

Perry Banks: "Lots of ways, most of the time I shoot pool in Atlanta every Thursday."

McGarity: "How do you make a living playing pool?"

Perry Banks: "I play for money."

McGarity: "What kind of automobile have you got?"

Perry Banks: "Don't have one."

McGarity: "How do you get back and forth?"

Perry Banks: "I have a friend who works at the rock quarry in Stockbridge."

McGarity: "Do you remember where you were on the date of November 7th last year?"

Perry Banks: "At the poolroom."

McGarity: "Perry on Thursday, November 7, 1974, Jerry wasn't at Mrs. Slaughter's that day, was he?"

Perry Banks: "I don't know whether he was there or not. I wasn't with him."

Mr. Myers re-directs examination of Perry Banks, "When you hunted the land off of Rock Quarry, did you ever use red shells?"

Perry Banks: "I used red and green shells."

Judge Sosebee: "Well, when did you last shoot any red shells?"

Perry Banks: "Probably last fall, when it was deer season."

Judge Sosebee: "Well, when would that be?"

Perry Banks: "It was in October I hunted in October, November 1974."

Mr. McGarity re-directs examination of Perry Banks, "Do you have a hunting license?"

Perry Banks: "I got my rabbit license on me now."

McGarity: "Well, you have to have something besides a rabbit license to hunt deer."

Perry Banks: "Don't need one, if they don't catch you."

***

Mr. McGarity calls T.K. Floyd as a rebuttal witness for the State of Georgia: "In your conversation with Perry Banks last Wednesday did you ever mention anything to him about railroading somebody?"

Sgt. Floyd: "No, sir. I never mentioned the word 'railroad' when speaking about Jerry."

Mr. Myers cross-examines Mr. Floyd, "Mr. Floyd, was it your testimony in this trial that you went there on Wednesday to question Perry because of the number of unanswered questions?"

Sgt. Floyd: "Yes, sir, it was."

Myers: "At this point and was it also your testimony that one of those unanswered questions was lack of a motive?"

Sgt. Floyd: "Yes, sir, I indicated a lack of motive, yes, sir."

Myers: "And was it also your testimony earlier that you do not usually continue an investigation after an arraignment hearing?"

Sgt. Floyd: "Not usually, no, sir."

Judge Sosebee: "Is that all for the prosecution?"

McGarity: "If Your Honor please, the State respectfully rests."

Myers: "Your Honor, the defense rests."

***

Judge Sosebee asks the jurors, "Are you gentlemen ready to give your closing arguments?"

McGarity approaches the jury box and begins, "Ladies and gentlemen of the jury. I want to thank you for your attention and the time away from your jobs and families it required for you to serve as jurors on this complicated case. It is the State of Georgia's burden to prove without a shadow of a doubt that Jerry Banks did kill Marvin King and Melanie Hartsfield as charged. I believe that we have shown that Mr. Banks was at the scene at the time of the murders; he had the opportunity to commit the murders; and that his shotgun was used to inflict the wounds that resulted in their deaths. We had an expert witness that testified that it was Winchester Western cartridges that were fired from Banks' shotgun, that inflicted the fatal wounds. The same shotgun in his possession on the night of the murders. Mr. Banks admitted that he removed Mr. King's billfold in hopes of finding money and threw it into the bushes. He lied to Det. Floyd when he accused another man of borrowing the shotgun and committing the crime. He said that he was hunting that day but there are no witnesses who can confirm his story. And, finally, the victim's car was found the following day near Mr. Banks' home."

Mr. McGarity pauses and fills his empty glass with water. He takes a few swallows and sets the glass back on the table. He looks and points at Jerry Banks and continues. "Mr. Banks is a vicious killer. He executed those people, a well-respected and talented teacher and musician. A family man with a lovely wife and four beautiful children. A young promising college student with the best years of her life ahead of her. It is your duty to find this killer guilty, get him off the streets before he kills someone else. What we need here is old-fashioned justice: An eye-for-an-eye and a tooth-for-a-tooth. The man has no regard for human life. Why shouldn't he give his own?"

Myers follows, "I too wish to thank you for your service and do not envy the difficult decision you have been asked to make. I will be brief. Without a doubt you must reach a conclusion that is inescapable. Jerry Banks is innocent. The evidence against Mr. Banks is very circumstantial. There are no witnesses who can attest to Mr. Banks firing the shots that killed the two victims. The State has not been able to provide a reasonable motive as to why Mr. Banks would have a reason to commit the crime. It does not make any logical sense that Mr. Banks would kill the two people, report the crime and then hang around to direct the police to the bodies. It would have been easier not to get involved and just go home. While at the scene not a single person noticed any blood stains on his person. His fingerprints were not found on the discharged shell casings. His fingerprints were not found in Mr. King's car. There were no items that belonged to the victims found at his home.

"Jerry's brother testified that he had been hunting in that area with the same shotgun, using the same type of cartridges several times. The latest being two weeks prior to the murders. The spent shells that were found and supposedly fired from Banks' gun were probably shell casings left behind from previous hunts by his brother Perry."

Defense Attorney Myers emphasizes to the jury that Banks could not have been the shooter, because he was not in the area at the time of the shooting. His neighbor testified that Jerry was at her house working in the backyard helping her husband and stayed to watch Another World. Which meant, he could not have left, until after three thirty in the afternoon.

Mr. Myers walks over to the evidence table to pick up Banks' shotgun. "Ladies and gentlemen, the weapon I am holding is an old shotgun. It is a family heirloom; it is a classic. But it is a tired-old gun. It has shot many a deer, rabbit and racoon. Its best days are behind it. At one time it was a reliable shotgun. If it were not for the black electrical tape holding it together, the gun would fall apart." Myers to show the gun's poor condition jurors, points the gun in the direction of Mr. McGarity.

Mr. McGarity jumps up and yells, "Now wait a minute! Stop pointing that gun at me. It may be loaded!"

He hurriedly walks over to John Hudson Myers and angrily jerks the shotgun away from him, "Young man, let's leave the gun on the table."

Mr. Myers replies, "My apology, I did not know you were so gun shy, Mr. McGarity.

"As I was saying, this gun could not have shot the two victims. The time it took to discharge a shot, remove the shell, reload and fire again, would have given the second victim an opportunity to attempt an escape. But the area where they were shot indicated that they were standing side by side, when they were shot. Even a slow person could have run twenty feet or so in that time frame."

Mr. Myers continues, "Jerry Banks is a young man. He has made his share of mistakes and he has paid for those mistakes. He has three children and a loyal wife. Based on the lack of hard evidence, it would be an injustice to find Jerry Banks guilty of this crime."

Judge Sosebee thanks the attorneys and calls a short recess so everyone can take a restroom or cigarette break or both."

CHAPTER 27 | Charge to the Jury,
First Trial

Up to now all the attention during the trial has been focused on questions by the opposing attorneys and the responses by the witnesses. Occasionally, Judge Sosebee asks a question or makes a comment. Everyone else in the courtroom sits and listens. Looking at jurors' facial expressions you know there are times when a juror wants to stand up and question one of the witnesses or the judge. By the end of the day their backsides are a little sore from all the sitting. They must wait on their turn to speak. Their opportunity comes after the closing arguments, any post-trial motions and Judge Sosebee's reading of the final instructions. The life and death decision will then be in their hands.

***

When court reconvenes at approximately 3 p.m., Judge Sosebee reads the Court's instructions as it relates to the law that apply to the facts of the case. "It is alleged that this defendant did on November 7, 1974, in Henry County, Georgia, unlawfully and with malice aforethought, kill and murder Marvin King and Melanie Ann Hartsfield with a certain shotgun. The defendant, Jerry Banks, has entered a plea of not guilty.

"The law provides that person shall not be convicted for any crime unless each and every element of such offense is proved beyond a reasonable doubt. If, after giving consideration to all the facts and circumstance of this case, you find your minds wavering, uncertain and unsettled as to what the truth is, then under the law, it would be your duty to find the defendant not guilty.

"If you find beyond a reasonable doubt that this defendant, Jerry Banks, did unlawfully and with malice aforethought kill Marvin King and Melanie Ann Hartsfield, you would be authorized to find the defendant guilty as charged. The decision must be unanimous."

The jury retires to the jury room to deliberate. After an hour and half, the foreman of the jury advises Judge Sosebee that they had not reached a verdict. Once back in the courtroom and seated in the jury box, the foreman rises and addresses the Judge: "Some of the jury members are getting hungry, can we take a break before it gets too late?" Judge Sosebee, with a grin says, "Mr. Foreman, I think the rest of us could use something to eat as well. Capt. Childs is ready to take you to supper. I caution you not to discuss the case until you return to the jury room."

Once back in the jury room, deliberation continues with little headway. After two hours and forty-five minutes, the foreman announces to the Judge Sosebee, that no verdict has been reached. Looking at his watch, he declares, "It's a little after nine o'clock and I am just thinking that maybe we might just recess until tomorrow morning. I will let the bailiffs and officers escort you to the Holiday Inn on Highway 155, where you can have a good night's rest. Mr. Bowen, see that you have all of them back in the courtroom at 8:45 a.m. Court will reconvene promptly." Judge Sosebee is anxious to bring this trial to a close.

***

Judge Sosebee tells the jurors to return to the jury room to continue their deliberations. "Hopefully, you can come to a decision this morning."

After approximately three hours the next morning the foreman slips a note to the bailiff sitting in a chair outside of the jury room, where he is guarding the door. It reads, "Your Honor, the jurors have reached a verdict." Where upon Judge Sosebee asks the deputies to fetch Jerry Banks from his jail cell behind the courthouse and to advise the attorneys, who are somewhere in the courthouse, that the jury has reached a verdict.

Twenty minutes later, all the attorneys are back in the courtroom. The jury enters the jury box and is seated.

Judge Sosebee asks, "Mr. Foreman, ladies and gentlemen of the jury, have you arrived at a verdict?"

"We have, Your Honor," responds the foreman.

Judge Sosebee instructs District Attorney McGarity to receive and read the verdict.

McGarity opens the envelope, scans the note, pauses and reads aloud, "We the jury find the defendant, Jerry Banks, guilty as charged."

Judge Sosebee addresses the Court: "The law provides that the jury may be polled individually, so I will proceed to do that. I will start with the foreman. Is this your verdict now? Did you freely and voluntarily agree to this verdict. He and all of the jurors individually respond, 'yes', thus validating the verdict.

"Ladies and gentlemen, you have found the defendant guilty of the charges of murder. The law places the responsibility upon the jury to determine what sentence would be imposed, the choices are life imprisonment or the death penalty. If you find the defendant guilty of wanton murder, Georgia law allows you to recommend execution by the electric chair. For the record you should know that the U.S. Supreme Court has imposed a temporary moratorium on executions. In 1972, the death penalty conviction appeal by an inmate named Furman, the high Court established specific requirements for the death sentencing. The U.S. Supreme Court ruled that unless a uniform policy exists of determining who is eligible for capital punishment, the death penalty will be regarded as 'cruel and unusual punishment'. The State of Georgia is in the process of having its eligibility standards ratified by the justices of the Supreme Court."

McGarity: "Your Honor, I tender into evidence another exhibit, which is a certified copy of a plea of guilty by Jerry Banks to involuntary manslaughter. In that on June 11, 1970, he shot and killed Robert Walker, without any intention to do so, and he was given a sentence of two years, seven months and seventeen days. He was released on January 18, 1972."

Judge Sosebee: "The Court will admit the certified copy. Mr. Myers, do you have, in the way of evidence, anything that you want to put in?"

Myers: "Not at this time."

***

The twelve-member jury had wrestled with the verdict and the sentence for over seven hours. Before casting the final vote, the foreman asked the jurors to bow their heads in silent prayer. "I do not want anyone to have any second thoughts if you decide to put the man to death," he says. Following the prayer, the jury voted and found Banks guilty of both murders.

The jury is instructed to retire from the courtroom and return to the jury room to deliberate the sentence. After thirty minutes they emerge.

Judge Sosebee: "The bailiff indicates that you have a question."

Foreman: "Yes, sir, Your Honor. Is it possible for you to explain to the jury that if a life sentence is invoked, what are the chances for parole? How and where is this sentence served?"

Judge Sosebee: "The only thing that I can say to you, Mr. Foreman, ladies and gentlemen of the jury, is that the Court would impose a sentence for life. This is as far as the law will permit the Court to comment. I will let you go to lunch. When you return go back to the jury room and deliberate over your decision."

***

After an hour of further deliberation, the jury finally reaches its decision.

Judge Sosebee asks the District Attorney McGarity to read the verdict of the jury.

McGarity nods and reads, "We the jury set the penalty at death. The offense of murder was outrageously and wantonly vile, horrible and inhuman in that it involved torture of the victims."

Judge Sosebee looking at Jerry Banks, "Would the defendant Jerry Banks, and his counselor please rise. The jury has found you guilty of the murders of Marvin King and Melanie Ann Hartsfield and sentences you to death. It is hereby adjudged by this Court that you be taken to the Henry County Jail and safely kept until you are transferred to the Georgia State Penitentiary at Reidsville, Georgia, where you shall suffer punishment of death by electrocution on the 28th day of March 1975, as provided by law, between the hours of 10 a.m. and 4 p.m. May God have mercy on your soul!"

A hush overcomes the crowded courtroom as Judge Sosebee announces the sentence. Hearing the verdict and the scheduled execution date, Jerry hangs his head, slumps back into his chair. John Hudson Myers, his attorney, grabs him by the arm and pulls him back up as Judge Sosebee continues to address the Court. Jerry Banks who has sat emotionless and sometimes disinterested as the prosecution attorneys introduced a host of witnesses, now cannot hold back his emotions. Attorney Myers shakes his head in disbelief. Virginia, sitting next to Perry, listens nervously to the reading of the verdict. They look at each other with overwhelming grief. Instead of hugging his wife and glad-handing his brother, Banks is handcuffed and escorted out of the courtroom. To avoid the horde of reporters the prosecution attorneys, Sheriff Glass and the deputies exit out of the back-entry way. A few minutes later, Jerry is issued a prison uniform and ushered into the bull pen. After he has finished dressing, he folds his street clothes and hands them to the guard.

Lawyer John Hudson Myers

"Please give these to Virginia. I won't be needing them for a while."

One of the older jurors, who was the most vocal in the jury room during the deliberations, did not mind expressing her opinion. She is the first to speak to the press, "The defense witnesses were not creditable. The man who said he had been hunting in the woods with the same shotgun and shells before the murders, got confused when asked to identify the color of his shell." One of the young jurors admits, "I had had trouble sleeping after viewing Det. Payne's gruesome photos of the bodies." Another juror says, "I had expected attorney Myers to pull a Perry Mason by introducing a plausible theory as to who might have committed the crimes. Perhaps call a surprise witness and get a confession. It never happened." Yet, another female juror says, "I wish that Banks had testified. I would have liked to hear his side of the story. Not testifying makes him look guilty. Innocent people don't hide behind their attorneys."

Perry and Virginia leave the Henry County Courthouse in tears.

CHAPTER 28 | Appeal to the Henry County
Superior Court

Jerry Banks' legal process has moved along with speed and efficiency. It takes one hundred and seven days from his arrest in December to the scheduled execution date in March. I ask an attorney where he thought Jerry Banks' case might be headed next. He explains it in simple terms so a lay person like me could understand, "There are three stages in the appeal process for the various types of petitions that can be filed. I will not bore you with all the intricacies and terminologies. If there are grounds and the judge or justices agree to hear your appeal, you first present your petition in the lower Court, Henry County Superior Court. If you lose in Superior Court, you then file your petition in the Georgia Court of Appeals or the Georgia Supreme Court. If unsuccessful, your last avenue of appeal is the high Court, the U.S. Supreme Court."

He continues by telling me the difference between the Georgia Court of Appeals and Georgia Supreme Court. "Both courts will review decisions involving possible errors made in the lower courts. However, the Georgia Supreme Court will have the final say in Georgia. Both courts are busy, so it is hard to gauge which court will grant a hearing and return a ruling the quickest. The legal system can be overwhelming at times. That is why lawyers have a separate library full of law books in their offices."

The death penalty sentence in Georgia carries an automatic appeal. Myers immediately files a motion in Henry County Superior Court. He expects a court date in the spring. Judge Sosebee will be the presiding Judge.

In 1974, 5,002 convicted criminals entered the Georgia Prison System. Of the total 47.8 percent were White and 52.2 percent were Black. The trend of more Blacks than Whites being sent to jail continues through the 1970s. That is not to say that Blacks commit more crimes or that they are more likely to get caught. The numbers do indicate when Blacks are arrested, they are more apt to land in jail and then have more difficulty getting released. It is not an encouraging statistic for Jerry Banks who is counting on an acquittal at the next trial.

**

After learning that Jerry Banks is found guilty, Andrew Eberhardt is surprised and stunned that he is not called to testify. Newspaper accounts refer to Eberhardt, the motorist who called police, as the "mystery man." Advertisements by Myers seeking his identity were not seen by those who were aware that Eberhart was the caller which was a surprise to Eberhardt since he told Sheriff Glass, his family and his friends of his encounter with Banks on November 7th. He cannot understand why he is labeled as the "mystery man."

Eberhardt, a Boy Scout leader, feels he has an obligation to provide the accused Banks with whatever assistance he could. According to the Boy Scout oath, "It is my duty to God and my country to obey the Scout Law and help other people at all times." Jerry Banks is no exception. He first drives to Forsyth on February 4th to meet with Judge Sosebee and personally inform him that he is the unidentified caller. After listening to Mr. Eberhardt's detailed account of what occurred, Judge Sosebee promises to pass the information to the attorneys. Then, in an effort not to offend the Sheriff, he calls Jimmy Glass. Mr. Eberhardt discloses to Sheriff Glass that he has spoken to Judge Sosebee about offering to testify. Sheriff Glass suggests he come to his office and relay the information to a detective who will prepare a written statement of what happened that night.

Banks' defense attorney, Myers, and Judge Sosebee now know the identity of the missing motorist. Myers has the new evidence for which he has been searching. He petitions the Court for a new trial. Judge Sosebee schedules the hearing to convene at the Butts County Courthouse in Jackson on Friday March 21, 1975. The City of Jackson is the county seat of Butts County, one of the four counties in the Flint Judicial Circuit. The Judge is scheduled to be in Butts County that week and agrees to hear arguments while there. Also present at the hearing will be District Attorney Ed McGarity and Sheriff Glass.

Mr. Myers' argument centers around the violation of the "Brady Rule." A 1963 decision by the U.S. Supreme Court requires prosecutors to disclose materially "exculpatory evidence" in its possession to the defense. "Exculpatory evidence" is defined as evidence in a criminal trial that is considered to be beneficial to the defendant and could bring into question the defendant's guilt. These include any deals the prosecutor might have made with potential witnesses whereby agreeing not to prosecute or granting leniency in exchange for their testimonies. It establishes specific rules of conduct by law enforcement and those who prosecute the accused.

The defendant in this case is a twenty-five-year-old Maryland man, John Leo Brady. He and an accomplice were accused of murdering a fifty-three-year-old man while attempting to steal his car. Each was tried separately; each was convicted and each received the death sentence. Brady's accomplice in the crime provided a written statement to law enforcement admitting that he alone had committed the murder. The prosecution withheld the written confession from Brady's defense attorney. The justices determined that had the jury known of the confession, Brady would probably not have gotten the death sentence. Brady was subsequently granted a new trial, acquitted and would lead a productive life. The high court's decision became known as the "Brady Rule" or the "Brady Law."

***

The hearing begins with Mr. Myers contending that if the testimony of Andrew Eberhardt had been presented it could have altered the jury's decision.

Myers: "If Your Honor pleases, the identity of the passing motorist who alerted the police and returned to the scene was never disclosed to me. This lack of knowledge is particularly detrimental to Banks' defense. The defense had advertised in the local newspaper seeking the identity of motorist, to no avail. What is most troubling is the fact that Mr. Eberhardt had communicated with the Henry County Sheriff's Department several times and offered to testify. Sheriff Glass stated under oath that he had not intentionally withheld any information at Jerry Banks' trial."

Judge Sosebee: "Sheriff, what is your response to Myers' allegation?"

Sheriff Glass: "That November 7th night was blur to me. I was not prepared for what I saw off Rock Quarry Road that evening. I was sort of in shock after seeing those unfortunate victims lying in the woods. I was in a hurry because I was already late to an important speaking appointment. At the stress of the moment, he could have talked to me that night, but I don't recall. In fact, I don't know who I talked with, much less, what I might have discussed that evening."

Myers: "I would like to enter into evidence an affidavit filed with the Henry County Clerk in Superior Court, whereby Andrew Eberhardt explains his activities on the evening of November 7, 1974. Mr. Eberhardt is unable to be here in person, because of his work-related travel commitments. I believe it is the same information that he has already verbally relayed to you earlier."

Mr. Myers and Mr. McGarity argue for and against the defense motion for the new trial. Judge Sosebee takes the motion under advisement and adjourns the hearing. He promises to render his decision later.

Shortly thereafter, Judge Sosebee meets with the attorneys in his Court. "Gentlemen, I am going to deny the motion for a new trial. There are several court cases that are on point and are the reasons for my decision. It has been repeatedly held in the courts that newly discovered evidence in itself is not necessarily a good cause for a new trial. Knowing who reported the crime to the police, would not have necessarily changed the outcome of the trial. Mr. Eberhardt's testimony did establish that Banks' purpose for being in the woods that day was to hunt. Eberhardt, unfortunately, cannot provide an eyewitness account as to what actually occurred off Rock Quarry Road that afternoon before he was flagged down by Banks."

***

After the hearing, Myers drives to McDonough to inform Jerry Banks that Judge Sosebee declined to grant a new trial. "I disagree with his ruling," he says. "It's hard to imagine that you, while hunting had a preconceived notion of finding someone to rob and then shoot them. Don't give up hope, Jerry. I am going to appeal the Judge's ruling. We will have another chance when our case is reviewed by the Georgia Supreme Court. Hang on, I will get you out of this."

***

It is rare that a local jurist gets national attention. I admit I was proud when the word reached my office that our Superior Court Judge Sosebee would be making a national television appearance. Judge Sosebee's tough stance on crime has made him a celebrity. In Forsyth, thirteen young Monroe County citizens were arrested for selling drugs. Some of the accused are from prominent families. The perception in small communities is that social standing and money guarantee a more favorable treatment by local judges. The same holds true for young offenders with parents, who are well-connected politically in the community. They always seem to get some type of probation or receive lighter sentences.

This was not the case as the convicted are collectively sentenced to sixty-seven years of straight time in prison. When news of the heavy sentences reaches Walter Cronkite's news desk at

CBS, he arranges an interview with Judge Sosebee on his national telecast. Mr. Cronkite, one of the most respected newsmen of his era, has a widespread listening audience.

Mr. Cronkite says, "Judge Sosebee, give our viewers an explanation of why you sentenced one of the city councilman's son and his friends."

"Mr. Cronkite, thank you for having me on your show. I watch it all the time," Judge Sosebee replies.

Mr. Cronkite nods, "Thank you. It's pleasure to have you on."

Judge Sosebee continues, "These convictions and sentences came as a result of drug selling. These were not little possession cases. These young men were responsible for ruining lives of many local individuals. I am talking about people who may be my neighbors, friends or their children attending our schools. The use of drugs leads to addiction. I do not enjoy sentencing anyone to prison, but I am hearing too many cases where the commission of the crime is influenced by drug use. Many are stealing to feed their drug habits."

As a result of his television appearance, Judge Sosebee's office is inundated with calls from all over the United States. Viewers from as far away as Hawaii and Canada all praise him for his hardline stance on drug pushers. The consensus is that they wish other judges would do the same. Many state that they are beginning to see the drug epidemic spread into their communities. "It is time to get tough," expressed a viewer in a letter to the network.

CHAPTER 29 | Appeal to the
Georgia Supreme Court

As promised, Mr. Myers appeals Judge Sosebee's denial to the Georgia Supreme Court. In his brief to the Court, he states that the concealment of the motorist was prejudicial to Banks' defense. On September 12, 1975, the majority of the justices disagree with Judge Sosebee's opinion. Consequently, the Georgia high court rules that Jerry Banks should be entitled to a new trial. The justices contend that the State of Georgia's evidence in the case is based exclusively on circumstantial evidence and the defense should have been informed of the identity of the witness who reported the crime.

Justice Jordan's seven-page decision highlights one major issue: "We think it was important to the theory of the defendant's case that the testimony of the passing motorist should have been made available to the jury. He was the person who could corroborate the appellant's statement to the police. The very heart of the appellant defense was based on the truthfulness and veracity of statements to the police during the investigation. The verification of certain facts made by the unidentified motorist could have bolstered the veracity of the appellant's statement. Without the testimony of the passing motorist, the jury might have well concluded that this mystery caller was a part of the deceptive scheme of the defendant to deceive and mislead the investigating officers.

Another trial would establish that the Sheriff and the investigative officers knew the identity of the mystery caller."

The ruling is a slap on the hand to the Sheriff and prosecutors whom the justices perceive to have intentionally withheld the information. The justices concur unanimously that based on the discovery of the identity of the passing motorist, there is sufficient grounds for a new trial. The ruling also overturns Jerry Banks' death sentence.

Myers and the Banks' family are elated with the ruling. The news could not have come any sooner for Jerry. He tells his attorney, "I was about to throw my Bible into the garbage. Up to now all my prayers have not been listened to. Finally, a new jury will learn the truth."

CHAPTER **30** | Second Jury Trial
Prosecution:
November 17, 1975

I admit that I had only a casual interest in the outcome of Banks'
first trial and had not formed an opinion as to his guilt or inno-
cence. Now that I had the opportunity to read the 300-page tran-
script of the first trial, I have become intrigued in Jerry Banks'
case. I begin to speak with deputies and those in attendance at-
tempting to keep abreast of the second trial. I have developed an
idea of the strategies the opposing lawyers would use to convince
the jurors. At the conclusion of the trial, I will be able to get feed-
back from one of the jurors who is an officer at my bank. I will
then find out if my assumptions were correct.

Attorney Myers has a second chance by way of another trial. He has the benefit of knowing what evidence the prosecution
will present and what testimony the State witnesses will give. His
mission is simple. Find credible witnesses who can discredit the
State's allegations and prove that Jerry could not have been the
shooter. The prosecution only needs to discredit Jerry's assertions
that he is innocent and show that his shotgun was used to kill the
victims and that he pulled the trigger.

When the Georgia Supreme Court ruled Jerry Banks was entitled to a new trial, it is the "Brady Rule" that gives Jerry Banks
new life. Like Leo Brady, Jerry Banks was denied prosecution's
knowledge of certain facts that could have exonerated him. The

decision prompts District Attorney McGarity and newly appointed Assistant District Attorney Hal Craig to prepare for another
trial. Craig is a rising young McDonough attorney with Henry
County roots. The trial is scheduled for November 17, 1975.

Before the trial begins, Hal Craig, at the direction of Ed McGarity, offers Jerry Banks through his attorney, John Hudson Myers,
a reprieve from possible execution. The State of Georgia would
exchange the likely death sentence for life imprisonment. As a
condition, Jerry Banks would have to plead guilty to the murders.

Myers tells Jerry the district attorney is offering a plea deal. He
is willing to recommend a life sentence, if you will admit to the
murders of the band director and the student.

Banks responds, "I'm not lying! I didn't kill those people. I
just found the bodies! Before, I did shoot my cousin, but I didn't
mean to! It was self-defense. I felt bad about doing it and expected some type of punishment. With my time in jail, I paid for that
mistake. But this time I'm innocent and I'm not confessing to
nothin'. I did not do it! It's no deal!"

"I understand, Myers says. "I believe the new witness who
called the police will convince the jury that you are telling the
truth. You do not have to make a deal."

**

The selection of the jury follows the same process as in the
previous trial. District Attorney McGarity collectively swears in
the jury candidates. By now everyone who keeps up with the local news, either via television or newspaper, is familiar with the
name Jerry Banks. They know he was found guilty and has gotten
a second trial mainly due to what many consider as a technicality.
When Mr. McGarity asks all those, who had formed an opinion
regarding the guilt or the innocence of the prisoner, sixteen candidates raised their hands. Another four candidates are disqualified
because they are either related to the accused, oppose to the death
penalty and/or are victims of a crime. Driving home the point,
Mr. McGarity wants to eliminate any candidates who might have
formed a bias but are reluctant to admit it.

Mr. McGarity addresses the juror candidates: "Now, there's no doubt, probably, most of you have read some of the newspaper articles about this case. Would the fact that you have some knowledge of the case prevent you from forming a true and just verdict for the defendant?"

No one else raises his or her hand asking to be excused.

Henry County Clerk of the Superior Court, Sara Taylor, calls the first panel of the qualified jury candidates to the box. Mr. McGarity and Mr. Myers ask each candidate the usual questions? "Is your spouse employed. Do you have any children? How long have you lived in Henry County? Are you employed? Where, and what do you do?" When the attorneys complete their questioning, Mrs. Taylor repeats the process three more times. Forty-eight potential jurors are profiled. After each side reaches their quota of strikes, thirteen individuals remain, one being the alternate.

The jury includes two employees from Delta Airlines, along with employees from Southern Bell, Atlanta Dairies and the City of Atlanta. There is a banker, a fireman, and a CPA. There are two housewives, two regional company managers and a businessman. The all-White jury of eight men and four women are selected with the unenviable task of determining the fate of Jerry Banks. It has been a year since the discovery of the bodies of King and Hartsfield. In the meantime, Jerry Banks still sits in the Henry County Jail.

***

On November 17, 1975, the second trial begins for Jerry Banks with high expectations. Those who closely followed the first trial, however, consider the evidence against the defendant as overwhelming. On the other hand, those who are less familiar and listen to the street talk, are puzzled why a hunter would rob a couple for a few dollars, execute them and then hang around to tell the police.

District Attorney Ed McGarity calls the same witnesses to testify for the State of Georgia as had testified in the first trial. John Hudson Myers elects not to call Gracie Slaughter or Perry

Banks this time. He is concerned that this jury may question their veracity as had the previous jury at the first trial. Instead, he intends to call Sheriff Glass, Andrew Eberhardt and may allow Jerry Banks to testify on his own behalf.

Mr. McGarity calls Det. Charles Richard Barnes to the stand as the State's first witness. His testimony is unchanged as are the testimonies of the other detectives, who testified at the first trial. Jurors are amused by Barnes' additional information about Jerry Banks' hunting dog. The puppy is the only known witness that could account for Banks' activities on the day of the murders.

McGarity: "At the time you arrived at the scene, did you see the dog there?"

Det. Barnes: "Yes, sir."

McGarity: "What size dog was it?"

Det. Barnes: "It was a small dog."

McGarity: "A small puppy?"

Det. Barnes: "Yes."

McGarity: "It wasn't a deer-dog, was it?"

Det. Barnes: "No, sir."

***

An avid hunter would ask, "Who brings a dog along on a deer hunt. The white tail deer are too smart to let a noisy dog sneak up and allow someone to shoot them. A trained hunting dog can flush out a rabbit or a bird, but not a puppy. Maybe that is why he never saw any deer." Even if you discount the presence of a so-called hunting dog, Jerry was dressed appropriately to justify his claim that he was hunting. He wore typical hunting clothes, an army field jacket, blue jeans, army combat boots, and some sort of knit cap.

Mr. Myers cross-examines Det. Barnes, "Det. Barnes, did you check Jerry Banks' shotgun to see if it had been fired? As a matter of fact, you didn't do anything with regard to this weapon, at all?"

Det. Barnes: "No, Sir."

Myers: "Did you look inside to see if there were any spent rounds in the chamber?"

Det. Barnes: "No."

Myers: "Do you know what happened to Jerry Banks after he had taken you to the bodies?"

Det. Barnes: "Yes, sir. Later Det. Payne took him down to the office for the purpose of getting a statement from him."

Myers: "What time was that?"

Det. Barnes: "Around midnight."

Myers: "Did you place him under arrest?"

Det. Barnes: "No, sir."

Myers: "When you picked him up did you ask him to bring his shotgun?"

Det. Barnes: "No, sir."

Myers: "Have you been able to determine how Mr. King and Miss Hartsfield got to that location?"

Det. Barnes: "They apparently got there by automobile. There were fresh tire tracks at the scene. The broken piece of the taillight cover that was found near blood stains came from King's car."

Myers: "Did the tire tracks match those tires that were on King's vehicle when you found it?"

Det. Barnes: "Yes, sir."

***

Mr. Myers has not been able to determine who took Jerry home after detaining him for five hours at the detective trailer. The trailer is divided up into three rooms. There are offices on each end and long open room in the middle. Detectives testified that Jerry was seen sitting in the front room by himself.

From the evidence presented at the first trail, the shooter forced the couple out of their car which was parked on the abandoned dirt road facing in northerly direction. The shooter or shooters would have been standing some distance behind the Opel. Mr. King and Miss Hartsfield were standing directly behind and near King's car when they were shot. One of the pellets struck and broke the rear plastic light cover, either through a direct hit or by ricochet. Each was shot in the back while standing on the dirt road. Since neither appeared to have reacted in any way before the first shots were fired, detectives assume they did not expect to get shot. Perhaps the shooter was known to them. Whoever moved the Opel, backed up, turned around and re-entered Rock Quarry Road. It was in the afternoon. No one reported seeing a red vehicle leave the old roadway and head north on Rock Quarry Road.

***

Sgt. Tommy Floyd, recently promoted to Lieutenant, is duly sworn, and is examined by Defense Attorney John Hudson Myers. Lt. Floyd and Det. Robbins did most of the field investigation. In the first trial, little was revealed about the numerous persons they questioned.

Myers: "Mr. Floyd, what was your role as the investigating officer?"

Lt. Floyd: "Well, interviewing witnesses, prospective witnesses, following leads, what have you."

Myers: "Would you share with us some details of the investigation."

Lt. Floyd: "I talked with people Mr. King was associated and worked with, I talked with members of his band, The Mark Five."

Myers: "In your interviews with these people were you able to establish a connection, a relationship between Jerry Banks and Marvin King or Melanie Hartsfield?"

Lt. Floyd: "No, sir. I was not."

Myers: "When you talked to the members of victim's and Banks' families, did you ask them questions relating to his character or personal disposition?"

Craig: "Your Honor, I object to that."

***

Jerry is sitting in the McDonough courtroom hearing testimony. All he can do is sit there and listen. There are times that he would like to stand up and holler, "I object," especially when a witness says something about him that is not true. It's a phrase that he has heard numerous times from Mr. McGarity. Jerry knows that his attorney is not going to let him take the stand. At times he is restless and becomes bored. His mind wanders. When Judge Sosebee sends the jury to the jury room in order to discuss a pending objection, he begins to reminisce about Virginia and the children.

He remembers the day he convinced Virginia to attend Lion Country Safari, touted as the South's most exciting tourist attraction and only four miles from their home. He had received a family pass for the extra loads of crush-n-run he delivered while his company did a paving job at the park. It was the last weekend of August as the pair, with Jerry Jr. and Elbert, turned left into the entrance on Walt Stephens Road. It didn't matter that the air-conditioner in the car did not work, they were excited to be there. With the speaker-box on the dashboard giving instructions, they were told about the animals which were located at each stop: elephants, giraffes, hippos and monkeys. The old lion that was standing in the middle of the road, oblivious to the traffic brought the frightened Elbert to tears when he showed his yellow teeth and licked the window. All was forgotten when Jerry Jr. and Elbert were allowed to ride the merry-go-round sitting on zebras instead of horses. Virginia held the brave Elbert as the carousel slowly rotated while the zebra moved gently up and down. The day came to an end as they listened to the Dixieland Band while enjoying Coca-Colas and peanuts.

Jerry's pleasant daydream is interrupted when Judge Sosebee instructs the bailiff to fetch the jury. "A few months ago, I spent an enjoyable day with my family. Today, my life is in a mess," laments Jerry.

***

Judge Sosebee: "Based on what the record now shows, the Court will sustain the objection. If it becomes material at some point, the Court will permit the question, but I don't see the materiality of it at this point."

The prosecution alleges that robbery was Jerry Banks' motive for the murders. Dr. Howard gives his detailed explanation of his findings in the performance of the autopsies. Defense Attorney Myers takes the cross-examination in another direction.

Myers: "I believe you indicated in your report that you found a watch, is that correct?"

Dr. Howard: "I believe it is. Marvin King had a Gruen watch on his left wrist that was in operating condition and Melanie Harts-field had a wristwatch in running condition on her left wrist."

***

In my opinion the killer or killers had no interest in remov-ing any of the jewelry from the victims. Hitmen will sometimes remove a personal item to prove to their clients that the targets had been eliminated. In so doing they could expect final payment without delay. Jerry Banks had an interest in King's wallet but passed on his watch. Little did he know that the original Gru-en watches were manufactured from 1904 through 1917 and are among the most expensive watches in America. Some of their val-ue is in the limited number in existence. Gruen moved to the U.S. and became one of the first U.S. watch companies to offer basic movements produced in Switzerland and assembled in the United States. Unlike the Swiss-made Rolex, which is still being manu-factured, Gruen ended all manufacturing in 1958 and the watches have become collectors' items.

If robbery was the motive for the killings, the thief was not aware of the value of the watch. Certainly, Jerry Banks probably never heard of a Gruen watch. Although the American-produced Gruens are less expensive than the earlier version, it is an expen-sive watch for a band director.

***

Court recessed until 9:30 a.m. Tuesday morning, November 18, 1975.

The next day Mr. Myers cross-examined Mr. Ray who was employed by the Henry County Sheriff's department as a detective, "Who drove you to Rock Quarry Road at four o'clock in the morning?"

Det. Ray: "I drove and there were several people with me. We'd made arrangements for some portable generated lights to be mounted on a pick-up truck in order to give us light to search the area. We walked from the pavement's edge down the old roadbed to the scene and past the scene until it makes a kind of horseshoe-type turn back to pavement. There was the driver of the truck, operator of the lights and several other police officers involved in the search."

Myers: "From the evidence, did you conclude that the King vehicle was present at the time of the shooting?"

Det. Ray: "Yes, sir."

Myers: "Did you notice any other tracks, tire tracks there besides the one that was left by the King vehicle and by the truck you were operating?"

Det. Ray: "No, sir."

***

Phillip Stewart Howard was instrumental in the discovery, test-firing, safekeeping and delivery of the shell casings to the crime lab. Six different spent shells are presented as evidence by the prosecution. Capt. Howard is cross-examined by Defense Attorney Myers.

Myers: "Tell the Court what you found at the scene and be specific?"

Former Capt. Howard: "On November 8th, Det. Ray and I found two Winchester Western Super X 00 Buck Mark V shotgun casings, 12-gauge."

Myers: "What time was it found?"

Former Capt. Howard: "I'd say we got back to the scene around first light, I imagine anywhere from seven-thirty to nine o'clock. I didn't make note of the exact time when they were found. No."

Myers: "How long after you found the shell did you continue

to search."

Former Capt. Howard: "Until about noon."

Myers: "So you searched the crime scene from four a.m. until lunchtime and found nothing but two shells?"

Former Capt. Howard: "Yes, sir."

Judge Sosebee: "How closely was the area searched immediately around where you say these shells were found?"

Former Capt. Howard: "Your Honor, we searched it close, but in that area were pines, honeysuckles, pine needles, briars. We searched it as best we could and of course, we returned another time and nearly clear-cut it."

Myers: "So you had the weapon in your possession then on November 10th?" Holding up a plastic bag, he asks, "Can you identify these?"

Former Capt. Howard: "Yes, sir. These are three shotgun casings, 12-gauge; one Peters, one Remington and the third is also Remington, that I fired in the rear of the trailer marked with my handwriting and initials on the back. They were transported to the Georgia State Crime Lab for firing pin and pressure checks."

Myers: "Now, where were the two shells that you found on November 8th? Where were they on November 10th when you fired the Stevens you took from Banks?"

Former Capt. Howard: "On December 2nd, the three shells fired from Banks' gun, were carried by Det. Robbins to the crime lab. The other two shells were already at the crime lab."

Myers: "Were you present when Det. Hart found the shell casing?"

Former Capt. Howard: "Yes, I was searching in the general area."

Myers: "How far from the location of the first two discoveries did you find this third casing?"

Former Capt. Howard: "I'd say it was approximately maybe ten feet."

Myers: "Now, how many people were involved in that search on that day, the day of December 13, 1974, just approximately?"

Former Capt. Howard: "Nine, approximately."

Myers: "How many people were involved in the search on December 8th?"

Former Capt. Howard: "Five."

***

When John Hudson Myers completes his examination of Capt. Howard, Judge Sosebee calls for a short recess. At this point in the trial, the defense has attempted to create suspicion regarding the discovery of the spent shells. Capt. Howard found one of the spent shell cartridges and had sole custody of his and Det. Ray's shell before having them sent to the crime lab. Myers also plants a seed in the minds of the jurors about the curious circumstances surrounding the discovery of the third shell by Det. Hart. After the discovery of the first two shells, there were two organized searches conducted by fourteen law enforcement personnel to find the remaining two spent shells. Finally, the third shell casing was located approximately ten feet from where Capt. Howard found the first casing.

***

Det. Paul L. Robbins is called to the witness stand and is cross-examined by Mr. Myers.

Myers: "Det. Robbins, you testified that the shell casings you took to crime lab are sitting on the evidence table. How do you know they are the same spent shells?"

Det. Robbins: "At one time they had a piece of tape around them, and it was marked but it's not on there now. But at first, they were marked 'Found at the Scene'. Those were the words."

Myers: "The identifying tape is gone. So, you cannot swear these spent shells here are the ones that were found at the scene?"

Det. Robbins: "But sir, they look the same."

Myers: "What else did you take to the crime lab?"

Det. Det. Robbins: "A pair of brown shoes, a pair of black patent leather boots, two pieces of paper towels, two plastic bags containing soil samples and a pair of sunglasses."

Myers: "Were there any fingerprints on those items?"

Det. Robbins: "I was told that there were no latent prints on the shell casings or any of the other items I carried to the lab."

Myers: "Were you present when Capt. Howard test-fired Banks' Stevens shotgun?"

Det. Robbins: "I was in the trailer and heard the shots."

Myers: "Could Capt. Howard have test-fired the shotgun on Friday the day after the homicides or what day was that?"

Det. Robbins: "It was late Sunday afternoon, November 10th, because I remember saying something to Capt. Howard about this is going to interrupt church services."

***

Forensic scientist Kelly Fite's testimony at the first trial was very damaging to the defense. He testified that all the spent shells that were sent to the crime lab had been fired from Banks' shotgun. He also testified that the victims were killed by a shotgun discharging 12-gauge Winchester Western cartridges.

Mr. Fite is questioned by Mr. Craig and by Mr. Myers.

Craig: "All right, what was the purpose of you examining Miss Hartsfield's red sweater?"

Fite: "Well, it was to get an idea or to determine the muzzle-to-target distance or the distance from the end of the shotgun to the clothing. Also, the examination of the hole would indicate to me the type of ammunition used to make this hole."

Craig: "And how did it do that?"

Fite: "Well, in Winchester Western type buckshot, they pack the buckshot in polyethylene granules, and this keeps the shot from banging against each other. As a result, the shots fire more accurately at the target. I noticed there are numerous particles of this polyethylene granules on the and around the entry hole in the back of the sweater. These are unique to Winchester Western."

Craig: "Mr. Fite, you have been mentioning the term, '00 buckshot.' "Now is 00 buckshot found in any other gauge other than 12-gauge?"

Fite: "No, sir, it's only found in 12-gauge. Number 1 buckshot comes in 16-gauge and Number 3 buckshot comes in 20-gauge."

Myers: "When did you fire the weapon that Det. Barnes brought you?"

Fite: "December 6th."

Myers: "You handled several. Is there any way that these shells could have been confused during your test?"

Fite: "No, sir. Mr. Barnes was present. It was fired and the cartridge cases were marked at that time."

Myers: "Mr. Fite, how many shotgun shells of this type do you look at, say, in a two-month period?"

Fite: "Probably ten different cases."

Myers: "Is there any way, medically or scientifically, that one could determine the age of a shotgun shell casting?"

Fite: "If you have modern cartridges and you store them, where they are not subjected to weather, there would be no way to tell, say to a year's difference in ages of them. But if they were subjected to weather and oxidation, there would be oxidation on the brass."

Judge Sosebee: "Mr. Fite, what about the spent cartridges that you have seen. Could you make a determination as to whether they had been out in the weather and if so, approximately how long?"

Fite: "Well, on November 9th, they showed no signs of oxidation, in fact, they were relatively shiny. There was no dust or dirt inside the cartridges cases to indicate they had been out, say in rain or wind or anything like this."

Judge Sosebee: "Did you have an occasion to examine the third cartridge at a later date that allegedly was found at or near the scene of the homicides in question?"

Fite: "Well, it appeared to have more oxidation on it than the other two cartridge casings. Of course, it was the same brand. It did appear to have more weathering on it than the two brought to me on November 9th."

Myers: "Is there any way, medically or scientifically, in your opinion as an expert, that you can tell whether the pellets found in a wound could be traced to any particular shotgun, if the person was shot with a shotgun?"

Fite: "No, sir, there's not."

Myers: "Is there any way, medically or scientifically, as an expert, to determine whether the Stevens shotgun discharged pellets that killed anyone or anything?"

Fite: "No, sir, there's no way."

Myers: "As to the polyethylene granules, were these granules found around any of the other wounds of Mr. King or Ms. Hartsfield?"

Fite: "Well, I don't recall. I am only certain about the sweater."

Craig: "The State rests."

CHAPTER 31 | Second Jury Trial
Defense

Up till now Jerry has remained in the bull pen most of the time waiting on the conclusion of his second trial. To an inmate jail time is a depressing time filled with prolonged boredom. Each day ends like it begins with little of consequence occurring in between. Highlights of the day are the visits from family and friends, a conference with the defense attorney or incoming mail. Time is spent reading, sleeping, playing cards, listening to music, watching television or staring at the walls. Jerry Banks gets little mail and when he does receive a personal letter, he seldom replies. Present circumstances have dampened his spirits and the desire to communicate with those outside the walls has subsided.

He does not mind sharing the cell with other inmates. Many are short termers who were convicted of minor crimes and are in for brief stays. Others, who are convicted of more serious crimes, are in for longer stretches. Jerry Banks does however commiserate with other inmates who are in the same predicament as he and share his interests. While in jail Jerry develops a friendship with the middle-aged, white inmate. They share two commonalities. Both are sentenced for murder, and both love major league sports.

Sporting events are important to Jerry Banks and his inmate friend. Whether it's Falcon football, Hawks basketball or Braves baseball, the competitiveness of the games provide them needed excitement and uplift their spirits. Avid baseball fans, they cannot wait for the first pitch of each game. Rainouts result in a dull evening for the two.

They looked forward to watching or listening to the Atlanta Braves during the past baseball season. While a game was in progress, they screamed at the umpires when a call went against the Braves. They yelled at players who struck out with Atlanta runners in scoring position or made errors that resulted in a run for the opposing team.

Before he was locked up, Jerry Banks watched most of the games. 1974 was a magical year for the Braves. He saw Hank Aaron break Babe Ruth's home run record. Just as Jerry Banks' life changed after his arrest, so did the lineup for the Atlanta Braves in 1975. Hank Aaron, who had contemplated retirement, opted to play two more years in Milwaukee, the Braves' former home. Without Aaron the 1975 season ended mercifully in October. It was a disappointing year as the Braves won only 64 games. Jerry Banks hopes his trial has a better outcome than did the Atlanta Braves' season.

***

There are no "smoke and mirrors" foreseen in John Hudson Myers' defense strategy. In fact, the defense has subpoenaed only two witnesses. The Justices of the Georgia Supreme Court granted Jerry Banks a new trial based primarily on evidence that was withheld from the defense. John Hudson Myers will save the "unidentified motorist" as his last witness. First, he will examine Sheriff Glass. Myers is determined to prove Sheriff Glass had intentionally withheld the name of a key witness, an unusual and risky maneuver. Under normal circumstances Sheriff Glass would be classified as a "hostile witness," antagonistic toward the defendant. In his capacity as Sheriff, he was responsible for locking up Jerry Banks, and now he is called on to defend him. I am perplexed by Mr. Myers' defense strategy. I ask myself, "Why doesn't he instead, present other witnesses or experts to testify on Banks' behalf?"

***

Mr. Myers swears in Sheriff Glass, and he takes the stand. "How long were you there that evening?" Myers asks.

Sheriff Glass: "About twenty minutes."

Myers: "Do you recall seeing a Henry County citizen by the name of Andrew Lake Eberhardt on November 7, 1974, the day of the murders, at approximately 6:30 p.m. on Old Rock Quarry Road?"

Sheriff Glass: "I do not remember seeing Mr. Eberhardt."

Myers: "Have you had the opportunity since November 7, 1974, to meet and talk to a Henry County citizen by the name of Andrew Eberhardt?"

Sheriff Glass nodding his head: "I have. He came into my office the day after our phone conversation."

Myers: "Did you have occasion to take a statement in the office on the morning of February 4, 1975?"

Sheriff Glass: "I had one of my detectives take the statement."

Myers: "Do you recall on March 21, 1975, during a hearing for a second trial, a question that was posed on direct examination to you by Mr. Ed McGarity? 'Have you withheld any evidence that would be beneficial to the defendant in the trial of this case?' Do you recall that question?"

Sheriff Glass: "Yes, sir, I recall it."

Myers: "Do you recall your answer?"

Sheriff Glass: "To the best of my knowledge, my answer was that I had withheld no information in regard to this case."

Myers stares at Sheriff Glass for moment: "That's all, Your Honor."

Andrew Lake Eberhardt, a sales representative for a construction equipment company, is called to the stand by defense attorney Myers. Mr. Eberhardt was a customer at my bank. I had the opportunity to refinance his antebellum-styled home on Jodeco Road. I learned of his encounter with Jerry Banks during one of his visits to the bank.

Myers: "Mr. Eberhardt, now while driving down the road did you have the occasion to be stopped or flagged down by anyone that afternoon or evening?"

Eberhardt: "Yes, I did."

Myers: "Would you tell us what you did after seeing this person attempting to flag you down?"

Eberhardt: "Well, I almost didn't stop and then I figured that it might have been a hunting accident, so I stopped to see if I could see what the problem was."

Myers: "Well, why did you think that there might be a hunting accident?"

Eberhardt: "Well, the gentleman had on hunting gear and a gun with him. He appeared to be a hunter. I knew people hunted in this area. The puppy was with him scampering around in the road."

Myers: "What did he say to you?"

Eberhardt: "He said that he had found two people who had been shot in the woods. I asked him if they were dead and he said, yes, they were. Then, he asked if I would call the police department and I told him, yes."

Myers: "What did you do after you hung up the telephone?"

Eberhardt: "I decided that it had been a good while since I had first stopped on the roadside and that he might think that I had not called anyone. He indicated when he first stopped me that he had stopped a previous car and that the driver said that he didn't want to get involved."

Myers: "He did not want to get involved?"

Eberhardt: "That was my understanding, yes. I forgot about that and then I figured that he might think I didn't want to get involved either. So, it was getting toward dark and cool that evening and I got my hat and my coat and my son, Lake Eberhardt, to go with me. We went back towards Hudson Bridge Road and back down the Rock Quarry Road."

Myers: "When you arrived at the place where this man stopped you, was he still there and was he alone?"

Eberhardt: "He and his little dog that was with him were still there."

Myers: "Did you have the occasion on November 7, 1974, to talk to Jimmy Glass?"

Eberhardt: "When he came up and went into the woods, I

didn't talk to him at first. While they were still doing things out there whatever they were doing, he came out of the woods, started up the street to leave. He mentioned he was going somewhere to a speaking engagement and that was the reason he was leaving."

Myers: "During the course of that evening, did you have occasion to tell any officer there, who you were and why you were there?"

Eberhardt: "I told the first two officers that came up why I was there. I don't recall whether we went into any detail as to who I was specifically. I told them that I was the one that had called the police and that was the reason I was waiting there on the side of the road."

Myers: "Did you ever have the occasion, opportunity to speak with Sheriff Glass?"

Eberhardt: "When I arrived back from Tennessee that week, my wife, Jo, showed me the Atlanta paper saying that Mr. Banks had been convicted and sentenced to death. Someone testified that they still didn't know who I was. That upset me and I worried about it all weekend. I went on the following Monday morning with my son down to Jackson, Georgia to see Judge Sosebee. I didn't know what else to do."

Mr. Craig cross-examines Mr. Eberhardt: "You do not recall the officer's name that you talked to at the sheriff's office?"

Eberhardt: "He didn't volunteer it and I didn't ask him."

Craig: "Now, I believe you said you had some conversation sometime during that night with Sheriff Glass at the scene, is that right?"

Eberhardt: "I said I'm the fellow that called, and I'm Andy Eberhardt and I'm married to your in-law, Jo Austin, something to that general effect. He shook hands with me and said something about it was a terrible thing. I don't remember exactly what he said, and then he indicated that he was late to a speaking engagement somewhere. He was in a hurry."

Craig: "Mr. Eberhardt, I believe you said you became upset with the fact that it seemed to be that no one in the sheriff's office knew who you were. Is that right?"

Eberhardt: "Well, I don't know whether upset is the word, I

was concerned about it."

Craig: "The main thing that you were concerned about is that your particular name had not come out. Your name was not in the newspaper, is that right?"

Eberhardt: "I don't care that my name wasn't in papers. It was indicated in the paper that the police did not know who I was. I had no reason for them not to know."

Craig: "I believe that's all."

Myers: "The defense rests."

***

The second trial ends without any melodrama. By now every living soul in Henry County is familiar with Jerry Banks and the murders. All jurors had given Banks the benefit of doubt about his guilt and had previously sworn to the Court not to have any preconceived bias. But as the trial reaches the end of the second day, the defense has presented little new evidence beneficial to Banks.

Banks' credibility is questioned early in the trial when testimony divulges that he had initially lied to Lt. Floyd about the wallet and then fabricated a story about loaning his shotgun to the probable killer. The State has proven that the shell casings found near the murder scene came from Banks' shotgun. There is just too much evidence that points toward a guilty verdict.

A legal expert questioned by a reporter is critical of John Hudson Myers' failure to challenge the possible illegal seizure of Jerry Banks' shotgun. He is of the opinion that Det. Barnes did not have proper search warrant. That being the case, the defense should have questioned the admissibility of the shotgun and the spent shells as evidence. Myers should also have asked why the shell casings were not held under dual control before being sent to the crime lab. No doubt, without the admissibility of the shotgun and shell casings, the defense would have the upper hand.

John Hudson Myers again has second thoughts about allowing Jerry Banks to testify. Myers is aware that the State presented the same evidence that had gotten Banks convicted at the first trial. He is confident, however, that he has created enough doubt in the minds of the jury, that Banks could not have been the shooter. Other than three spent cartridges that were supposedly fired from Banks' shotgun, the State's case against Banks is totally circumstantial.

Judge Sosebee reads the charge to the jury which is identical to the one he read at the first trial. He then sends them to the jury room around 5:30 p.m. to deliberate. The trial has taken two days. To no one's surprise, the jury reaches a guilty verdict in just two hours. It takes them another thirty minutes to recommend the death sentence, again, for the double murders.

***

I never know what goes through a juror's mind at the moment he or she casts the final vote on the sentence of life in prison or the electric chair. It takes only one dissenting vote to spare a young life. I was curious what comments the jurors who had served on the Jerry Banks trial volunteered to The Weekly Advertiser. *It is obvious from the quick verdict that they had no doubts about Jerry Banks' guilt.*

A reporter asks, "Any comment on why Banks reported the murders and remained at the scene?"

"Banks had time to hide the car off Tye Street near his home and return to the scene, so as not to look guilty," juror speaks without hesitation.

The reporter approaches a second juror: "What was your impression of Banks?"

"I figured Banks to be a 'cool cat.' He sat there the whole time and showed no emotion, even when they showed all those gruesome pictures," expresses the juror.

The reporter asks a third juror, a male: "What about the condition of the shotgun and the time it took for someone to fire it?"

"I personally examined the weapon. I think that a skilled hunter would have no problem in firing the gun. Also, to me, Fite's ballistics testimony was conclusive," says the juror.

The reporter continues getting responses to his interviews. "What clinched it for me, was the fact that Banks had already served time for murder," one juror says.

Another, a soft-spoken woman, adds, "I am concerned as to what is going to happen to the boy. But I owe it to the families to punish the one that had taken their loved ones away. I am glad that it was over."

***

Jerry Banks receives more bad news when the U.S. Supreme Court reaffirms the constitutionality of the death sentence if certain statutory changes are followed. In Georgia, the death penalty for murder is now allowable when at least one aggravating circumstance exists. The most common is when the offender has a prior capital conviction, is in the process of committing another crime, is in possession of a dangerous weapon or is committed for monetary gain. The death penalty also applies if the victim was a policeman, judicial officer or if the victim was tortured. Jerry Banks has a prior capital conviction and was in possession of a shotgun when he allegedly robbed the victims. He remains in his Henry County Jail cell, until his automatic appeal to the Georgia Supreme Court is heard. No one can foresee any reason for the justices to overturn the sentence a second time.

Jerry Banks' execution date will be rescheduled following the outcome of his automatic appeal.

CHAPTER 32 | Old Jail
in the Spotlight

Since his arrest in December 1974, Jerry Banks has been in the Henry County Jail. The facility had changed little since his departure in 1972. Since he was not eligible to post bond, he remained in the bull pen, until his appeals are heard. Now that he has been found guilty, his next stop is the Georgia State Prison, home of the State of Georgia's death chamber.

Jerry Banks knows something is up when inmates are ordered to tidy up the bull pen and the other cells. Jailers and trustees are busy sweeping and mopping hallways and bathrooms. The kitchen staff is straightening out the cluttered cabinets and hanging the pots and pans neatly on the proper hooks. Lt. Wendell Glass, the Sheriff's cousin, is responsible for the jail. He, obviously, is trying to impress someone.

A woman is stopped by a Georgia State Patrolman for going seventy-seven miles-per-hour in a fifty-five miles-per-hour zone and is charged with speeding. She is furious at being stopped. After giving the trooper a piece of her mind and threatening not to pay the fine, she is warned. After she tears up the ticket into little pieces and throws them at the trooper, she is arrested. Her temper and bad behavior land her in jail.

Upon release she learns that a newspaper office, *The Weekly Advertiser*, is nearby. She walks over and finds a reporter sitting

Rendering of Henry County Jail inspired
by inmate Clarence Holloman
aka "Washpot"

at her desk. She recounts her ordeal from the night before and voices her complaints. Most of her tirades include the exaggerations of what did occur. However, the lack of privacy for female prisoners gets the attention of the female reporter.

As a result, the newspaper's editor sends Betty Drake, its lead reporter, to investigate the matter. Betty Drake contacts Sheriff Glass and inquires about the incident. He invites her to come and personally inspect the jail.

Torrential rains greet Mrs. Drake as she enters the jail that afternoon. Lt. Glass is there to greet her and offers to escort her throughout the jail. The inmates are quiet, so the only noticeable sound is the rain hitting the three pots strategically placed underneath the roof leaks. The jail is clean, but the gray and off-white painted walls are drab, making the jail's interior appearance depressing. Bull pen and individual cells are furnished with beds, foam-rubber mattresses, blankets, and commodes. A separate shower facility is at the end of the hall.

Seven prisoners are in the bull pen, either playing checkers or watching television. Several inmates have books or magazines lying on their cots. Mrs. Drake imagines they were placed there to impress her. A delicious aroma emits from the kitchen, where "Miss Bertha" is standing over a simmering pot of butter beans. Flour, eggs, butter, and the appropriate utensils and pans are laid out for the preparation of a batch of biscuits. Helpers ("run-arounds" as the jailers call them) are busily assembling the silverware, cups, napkins, and the necessities for the evening meal.

After Lt. Glass answers all of Mrs. Drake's questions, he accompanies her to the front door. She promises him that her report will be in next Thursday's edition of the newspaper. Leaving the jail, she is thankful that her editor had not asked her to spend the night. The hour she spent inside was long enough for an innocent woman.

Based on Mrs. Drake's findings, the editor of the paper later publishes an editorial expressing the importance of a new jail facility and encourages the government officials to make its construction a priority. The editorial called the jail more of a historic landmark than an adequate prison facility. It is often too crowded and offers little privacy for inmates. Client-attorney meetings must be conducted in an empty office or an unoccupied cell. When these are in use, a conversation is usually handled by speaking in a low voice through the jail bars. There is no formal visiting room. The paper gives the facility an unofficial tagline; the "Old Jail."

***

At the conclusion of the Civil War, the U.S. Supreme Court ruled those prisoners in U.S. jails have no civil rights. A prisoner was considered a "slave of the state." For the next one hundred years, treatment of prisoners was at the discretion of those overseeing the prisons. The prisoner was at the mercy of the guard. When and what he ate, when he bathed and when he was allowed out of his cell varied from prison to prison, guard to guard. Medical attention, new sheets, clean prison clothes and visiting privileges often required a special favor or a small token. Once a prisoner went behind the walls little was heard from him. A prisoner made the news only when his or her escape attempt was successful.

The Justices of the U.S. Supreme Court became concerned with the poor facilities and harsh treatment existing at some of the State Penal systems. The Supreme Court of the U.S. decided in 1963, that state inmates should have the right to petition the Court and challenge both the legality of their sentencing and the conditions of their imprisonment. The decision, along with the civil rights movement targeting prison reform, opened the floodgate for petitions. Prisoners began to air their grievances about the conditions of their jails. Lawsuit after lawsuit is filed in the 1960s and 1970s. This reversal of the old law is welcomed by those on the "inside" but could not have come at a worse time for local government officials. County budgets are already strained, and jails are overcrowded. In most areas, crime is on the increase and public sentiment insists that judges hand down tougher punishment to convicted felons. As the "war on crime" intensifies, judges lengthen prison sentences to appease public outcry.

***

Not by his choosing, Jerry Banks does have a place to stay with three meals a day, paid for by the good citizens of Henry County. On the outside, however, many are having a difficult time. The jail is overcrowded with those awaiting trials for theft, check fraud, selling stolen goods or other unlawful acts. Henry County is amid an economic recession and experiences increases in the numbers of unemployed, bankrupt and dispossessed. Desperate persons resort to crime as a cure for their financial difficulties. Many of these unfortunate souls get caught and are sent to jail. The antiquated "Old Jail" is no longer adequate to handle the deluge of prisoners.

Up to now, Henry County government officials and the "Old Jail" have escaped the negative publicity experienced by other jurisdictions. Their good fortune can be attributed to the Chief Jailer, Wendell Glass and the guards who have a reputation of treating the inmates in a fair and humane way. With Bertha preparing the meals for the sheriff's department staff, jailers and the inmates, no one could complain about the meals.

That changes in September 1975. The Henry County Jail in McDonough is repeatedly thrust into the news. There are two jailbreaks, a pending suit by prisoners, a petition by the ACLU and the continuous pressure by the Grand Jury to replace the outdated jail.

Jerry is awakened Friday morning, September 19th, by the commotion at the jail. Lt. Wendell Glass is escorting Mike Offut from the shower, located immediately across a narrow hall from the bull pen on the western side of the jail. As he unlocks the gate to admit Offut, his cellmate Harold Rodgers bolts through the opening. Lt. Glass immediately pursues after Rodgers. Offut takes advantage of the unlocked gate and follows Rodgers. To the surprise of Ofc. Betty Peel, who is on duty, the pair run through a hallway connecting the cell area to the radio room. Lt. Glass catches Offut with minimal effort, but the twenty-one-year-old Rodgers is too quick for the slow-footed Glass. Rodgers is able to locate and press the button that controls the front door. Ofc. Maggie Cheek, who is attending to a female detainee at the time, is frantically yelling for Rodgers to stop. Ms. Cheek later tells Sheriff Glass, "I am so sorry. I could not catch up with the prisoner. I tried. It happened so fast, it's hard to remember all the details. Outside it was dark and foggy. Ofc. Peel joined me in the search in the nearby woods. We looked in the windows of the boarded-up abandoned house and walked around the little church next door. He just vanished."

Lt. Glass immediately issued an alert to all patrolmen on duty. The local search in the darkness is futile. But Saturday morning at the intersection of Jodeco Road and Interstate 75, a suspicious man is spotted by an officer as he stands beside the road. Rodger's escape was a spur-of-the-moment decision. He did not have time to dress. Wearing no shirt, no shoes, just blue jeans, Rodgers is tired, cold and hungry.

Fugitive Rodgers, approached by the officers, yells, "You got me."

He is returned to the Henry County Jail, where Lt. Glass is anxiously waiting for him.

Lt. Glass says, "Glad to have you back. You and Offut can add the escape attempt to the auto theft and forgery charges you already have."

Rodgers had managed to elude the police for twenty-four hours. He was able to travel eight miles during the night while barefoot. Quite an effort for a desperate man who was obviously not happy with the accommodations at the jail. Ten days earlier, inmates Thomas Hunter from Jonesboro and Willie Frank Mathis from Griffin cut their way out of their cell with a concealed hacksaw at 2 a.m. They managed to escape through the front door. They had more luck, as they are still at large.

Apparently, it does not take a "Houdini" to break out of the "Old Jail." Another jail escape by Mathew McLeroy's raises the number of breakouts to five in the last six months. The frequency and ease of the escapes bring into question the security of the prison. McLeroy overpowered guard Chester Collins Sunday morning as he let inmate trustees out of their cells. Collins was more surprised than hurt. McLeroy broke a window and fled through the main office.

McLeroy alias, Larry Martin, and his accomplice, Larry Brown, were awaiting extradition to Tallahassee, Florida to answer for numerous burglaries. When they were stopped on Hudson Bridge Road driving a 1975 Oldsmobile, the officer found stolen credit cards and illegal drugs in their possession. Despite roadblocks and a local manhunt, McLeroy vanishes. Henry County law enforcement never see him again.

Lt. Glass has a difficult time explaining the escape to the Tallahassee Police Chief. "You mean he broke a window and ran out the front door? What kind of jail are you running up there? He is considered a habitual offender and is one of our 'most wanted' criminals."

Jerry Banks thinks to himself, "It seems everyone is getting out of here but me."

***

Traffic in the jail has never been busier as numerous well-dressed individuals and groups walk through, inspecting the facility. Today, it is a collection of men and women with Grand Jury badges on their lapels, curiously looking around and talking amongst themselves. The Henry County Attorney and Board of Commissioners stopped by a few days ago. Last week, there were a bunch of lawyers who spoke to all the inmates and wrote down their complaints. Various rumors are spreading among the inmates as to what is going on. The curiosity is getting the best of Jerry Banks. He is able to get Lt. Glass' attention.

Jerry Banks says, "Mr. Glass, sir. How come so many people are coming in and looking at the jail. The inmates want to know if there is something wrong with the place. Especially, after all those men were able to escape."

Lt. Glass answers, "Mr. Banks, what we need is a new jail. I know you didn't sign the petition filed by the American Civil Liberties Union (ALCU). Representatives from the ACLU met with Henry County officials and went over the numerous modifications needed to bring the jail up to standard. One of which is the addition of the visitors' room."

Banks remarks, "Yea, I didn't want you and the guards to get mad at me. I like the idea of a nice place to meet with Virginia and the young'uns when they come to visit. My lawyer tells me that I'm going to be here until all of my appeals are heard."

***

Judge James C. Hill, who reviews the complaints in the ACLU petition, is pleased with the board's recent plans to upgrade the old facility, but that does not prevent him from ruling in July 1976 that the present jail will probably never meet current standards. Consequently, it cannot be used to house prisoners. The commissioners are given ten days to respond to the order. Thankfully, Judge Hill relents and gives Henry County officials until February 1, 1978, to rectify the problems at the existing jail or complete the construction of a new detention facility.

Government officials for years had set aside the replacement of the "Old Jail." Instead, they chose to use taxpayer money for other necessary projects. The newspapers began to criticize the commissioners for ignoring the need for the new jail. Grand Juries investigated the problem on numerous occasions and each time recommended that the commissioners should address the situation. The public sentiment, however, did not favor spending money on a new jail, while their own and the County's finances were under stress. Henry County struggled just to meet its operational budget and had no available funds to invest in a jail.

The Grand Jury viewed the problem as a humanitarian issue and urged all the churches and civic organizations to send delegations to inspect the jail and report back to their members its inadequacies. No separate facilities exist for juveniles or for women. Adolescents must be housed with older prisoners, when the few single cells are occupied, as was the case most of the time. Crowded conditions at the Jackson State Prison often left prisoners backed up at the Henry County Jail adding to its already crowded conditions.

The newly elected Henry County Board of Commissioners reasons the issuance of bonds as the logical means to finance the construction. Voters, however, consider the bonds a tax burden and soundly defeat referendums, including the construction of a new $900,000, sixty-five bed detention center which would more than triple the capacity of the present facility.

After the meeting, Chairman Findley is quoted in the newspaper as saying, "The jail is not just a problem for the commissioners alone. It is a problem of the people in Henry County. A jail is a necessary part of law enforcement. Without a place to lock up criminals, you cannot have effective law enforcement. The cost is greater to board prisoners in other jails than to keep them here. The taxpayer will be footing that bill either way."

Nevertheless, many of the voters interviewed by *The Weekly Advertiser* following the vote count, have various reasons for their negative votes.

- "I would have voted for it, if the amount is more reasonable."
- "I didn't reckon they have to spend all that money."
- "If folks don't like our jail, then they don't have to go there."
- "I just don't think we need a new jail."
- "Everybody at my church thinks a new jail is needed. But we don't need a million-dollar motel for inmates."
- "If they had asked for $500,000, I believe I would have voted for it."
- "The shape the economy is in, folks don't want to put that much money in."
- "We need better jail conditions, but not necessarily a better jail."

Since the three attempts to pass referendums to allow Henry County to issue new general obligation bonds had failed, the board is forced to seek other sources of funding. Fortunately, Henry County is awarded federal revenue sharing funds that can be diverted from other projects and used to build the jail.

CHAPTER 33 | The Power Struggle

The political climate in Henry County in the 1970s is influenced in part by a severe recession. People in general are unhappy. The stock market crashed in 1973 and does not recover until 1975. The value of my General Motors stock has dropped to less than $12 a share. I do not know how my friend L.P. McKibben, the Chevrolet dealer, is going to make it. In 1976 unemployment is hovering around nine percent. There is a shortage of gasoline as a result of the Arab nations' oil embargos. Short-term interest rates for loans are approaching sixteen percent, while fixed home mortgage interest rates are at twelve percent. During these turbulent economic times financial institutions stop lending, thus crippling many businesses. Many of my loan customers are past due with their loan payments. These poor souls are out of work and cannot pay their bills.

The Henry County government is in the same predicament as operating expenditures are exceeding county revenues forcing the governing body, the Henry County Commissioners, to raise property taxes and borrow money. Voters are angry and retaliate against incumbents, who they blame for the increases. These public officials are summarily voted out of office. There is tremendous pressure on the Board of Commissioners to freeze wages and control government spending. On the other hand, the county is growing, and citizens are demanding more and better services. The one area of most concern by the citizens is public safety, primarily police protection.

***

By Georgia law the sheriff is elected and operates his department independently from the county governing officials. The county commissioners, responsible for managing the affairs of the county, are also elected. Each official is accountable to the voters. The majority of the voters are the property owners who pay property taxes. How the property tax revenues are allocated is the responsibility of the Henry County Board of Commissioners through an annual operating budget. At a time when the commissioners are cutting operating costs, Sheriff Glass is spending more on public safety. The result is the police department, under Sheriff Glass, continually exceeds its budget. The Henry County Commissioners reason that in order to control the County's expenses, they must rein in the police budget. There exists a difference in financial priorities. Thus, a power struggle between the Sheriff and the commissioners ensues.

Chairman Hugh Findley, on behalf of the other members of the Henry County Board of Commissioners (which include Kelley, Cleveland, and Mitcham), is instructed to speak with Sheriff Glass and seek his cooperation in resolving the County's budget deficits. Chairman Findley meets with the Sheriff Glass for lunch at the Holiday Inn in McDonough. Sheriff Glass orders a country fried steak, French fries, green beans and is thinking about a slice of apple pie. It will depend on how the meeting goes and if Hugh is paying the bill. Jimmy Glass does not worry about his weight even though his doctor has encouraged him to watch his cholesterol. Hugh is anxious about the meeting and has little appetite. He orders a cup of vegetable soup and a salad. Following the meal, he gets to the point.

"Sheriff Glass, as I mentioned, we have a situation here that we need to address. Due to the hard times, our tax collections are down, and we cannot meet our budget. We have got to find a way to cut expenses. The commissioners adopted a tight budget last January. Your expenses thus far this year are exceeding the amount we have allocated for the sheriff's department," Finley says.

Sheriff Glass replies, "I know Hugh. I have spent money on fixing police cars and hiring more patrolmen. We have been issuing more citations in hopes that the extra ticket money would cover the increased expenses. It hasn't so far."

"Counting on ticket money to fund the department is not a good idea," Finley says. "I got a call from a gentleman from Tennessee who had gotten a ticket for going ten miles over the speed limit. He accuses Henry County of being a 'speed trap.'"

"Henry County has seven exits off Interstate 75," Sheriff Glass says. "There are all kinds of people traveling up and down the Interstate. Some are dope pushers, smugglers and law violators. I need the patrol cars and men to catch and keep them from doing harm to our citizens."

"Last year the county ran out of money August 1st," Finlay admits. "We had to go to First National to borrow $500,000, so we could operate until the tax money started coming in at the end of November. Some of that money we borrowed was used to pay you and your department's salaries."

"Hugh, crime is increasing here," Sheriff Glass responds. "Lately, we have been finding a stolen car or a dead body in Stockbridge about every month. The people are demanding that the police department put a stop to these crimes and put the criminals in jail. I am going to do what it takes to protect the people, who put me in office."

"Sheriff, I am paying for our lunches out of my pocket," Finley says. "Whether you like it or not, I intend to balance the budget one way or another."

***

True to his word, Mr. Findley asks and receives a motion at the first official board meeting in January to limit the Sheriff's powers. The newly sworn commissioners unanimously vote to create a Henry County Police Department which would operate separately and apart from the Henry County Sheriff's Department. The news comes as a shock to the citizens of Henry County and infuriates Sheriff Glass. A spokesperson for the commissioners says, "It is done for economic reasons."

The transition is set for Monday March 15th. The reorganization sees the number of personnel in the sheriff's department reduced to fifteen including cooks and secretaries. The sheriff's office will have responsibility for the jail, the courthouse and county buildings, serving papers and other related administrative functions. The criminal investigations and traffic enforcement would shift to the police department. The new police department will be headed by J.C. Floyd with a staff of thirty-five personnel. Six of them are detectives who would handle criminal matters.

***

The turmoil in the trimmed-down sheriff's department has just settled down when a letter accusing Sheriff Glass and his department of wrongdoing, is sent to the governor's office. The accusations are enumerated in a scathing article in *The Atlanta Journal* by a reporter named Ann Woolner.

It is customary at the Henry County Jail to give the inmates the daily newspapers once Lt. Glass, the jailers, and the other department personnel have read them. The rule is that the inmates who have spent the most time in the jail are given first claim to the newspapers. These include *The Atlanta Journal*, the evening paper, *The Atlanta Constitution*, the morning paper, and Thursday's local paper, *The Weekly Advertiser*. Jerry Banks is not much of a reader. He likes the comics and the sports section.

The article in question stems from a letter sent to the newspaper. It enumerates the following accusations:
- Using police cars to haul liquor and to hire prostitutes
- Planting drugs to frame a man
- Tearing up numerous traffic tickets for money
- Encouraging detectives to ease up on certain investigations

- Illegally helping people obtain driver's license, either for a fee or in hopes of obtaining votes for the Sheriff
- Stopping female traffic violators and promising to let them go in return for sexual favors
- Participating in or turning their heads to illegal gambling
- Tampering with evidence in a drug case so a felony charge could be reduced to a misdemeanor

Jerry Banks utters under his breath, "That doesn't sound fair. These people ought to be in jail with us! It's just not right for the Sheriff who put me in jail to do whatever illegal he wants to and nothin' ever happens to him. He would look good in orange."

The newspaper article surprises many people, especially the local die-hard supporters of the Sheriff. The Henry County Board of Commissioners holds a closed-door meeting to discuss how it should handle the appalling accusations leveled at the Sheriff and his department. Chairman Findley responds to a member of the press, who is seeking an official statement, "I called the governor's office during our meeting. He said his people will help us in any way to get to the bottom of it. The commissioners believe that these acts should be investigated by someone outside of our county."

As a result, the new Henry County District Attorney, Byron Smith, and the Henry County Board of Commissioners send a joint letter to Gov. George Busbee asking him to have the G.B.I. investigate these acts of wrongdoing that are levied against the enigmatic Sheriff and his department.

Sheriff Glass in a statement to *The Weekly Advertiser* says, "I am not guilty of any wrongdoing. There are those who are trying to discredit me, my family and friends before the election in an attempt to prevent me from serving a second term. I have confidence in the people of Henry County who I have served in their best interest, as I promised, when I ran for office four years ago. The people know that I have always been close to each of them, individually or by telephone, both day and night, twenty-four hours a day."

Apparently, three unknown disgruntled employees sent the list to the newspaper of what they considered to be unacceptable behavior by individuals in the sheriff's department. They admit that Sheriff Glass did not personally engage in all the activities but was aware that they were happening and did nothing to stop them.

District Attorney Smith presents the question of an investigation of Sheriff Glass and his department to the Grand Jury. A copy of the G.B.I. report is presented at the hearing.

Sheriff Glass has been in and out of the courthouse during the four days of interrogations and deliberations. He sits impatiently through Judge Sosebee's solemn charge to the jurors. To the jurors the week was one of intense pressure. With most of Henry County's citizens anxiously awaiting a verdict, the twenty-two men and women are of one mind in wanting to do the right thing.

Following closed door hearings for portions of four days, the Grand Jury clears Sheriff Glass on June 10th. Jurors are in total agreement that there is not sufficient cause to continue investigation of the Henry County Sheriff's Department and give Sheriff Jimmy Glass a clean bill.

Jury Foreman Hugh Thompson admits, "There were some things the jury was not satisfied with – in a moral or ethical sense. We didn't consider Sheriff Glass to be lily-white, and in the future, we encourage him to enter into a higher degree of professionalism."

Sheriff Glass is vindicated of improprieties. Nevertheless, challengers to the Sheriff's position in the upcoming primary use the negative information in a smear campaign against him. They say, "Where there is smoke, there is fire." Jimmy Glass publishes an open letter in *The Weekly Advertiser* in answer to political ads attacking his integrity. "My opponent's actions are typical of the desperate last-minute efforts by some candidates. They figure they can sway public opinion against me prior to an election.

"The commissioners have charged me with exceeding my budget. It's hard to keep from overrunning the budget when our police cars are in continuous need of repair. I feel that all counties should have their police departments under the sheriff. In Henry County it is cheaper to keep law enforcement under one roof. Besides, if the people are not happy with the job I am doing, they can vote me out."

Herschel Childs, Jimmy Glass' highest ranking deputy, is named permanent chief of police effective November 15th. Maj. Childs has been employed for the past five years as a policeman in this area. He served one year in the City of McDonough and four years with the Henry County Police and Sheriff's Departments. Prior to coming to Henry County, he worked as a policeman for the City of Anderson, South Carolina. He is respected by the patrolmen and detectives and has a good relationship with Sheriff Glass. Maj. Childs lives in McDonough with his wife, Elaine, a teacher at McDonough Middle School.

The issues the voters must decide are twofold. One, should the sheriff's department regain police powers and two, should Jimmy Glass be re-elected as sheriff. The support for Jimmy Glass is overwhelming at the 1976 general election in November. The majority of the voters want Jimmy to be their sheriff and they want him in charge of law enforcement in Henry County.

Voters show their support by giving Jimmy Glass eighty percent of the popular vote. The incumbent commissioners are not so fortunate. Four out of five commissioners are not re-elected. Only Bill Hinton who had openly opposed the separation is re-elected. Thus, 1976 is a turbulent year for Jimmy Glass, but he has survived. He has successfully fended off the efforts by his enemies to discredit and unseat him from political influence in Henry County.

A special bill is introduced that imposes strict budgetary requirements on the sheriff. The bill allows the Henry County Sheriff to oversee both departments and fix the salaries, subject to the final approval by the Henry County Board of Commissioners. Now without a doubt, Jimmy Glass is chief administrator of the both the police and sheriff departments. The bill does not eliminate the position of police chief, who remains accountable to the sheriff. The measure gives Jimmy Glass and his successors power to employ law enforcement personnel, establish police policies and submit one consolidated budget.

***

All the political maneuvering by the county officials and the Sheriff has done little to benefit Jerry Banks. It matters not who is running the place. The Henry County Jail is a miserable place to be confined. It has been Jerry Banks' home for the last two years. If his upcoming appeals are not successful, he is headed to Georgia's "big house" and his stint there will be short-lived.

Part III

Prison, Defense Team and Appeals

CHAPTER 34 | Trip to Washington, D.C.

Alex Crumbley lives in an unincorporated area of Henry County, more specifically rural Kelleytown. The Crumbley family is one of the first settlers in the County arriving in the early 1800s. Anthony Crumbley, of Scotch-Irish decent, moved to the Cotton-Indian River area near Tunis which today is McDonough. The Crumbley family can claim numerous relatives who live in the area.

Shortly after receiving degrees in journalism and law from the University of Georgia in 1966, he returns to practice law in McDonough. He is married to Claire, has a son Alexander, sister Carol, Dr. Foster's nurse, and a brother, Wade, who is an aspiring attorney. His law office is located at 80 Macon Street in McDonough.

Crumbley, as a young lawyer, was already developing an impressive resume, most notably being named the Flint Judicial Circuit's first public defender in 1976. An experimental program launched by the Richard Nixon administration to help indigent defendants who are filling the jails. As a lawyer and devout Christian, "He believes an indigent accused deserves the same quality defense as someone who has the means to pay." The program was being funded in part by the federal government, meaning by the taxpayers. The public defender's duties will take a burden from the courts since counsel for indigents has previously come from

218

the lawyers appointed by the court.

While at the Henry County Courthouse in late December 1976, he receives word from a deputy that Jerry Banks wishes to see him. It is the beginning of a relationship that provides Jerry with hope of a new trial and eventual release.

Banks began the conversation. "Mr. Crumbley, do you

Alex Crumbley

know who I am?" Crumbley tells Banks that everyone in Henry County knows who Jerry Banks is. Many newspaper articles have been written about the murder convictions. Banks tells Crumbley that he had not heard from his lawyer in a long time. The last conversation he had with Myers was about his upcoming appeal in the Atlanta court. Banks was told by attorney Myers that he should not worry, but he does worry. Banks learned yesterday his appeal was turned down from watching the news on television.

Crumbley tells Banks that he was right and he, too, had heard of the ruling by the Georgia Supreme Court, which did not overturn his conviction. Crumbley admitted that he did not know the details and had no idea what happened to Myers, but assured Banks that he would investigate the matter.

Banks became somewhat agitated, "Mr. Crumbley, does that mean I may still go to the electric chair. I pray to God, that you will help me." To calm Banks down and to mitigate his desperate plea, Crumbley informs him that his death sentence appeal now moves to the U.S. Supreme Court in Washington, the highest court in the land. There he will have another chance to have his sentence overturned.

***

The missing motorist's meeting with Judge Sosebee had set in motion the momentum for a new trial. The appeal process provides several avenues for defense attorneys to pursue. Jerry Banks was found guilty by a jury in Henry County Superior Court. Myers appeals the decision back to the lower Henry County Superior Court, where he cites the non-disclosure of the motorist as grounds for a new trial. When a new trial is denied by Judge Sosebee, attorney Myers files a perfunctory appeal to the Georgia Supreme Court. The Georgia Supreme Court is comprised of seven judges, who are elected statewide. Vacancies are appointed by the governor. By law, the Court must render a decision within six months. While waiting for that ruling, attorney Myers files a secondary notice of appeal on September 2, 1975, in the Georgia Court of Appeals. The case is to be heard on April 19, 1976. Myers has two appeals pending that likely will be denied.

Anticipating another defeat in the courts and no compensation for his efforts, the discouraged John Hudson Myers loses interest in Jerry Banks' defense. The original retainer the family had gathered up, is now long gone. Myers' visits to the Henry County Jail, which were already very infrequent, have now become nonexistent. Jerry Banks is searching for another lawyer.

Alex Crumbley developed a keen interest in politics at an early age. Some of his early Henry County ancestors, Anthony Crumbley and Ferdinand Crumbley, held public offices. As an active member of the Henry County Democratic Party, he joined other aspiring local politicians in organizing a fundraiser for Jimmy Carter, a dark horse presidential candidate to say the least. It is hard to imagine that a peanut farmer from Plains, Georgia could become president of the United States. In the South where Mr. Carter has accumulated some impressive credentials, he is a popular candidate. However, in the rest of the country, few have heard of him. A graduate from the U.S. Naval Academy, Mr. Carter was in the top ten percent of his class. He served in the Georgia Senate and as Georgia's governor. He teaches Bible study every Sunday morning at the Maranatha Baptist Church. Mr. Carter is known to be a down-to-earth, hardworking, honest person with Southern conservative values.

By Henry County standards the fundraiser is a success. Mr.

and Mrs. Carter are campaigning in Ohio, but one of Mr. Carter's campaign chairmen attends and makes a few remarks. The next day Crumbley receives a personal call from Mr. Carter thanking him for his efforts and support. Mr. Carter tells him that he expects to win the election. Mr. Carter asks him if he wants to attend the inauguration in Washington? Without hesitation, he accepts the invitation and assures Mr. Carter that he would be honored to attend.

On January 20, 1977, Crumbley does just that and attends the inauguration of President-elect Jimmy Carter, the first and only president from Georgia. It is a cold January day. The temperature never gets above 28 degrees. There are over 250,000 people there. All want to get a first-hand glimpse of the man, who has defied the odds and became the 39th president defeating Gerald Ford. The number in attendance turns out to be four times more than had attended Richard Nixon's inauguration.

Chief Justice Warren Burger administers the oath of office. President-elect Carter raises his right hand and places his left hand on his family Bible. A bookmark is strategically located in the book of Micah 6:8. *And what does the Lord require of you? To act justly, and to love mercy and to walk humbly with your God.*

Like all other past presidents, the inaugural speech is carefully prepared and emphasizes his and Vice President Mondale's goals while in office. President Carter states in his address, "The nations of the world might say that we built a lasting peace, built not on weapons of war, but on international policies that reflect our own most precious values."

While in Washington, D.C., Crumbley makes a visit to the U.S. Supreme Court. As a lawyer he has always wanted to tour the facility. His visual memory of the courthouse building has come only from pictures and television. He has another motive for being there. He wants to check on the status of the Jerry Banks' appeal.

To his surprise, the clerk in the record room is remarkably familiar with the *Georgia v. Banks* case. She tells him that John Hudson Myers has not filed a proper brief. The appeal caught her attention because it contained a poem. An unusual approach to such a life-or-death document. She further says that the automatic appeal to overturn Jerry Banks' death penalty in the U.S. Supreme Court is still pending.

An appeal of a murder conviction by an unknown Black man from a small community in Georgia would never have reached the highest court in the land if it had not been for the Court's concern of basic human rights. It began when the U.S. Supreme Court of the United States realized that its ruling in 1866, declaring that prisoners have no constitutional rights, was contrary to the U.S. Constitution and its Bill of Rights. The concept that a prisoner is "a slave of the state" is outdated and un-American. That changed in 1964 when a more benevolent U.S. Supreme Court ruled for the first time that state prison inmates have a legal standing in federal courts.

A short time later the U.S. Supreme Court does review Jerry Banks' appeal. Despite the new prisoner rights, successful appeals from convicted felons attempting to overturn their death penalties, especially paupers, are rare. John Hudson Myers does not make the trip to Washington. The standard defense in such an appeal petition is whether the criteria in the Georgia law for imposing a death penalty sentence is too broad and vague, thereby depriving the defendant, Jerry Banks, of his constitutional rights. The majority of the justices, however, think otherwise and on April 18, 1977, the U.S. Supreme Court rejects the appeal. Justices William J. Brennen, Jr. and Thurgood Marshall, both opponents of the death penalty, are the only justices who vote to set aside Jerry Banks' death sentence. The case now returns to the Georgia where the Commissioner of the Department of Corrections will reschedule the execution date.

The justices are divided over the constitutionality of the death penalty. Every death sentence appeal brings a new interpretation of the rights of a particular condemned prisoner.

I have often questioned whether the fear of an execution deters anyone from committing murder. If you look at the murder statistics, there is no direct evidence. At times, I believe our country would be no worse off without the death penalty but I can sympathize with those who seek vengeance when one of their loved ones is brutally murdered.

Leave it to the State of Georgia to have two landmark cases that are instrumental in settling the issue. First the 1972 Furman v. Georgia *decision the United States Supreme Court struck down all the various existing state death penalty rules and procedures in a five-to-four decision. The justices determined that there are too many inconsistencies in how the penalty is imposed. As a result, the high court formally established a moratorium on further executions until states can implement uniform guidelines for sentencing the death penalty.*

In my opinion, what has made our democracy so resilient is the decision of the Founding Fathers to include the Bill of Rights in the U.S. Constitution. Their wisdom has safeguarded the everyday citizen from authoritative abuse. Several additional amendments have since been adopted. The Eighth and Fourteenth Amendments apply to Jerry Banks as a convicted felon. For example, the Eighth Amendment states, "Excessive bail shall not be required, nor excessive fines imposed, nor cruel and unusual punishment inflicted." The amendment is intended to safeguard the convicted against excessive punishment. The Fourteenth Amendment states in part, "All Americans are entitled to equal protection under the laws. All persons born in the United States are citizens and cannot be deprived of life, liberty, or property without due process of the law."

The majority of the justices view capital punishment as unfair because it does not treat all the accused equally. They contend that present state laws violate a person's rights as provided by the Eighth and Fourteenth amendments. The justices consider the death penalty as "cruel and unusual punishment" which is not permitted under U.S. Constitution's Bill of Rights. Later, however, the U.S. Supreme Court reverses its position based on another Georgia Case, *Gregg v. Georgia.* By a seven-to-two vote the high court now deems the Georgia death penalty as constitutional because its statues call for separate proceedings for the trial and the sentencing. Jurors can evaluate the severity and the circumstances before rendering a verdict. At Jerry Banks' trial all the court-mandated guidelines were followed. The jury first determined Banks' guilt of the murders and then, based on the severity of the crime, recommended the appropriate sentence to the court.

***

The U.S. Supreme Court's decision is another blow to the defense effort by John Hudson Myers. Not only does the Court fail to spare Jerry Banks from the electric chair, but it legitimizes its use. It appears that Jerry Banks has exhausted all the realistic avenues for appeal of his death sentence. He will soon be transferred from the Henry County Jail to the Georgia Diagnostic Classification Prison in Jackson to await his fate. His family and friends' hope for an eventual release is fading.

Crumbley is disappointed and disgusted with John Hudson Myers' efforts in defending Banks. He feels that Jerry Banks' defense lawyer, Myers, abandoned his client. In response to a statement to a reporter who asked him about his fee for handling the Jerry Banks case, Myers replied, "I received a ten-dollar retainer, kettle of fish and collard greens." Even though he may not be getting paid for his services, any responsible member of the bar would have at least made an appearance at the appeal hearing. It is the second time Banks' attorney has not appeared at a hearing and second time he has failed to stand behind his client. It is now obvious that Banks has not gotten competent representation. Facing overwhelming odds, the best that can be done now is to have his death sentence commuted to life imprisonment.

Rumor has it that John Hudson Myers' legal reputation is further tarnished by an incident that occurred in Henry County. After visiting with Banks and one other client at the Henry County Jail, Myers was in a hurry to get back to Atlanta and is stopped for allegedly speeding. Noticing his suspicious behavior, the officer searches his car and uncovers more than one ounce of marijuana. Myers is arrested and subsequently charged with possession. He is later released on his own recognizance. However, if found guilty, Myers could receive a prison sentence and have his license to practice law suspended.

CHAPTER 35 | First Day in the Big House

Time in a maximum-security prison is well documented. Many inmates have kept diaries and were able to publish their experiences. It is a dangerous place filled with dangerous people. For many, survival physically and emotionally is a challenge. Jerry Banks's stay in the Jackson prison is no different.

New arrivals at Jackson's Georgia Diagnostic and Classification Prison are dropped off every Tuesday and Thursday. Transportation to the prison is by an off-white converted Bluebird school bus with barred windows; the rear emergency door is welded shut. The ride is quite long as the bus makes several stops at different county jails. Handcuffed and shackled, Banks sits on the last row with little to say. He has no desire to carry on a conversation with the passengers, especially the guards, who probably have nothing but contempt for him. For many passengers it is a one-way ticket with little certainty of a return trip.

The Jackson Prison is Georgia's largest maximum-security facility. Located in Butts County just off Interstate 75 in central Georgia, it is some fifty miles south of Atlanta. First opened in 1969, the prison has been home to some of the most dangerous inmates in the state's history. At the time, over two thousand adult males were incarcerated there. Jerry Banks' arrival brings the number of those who are on death row to seventy-six. For these prisoners, time for any type of reform has passed. The execution chamber, which had been housed at Georgia State Prison in Reidsville is in the process of being relocated to Jackson.

***

The unlocked front gate slides open after the transfer papers are verified by the attending guard. The bus continues to the transfer yard where other buses from other parts of the state have already unloaded their prisoners. After Banks enters, his shackles are removed, and he is instructed to walk down the hall toward two awaiting guards. The clanging sound of the gate slamming shut stuns Banks. It is a sound that first timers never forget. The reality of why he is here is no longer a bad dream but an evolving nightmare.

Jerry Banks, like the other arrivals, is processed: stripped of his clothes, thoroughly inspected for concealed items and disinfected. The attempt to smuggle drugs is a common problem with the addicts. Banks has never used drugs but is known to have a drink or two. He is issued a prison jumpsuit, underwear, white socks and shoes. Next comes the haircut, followed by a photo shoot. Frontal and profile facial pictures with a seven-digit number printed on the bottom edge becomes his ID for the remainder of his prison life.

Banks is given a bar of soap, toothbrush, toothpaste and one towel. The metal bed is covered with a thin mattress and an often-used pillow; he receives one sheet, a blanket and a pillowcase. His tattered and faded Henry County issued prison uniform and what few possessions he has are catalogued and boxed up. Death row inmates are not allowed to bring anything from the outside other than books. The prison provides reading materials and a Bible, if requested by the inmate.

Banks is escorted to a central meeting room by two armed guards. There he is joined by five other newly processed prisoners surrounded by additional guards. Banks is the only prisoner in the group whose destination is the death row cellblock. A tall, burly White guard begins shouting orders, "I have assembled you here to teach you some discipline. From now on you will address all the prison staff from the warden down to the cook as madam or sir! From now on, it will be 'Sir, good morning, sir'! How will you cons address me tomorrow afternoon?" After three attempts and several terse commands, the intimidated prisoners are able to shout in unison, "Sir, good afternoon, sir!"

Guard Burton Wilbanks resembles a heavyweight prize fighter who has lost most of his bouts. He is bald and his face is littered with scars. *I suspect when ugly baby Burton was delivered, his doctor slapped his behind and then gave his mother a bewildered stare. A look that meant, "How could you have brought this awful creature into the world?" And from Burton's demeaner, his parents probably had little use for the boy.*

He is one of the most frightening dudes Jerry Banks has ever met. Later it is learned that he was wounded during the Korean War after a grenade exploded in his fox hole. He left Walter Reed Hospital as a decorated Marine.

Guard Wilbanks then introduces the Warden, James Ricketts, who sarcastically welcomes the new prisoners to his "house." He enumerates the rules each inmate is expected to follow: "Prisoners must speak in a low voice during rest periods, after lights out, and during meals. Prisoners must keep the cell clean at all times. Beds must be made, and personal effects must be kept neat and orderly; floors must be spotless. Prisoners must not move, tamper with, deface or damage walls, ceiling, windows, doors, or any prison property. Smoking is a privilege. Smoking will be allowed after meals or at the discretion of the guards. Prisoners must never smoke in their cells. Mail is a privilege. All mail flowing in and out of the prison will be inspected and censored. Visitors are a privilege. The visit will be supervised by a guard. The guard may terminate the visit at his discretion. And finally, all prisoners must at all times obey all orders issued by guards."

Borrowing a line from *Cool Hand Luke*, "We will not have a 'failure to communicate' in this prison. Break the rules and your hard time will become harder. You will lose your exercise and visitation privileges. Troublemakers will spend a lot of time in solitary confinement. Do you understand?"

Banks is separated from the other prisoners and is accompanied by Wilbanks and two guards to his new home. "Just follow the yellow line," Wilbanks commands.

Death row inmates live in four pods of meticulously kept single-inmate cells measuring just six-and-a-half by nine feet. As Banks walks down the hall, he notices that each cell is furnished with a bed, sink, toilet and shelves. Shoes are placed under each prisoner's bed. The shelves contain books and magazines that he learns came from the prison library. Banks is surprised that some inmates have radios.

He asks, "Sir, how come some of these guys have radios?"

Wilbanks answers, "With good behavior maybe you will be allowed one someday."

In front of the cells is a narrow common area with tables and chairs. Mounted on the tables are black and white television sets that provide the only daytime entertainment for the attending guards and inmates.

Unlike the old Henry County Jail, Jackson Prison is cleaner and much bigger. All the cells look the same to Jerry with their drab, gray-painted walls. None contain windows and have only one overhead light controlled from the outside. The cell door is solid steel with a grate opening the size of a regular windowpane. A grate panel slides open, allowing the guards to pass food trays without unlocking the door. For a country boy who has enjoyed the wide-open outdoor spaces, this new home appears no bigger than a closet.

.

***

Jerry Banks is now the newest inmate on Georgia's notorious death row. He wonders, "Who were some of the others who had previously occupied his cell? What horrendous crimes did they commit? Could he be the only one that doesn't belong here?" One of the guards who has duty over this section of death row, considers these inmates to be a bunch of savages.

Having been found guilty of the brutal deaths of Marvin King and Melanie Hartsfield, Banks is in the company of the most vicious killers in Georgia. All have a date with the electric chair. In Banks' opinion these people may look and talk like him and his friends, but inside they are filled with evil. Some are the devil's rejects.

In the adjoining cell to his right, is twenty-three-year-old Timothy McCorquodale from Alma, Georgia. On the evening of January 16, 1974, he met seventeen-year-old Donna Dixon, a runaway, who hitchhiked to Atlanta from Virginia. The area of Peachtree and 10th Streets known as the "the strip" contains apartment houses, rundown motels, strip-clubs and bars. While at a bar, McCorquodale notices a girl flirting with two Black men. Later that night, McCorquodale convinces Ms. Dixon to accompany him to his apartment on Moreland Avenue along with his girlfriend and another companion. Tim McCorquodale perceives Donna to be a "nigger lover" and is determined to teach her a lesson. After arriving at the apartment, to her shock, he begins punching her with his fists and whipping her with his belt. All the while, he is yelling, "I hate niggers!" Lying on the floor, bleeding and in tremendous pain, Ms. Dixon begs him to stop. To shut her up, he proceeds to put a washcloth in her mouth and secures it with electrical tape and binds her hands and feet with her nylons. Not finished with the torture, he rips off her clothes, slices her breasts and pours salt on her wounds. He lights a candle and pours the hot wax on her body. The cruelty finally comes to an end after he finishes raping her.

After drinking two more Jack Daniels, McCorquodale becomes concerned that Ms. Dixon will report the attack. While she is still naked and lying motionless on the floor, he strangles her. Faced with the dilemma of having a dead body in his apartment, he recalls spotting a Dempsey Dumpster the day before in a remote area at the intersection of Slade Road and Highway 42 near Rex, Georgia. He throws her lifeless body into an old trunk. The next day, with the help of his companion, he loads the trunk into his van and heaves the body into the dumpster.

***

Tim McCorquodale is convicted of the brutal murder of Donna Dixon. Like Banks he is sentenced to die in the electric chair. Having run out of appeals, he gets transferred from Reidsville to Jackson Prison a month before Jerry Banks. He is considered a redneck and a loudmouth by the guards, who are stationed at death row block. He is always mouthing off to the guards about the food or his poor treatment. His demands to see his attorney have become tiresome. McCorquodale is labeled as a troublemaker.

Terrorizing new inmates is a tradition on death row. Young Jerry Banks is an easy target. No one is better at harassing inmates than McCorquodale. Although separated by a concrete wall and not able to make eye contact, the verbal abuse is only inches away.

McCorquodale yells out, "Hey you, Banks, what are you in for?"

"They say I killed two people in Henry County," Banks replies.

McCorquodale asks, "Did you, do it?"

"No, I am innocent. I was framed!" says Banks.

McCorquodale laughs and continues, "Everyone in here claims they're innocent."

Mitchell, a Black man, in an adjoining cell, sarcastically yells, "Leave the boy be. He has enough worries without listening to you."

William Mitchell is in Jackson Prison as the result of a vicious crime he committed on August 11, 1974, in South Georgia. Broke and in need for money, he figured the local convenience store would be easy pickings. He arrived early and waited for the store to open. Shortly after Mrs. James Carr and her fourteen-year-old son, Chris, unlocked the front door, Mitchell entered. Finding no one in the store, Mitchell pulled out his pistol and demanded money from Mrs. Carr. To his disappointment the manager had made a bank deposit the night before, leaving little in the cash register.

He then ordered the two to the back of the store in hopes of locking them in the walk-in cooler while he made his getaway. When he discovered that the cooler was not large enough, he shot both Chris and Mrs. Carr. He proceeded to ransack the store and grabbed all the cigarettes and beer he could haul. Concerned that the victims were still alive and could identify him, he returned to the storage room and shot them several more times. Miraculously, Mrs. Carr survived and testified against Mitchell.

Another inmate joins in the verbal harassment of Banks. The cell to his left is occupied by Joseph Mulligan who has been at Jackson Prison a brief time. He has a history of arrests, and his family considered him totally worthless. No one wanted anything to do with him although Mulligan did keep in touch with his younger sister who informed him of her marital problems with her abusive husband.

He and a friend, on April 12, 1974, decided to drive to Columbus, Georgia to visit Mulligan's brother-in-law and try to patch things up between the couple. Patrick Doe was an U.S. Army Captain at Fort Benning. During the visit, Doe revealed that he had filed a divorce action against Mulligan's sister. Mulligan became angered by the way Doe was treating his sister. "Doe ought to be punished for what he is doing to her." He told his friend.

Capt. Doe had made plans that evening to attend a party given by one of his friends. He invited Mulligan and his friend to accompany him and his female companion to the party. The three drove a short distance to pick up Marian Miller. Doe greeted her with an affectionate kiss and the four were apparently ready to party. When Doe started his car, the angered Mulligan, riding in the backseat, shot him in the back of head. When Marian began screaming and shouting for help, he unloaded his gun striking her four times.

Mulligan and his friend exited the car. But before leaving the scene, they were careful to wipe all the incriminating fingerprints from Capt. Doe's car. Unfortunately for them, one latent print remained on the left door window. Detectives were able to match the print with one on file with the F.B.I. belonging to Mulligan. After a quick arrest and trial, he was found guilty. The judge and jury showed no mercy and gave him the death penalty.

The three inmates continue to harass Jerry. The catcalls and laughter echo throughout the cell block. The guard on duty considers the banter between the inmates as harmless fun. He is pleased to have some amusement to an otherwise boring evening.

McCorquodale says, "Banks you are in fine company. Mitchell here shot a woman five times and killed her fourteen-year-old kid.

All over a few dollars, a handful of candy bars and a six pack of Pabst Blue Ribbon beer. Mulligan killed his sister's husband and a girlfriend because the husband was leaving her for another woman. I killed a woman because she liked niggers, like you."

Banks replies, "Just leave me alone. I don't feel like listening."

"You better enjoy our company," McCorquodale says. "You ain't getting out of here until the warden takes you to the death house. Then they are going to strap you to 'Old Sparky' and fry your brains. They will put an often-used sack over your head, so the people who come to watch, won't see your eyeballs popping out and the puke coming out of your mouth."

Mitchell laughing and shouting facetiously, "That's enough of that crap. Tell the boy how it is really going to be."

McCorquodale goes on, "When the man pulls the switch, the lights go dim as a jolt of 2,000 volts of electricity race through your body. First come the convulsions; your body stiffens like a board. Then you thrust forward. A minute-and-a-half later comes another jolt of 2,000 volts. This time you won't feel it because you are dead. People say that sometimes bolts of fire come out both ears after the second jolt. Then comes the smell of burning flesh. It's your flesh, but you won't know it. After the smoke clears the doctor comes in and pronounces you dead, as if there is any doubt. Then they put you on a stretcher and cover you with a white sheet. By then somebody behind the glass window yells, "The S.O.B. got what he deserved. I hope he rots in hell."

"I don't want to hear anymore," says Banks.

McCorquodale, laughing out loud, says, "Won't that be fun, boy? Your Black ass is going to be dead!"

Mulligan interrupts, "Yah need to settle down now. It's time to sleep. I hope you don't have any nightmares."

By nightfall Banks is exhausted, but sleep eludes him. He has many thoughts racing through his mind, not to mention the disparaging remarks made by the loud-mouth bigot in the neighboring cell. The cellblock is alive with chatter well into the night. He could not imagine what these condemned men must talk about. Then there are the noisy toilets; when flushed they sound like someone is being sucked down the drain. Banks had barely closed his eyes when he hears a commotion down the hall. An approaching meal cart with a noisy wobbly wheel is making its way toward his cell. The trustee pushing the cart and delivering the meals announces his arrival, "Wake up you cons, breakfast is served!"

CHAPTER 36 | More Appeals

John Hudson Myers half-heartedly navigated Jerry Banks' case through the legal system. Following his guilty verdict at the hands of the local jury at the January 1975 trial, Myers appealed the conviction to the Henry County Superior Court in March 1975. The testimony of the unidentified motorist, however, did not convince Judge Sosebee to grant a new trial. Myers then filed appeals in both the Georgia Court of Appeals and the Georgia Supreme Court. In September, the Georgia Supreme Court granted a new trial based on the United States v. Brady *case. The second trial in November 1975 resulted in another conviction. Myers again appealed to the Georgia Supreme Court and was denied in June 1976. In April 1977, the U.S. Supreme Court did not overturn the death sentence.*

The normal course of action for a convicted felon is to appeal, appeal and appeal until every option is exhausted. I do not know the record number of appeals filed by a death row prisoner, but it must be quite a few. The 1963 U.S. Supreme Court ruling gave prisoners the right to file habeas corpus *motions in the courts. Habeas corpus is a Latin term literally meaning "you shall have the body" (the right to physically appear in court). Many of those who are condemned to die spend their time reading law books in order to find a legal way out. Jerry Banks is depending on Alex*

Crumbley to find grounds for an appeal motion. Most of the time the motions fail to have merit and judges take little time in denying them. But with the large numbers of death row inmates with different and unique circumstances, coupled with liberal judges, an occasional appeal does get a favorable ruling. I am hoping Jerry Banks' case is one of those exceptions that will result in a new trial.

From what I have heard and read, the only links between Jerry Banks and the murders are the shotgun and red shell casings. There is no other physical evidence, or eyewitnesses that prove Banks was the killer. I am convinced there is more below the surface. When all the facts are uncovered and revealed, the truth will exonerate him.

Although Alex Crumbley's law practice is doing well and he is extremely busy, he begins to devote time to Jerry Banks' appeal. On May 6, 1977, he and his uncle, Ernest Smith, and Banks' former public defender, Buddy Welch, file a petition for a writ of *habeas corpus* in Henry County Superior Court. Buddy Welch would have been the court-appointed counsel for Jerry Banks had not his mother engaged John Hudson Myers. Crumbley had interned at Mr. Smith's law practice while in law school and considered Mr. Smith's experience to be invaluable at the hearing. One of their arguments asserted that the death sentence violated Jerry Banks' constitutional rights under the Eighth and Fourteenth Amendments. This is currently a commonly used ground for an appeal. Unfortunately, it seldom results in a favorable ruling.

Hugh Sosebee has served as Chief Judge for Flint Circuit for twenty-four years. He has just turned sixty-one-years-old and has not had a vacation in twelve years. Gov. Busbee appoints Sam Whitmire to fill his position effective January 4, 1978. Judge Sosebee continues serving as Senior Judge in the circuit. As a Senior Judge he will only handle a limited number of cases. These will be of his choosing and at his convenience until a permanent new second Superior Court judge is named. The newly in-coming Superior Court Judge Sam Whitmire from Barnesville presides over the hearing. On September 15, 1977, Judge Whitmire denies the appeal.

***

Welch meets Crumbley in his office to prepare a petition for another appeal. His secretary has prepared a fresh pot of coffee. Welch reaches into his shirt pocket and pulls out a nearly empty pack of Marlboros and says, "I need a cigarette. Can't drink coffee without a cigarette." Crumbley tells Welch that Dr. Blissit advised him to get some exercise. So, he buys a road bike and starts riding. Crumbley continues, "Early one morning last week, I was riding through a subdivision near the house. I noticed a silver-haired gentleman in a bathrobe shuffling his way to the mailbox, coughing, with a cigarette hanging out of his mouth. Just as I was passing, he reaches down to pick up the morning paper lying on the driveway. I guess he gets up early so he can read the obituaries to see if any of his friends have passed. He knows his days are numbered, but he hopes to outlive his pals. I share this observation with you in order to encourage you to stop smoking. Those cigarettes can't be good for your health!"

Undaunted Welch ignores Crumbley's lecture. They finalize the petition and file the appeal in Henry County Superior Court. The appeal of the conviction is based on grounds that Jerry Banks did not get a fair trial since he did not receive an adequate defense. The appeal petition states that attorney Myers did such an ineffective job, that Banks was denied his constitutional rights. They reason that Jerry Banks' circumstances of neglect were so blatant that they represent a classic case of injustice and incompetency. They base their allegations on the several glaring mistakes that the defense attorney made during the trials.

The petition purports that Mr. Myers should have raised a question concerning the constitutionality of Georgia's death penalty. He did not. There were instances of hearsay testimony that he should have challenged. He did not. He should have filed a timely petition to have the U.S. Supreme Court review the decision of the lower court, he did not.

***

In March 1978, the appeal hearing convenes with Judge Whitmire presiding. Jerry Banks is transferred from Jackson Prison to the Henry County Jail. After the opening remarks Buddy Welch swears in the first witness. In all the trials and appeal hearings Jerry Banks never testified. For the first time Jerry Banks takes the stand in his own behalf. There is apprehension about having Banks as the first witness. He is obviously nervous, but eager to have his say. Buddy Welch calls him to the stand and asks him to assess John Hudson Myers' handling of his defense.

Jerry Banks: "While I was a prisoner at Henry County Jail, my mother hired me a lawyer. I liked him and he seemed to be a smart man. He assured me that he would get me out of this here mess. We had talked about the appeals, and he promised to let me know how it went as soon as he knew something. The next thing I know I hear about the Georgia Supreme Court ruling on television and after that I never saw him again."

Welch: "Did you know rumors have it that Myers was paid $4,000 by family members to represent you during the trials and appeals? What kind of job did he do?"

Banks: "I admit that I was happy to have a Black brother as my attorney. Virginia tells me that he is a good Atlanta lawyer. I believed her until he doesn't get back in touch with me. By walking out on me he was not doing his job."

Mr. Arch McGarity, a graduate of Mercer law school and recently admitted to the Georgia Bar, is representing the State after the retirement of his father, Ed McGarity.

McGarity: "Your Honor, Mr. Banks had hired Myers not once but twice. If he thought his lawyer was doing a bad job, he should have fired him."

Mr. Crumbley and Mr. Welch call three expert witnesses to testify. First is Crumbley's former law professor from the University of Georgia, Ronald Ellington. He states that he read the second trial transcript and notes six points that Myers missed or omitted during the trial. "The preponderance of the six are sufficient to justify a new trial," he says.

They are confident that the two other attorneys, Austin Catts from Atlanta, and Jim Spense from Decatur, can convince Judge

Whitmire to support their contentions. They elaborate on the seven complaints that were submitted to the Georgia State Bar Grievance Tribunal on Jerry Banks' behalf. The tribunal is to decide whether John Hudson Myers should be disbarred. They mention the major grievances. Mr. Crumbley reads a line from the complaint to Judge Whitmire, "Myers is accused of 'abandonment' of his client and the acceptance of fees for services he did not perform." A decision is pending.

Mr. Crumbley also asked his friend and former jury commissioner Willie D. Lemon, (no relation to Virginia Lemon Banks), to testify. He heads up the citizen board who reviews the selection of jurors to the jury pool. In the second trial Banks had an all-White jury. As an expert witness he will point out the racial imbalance of the two juries that had served during the two trials.

Mr. McGarity objects to allowing Mr. Lemon to testify: "There is no evidence to indicate that the verdict was determined by a racist or prejudiced jury." Judge Whitmire agrees, and Mr. Lemon is not allowed to testify and is excused. Mr. Crumbley wraps up his final summation with a good feeling about their chances of winning Jerry Banks' appeal. On March 10th, however, Judge Whitmire denies the appeal.

Later the Georgia Supreme Court grants a hearing on the petition that Jerry Banks had ineffective counsel. On November 7, 1978, however, the Georgia Supreme Court upholds Judge Whitmire's ruling by a four-to-three vote. As a result, Judge Whitmire resentences Jerry Banks to the electric chair and a new execution date is set for June 28, 1979. Accordingly, on June 21st, Sheriff Glass receives orders to transport Banks back to the Jackson Prison where he is to await execution.

***

Meanwhile, attorney Myers is having his share of problems. He has not followed up on an earlier appeal that he had filed on behalf of Jerry Banks in the Georgia Court of Appeals. Such negligence is not looked upon with any favor by the busy appellate court. The Court notifies Myers that he has not submitted the proper paperwork, specifically the "enumerations of error and brief." Those should have been filed within the twenty days as required by law. He is given time to comply. Myers' response is totally unsatisfactory and fails to provide the Court with valid reasons for his inappropriate conduct. Subsequently, Mr. Myers is held in contempt and his name is stricken from the roll of attorneys authorized to practice in the Georgia Court of Appeals.

Mr. Myers also faces a more serious censure and the possibility of having his license to practice law in Georgia revoked. He is required to attend a "evidentiary hearing" to defend his conduct in the defense of Jerry Banks. He must show cause why he should be allowed to remain a member of the Georgia Bar Association. He enters the hearing room dressed as a priest, complete with a white collar, rosary and a borrowed Protestant St James Bible.

The chairman of the five-man tribunal reads the charges and asks Myers for an explanation. Mr. Myers responds, "Forgive me for I have sinned. I ask you gentlemen to grant me forgiveness." The unusual approach in a plea for mercy does not impress the members of the tribune. They vote to disbar him. John Hudson Myers can no longer practice law in Georgia. Unfortunately, it comes too late to help his client, Jerry Banks.

CHAPTER 37 | "It's That Time, Jerry"

Jerry Banks has had a few days to resettle into his new home at the Georgia Diagnostic and Classification Prison in Jackson. This will most likely be Banks' last destination. Crumbley has the occasion to be in Jackson and receives permission to visit Banks. The death row block is composed of small individual cells. Prisoners are watched constantly and are allowed to leave their cell for exercise only one hour each day. Inmates refer to prison as "the stir" because it's a place where you go "stir crazy." Confinement, loneliness, and despair are overwhelming.

Banks tells Crumbley, "If I have a choice, I want to end it all right now. I no longer have a reason to live. I am going to die. It might as well be now." For an innocent man, awaiting execution must be a horrifying experience. Banks refuses to discuss his time at Jackson Prison with Crumbley or anyone. The Warden, Dr. James Ricketts, knowing the fragile mental state of new inmates, encourages the prison chaplain to visit new death row inmates immediately upon arrival.

***

My family friend and fellow church member, Dick Tolcher, has dedicated his time to the prison ministry for many years. He shared with me the discussions he had with the poor abandoned souls who are incarcerated in the Jackson Prison. Counseling those on death row has been especially challenging but rewarding, he says. The chaplain must act as a preacher, social worker and psychiatrist. The chaplain offers counseling to those inmates who seek guidance through dialogue. An inmate is allowed to select a minister, priest or a church representative of his faith. For those with no religious preference, the prison chaplain is there to offer basic counseling.

To new arrivals, the reality of confinement to a lonely cell presents a hopeless situation. Knowing that death sentences are seldom overturned, few inmates are emotionally prepared to accept death as punishment for their crime. While most have no or little religious upbringing, the possible existence of a forgiving God offers a means to cope with despair. Private meetings with a sympathetic chaplain give the condemned inmates the opportunity to express their feelings. Unlike a defense attorney, the chaplain is better equipped to inform the inmate as to what he can expect while he is within the confines of the prison.

The prison chaplains like Dick Tolcher, a Catholic Deacon, make regular visits to the death row cell block. Unlike priests, ordained Deacons cannot perform Catholic services. Their responsibilities are limited to assisting the priests with their duties. Deacons are allowed to marry and hold non-cleric jobs. Deacon Tolbert is married and the father of six children. He makes it his personal mission to provide advice and comfort to the downtrodden prisoners.

On this day, a chaplain introduces himself to the newest inmate, Jerry Banks. At first Banks is a little apprehensive to speak to his so-called spiritual friend, especially a Catholic. As a Southern Methodist, he knows little about the Catholic faith. He has heard about confessions, nuns and all the kneeling that goes on in that church. He reasons, however, that speaking with anybody is better than staring at the blank walls all day. Banks describes to the chaplain the rude welcome he received from other inmates when he first arrived. He tells how one of the inmates described what happens to the condemned once the switch is pulled. Banks described the encounter as just awful.

Banks tells the chaplain, "I am innocent and do not belong in this here prison. I am not like the other bad men that are in here."

"First of all, I want you to know that there have been no executions here and to my knowledge, none are scheduled. In fact, there have been no executions in the United States since June 1967. It was in Arkansas. You must have faith and trust in God. Jerry, I don't know how folks get through life without God. Doing time without God is nearly impossible. Through your belief in God and his teachings you will find peace. The Bible tells of cases where Jesus performed miracles. He brought Lazarus back from the dead and spared Barabbas from crucifixion. Maybe God will send a guardian angel to Jackson, Georgia to help you find a path out of here," replies the chaplain.

Banks continues, "My new attorney tells me that I have a good chance of getting another trial. But after losing two appeals, I don't think it's gonna happen."

"Don't sit here feeling sorry for yourself. Read the *Book of Job*. A man lost everything and was tempted by the devil, but he never lost his faith. For his strong belief and trust in God he is awarded a special place in heaven. What you are going through now doesn't compare to the suffering the families of the victims have endured. God does offer forgiveness to those who ask. Your final walk will be much easier if you and your conscience are at peace," assures the chaplain.

Jerry takes his first meeting with the chaplain to heart. He starts reading the Bible. His anger slowly subsides. "Jesus didn't forsake me. I have forsaken him. I should have listened to my mother. I am gonna start praying again like I used to when Mama made me," proclaims Jerry. His desire to survive the ordeal is strengthened by his desire to be reunited with Virginia and his young'uns. He writes a passage in his prison Bible asking God to watch over and bless his family.

Banks asks about the meaning of the "death watch" and is told by the chaplain as to what will happen. "The process of execution in the State of Georgia is well documented. Once a judge signs an execution order, the warden will meet with the inmate to read him the order. He will give him a copy and ask if there any questions. He then will be moved to a private holding cell with a sink, toilet, and shower, a so-called medical observation area. There is a small area immediately outside of the cell where two corrections officers will be stationed to watch the inmate day and night. The guards who sit in the observation room look through a one-way glass window. The officers call their assignment, the 'death watch.' There is no clock on the wall, but the countdown will have begun. The execution date is then usually two weeks away.

"A few days before the scheduled execution date the guards will move you from the medical observation room to the 'death house'. The twenty by twenty-foot structure is where state-ordered executions are carried out. It is a single-entry fortified building accessed only through the prison yard. On execution day, witnesses to the execution are immediately escorted to a viewing room. Victim's families and other invitees sit on three sixteen-foot wooden benches. A large one-way glass window separates the seated onlookers from the execution chamber. They can see you, but you can't see them.

"Inmates are allowed to select the menu for their last meal served on execution day. After the final meal, the inmate has the opportunity to write a statement which can be read aloud. A prison official will tape record the reading and store it in the prison archives."

Banks pauses, "Can I write a poem? Yea, I will write a poem to Virginia like I use to."

The chaplain goes on. "The prison barber will come and shave your head. Once the final appeal is denied, the warden and the chaplain will come to your cell and let you know that your time has come Jerry.

"From there it's like a ritual. Each guard who volunteers has a specific duty. The whole procedure is rehearsed in advance so, there can be no slip ups. Once the condemned inmate is escorted to the chair, two guards will hoist him onto the chair. Ironically, the wooden chair was built by prison inmates from Georgia pines. Then a group of specially trained guards straps the inmate in the chair, they call 'Old Sparky'. There are ten leather straps that fasten arms and hands securely on the armrests and around your body. If you wish, two minutes are reserved to read the final statement followed by a prayer before the warden reads the execution order.

"The prison doctor administers a strong sedative an hour before hand to relax the condemned. A guard then places the hood over the head. All the guards will leave the chamber. The prison electrician attaches two electrodes to wet sponges at the top of the head and on the right ankle. The execution is over in a few seconds. You should not feel pain," explains the chaplain.

In disgust Banks comments, "Then I'm dead and gone!"

"I have faith in the Lord," assures the chaplain. "If you are innocent as you say, the truth will come out. Trust God. You will not die in the electric chair."

***

Jerry Banks has been in and out of death row for three-and-a-half years. The lengthy appeals process, the new trials, and the stress from not knowing have taken their toll. He has become the victim of a mental health condition that afflicts people who sit on death row for an extended period. This psychologically debilitating issue is caused by a variety of factors: limited exposure to sunlight, isolation, and confinement.

Banks is showing typical symptoms of one who is suffering from death row syndrome. His mental health has deteriorated. He has been under constant observation. He is sleep-deprived as he is frequently awakened for regular bed checks. Although the outward signs are not clearly visible, mentally he has become psychotic. His demeanor is such that he easily becomes agitated and depressed. His depression is accompanied by self-destructive tendencies. Banks has become a very unstable person. Even if his life is spared, his mental state is likely permanently impaired.

CHAPTER 38 | The New Defense Team

Alex Crumbley has been a friend for many years. I had the honor of attending his swearing in by Gov. George Busbee at the State Capitol in March 1976 as Superior Court Judge. At the age of thirty-six he succeeds the retiring Judge Hugh Sosebee. His wife, Claire, and my wife, Lyndy, share a special relationship as Henry County Master Gardeners.

The newly appointed Superior Judge is flattered by an article in the newspaper that mentions him as being one of the youngest Superior Court Judges in the State of Georgia. In another news article in *The Weekly Advertiser* a local reporter quotes a clerk in the Henry County Courthouse. "What do you think of Mr. Crumbley being named as the new Judge?" The usually soft-spoken court employee says without reservation: "He is an energetic and capable man. His roots and a large portion of his legal background lie in Henry County. I think Gov. Busbee picked the right man."

The appointment fulfills Alex Crumbley's lifetime dream. From the time he entered Henry County High School he worked during the summers and sometimes after school. He would help his uncle, Ernest Smith, at his law practice in McDonough. The only job he ever had, which was not in a law office, was for his uncle, Sheriff Hiram Cook. He spent one summer working in the sheriff's office.

As a Superior Court Judge, Alex Crumbley can no longer actively participate in the practice of law. Consequently, he petitions Judge Sosebee to remove him as Banks' defense counsel. His clients will have to find other lawyers to represent them. Alex Crumbley had become attached to Jerry Banks as a victim of the complex judicial system. He is empathic toward him and his family and feels he deserves another day in court. He is determined not to have Jerry Banks abandoned by his defense lawyer again.

He urges two of his fellow lawyers, Buddy Welch and Steve Harrison, to meet with him for breakfast at a small diner in front of the high school. Food Village is a convenient place to meet and talk. He hopes to persuade them to represent Jerry Banks in his absence. Even as competing lawyers, Crumbley has a close relationship with them. Welch and Crumbley have both worked in Earnest Smith's law office after finishing law school. Harrison and Crumbley attend St. Joseph Episcopal Church. All three are University of Georgia grads. The trio is seldom together when the subject of the UGA "Dawgs" is not mentioned.

To the chagrin of Buddy Welch, Crumbley mentions that there are no public defender monies available nor can Jerry or his family pay legal fees. It would strictly be a *pro bono* case. The objective would be to get Jerry Banks' conviction overturned, but at a minimum to get his sentence commuted to life imprisonment. It would spare him from execution and give him a chance for parole.

Crumbley tells them that the case is like a jigsaw puzzle with several missing pieces. Many facets about the murders just do not make sense.

- Why did it take until the next morning to locate the spent shells? These shells should have been found that evening somewhere near where the victims were shot.
- Why did Banks hang around after he found the bodies?
- Why did not Ofc. Tomlinson see blood stains on Jerry's clothes when he met him on Rock Quarry Road? It would have been highly unlikely for someone to shoot two persons at close range, drag their bodies through the brush, and remain void of blood stains.
- If Banks moved King's car, would not he have taken his

dog. He was attached to the animal and did not want his puppy to get run over in his absence.

- Why weren't there fingerprints and dog hairs found in the car?
- If Jerry was flagging down cars while standing on the side of the road, why didn't other passing motorists see him?
- Why did it take two organized teams and countless individual searchers over a month to find three shell casings located only thirty-five feet from the actual shooting?
- Why was the fourth shell never found? Maybe the detectives have not divulged all they have uncovered in their investigation.
- Why does a band director keep a loaded gun in his car? If he feared for his life, why didn't he use it to defend himself?

Another interesting development occurs while Judge Crumbley is at the Henry County Courthouse. He receives some interesting information during the informal reception following his swearing-in ceremony. Cindy Glozier, a reporter from *The Weekly Advertiser*, approaches and begins telling him about an unusual discussion she had with a reliable source concerning the shooting. This person had heard shots at the time Marvin King and Melanie Hartsfield were supposedly slain. Apparently, the incident was reported to Jimmy Glass, but the call was never mentioned during the trials.

From the onset the new defense team has a formidable task in mounting any kind of winnable defense. They must start over from scratch with limited amount of time before an execution date is scheduled. Nevertheless, the young lawyers begin their work with high expectations. Judge Crumbley's brother, Wade, finishes his law studies at the University of Georgia Law School and passes the bar exam. He becomes a partner in the law practice, now Crumbley & Crumbley. With his brother's blessings Wade becomes the third member of the defense team. Wade Crumbley is anxious to put his newfound knowledge to work and test his lawyer skills on this important capital case.

Wade Crumbley and Steve Harrison meet at Buddy Welch's

office to go over a strategy to get Banks out of prison.

Buddy Welch says, "If we are going to get anywhere, we need to talk to everyone Mr. McGarity called to testify at the second trial. I am not bashful in interviewing the Black police officers, Ofc. Tomlinson, Ofc. Lemon and Ofc. Glover. It's been three-and-a-half years since they investigated the murders. Maybe they have some second thoughts about the outcome and will divulge some inside information to us. Perhaps their compassion for one of their fellow brothers will outweigh their fear of getting fired by Sheriff Glass."

Welch questions Ofc. Charlie Tomlinson who was the first officer to arrive at Rock Quarry Road and found Banks and his dog standing on the side of the road; Ofc. Johnny Glover located King's Opel off Tye Street in Stockbridge; and Ofc. Lemon, a member of the police force, who was not involved directly with the investigation, but had knowledge of the goings-on at the department.

Tomlinson responds, "I saw Banks standing on the west side of the road in his hunting outfit. We stood there talking until back-up arrived. Once Det. Barnes joined me, we followed Jerry to the blood-stained roadbed and then to the bodies. Det. Barnes lifted the blanket. It was horrible."

I have known Charles Tomlinson for many years, as a police officer, and inspector in the Henry County Building Department. He said to me the guards told him that Jerry Banks was a quiet and model prisoner while in the Henry County Jail. He had the occasion in July 1977 to escort Jerry to his sister's funeral service at Bentley Hill Methodist Church. Mary Jo had been suffering from an extended illness. He also said that he had the chance to get acquainted with Jerry and questioned whether he was the type to execute someone. Charles is a very compassionate individual. As a police officer, he would rather give you a warning than write you a traffic ticket.

***

Word quickly spreads that a team of lawyers are questioning all the officers and detectives about their involvement in the investigation. They are hoping to uncover evidence that would cast a shadow over the testimony given by them at the trials. Capt. Sugg Howard, who led the investigation, left the department immediately after the conclusion of the trial. Det. Bill Hart, who found the third dispensed shell casing, also left the department shortly after the first trial.

I wonder if these gentlemen were fired by Sheriff Glass or left on their own accord? Both had found evidence damaging to Banks' defense. One would assume they should have been applauded for their fine work and promoted rather than dismissed. The team knows they must find Howard and Hart which would require a lot of legwork. The representation of Banks is important, but they cannot ignore their paying clients. They cannot effectively represent both without help. An immediate priority is finding a private detective who has the time to run down leads and locate witnesses. Something Myers had not done.

Doug Moss has developed a reputation of being the best private investigator in the State of Georgia. As a former detective he is well-connected with law enforcement personnel throughout the state. His number one client is Bobby Lee Cook who handles mostly high-profile cases. The character in the Matlock television series, played by Andy Griffith, is fashioned after Bobby Lee Cook. His defendants all have money and seldom question his exorbitant fees. Usually, the evidence against his clients is so overwhelming that large prestigious Atlanta firms generally shy away from taking such cases. Many of Mr. Cook's past clients faced similar overwhelming odds as does Jerry Banks. The defense team reasons that, with the help of Doug Moss, they can prepare a stronger defense.

Moss, about forty-years-old, is a tall, bespectacled, wide-shouldered, burly man. Moss is all business when it comes to his detective work. He is not cheap, by any means. Once Welch informs him that they are working for free, Moss agrees to reduce his fee. Moss guarantees that he and his agents can find anybody if they reside in the continental United States and are still alive.

Moss calls Wade Crumbley a few days later, "Wade, I have good news. I found Bill Hart in Clayton County. I sent an agent to his house to confirm that he was still living there. He admits leaving Henry County Police Department because he was unhappy with how police matters were being handled. When he was offered a security guard position at Clayton State Junior College, he left. Clayton State was gaining enrollment and needed to expand its security staff."

"That's great. Does Bill Hart know why you were looking for him?" asks Crumbley.

Moss continues, "He was told that it had to do with the Jerry Banks case. He appeared to be a little out of sorts when he heard the name Jerry Banks. He did not open up to the agent. He asked if somebody would be contacting him. The agent replied in the affirmative."

"What about Capt. Howard?" inquires Crumbley.

Moss replies, "I am getting around to him. I knew that he went to work for the Clayton County Coroner's Office after he gave his notice to Sheriff Glass. He did not stay there very long. I figured that he probably went to work for another police department. I checked with the Fraternal Order of Police to see if he had applied for financial help. No luck. I called my gal at the State of Georgia Unemployment Office to check if he had filed for unemployment benefits. No luck there, either. I discovered that he had moved. I checked with his old neighbors and none of them knew where he went. If his children are attending public schools, there is no enrollment record. It may take a while longer, but I will find him."

***

Wade Crumbley, using the information Moss has given him, calls Clayton State and learns that Hart works the evening shift from 4 p.m. to midnight. Crumbley and Harrison surprise Hart at the college the following day.

Hart says, "I have been expecting you. I have a file that you may want to look at. It should help you with Banks' defense."

Harrison, opening the manila file folder is shocked, "This is a police file on the Banks investigation. What are you doing with this!"

Surprised Crumbley adds, "The more important question is why did you keep this information?"

"At the time it was the most important case I had ever worked on," Hart says. "By keeping the notes, I could reflect back on the work I did. I figured one day I might write a book about my experience as a detective. I always enjoyed reading detective mysteries. Sherlock Holmes is my favorite.

"The detectives and I talked to many prospective witnesses. The police department received several calls from citizens that had information about the case. All the detectives knew who the witnesses were and the information they had given. As the trial unfolded none of these witnesses were ever called to testify. I found that to be strange. I was worried that someday somebody was going to come around and ask questions."

Without hesitation Harrison replies, "And here we are."

"Once Banks was convicted the file became more than just a keepsake. I decided that a copy of the entire file could be helpful to have when somebody starts accusing me of conspiring to conceal evidence. I will give you a copy of the file voluntarily with the promise that you do not involve me in your investigation. I have a family and I do not want to embarrass them with my past," admits Hart.

Wade Crumbley adds, "We will do our best. You have been a big help."

To the surprise of the defense team, Hart's file contains the names of numerous witnesses, who had contacted the police department to report specific information about the murders. Other than Eberhardt, none of these names was given to defense attorney Myers. Whether it was intentional or an oversight, the defense team is determined to find out why. With Jerry Banks' execution date set for June 28 and fast approaching, the defense team had little time to waste. In May and June 1979, Wade Crumbley, Steve Harrison and Buddy Welch divide up the names mentioned in the file and begin to interview each one individually. Their goal is to find new witnesses for the defense that could validate Banks' claim of innocence.

***

Raymond Leon Scruggs lives on Chestnut Drive in unincorporated Flippen. He is forty-eight-years old and works at the Lakewood General Motors Assembly Plant. On the day of the murders, he was traveling on Hudson Bridge Road and noticed some activity around a small station wagon. He caught a glimpse of two White men arguing, while a woman remained in the wagon. Scruggs reported the incident to the police, who took his statement. Capt. Howard and Sgt. Floyd signed his statement on behalf of the police department. Steve Harrison calls Mr. Scruggs about his statement to the police concerning the Jerry Banks case.

Scruggs comments, "Cap'n, you can call me, R.L. Yes, I have tried to get the police to investigate the disturbance I saw on Hudson Bridge Road, not far from the Interstate, on the afternoon of the murders. I guess the two men were fighting over the woman in the car. From what I have read in the newspaper about the murders, the wagon may be same make as the band director's car. Maybe it was the White men that killed them, not the Black man, Banks."

Harrison asks, "Tell me why you were on Hudson Bridge Road that day?"

"I had been over to Interstate 75 to get some gas and we, the boy, who helps my wife out at the store, and myself were cutting over to Highway 42 on our way to Decatur. My wife had sent word for me to come by the Majik Market store that she runs," replies Scruggs.

Harrison continues, "So what did you see that day that caused you to call the police."

"Well, we were going down Hudson Bridge Road toward the Interstate and I had me a drink. While I was pouring this drink, the boy that was driving me said, 'Let's stop and watch that cop and that guy fight.' The White men appeared to be fussing and I thought that they were going to fight. The boy who was driving wanted to stop but I said no! I thought it was the police in an unmarked car. What do you want to do, get us both locked up?' I said," responds Scruggs.

Harrison says, "What happened next?"

"Cap'n, we noticed a station wagon and a dark colored Chevrolet. This car was parked in the open field off the right side of the road before you get to the overhead bridge off Hudson Bridge Road where the road crosses over the railroad tracks. The Chevrolet with the radio-looking antenna was right against the rear bumper of the station wagon.

"The station wagon appeared to have a woman inside and two men outside. One man got out of the Chevrolet and was leaning against the station wagon on the passenger side and speaking to the other man through the rolled down window. The driver of the station wagon got out and continued jawing with the other man," says Scruggs.

Harrison asks, "You say the driver of the so-called police car was arguing with the man who had gotten out of the little station wagon? At the same time, the woman in the wagon had ahold of his arm trying to pull him back in. Mr. Scruggs do you think that the two men were fighting over the woman?"

"It's possible, Cap'n. It sure looked like they were having a heck of an argument," Scruggs answers.

Harrison continues, "Did you tell this to the police?"

"Yeah, so, I went on to Decatur and a couple of days later I went to the McDonough Police Station and told them what happened," says Scruggs.

Harrison poses another question, "What color was the station wagon?"

Scruggs: "Not sure, I was studying the fight. I know it was a darker color, maybe dark red," says Scruggs.

Harrison asks, "What was the detective's response when you told him what you saw?"

"He said they would check it out," Scruggs says. "When I called back later the detective said they found no connection with the men fighting and the murders."

Harrison tells Mr. Scruggs that he may need him to testify if there is another trial and thanks him for his help.

***

Moss calls Wade Crumbley to give a report on the missing Sugg Howard who is now doing construction work. He left the Clayton County Coroner's Office and landed at Georgia Power.

Moss continues, "While I was doing a background check on Howard, I found some disturbing information that you may find helpful. Howard was previously employed by the Morrow Police Department. While there, he was accused of misrepresenting the State's evidence during a trial. Interestingly, it was a case involving shotgun shells. He testified that the spent shell that supposedly came from the murder weapon was green. The witness disputed Howard's testimony and proved that he only fired red shotgun cartridges from his gun, not green as claimed by Howard. Those familiar with case suspected the detective had probably tampered with the evidence. I was also told that he had been indicted and then convicted of second-degree forgery in Cobb County. You will need to check that out to be sure.

"I also had an interesting conversation with one of your Henry County Commissioners, Bud Kelley. He remembers hearing gun shots behind the Henry County Courthouse on Friday, one day after the murders. Mr. Kelley arrived at the courthouse as it opened around 8:00 a.m. to take care of some County business. He thinks those shots must have come from the shotgun that Capt. Howard fired. By the way he is living in Waynesboro near the Georgia Power Plant there."

"If that is true, it means Capt. Howard had lied," responds Wade Crumbley.

Moss counters, "Proving it may be difficult."

***

The now-Judge Alex Crumbley had asked Steve Harrison to call Cindy Glozier. She returns Steve's call and repeats the gist of a discussion that she had shared with the Judge earlier. In the process, Harrison arranges a meeting with Chief Collier and Paul Collier, Jr. in Stockbridge.

The City of Stockbridge Police Department is headed by Paul Collier, Sr., assisted by his son Paul Collier, Jr., the city's lone patrolman. Steve Harrison makes the ten-mile drive from his Mc-Donough office to Berry Street in Stockbridge. The police station and municipal building are located across the street from the old Stockbridge Train Depot. Chief Collier and Paul Jr. are expecting him.

Harrison says, "Cindy Glozier from *The Weekly Advertiser* tells me that you heard shots on the day of King and Hartsfield murders."

"Yes, I did," replies Chief Collier.

Harrison continues, "As I mentioned on the phone, a team of McDonough lawyers are representing Jerry Banks. He's sitting at the Jackson Prison facing a possible execution in June. We think he is innocent. We uncovered a secret police file that listed you and others who had offered information to the sheriff's office or to the one of the detectives. The conversations and statements were kept hidden and were never mentioned during the two trials. What you heard that afternoon might help our defense."

"We heard gun shots on the afternoon of the murders, November 7, 1974. I was surprised that the information and evidence that I gave to the sheriff's office following the murders was disregarded, especially since it came from a fellow law officer.

"Harold Rape, Paul Jr., and I were at the Stockbridge city dump on Railroad Street preparing to do some target practice. As you know, my friend Harold is a Georgia State Game Warden. He popped into the office that afternoon and asked if we could join him to test-fire his new 44-magnum pistol. I told him that we would have to hurry because we had school crossing duty and that school would be letting out soon," says Chief Collier.

Harrison asks, "What time was it when you heard the shots?"

"It was about 2:30 p.m. or so. We were in the process of setting up some glass bottles and tin cans as targets when we heard shots," Chief Collier replies. "They were faint but loud enough to hear, so we knew they were fired at a distance. Since it was hunting season, we didn't think much about it at the time. When I later heard on my police radio that someone had been killed that same afternoon, I remembered hearing the shots. Railroad Street is a few hundred yards from Rock Quarry Road and is a mile from where the murders took place. Those shots we heard must have come from that shooting."

Harrison asks, "Could you recognize what type of gun was fired?"

"It sounded like a shotgun to me," interjects Ofc. Collier.

"It sounded like an automatic or a double-barrel shotgun because it was fired rapidly, bam-bam and bam-bam," adds Chief Collier.

Harrison continues, "What direction would you say the shots came from?"

"I'd say in the area to the south of the dump toward the Interstate where it is mostly woods. The shots came from that direction. I am reasonably sure that those shots came from a double-barrel shotgun fired by one person," replies Ofc. Collier.

Harrison asks, "The shots you heard, could they have come from a single-barrel shotgun?"

"From what I read in the newspaper later, Banks' old 12-gauge had to be breached and manually reloaded after each round. The shots we heard could not have come from Banks' gun. I might have a different opinion if there were two shooters firing single-barrel guns, simultaneously," answers Chief Collier.

Harrison goes in another direction. "I also read in the report that you and George Hart went to the murder scene and found some shotgun shells."

"On Saturday, two days after the murders, George Hart, the Mayor of Stockbridge at that time, suggested that we go to the murder scene. Although the King and Hartsfield murders occurred on the abandoned dirt road, not in the City of Stockbridge, the location is just a short distance outside of the city limits. Since we don't have many murders in Stockbridge, we both were curious and wanted to look around.

"We were walking down the old Rock Quarry Road near where the bodies were discovered. Mayor Hart saw two newly discharged green shotgun shells on the shoulder of the road in a grassy spot partially covered with pine needles," Chief Collier says. "I knew it was the right location because there were Polaroid film strips and burned flashbulbs scattered about. Since the shells were found only twenty-five feet from where one of the victims was killed, we were surprised that the detectives did not find them. Mayor Hart made a statement to the effect, 'I think some of those people looking for evidence need glasses. The detectives might have an interest in them.' I called Jimmy Glass' office to report the find. I put the spent cartridges in a manila envelope, identified the contents and left it on my desk.

"The following Monday or Tuesday someone came to my office and picked up the envelope," he says.

Harrison asks, "Did you or Mayor Hart ever hear back from anyone at the sheriff's or police departments?"

"No, sir," says Ofc. Collier.

Harrison tells them he might need an affidavit from them for the scheduled hearing with the judge. "With the new witnesses and evidence, we hope the judge will grant a new trial," Harrison says.

***

Buddy Welch and Wade Crumbley learn from the Hart file that a Dean Floyd had contacted Sheriff Glass and reported hearing shots around the time of the murders. Shortly thereafter, while driving, he noticed a suspicious person parked on the side of the road near the crime scene. Mr. Floyd meets Wade Crumbley in the parking lot of the Matador Inn. The motel is located at the Interstate 75 exit and Hudson Bridge Road not far from the murder scene. There he explains what he remembers had happened the afternoon of the murders.

Dean Floyd begins, "Yes, I was outside, building a calf pen for the eleven feeder steers that I bought at the Mid-State cattle auction in Jackson."

Crumbley says, "When I was growing up, I visited the J.C. Carter dairy near my home. I observed how they raised their calves in portable pens. I learned all about raising calves that day. What is the location of the calf pen that you were working on?"

"It's on Hudson Bridge Road, east from its intersection with Flippen Road not far from the Broder's dairy," answers Dean Floyd.

Crumbley asks, "What happened next?"

"I was about to put up the tools and get ready to pick up my son from Stockbridge Elementary School when I heard the shots. There was a bang-bang, a pause and then another bang-bang. It sounded like an automatic shotgun," Dean Floyd replies.

Crumbley inquires, "Are you sure it was a shotgun, that you heard?"

"Yes, I have been hunting all my life and I certainly know the different sounds that you hear when you shoot a rifle or a shotgun," answers Dean Floyd.

Crumbley continues, "The murders of the band director and his student were terrible. I assume you know about where it happened. How far would you imagine it is from the calf pen to the murder scene?"

"I say it is about a mile," says Dean Floyd.

Crumbley continues the questioning. "You mentioned that you noticed a man holding a shotgun on Rock Quarry Road."

"Yes, on my way to the school I headed east on Hudson Bridge and crossed over the Interstate bridge. As I was about to make a left on Rock Quarry Road, I saw a black van on top of the bank and a White person standing by the van. He had on hunting clothes and was holding what looked like a Browning Automatic shotgun or something like that. It was really shiny, with a brown stock, and the man was standing there smoking a cigarette," answers Dean Floyd.

Crumbley asks, "How long after that did you decide to contact the police?"

"Since the man on the bank was about a quarter of a mile from where those people were killed, I thought it was important that the law folks know about it. So, the next night I personally called Sheriff Glass. I gave him my name and told him the same story that I have told you," Dean Floyd replies.

Crumbley, surprised, asks, "What was his response?"

"He said don't worry about it, Brother Floyd, it's already took care of, and I went about my business," responds Dean Floyd.

Crumbley says, "You have been a big help. I may need for you to put all this in writing."

***

Buddy Welch is able to find Grady Blankenship at a construction site of a house that he is building for a friend of the Banks family, ironically on Banks Drive. J.C. Banks had subdivided his property on Flippen Road and put in a short street so their children could have a future homesite. Blankenship and his crew were framing this house.

Grady Blankenship began as a framing contractor and later started building custom residential homes. Grady, an affable sort, was a frequent visitor to my office at the bank. He was married to Lena Jo, a classmate few years ahead of me at Henry County High.

Blankenship asks, "So what's up, Buddy?"

Welch begins, "Some attorneys and I have gotten involved in the Jerry Banks case. We have uncovered some new evidence that will probably get him a new trial. I have read the statements that you, Mike and, the others gave to the detectives. I need to know in more detail what transpired on the day of the shootings. You say you think you heard the shots that killed the band director and one of his students?"

"Yes, we were framing a house on Banks Road at the time. It was the first house on the left after you turn off Rock Quarry Road onto Banks Road. We were putting the decking on the roof. I was the 'saw man', so I was on the ground. Mike Taylor and his brother, Gregg, were on the roof nailing down the plywood. Keith was handing them the lumber. It was after lunch, I would say around 2:30 p.m., when we heard the shots. Mike is an avid hunter and knows his guns. He said it was double-barreled shotgun," Blankenship answers.

Michael Taylor and his crew framed my father's home and mine. He was an avid hunter and expert on shotguns. Few people have more personal knowledge in recognizing the type of firearm being discharged than Mike.

Welch continues, "From what direction did the shots originate?"

"They came from the direction of the new hospital, Henry General." Blankenship paused and shouted, "Mike and Keith, stop what you are doing and come down here. Buddy Welch is asking a few questions about the King and Hartsfield murders."

Welch says, "I am going to imitate the firing of a shotgun and I want you to tell me whether or not these are the types of gunfire that you heard. The intervals of the gunfire are bam-one-two-three-four-five bam; bam-one-two-three-four-five bam; bam-one-two-three-four-five bam."

"Well, based on what I remember, it seemed like it was faster than that. I heard four shots," Taylor replies.

"Yeah, that's how I remember it, too," adds Blankenship.

Welch then says, "So you reported the incident to the police."

"The next day, after we heard about the murders, my wife Lena Jo suggested that I call the police and let them know what happened. Before I could go down to the police station in McDonough, two detectives came to the job site. They said that they were talking to all the neighbors and asking if they saw or heard anything on the afternoon of the murders," Blankenship replies.

Welch asks, "Do you remember who they were?"

"I think his name was Lemon, but I am not sure. He was sort of big fellow, looked like he hadn't missed a meal." Blankenship says.

Welch smiling: "Like you Grady?"

"No, he was bigger than me. Anyway, he said he would inform the other detectives." Blankenship answers.

Welch tells Blankenship that the man's name is Bobby Lemon. He now works in the sheriff's office. Welch continues the questioning by asking him if he heard any other gunshots that afternoon.

"No, we were doing a lot of hammering. If there were any, we didn't hear them," adds Mike Taylor.

Welch asks, "Are you willing to testify, if we can get the judge to retry the case?"

"You bet" is Grady Blankenship's reply.

***

The three lawyers who have become investigators decide that the information about the shotguns, if true, would rule out the possibility of Banks' gun having been used to commit the murders. Except for Blankenship and the framing crew, the other witnesses who claim they heard the shots, were some distance away from where the murders took place. Did they hear the fatal shots fired by the murderer or did they hear the shots from a nearby rabbit or deer hunter? They need to find out for sure. At the suggestion of Buddy Welch, who owns several shotguns and often hunts, they should conduct a test-fire of his 12-gauge to see how far the discharge sound travels.

Welch meets with Crumbley and Harrison and explains his plan. "Here's what we are going to do. Let's drive to Stockbridge this Saturday. I will take my 12-gauge shotgun. Drop me off on Rock Quarry Road. One of you go to the Stockbridge city dump and the other go to Banks Road where Blankenship's crew was framing the house. Wait there twenty minutes and then come back and pick me up. I'm going to fire my double-barrel Remington two times."

Harrison, who is driving, leaves Banks Road and picks up Crumbley from Railroad Street. They return to meet Welch who is standing on the side of Rock Quarry Road just as Banks had done four years earlier. Harrison proceeds to tell Welch, "I parked on the shoulder of Banks Road near the house. I clearly heard the shots."

Crumbley announces to the others. "Today at the dump, the shots I heard were very faint. It could have been different in 1974. Banks' shotgun and cartridges could have had a louder discharge. You never know."

Welch instructs Crumbley and Harrison to go to the site where Dean Floyd had built his calf pen. "I will give you fifteen minutes to get there, and I will fire the shotgun again."

Harrison speaks as he and Crumbley return to pick up Welch, "We heard the shots, but they were not very loud. Yes, we clearly heard the gunshots. We now have credible witnesses. Their testimony of hearing rapid fired shots should help our cause."

***

The same day Banks discovered the bodies of Marvin King and Melanie Hartsfield, Stephen Jeffrey Lee was found in his Roswell Road home lying face down on a waterbed. He had been shot once in the forehead and once in the back of the head. Lee was the manager of General Recording Company which had several pop chart hits including "Rose Garden" recorded by Lynn Anderson. He was well known to local performers and musicians.

There were three other murders on November 7, 1974 besides Marvin King and Melanie Hartsfield in Stockbridge:
* Carswell and Mandy Carr in Milledgeville
* Eugene Barge in College Park
* Stephen Jeffrey Lee in Atlanta

Investigators had ruled out any connection between the Carr and the Barge victims. Although somewhat far-fetched there appear to be some similarities between the Lee and King murders. In mounting a defense, Jerry Banks' lawyers contact law enforcement outside of Henry County. Welch solicits the help of his friend and fellow Henry Countian, Larry Ellington.

Charles Lawrence Ellington, known as Larry, was born and raised in McDonough. Upon graduating from Henry County High School in 1964, he joined the Marine Corps. After his tour of duty which included Vietnam, he began his law enforcement career with the City of Atlanta Police Department. While working as a policeman, he attended Georgia State University, earned his degree and was promoted to Sergeant.

"Do the G.B.I., F.B.I. or other agencies have any information that might help our case," Welch asks Ellington. "Since both victims were killed execution-style and Lee and King were in the music business, we were wondering if there is a connection."

Ellington replies, "I can tell you that Lee's investigation is under the watchful eyes of the boys higher up. General Recording Company is owned by a suspected criminal, Mike Thevis, a member of the Dixie Mafia. Known for their involvement in porno and drug-related businesses in Atlanta, the bureaus suspect that he or members of the organization might be responsible for the murder of Stephen Lee. He might have gotten crossed up with someone in the organization and was silenced.

"At first my sources surmise, since King was a musician, there might be a connection." Ellington continues, "After further investigation, the agents could not find any evidence that link the murders of King and Lee.

"Sorry, Buddy, that is the best I can do."

***

The defense team knows it will be difficult to discredit the testimony of Kelly Fite. The shell casings that he tested were most likely fired from Banks' gun. When and by whom is the question. Banks emphatically denies firing his shotgun. He claims that he and his dog never saw a deer. To find the answers they know that they must confront Phillip S. "Sugg" Howard and get him on the witness stand. Upon learning that Howard is working for Georgia Power, all three attorneys of the defense team drive to Waynesboro in hopes of finding Howard at his home. Their mission is to confront him about tampering with evidence..

CHAPTER 39 | The New Jail

I had the occasion to visit the old jail during my senior year in high school. I was escorted there by a police officer after having been stopped for excessive speeding in the city limits of McDonough. In all the years the school bus drove by the fifty-by-fifty bricked jail building with bars covering the windows, I never envisioned being locked in there. But now I was only minutes and a few steps from entering the bull pen gate. Fortunately, I never made it past the front office. I received a speeding ticket, a lecture and a warning. "If we catch you driving that fast in our town again, we will lock you up, you hear!" I was relieved and headed home staying under the speed limit.

Although the commissioners authorized various upgrades to the "Old Jail" to defer the greater cost of new construction, the ACLU alleges it is still deficient. The February 1, 1978, deadline for shutting down the facility is fast approaching. The architect's design plan for the new jail is nearly finished. Nevertheless, in November 1977, Federal Judge Hill affirms his earlier ruling and orders that the "Old Jail" be closed. Sheriff Glass is disappointed with the Judge Hill's decision. "I don't know where I can send my prisoners or how I can pay for their board," he vents.

The saga continues as a different Federal District Judge, Harold L. Murphy, on February 21, 1978, grants a 30-day extension after hearing the pleas from the new Henry County Chairman Frank Tingle, Sheriff Jimmy Glass and now County Attorney Edward McGarity. Mr. McGarity is asking for an eighteen-month extension to get sufficient time to obtain the federal funding needed for the construction.

McGarity replies in a despairing manner, "Your Honor, Henry County is $1,500,000 in debt and the taxpayers will not approve any further tax hikes." Sheriff Glass likewise seeks understanding from the Judge, "The jail had been at the twenty-prisoner capacity for some time. We have several prisoners sitting in other prisons that is costing the County $10 a day per inmate. Several of my prisoners are awaiting transfer to Jackson Prison but they say that they don't have room. So, they sit in my jail." One of those inmates referred to in Sheriff Glass' rebuttal to Judge Murphy is Jerry Banks.

To bring the matter to an eventual end, the sympathetic Judge gives Henry County forty-five days to advertise, receive bids and enter into a contract to construct a new jail. Judge Murphy sternly declares from the bench, "There will be no further extensions. Do you gentlemen agree?" Mr. McGarity speaks next, "Thank you, Your Honor. We will do the best we can. We will continue to make the jail our top priority."

In haste, the Henry County Commissioners consider three bids and award the $677,598 contract to Mark Buttrill of M.W. Buttrill Construction Company from Decatur. Mr. Buttrill's company is the south side's most prominent church builder and had recently completed the construction of The First State Bank's Fairview Branch Office.

He is instructed to begin construction of the new jail immediately. It will be located on county land below the administration building near Phillips Drive. County Attorney McGarity proudly states, "The jail should be ready for occupancy within a year."

***

On June 29, 1979, the new jail is dedicated at a special event whereby the public is allowed to tour the new facility. It has been approximately one year since the judicial order gave the Henry County Commissioners forty-five days to begin construction of a new jail. Mark Buttrill, the contractor, is able to bring the new detention center in on time and on budget.

As a bank CEO, I, along with local public officials, lawyers and other dignitaries, receive formal invitations to a reception prior to the public tour. I ask my wife, Lyndy, to join me at the reception. As director of the Henry County Mental Health and Substance Abuse Center Lyndy had visited the Old Jail to evaluate disturbed prisoners for involuntary commitment to the West Central Regional Mental Health Hospital in Columbus, Georgia for treatment. She was curious to see the enhancements in the new jail. She agrees to come.

Sheriff Glass makes a few remarks. "I can't tell you how happy I am to finally get a new facility. It will house sixty prisoners. Our old jail had outlived its usefulness. It has been overcrowded and many of our new arrestees were being sent to other jails outside of the county. At a great expense to Henry County, I might add. The old jail had many security issues. You may not know this but escape attempts had become more and more common over the years. Fortunately, most were caught almost immediately. However, we did have a few to get away. I can tell you that this new facility is escape proof. Please take a tour and see how all future jails will be built."

Police Chief Herschel Childs proudly shows off the new prison cells. All cell doors are open and available for inspection. He invites a church member to enter one of the cells. When he walks into the cell, Chief Childs closes the door behind him and quickly locks him inside. "Have you ever been in jail?" he asks. The surprised visitor replies, "No, I have not. What am I in here for?" Herschel responds in a joking manner, "Forgetting your wife's birthday last week! Well, now you can tell everyone that you were the first inmate in the new Henry County Detention Center." Everyone is amused, including the soon-to-be released grinning church member.

The following week, the prisoners in the "Old Jail" are transferred to the new detention center. The transfer occurs without incident. One of the prisoners who had served time in several prisons for burglary and an assortment of other petty crimes is familiar with how the locks function. He had been successful more than once in compromising cell door locks. One night, after everyone is asleep, he escapes from his cell. He reaches through the bars and shoves a twisted wash towel tip into the lock mechanism. After several attempts he forces the bolt to slide into the open position. The guard at the front gate, however, is able to apprehend him before he can exit the facility. As a result, Sheriff Glass summons the contractor and keeps him there day and night until all the locks are tamper proof. Angry Sheriff Glass expresses his displeasure, "You promised me, Mr. Buttrill, that this place is totally secure! You better make sure that no one else gets out so easily."

The "Old Jail" now sits empty for the first time in ninety years. It will no longer be the home of law breakers. Sheriff Glass announces that the building will be converted into offices. When finished, it will become his office and accommodate the other members of the sheriff's department. When I mention to Lyndy the relocation of the sheriff's department to the renovated old jail building, she responds by saying, "How appropriate."

If Jerry Banks is granted a new trial, he will be transferred to the new detention center for his scheduled trial date. He would gladly give up his death row cell at the Jackson Prison for a modern jail cell in McDonough.

CHAPTER 40 | Ku Klux Klan

From the onset there was a great deal of speculation about who committed the King and Hartsfield murders. But after two trials and two convictions, most assume that Jerry Banks was the killer. Public interest in the Jerry Banks story has all but subsided after the Georgia Supreme Court failed to grant a new trial after his second conviction. To the investigators, district attorneys and the jurors, it is a clear case of a robbery gone bad and murder. The evidence is irrefutable. There is sympathy for the young man, but the poor families who lost their loved ones are entitled to justice.

Meanwhile, rumors are circulating that the defense team is stepping on a lot of toes. They are leaning on the police officers and detectives to divulge hidden details about the investigation. They pledge anonymity to those who will come forward to identify the ones who took part in the alleged conspiracy. They are confident that someone in the ranks will speak up. The strategy shows promise as names of possible witnesses are soon brought to the attention of the defense team. Their success, however, does not come without some threatening consequences.

***

The defense team decides that stirring up public interest in Jerry Banks would be the logical first step. Targeted publicity can change public opinion about the fairness of the trials. Interviews with newspaper reporters revealing the existence of new surprise witnesses should bring into question whether Jerry Banks is the real killer of King and Hartsfield. The strategy works as all three lawyers are quoted in the paper or heard on the local news broadcasts. Old photos of handcuffed Jerry Banks being escorted to jail by a contingent of police officers make the front page. In the same article are the pictures of the three lawyers. Everyone knows who they are and what they look like.

Defense attorneys are duty bound to represent their clients by utilizing all legal avenues allowed to them. But when the convicted client is probably guilty, then the goal shifts to finding loopholes or technicalities in the arrest or trial process. It is an unorthodox means but a legal way to get at a minimum, a reduced sentence. An established lawyer would not take on such a case, but these are young and brash lawyers. Not far removed from law school and ready to conquer the legal system, they are eager to win a major case. Oblivious to the consequences, they are seeking evidence beneficial to their client, even if the discoveries embarrass the Sheriff and his investigative team.

The testimony of new witnesses could jeopardize the prosecution's ability to reconvict Jerry at a future trial. This effort does not sit well with some in the old establishment. These folks are of the mind that justice has already been done. A Black man with a prior police record has killed two innocent White people. These law-abiding citizens do not want to see Jerry Banks released from prison, especially if it is the result of some loophole or technicality. They know that the young lawyers are smart and ambitious. Some say these students are taught in law school to manipulate witnesses, discredit evidence and portray their guilty clients as choir boys. There is a small group of people in Henry and surrounding counties who consider themselves as watchdogs of injustices in the legal system. Their mission is to protect those who are about to be wronged. "It's time to get the Klan involved," they say.

The Ku Klux Klan had been around since the post-Civil War days. The Klan was founded in Tennessee and spread primarily in the South. Since the members are sworn to secrecy, few know who they are. They may be neighbors, fellow employees, or the usher at church. Although some suspect that law enforcement is sympathetic toward Klan activities, it is hard to prove. The Klan has an extreme dislike for Blacks, Jews and Catholics in that order. It has a history of violence and lynching in the deep South. Cross burning and parades are used to show their presence in the communities. The modern Klan, however, uses intimidation to communicate its disapproval of subversive actions by individuals who threaten their Southern values.

The local Ku Klux Klan in Henry County is not considered an aggressive group, unlike those in neighboring Spalding County, which has been rumored to resort to violence to enforce adherence to the long-established White-man rules. The Henry County Klan can be intimidating and have a degree of political clout. Most are racist, die-hard segregationists, and join the Klan for the fellowship. Many enjoy wearing the robes and listening to the emotional speeches at the Klan rallies. The passage of the Civil Rights Act in 1964 enhanced interest in the Klan and increased membership. Atlanta has become the "Cradle of the Civil Rights Movement." The degree of hate and dislike of Blacks varies from one Klansman to another. However, all have one common bond. None want to see the Southern way of life change. They resent those who wish to change it.

This view helped elect Lester Maddox as Georgia's Lieutenant Governor. The most popular Democrat in Georgia, Mr. Maddox came to prominence as a staunch segregationist when he refused to serve Black customers in his Atlanta restaurant. Later he is elected governor.

In the Banks case, the Klan's plan of action is not to carry out violence. Instead, a respected member first makes a polite call to question the reasons for defending a convicted Black man. Then, they make a second call and send a stern letter to each lawyer expressing displeasure for their un-American actions. If necessary, a vehicle parade in full dress passing by an attorney's home would be the final step. By instilling fear, the crusading lawyers are expected to back off.

Members of the local chapter of the Klan meet on a farm off a dirt road in McDonough. Some twenty vehicles, mostly pickup trucks, assemble in the pasture. The Grand Wizard informs the Knights of the purpose of their mission. Standing on a bale of cotton he shouts to his robed and enthusiastic audience, "Our purpose tonight is to discourage these misguided lawyers from trying to free a murderer. A Black man who has already killed three people would kill again if let out of prison. We must protect our wives and children. This killer must not be let out of prison. He needs to find his Maker by way of the electric chair. We want no violence. Our objective is to show the lawyers the wishes of the local silent majority."

I remember as a young boy witnessing a parade of cars driving down now Flippen Road. My sister, Margie, and brother, Joe, and I had set up a table from which we were selling ears of corn freshly picked from the corn field. We never made any money. Maybe it was because the corn ears were not ripe or there was no traffic on the rural road. Then came a parade of passenger cars and pickups with occupants dressed in white robes and were wearing pointed hats. The caravan resembled a funeral procession with some honking their horns while passing. At the time we had no idea who these men in the caravan were or what they were doing on this country road. Later I learned that the group was having a rally at a neighboring farm. Some years later I recall seeing the remnants of a burned cross in front of a church attended by Blacks on Red Oak Road. My introduction to the "men under the sheets" left a lasting impression.

I suspect many Klansman are avid hunters. I often wonder when I see a pickup truck with a gun rack. Is the driver a member of the Klan? The same is true for any vehicle displaying a flag, license plate or a decal recognizing the Confederacy.

I was disappointed. Although some waved, none stopped to buy our ears of corn.

In the news is the story of Raymond Head who had crosses burned in front of his house and his dry-cleaning business while running for a Griffin Council seat. The Klan's attempts to discourage his candidacy for public office were unsuccessful, and Mr. Head later became the first Black mayor of the neighboring City of Griffin.

The defense team receives anonymous letters and phone calls threating them to stop interfering with justice. They are told questioning the veracity of the dedicated and underappreciated police is a serious infringement of their rights. It's not acceptable to undermine the accomplishments of the sheriff and his department. But they are not deterred by the subtle threats from the Klan. While it does make them a bit nervous, fortunately, no harm would come to them.

CHAPTER **41** | August 1979: Superior Court
Hearing

For Jerry Banks, the wheels of justice turn slowly. On June 18, 1979, the defense team files for an extraordinary motion declaring that Banks' rights are being violated. Superior Court Judge Whitmire grants a hearing and stays Banks' execution ten days before the scheduled date. Jerry Banks is transferred to the new Henry County Detention Center while the Henry County Superior Court Judge determines the merits of the motion for a new trial.

This petition seeks another trial based on newly discovered evidence. If the concealment of one witness, Eberhardt, is enough to get Banks a second trial, the plethora of new witnesses should likewise get him another. The hearing does not address Banks' guilt, but whether he has gotten fair trials. There is no jury. The decision rests solely with the judge.

Jerry Banks and his attorneys are back in Henry County Superior Court seeking a new trial for the third time. For the State it will be déjà vu for the individuals involved: the same judge, same witnesses, same testimony, and same evidence. I am told that this hearing, however, will not be like the other two. The defense intends to introduce new witnesses and additional details relevant to the case. Many of these witnesses will be making their first appearance and will provide testimony that Judge Sosebee has not heard in previous trials. I am told the defense team will have expert witnesses who will refute the testimony of the State's expert witnesses. It is quite a contrast from the previous two trials when the defense called a total four witnesses, one being Sheriff Glass. I hope for Jerry Banks' sake that their testimony will lead to a different outcome.

***

From left to right: defense attorneys, Buddy Welch, Steve Harrison, Wade Crumbley and the accused, Jerry Banks

The hearing begins on August 13, 1979, in the Butts County Courthouse. (The Henry County Courthouse is in the process of being renovated making courtroom space unavailable.) Senior and now part-time Judge Hugh Sosebee presides. In July, Hal Craig was appointed as Assistant District Attorney. He will represent the State, while attorneys A.J. Welch, Jr.; Stephen P. Harrison; and Wade M. Crumbley will represent the defense. Tommy Floyd left his position with Henry County Police Department after seven years to become the first investigator for the Flint Judicial Circuit. The defense intends to overwhelm the Judge with twenty-six witnesses, either in person or by deposition. The prosecution expects to introduce only one new witness.

***

Welch: "We'd like to invoke the 'rule of sequestration' as to the witnesses. I would like to ask Your Honor to instruct the witnesses, once a witness has testified, to be placed in a separate room and not be allowed to discuss his testimony or the facts of this case from this point forward until the hearing is concluded."

Craig: "Your Honor, I have no objection to the rule; however, I ask that Mr. Floyd be excluded since he is assisting me in the presentation of this case."

Judge Sosebee: "I'd like to limit the objections through one counsel for each side. I will allow different attorneys to question witnesses provided only one attorney questions that particular witness.

"If we are in agreement, do you gentlemen want to call your witnesses now and let them stand as their names are called and remain standing until all of them have been called so we can see who is here."

Welch: "Those that are not standing are on call and can be here in short notice."

Judge Sosebee: "Now, you have a large number of witnesses standing and some that will be on call. Now, it's going to be rather difficult to find a place that's comfortable for all these witnesses. I don't know how long the testimony will be from any one of the witnesses, but I just anticipate it will be rather lengthy and I don't see any likelihood of us finishing today.

"Let me instruct all of these witnesses. You will have to remain outside the courtroom while the case is being presented unless you are exempt. Now it also means that you should not, under any circumstances, discuss your testimony with anybody as to what was said or went on in the courtroom.

"Before you get started, we need to bear in mind so far as this trial here is concerned, the case is not being re-tried. The Court is here to hear the 'extraordinary motion' for a new trial based upon contentions that there is newly discovered evidence available that was not made available earlier. This information was wrongfully withheld from the defendant and his attorney before the time you gentlemen discovered it. Let's be efficient with the time. If you get carried away with your questioning, I will stop you. Is that understood?"

Mr. Welch calls Mr. Tommy Floyd to the stand: "During the course of your investigation, Mr. Floyd, did you or any member of the Henry County Police Department take a statement from Mr.

Leon Scruggs and if so, was this information ever given to Jerry Banks or Mr. Myers?"

Floyd: "Yes, sir, a statement was taken, but I am not sure that it was given to Mr. Myers."

Welch: "Mr. Floyd did you do any investigation into what Mr. Scruggs had mentioned in his statement?"

Floyd: "Yes, sir, we tried to determine who was in the two vehicles, but there was no way to find out."

Welch: "During the course of the investigation, Mr. Floyd, did information come to you that the Henry County Police Department had received information or taken statements from four carpenters that were working on a house on Banks Road on the day of the murders?"

Floyd: "It was my understanding, although I didn't talk to them, that Grady Blankenship and his workers heard some shots on the day that the murders were committed on November 7th. I believe Det. Bobby Lemon told me and I understand he talked to those people."

Welch: "Was the information concerning the shots used in the investigation in any way?"

Floyd: "Well, it was used by Dr. Howard. The information helped him determine the time of death."

Welch: "Was the information concerning the statements from Mr. Blankenship and his carpenters ever disclosed to Mr. Banks or Mr. Myers?"

Floyd: "I don't recall."

Welch: "Did you go back to the crime scene near the blood stains to simulate the murder?"

Floyd: "Yes, as I recall, I fired in the direction where I surmised Miss Hartsfield and Mr. King were standing. I then fired in the area where I thought they were laying."

Welch: "What did you do with the spent cartridges?"

Floyd: "I ejected the shells. I had a pump shotgun. I ejected the spent shells onto the ground. I picked up the shells and threw them as hard as I could in the general direction where the other shells were found. I was trying to see how the killer disposed of his shells. Whether he walked over there to discard shells or picked them up and simply threw them. So, I threw them, which I had suspected the killer had done. The shells landed in the same general vicinity that the other shells were found."

Welch: "Did you pick up shells after you completed the experiment?"

Floyd: "Yes, sir, as far as I know, we got them all."

Welch: "So, you had to see if you could find the other shells, the missing shells, by throwing your spent cartridges into the bushes. You were hoping that the missing shells would be there, didn't you?"

Floyd: "I think I know where you are going. The shells that were found were red shells. The shells that I fired were green shells. I mean, we knew exactly which shells I fired."

Welch: "Well, how do you know, Mr. Floyd, if these people weren't killed with green shells?"

Floyd: "I don't know, sir."

Welch: "All right, sir. Mr. Floyd, during your investigation of this case, did you obtain any other information that would have been exculpatory for the defense, counsel for the defense or Jerry Banks himself in defense of his case at either one of the two trials?"

Floyd: "There are some statements from Mr. King's, ladies that he knew. Upon taking these statements, I learned that the personal information acquired during the background checks was fairly sensitive. These ladies were told that none of this information would be revealed unless instructed by the Court. I would not disclose the material unless I was legally obligated to do so."

Craig: "Your Honor, as Mr. Floyd said, I think he's probably asking for some direction from the Court. This was background information into the personal lives of the victims and doesn't directly deal with anybody that could have committed the murders."

Judge Sosebee: "If you are making an objection, I will need to make an inspection of the statements before I can rule."

Craig: "Well, I would request that it be done prior to turning them over. I have no objection to the Court looking at them, it's just our opinion that they deal with matters of a personal nature. Some of these people were not married then but may or may not be married now. Some have children. We just don't think this information would lead anywhere and for that reason, we just don't want to air it in public."

Welch: "Well, if Your Honor please, I'm not here to embarrass anyone, but I am here to get the true facts of this case. We have a man that's sentenced to death."

Judge Sosebee: "I will inspect these statements and then see where we are after that. Let's suspend with this line of examination for the time being."

***

Mr. Floyd's testimony regarding the discharged shells being tossed into the bushes by the shooter, might explain whose green shells former Mayor Hart found. Mr. Floyd could have inadvertently failed to recover two of the green shells he used in his experiment. Then, it is also possible that the spent shell cartridges Mayor Hart discovered were fired from the killer's shotgun. That would mean that it was the green cartridges that were fired at the victims, not the alleged red shells.

The hearing continues all day and finally recesses at 6 p.m. The defense calls former Stockbridge Police Chief Paul Collier, Sr., former Stockbridge Mayor George Hart and former Stockbridge Police Ofc. Paul Collier, Jr. to the stand. They repeat the same story that that they mentioned earlier to Steve Harrison at the Stockbridge Police Station.

Dean Floyd testifies he had heard the gun shots that sounded as if they came from an automatic shotgun. Grady Blankenship, Mike Taylor and Keith Ayers convincingly detail the shots that they heard as being rapidly fired. Gregg Taylor, a member of the framing crew, who could not attend and had his notarized affidavit read in court, confirms what the others had heard.

Mr. Wade Crumbley calls former State witness, Dr. Larry Howard to the stand followed by Kelly Fite. Dr. Howard had performed the autopsies on King and Hartsfield and Mr. Fite was the firearm specialist. Their testimony, as the expert witnesses, had linked Banks' shotgun and ammunition to the murders. The defense introduces its own expert witness. Dr. Joseph Burton is a former employee at the Georgia State Crime Laboratory. While there, he performed 5,000 autopsies and investigated approximately 15,000 cases. He is now an instructor in forensic pathology at the Emory University School of Medicine.

***

Crumbley: "Dr. Howard, let me begin by asking you this. Does the Winchester Western shell have any kind of polyethylene packing in with the shot?"

Dr. Howard: "Yes, it does."

Crumbley: "Now based on your examination of the bodies and examination of the wounds, would you say that all of the wounds have been inflicted with this type of shell? This brand of shell that has the polyethylene packing. Then why did you not find polyethylene packing in and around all the wounds?"

Dr. Howard: "That depends on several factors. The distance the shots were fired would determine whether the light-weight wadding reached the bodies. As to the granules, those could have passed through or bounced off."

Crumbley: "You found wadding and granules in the female victim's wound and on the red sweater."

Dr. Howard: "Yes, I did."

Crumbley: "Then would you say that it is more than likely that all four shots were not shot with the same type of cartridge, the red ones."

Dr. Howard: "It's not out of the realm of possibility."

***

Crumbley: "Well, let me ask you this, Mr. Fite. Do you have an opinion about how long it would take to fire that weapon, breech it, remove the shell, insert another shell, close the breech, cock the hammer and fire the second time?"

Fite: "Well, as someone that is familiar with the gun, I would say five to seven seconds."

Crumbley: "I want you to assume that two people were shot with a shotgun two times each and I want you to assume that there is evidence that the shots which killed the victims were fired in rapid succession, say all within a period of five, six, seven, eight seconds. Do you have an opinion about whether a person using that shotgun could have inflicted the wounds in the manner I have described?"

Fite: "I wouldn't think so. I would think it would take a repeating-type weapon to fire shots in that time span."

Crumbley: "Now, let me ask you this: do shells like that, or did they in 1974, contain white polyethylene packing in with the buckshot?"

Fite: "Yes, sir."

Crumbley: "Let me ask you this: in 1974 were there any other brands of buckshot shells of which you were aware that did not contain any sort of polyethylene or other filler material with the buckshot?"

Fite: "Yes, Federal did not have a packing at the time and does not have it now, that I know of."

Crumbley: "Then, what color is a Federal 12-gauge buckshot shell and was it the same in 1974."

Fite: "Red."

Crumbley: "Do you have an opinion about whether it is more or less likely that Remington Peters' shell of that type would leave traces of the polyethylene at a similar range of five feet?"

Fite: "I think it would probably leave there a black residue as did the Winchester."

Crumbley: "Did Winchester manufacture another type of shell that had the white polyethylene packing?"

Fite: "There's a Winchester 00 Buck and a Western 00 Buck. Also, there is the Winchester Western Magnum."

Crumbley: "Now, let me ask you this. In 1974 was there any method at all to determine how long a spent shell casing had been lying outside?"

Fite: "Well, yes, the natural observation of evidence found at the crime scene. There could be spider webs and dust inside the shell or oxidation of the cartridge casings. Things like this, of course."

Crumbley: "Do you remember what the condition of these shells were when you first looked at them?"

Fite: "Yes, sir, they were shiny and appeared to be relatively fresh."

Crumbley: "Now, Mr. Fite, I want you to assume that a person that picked up these shells in the woods, and carried them around while looking for other shells, would tend to destroy any evidence of dust or anything else that might be on the inside of the shell?"

Fite: "Yes, sir, that's possible."

***

Crumbley: "Dr. Burton, when you examined the shotgun, the one that is the alleged murder weapon, did you encounter any difficulty?"

Dr. Burton: "When I breeched it the first time, it fell apart, yes, sir. I tried again and it fell apart about half the time. The stock on the gun is loose."

Crumbley: "Is it your opinion that this shotgun in this condition is unstable to shoulder, aim, and fire. And it is not capable of being fired rapidly?"

Dr. Burton: "Yes, sir."

Crumbley: "Now, Dr. Burton, I want you to assume that you have two people shot four times with a shotgun, twice each. I want you to further assume that there is some evidence that the shots which killed the victims were inflicted, all within say five, six, seven, eight, maybe ten seconds. In your opinion, is it possible that somehow this gun could have inflicted the wounds in the manner I have described?"

Burton: "I would say it would be virtually impossible in less than approximately ten seconds."

Crumbley: "To your knowledge was there a shell manufactured by any other maker of buckshot shells in 1974 or say five years prior to that, that did not have any sort of filler material?"

Craig: "I object to this line of questioning about other brands of shells."

Crumbley: "If Your Honor please, what I am trying to establish is that perhaps the two shells George Hart says he found at the scene could have been more likely the shells which inflicted some of the wounds on the victims. They were of the same type. The same type that had none of this filler material. Dr. Howard has testified that he found no such material on three of the wounds. What I am attempting to show is that it is more likely that the green shells that George Hart found are the shells that inflicted those wounds rather than the red Winchester Western."

Judge Sosebee: "Since no one has produced the shell casing Hart found into evidence, I will sustain the objection for now."

***

The defense team attorneys then proceed to determine who in the district attorney's office has knowledge of the exculpatory evidence in the form of statements made to detectives–some of which were written down, some were not. They subpoenaed a host of people. First to testify are the prosecuting attorneys, Ed McGarity, who recently retired as Henry County District Attorney; Kenneth Waldrep, who was the assistant district attorney; and current District Attorney Hal Craig. Wade Crumbley examines Mr. McGarity and Mr. Waldrep, while Steve Harrison examines Mr. Craig.

All three gentlemen are asked the following questions:

- Did you have any knowledge of statements given to officers of the Henry County Police Department or Henry County Sheriff's Department regarding witnesses who had heard shots in the area where the bodies were found?
- Did you have any knowledge that Mr. George Hart had found some shotgun shell casings at the scene of the murders?
- Did you have any knowledge that a statement had been given to Mr. Tommy Floyd and Capt. Howard by Mr. Leon Scruggs that he had seen a man and a woman in a small station wagon, another man in a yellow with brown or cream-colored automobile stopped on the side of Hudson Bridge Road?
- Did you have any knowledge that Mr. Dean Floyd had in-

formed Sheriff Glass that on the afternoon of the murders that he had seen a black van parked on the side of Rock Quarry Road near the intersection of Hudson Bridge Road?

• Were you made aware that four carpenters building a house on Banks Road, Grady Blankenship, Mike Taylor, Gregg Taylor and Keith Ayers had all given statements to Officer Lemon that they heard shots on the afternoon of the murders?

All testify that they could not remember being made aware of those statements.

Next came the detectives and officers who were involved in some facet of the investigation of the murder case. Charlie Tomlinson and Bobby Lemon confirm that they had taken the statements from the four carpenters. Ofc. Lemon divulges, to the surprise of the Judge, that he is a relative by marriage to Jerry Banks. Banks had married his first cousin. Mr. Lemon testifies that he has no knowledge as to Jerry's guilt or innocence. He tells the Court that he has mixed feelings toward Jerry. When he heard that Virginia was pregnant, he was disappointed in him. But after he married and stayed with her, his opinion of him improved. However, when Jerry Banks shot Robert Walker, he lost all respect for him and was too embarrassed to tell people of his connection with Jerry. When Ofc. Lemon was asked, if Sheriff Glass knew of the family relationship, he said he wasn't sure. But he mentioned that Sheriff Glass took him off the murder case almost immediately.

***

Buddy Welch has the privilege of examining Sheriff Glass. Mr. Welch tries to determine what Sheriff Glass remembers about conversations he or his officers and detectives had with witnesses, who saw or heard something relating to the murders.

Welch: "Who was in charge of the investigation of the King and Hartsfield murders?"

Sheriff Glass: "At the time I went to the scene, the detectives were already there, and they were already working on the case. Capt. Howard stated that he would handle it and I was going to assist. I did not, as you would say, fully turn it over to them."

Welch: "Sheriff, do you remember talking with Stockbridge Police Chief Collier or his son, Paul, at some time after the murders?"

Sheriff Glass: "No, sir, I do not."

Welch: "Sheriff, do you remember receiving a call from Dean Floyd about a black van he spotted in the crime scene area on the afternoon of the murders?"

Sheriff Glass: "I do not know Mr. Floyd and do not recall having a conversation with him."

Welch: "Thinking back, do you recall speaking with Andrew Eberhardt the evening of the murders?"

Sheriff Glass: "I just remember meeting him after the first trial."

***

Steve Harrison asks Phillip Shug Howard if he had kept his boss, Sheriff Glass, informed as to the progress of the King and Hartsfield murder investigations.?

Howard: "Yes, sir."

Harrison: "Do the names Dean Floyd, Paul Collier, Leon Scruggs and Grady Blankenship mean anything to you?"

Howard: "I may have seen one of those names in a report, but as of this time right now, I couldn't remember if I was given a report that included those names. I don't think so."

***

Steve Harrison also questions former Det. Ted Ray, Det. Bill Hart and now Sgt. Glover. All three are asked if they had any conversations with Paul Collier, his son, or George Hart about hearing gun shots the day of the murders or finding spent cartridges on Saturday following the murders. All admit that they had no knowledge of those facts. Mr. Harrison asks if anyone of them picked up the envelope with spent shells inside from the Stockbridge Police Station. All respond in the negative.

***

Mr. Wade Crumbley examines Det. Paul Robbins. Mr. Robbins was born and raised in Henry County. He, Det. Payne and Sgt. Glover are the only ones who worked the King and Hartsfield murders and are still employed by the Henry County Police Department.

Crumbley: "Mr. Robbins, did you ever take a statement from Leon Scruggs?"

Det. Robbins: "There was a statement given by Leon Scruggs. Now, I know about the statement. I'm not sure whether I'm the one who actually took it or not, but I remember there being a statement by Mr. Scruggs."

Crumbley: "Do you remember whether you ever told anybody about it?"

Det. Robbins: "Whether I took the statement or not, everybody that was involved in the case would have been told about the statement."

Crumbley: "Would that include the district attorney?"

Det. Robbins: "I don't know about that; I think the statement was put in a file which everyone had access to."

Crumbley: "Did you ever tell Sheriff Glass about it?"

Det. Robbins: "Don't know whether I told him directly, sir. It was put in the file."

Crumbley: "Were you aware of a statement taken by Det. Lemon?"

Det. Robbins: "Yes, sir."

Crumbley: "How did you come to learn about the statement?"

Det. Robbins: "Because we all were assigned on this case, we all worked on the case, and we kept abreast of what was happening in the case. Whenever someone took a statement, there were four different copies of that statement and each one of the investigators got one. Everybody got a copy of the statement so that everybody would know what everybody else was doing. There was one copy for every team of investigators."

Crumbley: "What was the normal procedure when a detective took a statement? What did he do with it?"

Det. Robbins: "The detective would write it down in long hand

and give it to a secretary to type. The white copy stays in the original folder, a green copy went to one folder and a pink copy went to another folder and so forth. The folders were then given to the detectives that worked on the case."

Crumbley: "Did copies automatically go to the defense attorney or the district attorney's office?"

Det. Robbins: "No, sir, unless they asked for it."

Crumbley: "Where was the original kept?"

Det. Robbins: "They were kept in Capt. Howard's office in his desk."

Crumbley: "Do you know whether or not Sheriff Glass was ever informed of what was going on in this investigation?"

Det. Robbins: "I am sure he was informed but I didn't inform him. I reported to Capt. Howard, and he reported to Sheriff Glass."

Crumbley: "Mr. Robbins, let me ask you this. When you and Det. Floyd went to the site to recreate the murders, did you and he pick up all the spent shells after firing the shots before you left?"

Det. Robbins: "We fired those shots in and around the old roadbed. The discharged green shells were easy to spot."

***

Cindy Glozier was the reporter for *The Weekly Advertiser* assigned to the Jerry Banks case. In August of 1978, she wrote a series of articles taking the reader from the time of the murders through Banks' second conviction. Her investigative research gave her the opportunity to accumulate details that were not public knowledge. She confirmed that Chief Collier mentioned to her hearing what he thought were the shots that killed King and Hartsfield and that they were fired in rapid succession. Buddy Welch questions her about some of the discussions she had with Police Chief Collier.

Welch: "Do you mind saying how you first learned that information?"

Mrs. Glozier: "I was covering a story in Stockbridge. I was discussing the King and Hartsfield murder case with Paul Collier, Sr. He said, 'I believe that I heard the shots.' I said, 'Really!' and he said, 'Yeah.' During the discussion I asked him what were the shots like? He said, 'They were fired in rapid succession.' That was the extent of it."

She goes on. "Mr. Collier told me that he went up to Sheriff Glass with the information and that he told Sheriff Glass that he had thought he had heard the shots. There's no proof that he did, but he thought he had heard the shots from the dump."

Welch: "Did you talk to Sheriff Glass about it?"

Mrs. Glozier: "Later, when I interviewed Sheriff Glass while gathering material for the feature stories which I had planned to publish in the upcoming edition of the newspaper, I spoke with the Sheriff."

Welch: "What was his response?"

Mrs. Glozier: "He didn't believe the information was true and considered it as an unimportant item in the overall investigation. He asked me if I knew how many crank calls, he gets. He said, 'I once had an old lady call me to report that she had been abducted by aliens, taken to the spaceship, and molested.' He said he told her that he would contact the F.B.I., UFO Squad. Of course, such a squad does not exist. I told him that would make quite a story!"

Welch: "Did you receive any other tips from your sources?"

Mrs. Glozier: "No, I didn't. The only other thing in connection with the case, during the time of the publication of the stories, was a number of telephone calls from people in the middle of the night, who told me to leave the story alone. One caller said that my continued interference could be dangerous to my health!"

***

In June 1979, District Attorney Hal Craig, with help from Bobby Lemon and Paul Robbins, decides to determine if it is possible for someone at the Stockbridge city dump to hear gunshots a mile away. It is a similar experiment the defense team had already conducted. The elevation of the murder scene is about 720 feet above sea level according to topographical maps. The dump is of similar elevation. However, there is a hill between the two locations. When traveling north on Rock Quarry Road, crossing

Rum Creek, passing the Broder corn field and the old Clark dairy, there is long, steep hill before you reach Banks Road. From there to Railroad Street, Rock Quarry Road gradually descends. In between the two points the landscape is comprised of mostly trees.

Paul Robbins drops off Hal Craig and Bobby Lemon on the old, abandoned Rock Quarry Road, the site of the murders, then continues ahead to the City of Stockbridge dump. It is approximately three o'clock in the afternoon. They synchronize their watches. At approximately 3:15 p.m., Lemon fires four rounds from a 12-gauge shotgun using 00 buckshot. Immediately after firing the gun, the pair contacts Paul Robbins by radio. Robbins informs Craig that he did not hear the gun shots. The experiment is tried again as another round is fired. They conclude Chief Collier could not have heard the shots.

There are several factors that can influence the results. The murders occurred in the fall when the hard wood trees had less leaves. The murders occurred five years earlier when there was more open land between the two sites. The weather could have also been a factor. The Craig experiment was not as thorough as the Welch experiment. Nevertheless, Lemon's explanation of the experiment while on the stand puts a damper on what had been a convincing strategy by the defense.

When the subpoenaed John Hudson Myers fails to show, District Attorney Craig calls the last witness. Harold Rape, who accompanied the Colliers to the dump site, also testifies that he did not hear the shots. Mr. Rape admits that he was wearing ear plugs while he was shooting. He also admits that his hearing is less than perfect.

What is missing from Mr. Craig and the detective's experiment are that Buster Lewis or Banks Roads sites were not included. Both were closer in proximity to the location of the murders than was the city dump. The shots were heard at these locations.

Whether or not the gunshots were heard at approximately 2:30 p.m. by the six witnesses, whether the green spent shells belonged to Tommy Floyd or the real killer, or whether the suspicious characters spotted in the vicinity had anything to do with murders is not the deciding factor.

The issue at hand is that this information was not made available to the defense and consequently was never heard by the jury. Ultimately, it is the jury who should have decided the merits of the concealed information.

The defense team asks Judge Sosebee to rule on a motion requiring the District Attorney Hal Craig and investigator Tommy Floyd to open the files of the investigation to the defense. Is there other information that will create reasonable doubt as to Banks' guilt? Had the defense team known the existence of all the evidence buried in Capt. Howard's file and shown it to the jury, it could have produced a different verdict. The presiding judge of the March 1975 hearing did not believe the testimony of a passing motorist warranted a new trial. Will the same judge, who has just listened to the testimony of another group of witnesses, render a different ruling? Or will it require the Georgia Supreme Court to overturn his decision once again?

***

Judge Sosebee denies the motion for a new trial. He states that the testimony from the new witnesses would not have resulted in a different verdict. After inspecting the prosecution's case file, the Judge also refuses to include its contents into the trial record. He considers the information in the file as sensitive and personal and has no real bearing on the case.

I was told by someone close to the case that Wade Crumbley met with Judge Sosebee in his private chambers after the hearing.

Judge Sosebee told Mr. Crumbley that he thought the defense team did a good job during the hearing and should be commended for their efforts. It was the first time the power structure in Henry County was tested under oath. They appeared to be extremely uncomfortable while on the stand.

Wade Crumbley politely questioned Judge Sosebee's decision not to grant Jerry Banks a new trial.

Judge Sosebee stated that he believed his decision was the correct one. Jerry Banks had been tried in his Court two times. He had been found guilty both times. Not by him, but by a jury. The hard evidence against Banks was undeniable. Two juries believed he is the killer. As judge I would be doing the citizens and taxpayers of Henry County a disservice by ordering a new trial.

He told Mr. Crumbley that he would have another chance with his appeal to the Georgia Supreme Court. He concluded by saying that one day Mr. Crumbley might become a judge and will have to make the same difficult decisions. With that, he headed to Monroe and wished him the best with the appeal.

CHAPTER 42 | Sugg Howard's
Sleight of Hand

Those who have worked with Sugg Howard have him pegged
as a rogue detective, a "Harry Callahan" type. Like *Dirty Har-*
ry he always got his man. Capt. Howard was hired by Sheriff
Glass because of his law enforcement experience. Henry County
is quickly changing from a rural to an urban community. Interstate 75, which runs through the heart of Henry County, is a cat-
alyst for growth. With growth come traffic issues and increased
crime. The County needs a veteran policeman, and Phillip Sugg
Howard is Sheriff Glass' choice. He has twenty-two years of law
enforcement under his belt. He is promoted to captain with the
responsibility of supervising the small group of patrolmen and
detectives. Henry County is a large county with four incorporated
cities. Some of the cities have their own police departments who
handle police matters within their city limits. However, the authority of protecting the citizens of Henry County is vested in the
sheriff and the personnel he supervises.

Capt. Howard comes to Henry County in June 1973 and is assigned by Sheriff Glass to be the lead detective in the King and
Hartsfield murders. The Sheriff was impressed with Howard's past
high percentage conviction to arrest rate. In less than ninety days,
his team arrests a suspect and brings him to trial. The evidence
the detective team presents at the trial is so overwhelming, that

the jury needs little time to convict. A job well done. Case closed.

***

Sugg Howard is from the old-school. He believes that crooks need to be in jail. The no-good trash who can't hold down jobs and are always in trouble with the law don't belong on the streets. They are the ones who commit the crimes. Howard knows that eighty per cent of the young punks he has arrested are school dropouts. Most of them never amount to anything. What infuriates Howard more than anything is to see these good-for-nothing bastards get released from jail on some technicality. Howard has been heard saying, "That's not justice and something needs to be done. The public demands it. I consider it my duty to do whatever is necessary to put and keep criminals in jail."

A lot has changed since Howard began his career in law enforcement in 1952 and advanced to the rank of detective. The courts established rights for criminals and prisoners. Then, there is the "Brady Law" that makes it unlawful to hide evidence or conceal witness information, especially if it helps the accused. The Miranda Rights must be read word for word before an arrest is legal. Search and seizure procedures have become more complicated. Lawyers now had an arsenal of ways to get defendants off. To Howard the bad guys have more rights than do the police.

Circumstantial evidence is not always enough to get a conviction. It takes hard evidence to convince a juror. Sometimes hard evidence is difficult to find. Eyewitnesses, fingerprints, ballistics and murder weapons linked to the suspect are not always available. When the police are certain that they have their man, the old-school method is to coerce a confession. If that fails, a more devious approach is necessary: manufacturing of evidence.

Howard feels the label "bad cop" is unfair. Yes, sometimes there is a remote possibility that the accused is framed and innocent of the crime for which he is charged. But, the accused's arrest record, and his obvious past criminal activities, suggest that there are certainly other crimes that he has committed. Crimes for which he was not caught. It all evens out in the end. Justice has been done.

Although Howard has many years of experience, he seldom stays in any one place extremely long. Whether it is more money, a better position or dissatisfaction with supervisors, Howard moves around quite often. Before coming to Henry County, he worked for the City of Morrow for two years and one year for the Clayton County Police Department. Likewise, his stay in Henry County lasted only one year. It is rumored that his old-style detective mentality has gotten him crossways with past supervisors.

In 1973, while working for the City of Morrow, Howard was a detective on a murder case: a man was killed with a shotgun. Howard testified that the red shell casings that were found were fired from the defendant's shotgun. The defense proved that the cartridges that killed the victim were green and could not have been fired from the defendant's shotgun. It was assumed that Howard had tampered with the evidence. As a result, the defendant was found not guilty.

***

The defense team meets to discuss the revelations that Doug Moss reported to Wade Crumbley.

Welch begins, "I checked on Sugg Howard. He indeed was accused of tampering with evidence in Morrow and was dismissed accordingly."

"You don't think he mishandled the evidence in our case, too, do you?" Harrison asks.

Welch continues, "Let's go back and rehash what the detectives told the Court about the spent shells. According to Howard's testimony the murders occurred on a Thursday, two shells from Banks' gun were found in the woods the next day and sent to the State crime laboratory on Saturday, November the 9th. Banks was asked to turn in his gun on Sunday. On Sunday afternoon, Howard fired three shots into the dirt pile behind the detectives' office. These shell casings were kept in his desk for nearly a month before they were sent to the lab in December."

"I can't believe that the detectives would lie about witnessing

Capt. Howard test-firing Banks' shotgun on Sunday," comments Crumbley.

Harrison adds, "I can't either. I think he probably did fire the shotgun on Sunday as well. What does Jerry Banks say about when the shotgun was taken?"

Crumbley continues, "He says, he was watching television when the detective came to the house to accompany him to the police station to give a statement. While he was changing clothes in the bedroom, he thinks the detective spotted the shotgun. But he is not sure whether the gun was taken then or by someone else later in the morning. His hunting jacket with the unused cartridges was hanging in the same closet next to the shotgun. The shotgun was back where he remembers leaving it when he woke up late Friday morning. He was surprised, however, when a detective asked to pick up the shotgun again the following Sunday afternoon."

"What if Howard or one of the detectives confiscated Banks' gun the night he was picked up to give his statement? While he sat alone in the detectives' trailer, there was plenty of time to test-fire his shotgun before Banks was returned home early Friday morning. Whoever confiscated the shotgun could have returned it unbeknownst to Banks. That means that Howard could have been in possession of the spent shells fired from Banks' shotgun, when he arrived at the murder scene that Friday morning," Welch suggests.

Crumbley asks, "How did Howard know what type of ammunition Banks was using?"

"He got that information from those who witnessed the autopsy. Plus, when the gun was picked up, some cartridges were taken too. If the murders were committed by a professional hitman, wouldn't he have picked up his spent shells? Why take a chance and leave any incriminating evidence behind," replies Welch.

Harrison asks, "So you suspect the Sugg Howard planted shell casings that were fired from Banks' shotgun?"

"It may be a little far-fetched. But think about this. If Sugg found out or was told that the Jerry Banks who reported the murders was the same Jerry Banks who had been recently released from jail for shooting his cousin. That would make Banks a logical suspect," Welch suggests.

Crumbley adds, "That would be highly speculative."

Welch says, "Ask yourself, why does Sugg Howard wait until Saturday to deliver the spent shells to the crime lab? Why did he not take them up there on Friday, the day they were found? Is the crime lab open for business on weekends? Where is the fourth shell?"

"Here is another thought. Let's suppose the detective who picks up and returns Banks to his home, finds spent shells at his house. Maybe the kids were playing with them, and they are laying there in open view. Maybe he picks them up and gives them to Howard," suggests Harrison.

Welch adds, "Another coincidence—Bud Kelley told Dean Moss. You remember he said the test-firing took place early Friday morning. If that is the case, Howard most definitely had the spent shells in his possession, prior to returning to the scene—during the trials it was never revealed who took Jerry Banks home after he gave his statement. Banks couldn't remember who but knew it was around five in the morning. That was about the same time that Capt. Howard and Det. Hart probably arrived at the murder scene. Banks' house and the murder scene are only minutes apart. It is possible that one of them may have dropped off Banks at his home. While at the house there was the opportunity to return the shotgun without Banks knowing it."

Crumbley remarks, "If these allegations are true then we need to expose Howard."

CHAPTER 43 | The Motive

The most baffling and troubling aspect of the Jerry Banks case is the lack of a motive. Both Capt. Howard and Lt. Floyd testified that they had difficulty determining a clear-cut motive. Eventually, the detectives assumed that a botched robbery was the reason for the killings even though no stolen items belonging to the victims were discovered on Jerry Banks' person or at his home.

Over the years I have heard several possible motives. Most are too improbable to be plausible. To a suspicious mind the murder of a man and a woman found in a secluded spot had to be a crime of passion committed by a jealous boyfriend, a betrayed spouse or an embittered business partner. The incident was not a random shooting but a planned murder. Not by a hunter who by happenstance chose to rob unsuspecting passengers in a parked vehicle. The murder most likely was committed by a professional hitman. Marvin King and Melanie Hartsfield were executed, shot from the rear into their torso and again to the back of their heads at close range.

I remember asking a retired detective if he had any idea what the probable motive could have been. He said "Most murders he had investigated were committed because of dollars, dames or drugs." I was initially afraid to speculate, if one or any of those three had gotten them killed. As it turned out, he was right, one probably did. I suspect it was drugs.

During my college days at the University of Georgia in the 1960s, intoxicants were beer and liquor. Drinking alcohol had become part of the college scene. But by the 1970s, the post-Vietnam era, the recreational drugs of choice had switched to marijuana and cocaine. The "buzz" from drinking alcohol was replaced by the getting "stoned" on pot. Instead of getting drunk on Budweiser or daiquiris, people were "snorting" cocaine and getting "euphoric highs" from hallucinogenic drugs. Addiction to these drugs was no longer limited to the people in the inner cities who would steal to feed their habit. Drug use spread to the suburbs and to upper-class neighborhoods. People of means and fame were regular users. Athletes, movie stars and performers relied on drugs for creativity and to improve their performance. The rapid increase in the use of drugs became a national health problem. To combat the epidemic and related increases in petty crimes, Washington appropriated money for a program called the "War on Drugs." There was a national effort to stop the distribution and catch those responsible.

Recreational drugs and alcohol are always present at parties where there is music and social interaction. Performers and musicians are exposed to this culture, and many are active participants in their use.

***

In addition to being a music director for Jonesboro High School, Marvin King was an accomplished musician. He used his moonlight hours to perform in a small rock 'n roll band. At these events drug use often occurred.

It was in the summer of 1974 when I met Marvin King while he was performing at the Lake Spivey Country Club near his home. My neighbor, Rudy Kelley, introduced him to me. Rudy told him that I was a former high school teacher and that we would have something in common. Marvin was pleased to hear that six of my siblings were members of the Stockbridge High School marching band.

Such an event could have set the stage for Marvin King's eventual tragic death. It was not out of the realm of possibility that Mr. King witnessed a band member making a drug buy in the Lake Spivey parking lot, later catching him snorting cocaine. As a teacher, Mr. King would have considered such behavior as unacceptable. He recognized the drug pusher as the same fellow he had seen hanging around Jonesboro High's football field, after band practices. He mentioned the incident to the authorities and voiced his concerns about drug pushers infiltrating their school. With encouragement from Mark Foster, a full-time policeman with the City of Griffin and leader of the band, he contacted local law enforcement and agreed to assist in the capture of the drug pusher.

Some weeks later Miss Hartsfield, who was babysitting for Mr. King, accompanied family members to the Dairy Queen for an ice cream treat. While they were waiting in line at the walk-up window, Mr. King noticed a fellow leaning over and talking to someone sitting in a parked car. It was the drug dealer. Miss Hartfield had also seen him hanging around Clayton State between class changes. They assumed the long-haired young fellow must be pushing drugs at both schools. "How many students at the schools were enticed to experiment with drugs by this fellow," King wonders.

Based on the information from Marvin King, Capt. Berry from the Clayton County Police Department assigned undercover agents to stake out the schools. A short time later, the drug dealer was arrested. The kingpin behind the drug trafficking, however, remained anonymous.

During the remainder of the summer, Marvin King took every opportunity to learn about the drug activity in Clayton County, especially when it involved students. He became a secret informer for the narcotics squad and was invited to participate in some of its drug raids. As a performing musician Mr. King had a perfect cover and was already familiar with the drug culture. Apparently, he was getting dangerously close to learning the identity of some of the wealthy players profiting from the drug business. He and Melanie Hartfield had to be silenced.

Such clandestine activities by informers are seldom made public. As a result, Marvin King's involvement was not mentioned during the Jerry Banks trials.

CHAPTER 44 | A Path to a Third Trial

For obvious reasons, Alex Crumbley, now a sitting Superior Court Judge, recused himself from presiding over Jerry Banks' hearing for a new trial. The task went to part-time and Senior Judge Hugh Sosebee who heard the arguments from the defense team. He finally ruled on January 15, 1980, to deny the motion for a new trial.

Citing failure to comply with the "Brady Law" as the cause, the defense team petitions the Georgia Supreme Court and is granted a hearing. The "extraordinary motion" as it is called, for a new trial is argued on May 13, 1980, in front of Chief Justice Hiram K. Undercofler. Henry County District Attorney E. Byron Smith, Assistant District Attorney Hal Craig, and Attorney General Arthur Bolton represent the State of Georgia.

The petition identifies a cache of new evidence that has surfaced after the second trial. Again, the Georgia Supreme Court is asked to review the omissions and errors of Jerry Banks' previous trial. The primary issue is the suppression of evidence. The team hopes that the testimony by those who reported hearing shots fired in rapid succession the afternoon of the killings, would rule out Jerry Banks' breach-loading, single-shot shotgun as the murder weapon.

The justices take into consideration testimonies of the four carpenters, who were framing a house, a farmer building a calf pen and two city policemen all of whom heard shots at the time of the shootings. In addition, there is testimony from two motorists, who spotted suspicious individuals in the area of the murder scene. There are statements from two individuals who found other spent cartridges near the apparent location of the shooting. The most convincing testimony came from ballistic experts who testified that Banks' shotgun could not have been fired in rapid succession, that no less than five seconds was necessary to break the gun, throw out the spent shell, reload and re-fire. The timing could have been longer if considering that the stock was loose. When test-fired, the shotgun came apart fifty percent of the time upon breaking. The ejector no longer threw out the empty shells after firing. The ballistics experts also noted that only one of the wounds contained the white polyethylene packing granules unique to the Winchester-Western 00 shells that were linked to Banks' shotgun.

As a result, the Georgia Supreme Court on June 9, 1980, re-verses the Henry County trial court ruling and orders that Jerry Banks receive a new trial. Only one justice dissents. The State's high court rules: "Given the circumstantial nature of the case against him, we cannot say that the new evidence would not have resulted in a different verdict. This is especially true, where, as here, there is so much new evidence. Thus, creating real doubt that Jerry Banks has heretofore received a fair trial."

Jerry Banks is subsequently transferred, once again, from Georgia Diagnostic and Classification Prison in Jackson to the Henry County Detention Center to await a new trial.

***

The new trial ruling by the Georgia Supreme Court remands the Jerry Banks' case back to the Henry County Superior Court. Judge Andrew Whalen from the Griffin Judicial Circuit will preside over the third trial tentatively scheduled for January 1981. Judge Wha-len schedules a pre-trial hearing. Most of these hearings give the judge, prosecuting attorney and defense attorney time to discuss the charges, review the evidence and subsequently make motions.

The judge would lay the foundation as to how and when the case would be tried. During the hearing, the opposing attorneys have the opportunity to negotiate a plea bargain for the defendant.

Judges Sosebee and Whitmire had presided over the previous jury trials and the local appeals. The outcomes of those did not favor Banks. When it was announced that a different judge from outside the circuit would hear the case, I and the defense team were cautiously optimistic. Having a judge who is introduced to the facts of the case for the first time and has no preconceived knowledge of the intricate and complex details would most likely benefit Banks.

In the meantime, the much-discussed King and Hartsfield murder investigation and trial continue to make front page news. All the details of the gruesome murders and testimony of the witnesses are told and retold. People read with keen interest all the pre-trial hype in the papers. It is the type of information that gets ingrained in one's memory. For the detectives and attorneys six years have passed. They have experienced numerous other arrests, trials and convictions since the 1974 murders. None, however, compared to the King and Hartsfield murders and the subsequent arrest and convictions of Jerry Banks.

Welch, Harrison and Wade Crumbley have waited for more than two years for this moment. It is obvious that the three attorneys are well-prepared. The three have spent countless hours and money in preparation of doing what John Hudson Myers was unable or unwilling to do: get Jerry Banks acquitted. The number of subpoenas issued to potential witnesses far outnumber the total from the previous trials. They plan to bombard Judge Whalen with a slew of motions. It should be an interesting hearing and with much more drama, one that could not have been written better by a Hollywood movie scriptwriter.

***

The November 3, 1980, pre-trial evidentiary hearing permits the defense team to explore the possible violations of the "Brady Rule" by the investigators and the prosecution. The thrust of the hearing will be to identify evidence that was known but not revealed to the defense. The defense has several motions to present. The Georgia Supreme Court, in its ruling, allows the defense team a great deal of latitude in calling and questioning witnesses. Taking advantage of the opportunity, the defense team files a fourteen-page request for information. It includes numerous questions for the detectives about facts that may have been uncovered while investigating the case but were not made public. The answers could be useful to the defense. It puts the burden on the investigators to disclose all. As witnesses for the prosecution, the detectives would be subject to impeachment if their testimony is untruthful. Accordingly, the judge could throw out their testimony and consequently weaken the State's case against Banks.

Crumbley: "Your Honor, we have subpoenaed—I don't exactly know how many—somewhere in the neighborhood of thirty witnesses. Some of them are not here."

Judge Whalen: "It appears you have subpoenaed a bus-load of folks."

Crumbley: "Jim West, who has information about Mr. King, has pneumonia and is not here. Dean Floyd is here. Greg Taylor is in the U.S. Air Force. We intend to use his deposition. Charles Thompson and Rose Fisher are here. Leon Scruggs has brought us a doctor's excuse. He is recuperating from back surgery. He is an important witness. Paul Collier, Sr.; Paul Collier, Jr.; Grady Blankenship; Randy Rivers; Billy Payne; Robert O. Lynch; Andrew Eberhardt; Bud Kelley; Bobby Lemon; Edward E. McGarity; Paul Robbins; Johnny Glover; Jimmy Glass; Tommy Floyd; Hal Craig; Charles McCarter; Mike Taylor; and Keith Ayres—all these witnesses are here or available on short notice. Your Honor, neither Mr. nor Mrs. Walker can be found."

Judge Whalen: "Are they important witnesses?"

Crumbley: "From the investigative files obtained from detectives, a report stated that Mr. Walker and his wife had seen King's car along with an unidentified vehicle parked off of Hudson Bridge Road shortly before the murders. We believe that their testimony would be relevant and necessary to these proceedings. I understand they have moved, and no one knows where they are.

"Jim Stewart was a reporter with *The Atlanta Constitution* and presently resides in Massachusetts. He has agreed to fly down, but the Court would have to bear the expense."

Judge Whalen: "What is the nature of his testimony?"

Crumbley: "He will testify concerning certain statements that were made to him by Sheriff Glass and Mr. P. S. Howard. The same is true for Allan Lipsett who is also a newspaper reporter. He lives in Kingsland. It would cost $190 to fly him in."

Judge Whalen: "Go ahead and pay for their travel."

Crumbley: "Mark Foster, C. R. Barnes, Judge Hugh Sosebee, Kenneth Waldrep, Keith Martin, Ted Ray, Bill Hart, Bill Berry, Ray Foles and John H. Hart are here. But we have spent a great deal of time and energy trying to locate Mr. Sugg Howard. His testimony as chief of detectives is absolutely necessary. We know where he lives, but the local sheriff's deputies are unable to serve him. We are told by the Early County Sheriff's Department that they have a warrant out for him. He appears to be a fugitive from justice. They will continue to look for him."

***

The defense team had anticipated that former Capt. Howard would be reluctant to come to Henry County and testify after they confronted him in Waynesboro, Georgia. Returning from his construction job at the Georgia Power Plant, Sugg Howard was surprised to find the defense team parked in his mobile home driveway. He denied tampering with the shotgun shell casings and had a sudden lapse of memory when asked about the undisclosed witnesses. A good investigator knows when a suspect is probably lying. The eyes and body language are the best clues. The constant blinking, avoiding eye contact, fidgeting movements are always good indicators. Sugg Howard exhibited most of those characteristics when peppered by Buddy Welch's hardline questions. Welch is a master at intimidating witnesses and making them feel extremely uncomfortable. Howard's telltale signs combined with his nervous behavior convinced the defense team that he was hiding something. They could not wait to get him on the witness stand.

Crumbley continues to identify the list of subpoenaed witnesses; "Ed Jones, Charles Moss, Kelly Fite, and Dr. Howard are on call, as are Catherine Churchill, Roger Parian, Elizabeth Thompson, Steven T. Carpenter and James Howard. All are employees with the Georgia Crime Lab. Gary Hendricks, Dr. Allan Pierce, a professor at Georgia Tech, and Dr. Burton are on call. The next witness, Eddy Buchannan lives somewhere in California. He was with Leon Scruggs. Again, it is the defense's position that all these people need to be found. It would be prejudicial not having them testify and thus not allowing Banks to receive a fair trial."

Since the transcript of the previous hearing includes the testimonies given by those who had heard gun shots, those witnesses are excused. The remaining witnesses are sequestered.

Mr. Wade Crumbley, leads off by naming the forty-four requests for information, documents or physical evidence that the defense insists it is entitled to under their interpretation of the Brady decision. The first matter addresses the admissibility of the shotgun as evidence. Knowing when the shotgun was first taken from Jerry Banks would be a key point. Det. Barnes is examined and reiterates that it was taken at the request of Capt. Howard on the afternoon of Sunday the 10th. In rebuttal, Jerry Banks is called to testify. He tells the Court that he recollects that his shotgun was picked up on Friday morning the 8th. Banks, however, is very vague on the details and cannot identify the officer who came to his house. He remembers being alone. The children were next door and Virginia was at work. Banks also testifies that he was not given a search warrant nor was he told that he had the legal right to refuse the surrender of the shotgun. Banks further states that the gun was probably returned sometime while he was in McDonough giving his statement at the detectives' trailer.

The defense team's strategy is to ask a litany of questions seeking specific answers from those who participated in the two trials. Included in the process are Judge Sosebee, the district attorneys and their assistants, Sheriff Glass, all the detectives, members of the press and the Georgia Crime Lab. All are quizzed in hopes that their answers will shed light on some of the remaining mysteries of the murders. At the same time, the defense team is attempting to impeach those they can prove provided false testimony. The most often asked question to those under oath is, "Did you conceal, destroy or tamper with any of the evidence?" The standard reply is "no," or "I don't recall."

Sheriff Glass is asked if he, or if he knows who, interrogated serial killer John Paul Knowles. Is there a written statement concerning Knowles' possible connection to the King and Hartsfield murders? If the police officers believed he was a suspect, that would be exculpatory evidence. Sheriff Glass responds in the negative.

Mr. Welch questions members of the crime lab about the list of missing evidence. No one has any knowledge as to who misplaced or discarded the items on the list Mr. Welch provided the Court. The members of the press, Robert Lynch and Allan Lipsett, are asked where they obtained the information for their newspaper articles. Is there a secret informant? No one had any knowledge of a "deep throat."

Mr. Wade Crumbley asks Kelly Fite if he examined the red 12-gauge shotgun shell casing that was taken to the crime lab by Ed Jones and Jim Howard on December 13, 1974. The two gentlemen were employed by the Georgia Crime Lab and were participating in the search. Upon referring to his official report, Mr. Fite replies, "In my opinion, it was not shot from Banks' gun. The cartridge casing had similar markings but was old and the area around the primer was rusted. The compression was completely different from his test cartridge casings." In previous testimony, he had stated that all the shell cartridges delivered to the crime lab and tested were a likely match. Apparently, Mr. Fite was wrong about the third shell casing.

As a further example, too many statements from witnesses were concealed from the defense, Mr. Welch examines a previously undisclosed motorist. Mr. McCarter was driving south on Rock Quarry Road when he spotted Jerry Banks standing on the shoulder. He reported the sighting to Randy Rivers, the police department's spokesman, and Det. Billy Payne the day following the murders. Mr. McCarter agrees to testify.

McCarter, "Saturday, the next day, the three of us along with Det. Barnes went to the site and looked around. From there we went toward a field road that turned off Banks Road which runs in the direction of Tye Street. The area is where King's car was discovered." Mr. McCarter had not been asked to testify at the two earlier trials.

The existence of the shoe prints was not mentioned in the previous trials. Defense Attorney Welch questions former Lt. Tommy Floyd about the footprints.

Welch: "Mr. Floyd, tell the Court if you or anyone did investigative work on the shoe or boot prints left at the scene?"

Floyd: "There were a set of shoe prints found at the murder site and at the location where Marvin King's car was found, both prints were similar."

Welch: "What were the measures taken to record these prints?"

Floyd: "Well, after checking both sites, we determined they were very similar, and Capt. Howard instructed me to just draw a sketch of the prints on a piece of paper."

Welch: "Did you have the occasion to take Mr. Banks' boots to the murder scene and to the site of King's abandoned car to see if it was his boots that left a similar indentation?"

Floyd: "No, I did not, and I do not know if anyone from law enforcement checked out Banks' boots."

Mr. Welch asks Mr. Floyd if other suspects were considered. "Mark Foster was questioned more than once, but he was not considered a suspect," Mr. Floyd tells him. "Mamian Webster, Banks' cousin who initially said that he was with Jerry Banks on November 7th, was questioned several times. We figured he was mistaken about being with Banks that particular day because the weather wasn't like he described when questioned. We subsequently removed Mr. Webster from our suspect list."

Welch: "You removed Mamian Webster from the suspect list even though he admitted accompanying Banks on the hunting trip. You say he couldn't remember the weather conditions that day. Was that the sole reason?"

Floyd: "No, when we learned that Webster owned only a 16-gauge shotgun, we knew he could not have been the shooter. So, we turned our attention to Banks."

Welch: "Tommy, do you have knowledge of any information

about Mr. King or Miss Hartsfield that the defense should know?"

Floyd: "Since the victims were residents of Jonesboro and Morrow, the Clayton County Police Department did their own investigation. Their main focus was to determine who had a motive to kill them. The execution-style murders led them to believe that a paid hitman may have been the killer. I was told the Clayton County detectives also contacted the G.B.I. and inquired about the possible involvement of criminal organizations. There are known rings in Atlanta that deal in stolen goods, loan sharking, pornography and illegal drugs. Capt. Berry told me that Marvin King had earlier provided information to his department that led to the arrest of a drug pusher. After questioning the arrested, his detectives found no reason to think the drug pusher was involved in a so-called revenge killing of King and Hartsfield. Furthermore, prior to their deaths, neither had reported any threats against their person to the police department."

Mr. Floyd is asked if the area where King's car was found was a frequent parking spot used by them. He states that there is no evidence of that being the case. He also asked about the details of a 25-caliber pistol that was found in King's car.

Mr. Floyd says, "The gun was turned over to Mrs. King."

Mr. Floyd was further asked, "If the fact that Mr. King had a gun in his car, didn't it raise the question, why didn't he defend himself?" Mr. Floyd, shrugging his shoulders, offered no explanation.

Mr. Floyd does reveal new facts about the investigation, some of which can be considered as exculpatory. When asked why the police department had concealed information, Mr. Floyd sums up his testimony in a terse response, "Frankly, Mr. Welch, in 1975 I had never heard of the word 'exculpatory' much less knew what it meant."

The pre-trial hearing concludes on Monday evening, November 3rd. Witnesses who are unable to attend can expect to be subpoenaed to testify at the future jury trial. In total, the defense team files sixteen motions. Judge Whalen rules on seven of the motions and indicates that the rulings of other nine would be forthcoming at later dates. The defense does not expect to get favorable rulings on all the motions, but because of the Brady decision they have obtained the answers to some pertinent questions useful in the upcoming trial.

Mr. Harrison's motion to suppress the introduction of Banks' shotgun into evidence is overruled. Mr. Wade Crumbley's request for copies of all the investigative files held by the district attorney's office related to the Banks' case, be turned over to the defense. These would include written or oral statements made to police by private citizens who were never mentioned or introduced during the trials. Judge Whalen overrules the motion but does allow the Court to conduct an inspection of the district attorney's files to determine if there is anything in there to which the defense is entitled.

Judge Whalen grants Mr. Welch's motion to classify Jerry Banks as a pauper, thereby requiring the Court to pay the expenses of an expert witness and an investigator. Mr. Welch informs the Judge, "There are another sixty or seventy witnesses out there who my team and I were unable to contact. Furthermore, the defense should have the right to have physical evidence examined by someone outside of law enforcement." Judge Whalen caps the amount for expert witnesses at $6,000.

The prosecution is ordered to deliver to the defense team a complete copy of written scientific reports that it intends to introduce against the defendant prior to the trial. The defense can then engage an expert of its choice to make an independent examination of those items of evidence. Judge Whalen does not fix a dollar amount for which Henry County will be responsible, but the County will be required to pay a reasonable amount for the service. Judge Whalen, however, does not go along with the defense requiring Henry County to pay the cost of another investigator to aid in the preparation of the defense. The pauper status motion takes some of the pressure off the defense team in finding the money to pay these experts.

The final motion is delivered in a climactic fashion by attorney Buddy Welch who states, "The charges against Jerry Banks should be dismissed because the prosecution has lost or disposed of certain evidence. These include items that were presented as evidence at the first two trials. The length of time that has lapsed make it difficult for witnesses to recall all the details of the case. The obvious prosecutorial misconduct by concealing evidence from the defense would constitute double jeopardy if Jerry Banks is tried a third time."

The dismissal is a long-shot motion since Banks was never acquitted at either trial. Judge Whalen takes the motion under advisement.

In December Judge Whalen denies the motion and states that the trial will go on as scheduled.

Part IV

Release and Vindication

CHAPTER 45 | Meeting with District Attroney

A June 1980 petition to the Georgia Supreme Court resulted in a ruling that gave Banks a new trial. The justices determined that Jerry Banks was denied his rights under the provisions of the "Brady Rule." The pre-trial hearing before Judge Whalen on November 3rd gave the defense team the opportunity to visually dig into the files of the prosecution. They were also able to question numerous witnesses about details of the case that had not been previously revealed. The defense team senses that they have successfully dented the armor of the State of Georgia's case against Jerry Banks. Witness credibility and the legitimacy of the physical evidence were put into question. Nevertheless, the motion to dismiss the indictment against Banks was denied by Judge Whalen.

Those who closely followed the pre-trial hearing assumed that Banks would be granted a third trial. I have never known or heard of an accused being tried three times for the same crime, convicted twice and sentenced two different times to die in the electric chair. I guess Jerry Banks is on the verge of making judicial history in Henry County. I asked some of the older practicing attorneys if they could recall another situation like defendant Jerry Banks' multiple trials. No one had any recollection of a defendant being tried by a jury three times, but it was about to happen in Henry County Superior Court.

The decision comes as a surprise to the townspeople. There are those who think if the appellate courts continue to find errors in the lower court rulings, then Banks must not have gotten a fair trial and deserves another; there are those who think he is guilty, and a third jury trial is waste of taxpayer money; and then there are those who have no opinion or could care less. The third trial is set for January.

***

It has been nearly six years since Jerry Banks was convicted of the murders. Much has changed with the participants who investigated the murders, prosecuted the case and defended Banks. Most of the detectives who found the key evidence are no longer employed by the Henry County Police Department. Capt. Howard left immediately after the first trial, Det. Hart a few months later and Det. Ray the following year. The lead investigator, Lt. Floyd, is now an investigator for the Flint Judicial Court and assists the district attorney's office. Sheriff Glass lost control over the police department and his duties are limited to the jail and courts. The construction of the new detention center is complete and scheduled for occupancy. Jerry Banks original defense attorney, John Hudson Myers, is long gone. In his stead is an energetic team of lawyers who are determined to get Jerry Banks acquitted.

The news of a new trial does not sit well with all the witnesses. Most have already been subpoenaed multiple times to testify in the Banks case. Seldom are members from the crime lab expected to testify on the same case so many times and so long after the crime was committed. Each time during such a process, physical evidence was packed up, transported to court, examined, repacked and transported back to the crime lab. It is no wonder that evidence got misplaced or lost. Details of murders have become vague in the minds of the investigators. Those without notes have a hard time remembering the details. The defense team knows the State's case against Jerry Banks is in jeopardy. They meet with District Attorney Smith to persuade him to make a deal and avoid a third jury trial.

***

Buddy Welch and Wade Crumbley confront District Attorney Byron Smith in his office. "You have listened to the new witnesses at Judge Whalen's hearing and are familiar with their testimonies. Since the hearing, we have learned of other possible witnesses who we can subpoena for the defense," they tell him.

Crumbley continues, "There is new testimony from Kelly Fite where he testifies that one of the shell casings brought to him and tested was not fired from Banks' gun. He also mentions that the wadding, inherent only to Winchester Western cartridges, was found only around one of the wounds. Not all four, which should have been the case. Our expert testified that Banks' old shotgun, in its present condition, could not have been fired in rapid succession, thus confirming what our witnesses heard. The body of new evidence gives rise to the fact that in all probability Jerry Banks was not the shooter."

Welch with a stern expression says, "Byron, when we go to trial, I will present the former Stockbridge Police Chief, the former Mayor of Stockbridge, and a former Henry County Commissioner as witnesses. These people are respected in Henry County and have no personal agenda for not telling the truth, even if it embarrasses some folks."

Smith replies, "If you are talking about those who heard the gun shots, Hal Craig proved that the Colliers could not have heard gun shots while at the city dump. It is too far away."

Welch continues, "Well, we have an expert witness who will testify that on a cold day gunfire can be heard a distance in excess of a mile away. Plus, it will be hard to dispute the testimony of the carpenters who were eight hundred yards away and much closer."

"I believe the citizens of Henry County deserve another trial. My office is duty-bound to keep violent criminals in jail," Smith says.

Welch goes on, "Nevertheless, the number of new witnesses who have come forward since the last trial will overwhelm the jurors. We will use words like 'railroaded', 'framed' and 'conspiracy' in our address to the jury. They will feel compassion for a young Black man who they perceive to have been wronged by the legal system."

"That's a chance we'll have to take," replies Smith reluctantly.

Welch continues the persuasion, "I must tell you that we have done an extensive background check on former Capt. Howard. You are not going to like what we have uncovered. Once all our evidence is presented in Court, the newspapers are going to have a field day. It will be an embarrassment to those in the district attorney's and sheriff's offices."

Crumbley adds, "Criminal charges may be forthcoming against some of the individuals who obviously lied under oath. The ACLU and the NAACP will be down here. There will be lawsuits. Do I need to go on?"

Welch follows. "Without definitive evidence that the spent shells came from Banks' gun, the State just doesn't have a case. We may not be able to prove that Capt. Howard tampered with the shells, but his prior misconduct will certainly discredit him. He committed perjury in two previous cases, one involved a shotgun and he pleaded guilty to a forgery charge. If the State tries Banks again, I don't think you are going to get a conviction with tainted evidence. Your solid case against Jerry Banks has been compromised."

"Byron, I think it's time to put this matter to rest," Crumbley pleads. "It's been six years. Everyone involved with the case has made mistakes. I am talking about the Sheriff, the detectives, the district attorneys, the crime lab, the judges, the defense attorneys, (including us) and Jerry Banks. Admit it. The young man did not get a fair trial."

District Attorney Smith, who inherited the case, did not particularly like what he was being told, but he knows it is true. Having sat through the pre-trial hearing and seeing his prosecution case against Banks ambushed by the defense team, he knows he faces an uphill battle.

Smith tells the three defense attorneys, "I will discuss our options with Judge Whalen."

Three days after the meeting, Byron Smith announces he will not prosecute the case. On December 21, Judge Whalen signs the order to drop the indictment and to release Jerry Banks from prison in time for Christmas.

CHAPTER 46 | The Drug Bust

While Jerry Banks and the defense team were anxiously waiting on Judge Whalen's ruling on their petition for a new trial, a secretive meeting was taking place in Sheriff Glass' office.

Attorney Larry Tew meets with Sheriff Glass and tells him that he has clients who want to fly a shipment of prescription medication to Henry County. They can sell them on the black market in the Atlanta area and make a bundle of money. Larry conveys to Glass that for him to get involved, he needs a partner. "They would like to land at Berry Hill Airport. They will pay us $30,000 if no one gets in the way of the delivery. Are you interested?" asked Tew.

Sheriff Glass replies, "You don't need me. Nothing ever happens at that airport."

"That's just it. It is a fly-in airport," Tew tells the Sheriff. "The residents are a close-knit group. They all know one another, and all recognize one another's planes. When an unidentified plane lands at Berry Hill, somebody is going to get curious, especially if it's unloaded after dark."

Sheriff Glass follows, "You know you can be in a heap of trouble if you are found out. But should you decide to go through with this, I can look the other way. However, I expect some money for my participation. I will get the cooperation of Bill Hinton, whose family owns Berry Hill Airport and Chief Herschel Childs."

A few months later in the spring of 1981 a small plane, white with blue stripped wings buzzes overhead and circles the quiet "fly-in" community visible from Millers Mill Road in Stockbridge. Berry Hill Airport can best be described as a landing strip with a small hanger that is partially surrounded by modest homes. Most of the residents own small airplanes or work at William B. Hartsfield Atlanta Airport. All have a special connection or attraction to aviation. Berry Hill sits on thirty-three acres and has a 3,000-foot runway. Flight traffic is light at Berry Hill, but out-of-state aircraft do land from time to time.

The plane taxies to the end of the runway and stops in the grassy area away from the other planes perpendicularly parked and tied down along the runway. For some unknown reason, the pilot remains in the plane. After sunset, a homeowner notices the pilot unloading the cargo into a van. As the van speeds away, the plane takes off. The suspicious onlooker reports the incident to the Henry County Sheriff's Department. He is told that an officer is in the area and would investigate the matter.

***

Larry Darwood Tew from Dothan, Alabama is a partner in a small law firm in Stockbridge. His law office is located on Highway 42 in the City of Stockbridge next to The First State Bank. He passed the Georgia Bar in June 1974 and later is elected Henry County Probate Judge. Lawyer Tew represents two clients: Ed Black from College Park and his friend, John Hathorn from Florida, who are in the drug smuggling business, particularly Quaaludes. They are a good team and have made a lot of money. They are careful and go out of their way to cover all the bases. The success of their mission hinges on the cooperation of local officials.

In 1972, Quaaludes are one of the most frequently prescribed sedatives in the United States. Doctors prescribe them to promote relaxation and sleepiness. In some patients it produces a feeling of euphoria. It is the euphoric effect that make it a popular recreational drug. With increased use, it became apparent to doctors that Quaaludes were addictive. The Federal Drug Enforcement Agency now considers Quaaludes a dangerous drug and illegal to possess without a prescription.

Tew says, "Sheriff, the way a lot of people see it, pill-popping and pot-smoking have become commonplace on the college campuses. The kids have money, and they can't get enough of the stuff. I think alcohol is more dangerous than marijuana. There is no law against being intoxicated, but you can go to jail for smoking pot. It does not make sense to me. One day marijuana will be legalized."

His partner, Hathorn, arranges for another shipment and recommends that Black contact an individual named Ron Hoover to find a pilot. Hoover is familiar with rogue pilots who handle such flights without asking too many questions. Hathorn is unaware that Hoover had become an informer for the Federal Drug Enforcement Administration (D.E.A.). When the D.E.A. learns that Henry County officials might be involved, the agency arranges a "sting" operation to catch the conspirators in the act. Hoover recommends a pilot named Charles Overstreet.

On October 20, 1981, Charles Overstreet, Ed Black and Larry Tew meet at the Holiday Inn in McDonough, where it is determined that the cargo has shifted from marijuana and unknown pills to cocaine and Quaaludes. It is not what Tew is expecting, but he is agreeable to assist with the shipment. The trap is now set.

Overstreet begins, "If all goes well, it should arrive on Tuesday, November 3rd. The shipment is being transported by boat from Colombia to Bermuda. I will fly the cargo to Berry Hill Airport. My plane is a 421B twin engine Cessna. It is the fastest Cessna they make, and it can land on the short runway. I will be carrying extra fuel, so I can make the trip without refueling. Since it will be a tight landing, I prefer to bring the plane down when visibility is good, that is during daylight. To not draw suspicion, the plane cannot be unloaded until after dark."

"We are going to provide protection from the time the plane lands until the cargo reaches its destination in Atlanta," Tew replies. "Bill Hinton will make sure none of the locals at the airport interfere. Chief Herschel Childs will be on watch and will es-

Sheriff Jimmy Glass

cort the load to Fulton County. Sheriff Glass will monitor radio traffic and alert me if any police activity is occurring in the area."

On November 3, 1981, the Cessna circles Berry Hill Airport as expected. It is near nightfall, and the airport office is closed. Only Hinton remains in his office working on an appraisal that is due the next day. As planned, Chief Herschel Childs and Larry Tew are there. They know that Overstreet is flying the twin-engine Cessna that is about to land. Childs sits in an unmarked police car at the end of the runway. He is strategically parked out of view from any curious homeowners. Tew is there to pick up Overstreet. They are to meet the buyer's representative in Room 107 at the Best Western Motel on Highway 138 in Stockbridge. There they expect to obtain information about the time and place of the payoff. Childs stays with the plane until the cargo could be unloaded. All is quiet at Berry Hill as the sun is setting behind the tall pine trees that separate homes from the airport. The buyer's representative, Larry Sproat, arrives a short time later and greets Tew and the pilot.

Sproat says, "Yes, after the shipment is delivered, your money will be delivered to a Holiday Inn on Delk Road."

Childs helps Sproat stack the twenty-four pieces of luggage into the rear of the van. Childs follows the van as it exits onto Kittyhawk Drive and heads north. Traffic is light on Interstate 75 and the trip to the Cleveland Avenue destination goes without interruption.

***

Tew and Childs are sitting on a couch, cheerfully conversing with Overstreet. They are confident that they are about to receive more money than they will make on their regular jobs the next six months.

Unbeknownst to Childs and Tew, the plane was loaded with suitcases filled with flour. Overstreet and Sproat are undercover D.E.A. agents. Tew and Childs are the unfortunate victims of a successful "sting" operation. By accepting the manila envelope from Sproat, Tew takes the bait.

Childs nearly collapses from the shock of being arrested. He blurts out, "What will this do to my wife, Elaine? What will the other officers think? How can I ever face my friends and church members again?"

Agent Sproat quickly replies, "You should have thought of that before you started smuggling drugs."

Escorted to an adjoining room and separated from Childs, Tew quickly agrees to cooperate. Tew admits that he, Childs, Glass, and Hinton are all involved in the scheme. Childs also confirms that he and Glass are involved. Tew and Childs agree to make recorded telephone calls to Bill Hinton and Sheriff Glass. The next morning Bill Hinton and Sheriff Glass are arrested.

The trap was set, the bait was taken and now all are caught. The recorded conversation between Childs and Glass seals the case against the Sheriff. It turns out to be very damaging evidence during the trial.

It is surreal to see beloved Sheriff Jimmy Glass escorted in handcuffs to the unmarked black sedan and driven to the federal detention center in Atlanta. It is a day I will not forget. It is Friday, the day before the long-awaited Georgia-Florida football game. Many local Bulldogs fans including myself are preparing to head to Jacksonville to attend the game and partake in what is called the "greatest outdoor cocktail party." Those who get up early to begin their trip, are shocked at The Atlanta Constitution's *front-page headline,* "Feds Arrest 3 Officials in Henry Co."

The drug bust and arrest of Henry County officials make the national news. Federal officials identify those arrested as State Probate Judge, Larry D. Tew, 36; Henry County Police Chief Herschel L. Childs, 43; County Sheriff Jimmy H. Glass, 47; and the former Henry County Commissioner and Manager of Berry Hill Airport, Bill Hinton, 47. A Justice Department spokesman reports at a press conference, "The case against the four prominent Henry County men resulted from six months of undercover work. The accused are not alone. At least forty Georgia lawmen or public officials have been charged with serious drug offenses in the last two years. In North Georgia, Federal Agents are now pursuing hard drug smugglers who are transporting the illegal cargo, by trucks, cars and planes, a more difficult task than chasing the North Georgia moonshine runners in their souped-up Chevys as in years past."

An agent with the D.E.A. was quoted as saying, "These boys were easy targets. The lure of quick and easy money obstructed their sense of right and wrong. It was just a matter of time before they were caught."

I am terribly disappointed that the four gentlemen who I had held in high regard are facing lengthy jail sentences. Larry Tew had married a high school classmate. He and I are active Lions Club members, and his law office is located next to the bank. Bill Hinton is the bank's real estate appraiser. Jimmy Glass' wife Martha, heads data processing relations for Trust Company Bank. She is a regular visitor to the bank and its bookkeeping department. I vividly recall applying for a notary designation at the Henry County Clerk's Office. The application required two Henry County citizens to vouch for an applicant's integrity and honesty. Jimmy Glass and Herschel Childs, who were in the Henry County Courthouse signed my affidavits.

***

On March 8, 1982, Jimmy Glass' drug conspiracy and extortion case goes to trial. The other defendants have pleaded guilty and have agreed to cooperate with the federal prosecutors in convicting Jimmy Glass. The most damaging evidence is the fifteen-second tape recording between Childs and Glass, in which Glass acknowledges the payoff for drug delivery at Berry Hill Airport.

Relying on Sheriff Glass's local popularity, the defense counsel calls many individuals to testify as character witnesses on behalf of Glass. Three of Georgia's most powerful and influential men—Georgia House Speaker Thomas Murphy, ex-U.S. Sen. Herman Talmadge and Georgia Appeals Court Judge Kelley Quillen—all vouch for Glass' good name and character.

Glass does testify in his own defense. One reporter covering the trial is quoted as saying, "In listening to Sheriff Glass defending his actions, is like the Uncle Remus stories of *Br'er Rabbit* and *the Tar Baby*. As Jimmy Glass's attempts to extricate himself from the morass created by the prosecution witnesses, the more he struggles…the stickier things get."

In his remarks to the jury, the prosecuting attorney stated that Jimmy Glass is the man who 'cracked the whip' in Henry County. Herschel Childs referred to Glass as the 'super chief'. Glass had a reputation of losing his temper. "You just don't want to get on the bad side of Glass," he says. "Childs didn't, even when he didn't agree with what Jimmy Glass was doing."

After twelve days of trial and deliberating for eleven hours, a federal court jury of seven women and five men find Jimmy Glass guilty on all counts. These include conspiring to import cocaine and Quaaludes and the use of his office to extort payoff money. Judge Moye sentences former Sheriff Jimmy Glass to thirty-five years in a federal prison and fines him $35,000.

CHAPTER 47 | Jerry Banks' Release:
December 22, 1980

The Georgia Supreme Court overturned Jerry Banks' double-murder conviction and the fast-approaching execution date was suspended. With a new trial anticipated, Banks is moved from his death row cell at the Georgia Diagnostic and Classification Prison to the new Henry County Detention Center—a welcome change if moving from one prison to another can be considered a positive step. His three attorneys had done their jobs. They found witnesses and uncovered facts that Myers had overlooked. The feel-good story of the year makes front page headlines in *The Atlanta Journal-Constitution*. *The Henry Herald* covers the story with two full pages with the news of Jerry Banks' release. The Anti-Death Penalty Groups rejoice over the news. This is a candle-light vigil that will not occur. It has been a rough ride on a rocky road for the now twenty-nine-year-old family man. From here, it should be smooth sailing. After six years and eleven days Jerry is free.

***

Wade Crumbley, Steve Harrison and Buddy Welch rush over to the Henry County Detention Center after they receive a call from Judge Whalen's legal assistant. She eagerly confirms what they had hoped, "Judge Whalen has signed the motion to dismiss the conviction against Banks." They pick up a copy from Sara Taylor's office and deliver the order to the chief jailer with instructions to process immediately. Being Christmas week, the Judge wants to dispense with as much of the Court business as possible. He and his staff plan to be on leave through Christmas and not return until after the first week in January. The depressing business experienced by Judge Whalen in his Court offers little motivation for him to get into the Christmas spirit. But today, the release of Jerry Banks puts him in a holiday mood. A mistreated and almost forsaken inmate has found freedom.

Jerry Banks is told only that the District Attorney Smith is seriously considering not to pursue a third trial. Even if true, he has learned from past experience that promises made by attorneys, do not always materialize. He had been a victim of false hopes too many times. He resigns himself to the fact that it will be next year at the earliest before he can expect a release date, if at all. The reality is he will spend another Christmas Day in jail. "They lock you up in a hurry, but they are slow to let you out," Banks complains.

It is Monday, the 22nd of December 1980, three days before Christmas Day. Jerry is brought to the conference room. To his astonishment his defense team is there waiting for him.

Crumbley begins, "Jerry, Buddy, Steve and I thought that we would surprise you. What do you want most for Christmas?"

Perplexed but without hesitation Jerry exclaims, "I would like to get out of here, go home and never come back to this jail or any jail ever again!"

Enthusiastically, Welch says, "Well, pack your bags and let's go!"

"Oh, my God! You mean now?" asks Banks.

Welch responds, "As soon as you sign the discharge papers. When you are ready, Wade, Steve and I will take you home. Jerry, I have never seen you with such a huge grin!"

It is an emotional visit for all four. To Jerry Banks, it has taken what seems like an eternity to savor this long-anticipated moment. He cannot wait to see Virginia and the three children. They have been married for eleven years. She has not abandoned him, as had many of the other inmates' wives. Virginia has spent many a Sunday after church at the prison's visiting room talking with Jerry. She knows everything about the prisons, the guards and names of some of the inmates. She has learned about the appeal process and Jerry's friendship with the chaplain. She can recite the first question Jerry asks, when she visits. "Tell me about brother Perry, cousin Mamian and what is happening at home."

It was 3:30 p.m. when the car enters Banks' driveway. "The old place needs a little work," he murmurs to himself. "Well, I guess I will have the time to do it, now." Virginia, with the children tagging along, runs out to the car to greet Jerry. Filled with excitement, all are jumping up and down as they surround him.

Felicia says, "It's Daddy! He's home! Is Daddy here to stay?"

"Yes, your father is home for good. He doesn't have to go back," Welch enthusiastically replies.

Each takes a turn sharing hugs and kisses with their misty-eyed and speechless father. Buddy, Steve, and Wade look on and savor the experience. Later Jerry's mother and Perry come by. It is an overwhelming day for Jerry.

***

Jerry has become quite a celebrity. Historically, many have been condemned to die in the electric chair and few have had their sentences commuted to life. But only two in Georgia have had their charges dismissed and were allowed to go home. Jerry Banks is one of them. The baffled detectives now have no new leads, no suspects and an unsolved double murder "cold case" back on their hands. Scott Newell, a reporter from *11 Alive News*, interviews Banks at his home shortly after his release. Jerry is sitting comfortably on the living room couch, relaxed, legs crossed and left arm lying on the armrest of the couch. On the other end sits the reporter holding a microphone. The camera man is only about eight feet away. Jerry Banks notices the blinking red light as the reporter begins talking. He hopes his mother, Nannie Dodson, Virginia's Aunt Opal and all his friends will see him on television.

Newell pointing the microphone toward Jerry, "What was your

reaction when you were told that you were a free man?"

"I can't believe it at first. Mr. Welch assures me that it was true. The guard at Henry County Jail tells me it's a miracle. He said for me to stay out of trouble. He did not want to see me back in his prison," responds Jerry Banks.

Newell asks, "Do you believe it now?"

"Once my lawyers dropped me off at my home and there were no police around, I knew it was for real," answers Banks.

Newell continues the interview, "Do you, Mr. Banks, have any hard feeling or bitterness toward those who put you in prison and kept you there so long?"

"I keep no grudges," says Banks. "In the end I knew it would all work out. The chaplain told me to keep the faith and I did. I am happy to be home. I can't sit here and tell you that I believe in God and at the same time say that I am angry at anybody. People are human, they make mistakes. By being innocent, I was sure I would get out someday."

Newell, looking over his shoulder, says, "I hear some giggles in the background."

"Those are my three young'uns. They say that they want to be on television," proclaims Banks with a grin.

Newell responds, "Bring them out. The television audience might like to meet your family."

"This is Felicia," Banks says as she runs and jumps on his lap. She is eight years old. Right behind her comes nine-year-old Elbert who tells his little sister to move over. He also wants to sit on Daddy's lap. Eleven-year-old Jerry Jr. is the last to come into view of the camera. He shyly stands near his daddy beside the couch. Virginia, who is in kitchen preparing some snacks, does not want to be interviewed and stays out of sight.

The reporter has spent about an hour talking and filming Jerry and the children. On the noon and evening news the next day the story airs on Channel 11. The news story, which also features Buddy Welch, lasts only five minutes. To Banks it is worth every minute. His life appears to be good again.

Many of his old church members, the pastor and old friends come by to share in his joy of freedom. Charlie Tomlinson, who was one of the first patrolman to find Banks standing on the side of the Rock Quarry Road, drops by. Ofc. Tomlinson carries the guilt shared by the other Black officers, who think the department treated Jerry unjustly. He is a compassionate man and feels he personally owes Jerry. He does not know how he or the police department can ever repay him. But he is there to offer whatever support he or his family might need to help Jerry readjust to life outside of prison.

Banks' lawyers, who have personally spent thousands of dollars and countless hours of time to get Banks released, chip in to buy each of the children a gift. Little did they know, Christmas Eve and Christmas Day will be the last joyous days as reality begins to set in for Jerry.

***

Prior to Jerry Banks' entrance into the prison system, he was an immature young man. He had not fully grasped the consequences of dropping out of school and providing for a family. He loved his wife, Virginia, and he enjoyed having the children around. The economic times had reduced his construction work hours and his paycheck. Thus, his family did not have much money. Opal and other family members were always having to help with the household expenses. Nevertheless, Banks was always optimistic that a brighter future was just around the corner.

Today Jerry Banks is a different person. His self-confidence is gone. He is a broken man. The years of close confinement have created a disturbing paranoia. Jerry fears for his life. He perceives that there are people who want him dead. He meets with cousin Mamian Webster who he has not seen since his arrest. Mamian stayed away because he was afraid that sooner or later, he would be implicated in the murders. He did not want to risk facing what poor Jerry was going through. Everyone knows that he and Jerry were close and often hunted together.

Jerry embraces Mamian, "It's good to see you, man."

"I am so sorry for what happened to you," Mamian says. "I was too afraid to come and see you. I thought they might arrest me and put me in jail with you."

Jerry sympathetically answers, "That's okay man. There's nothin' that you could have done for me. I should never have gone hunting that day by myself. Since then, I feel that everything has gone terribly wrong for me."

"Jerry, you have always been right, but that time you should have left and not waited around for the police. That was a mistake," says Mamian.

Jerry says, "Mamian, I need your help. There are people that want to kill me. The Klan wants to hang me. Now that I am out of jail, the same people that killed the teacher and student are going to come after me. There are those in the victims' families that think I should not have gotten released. They hate me and they are looking to get even. And another thing, there are these people at the police station who think I am a threat to them. As long as I am alive, someone is going to investigate those police who framed me. I'm scared."

"Yes, somebody should be punished for what they did to you," says Mamian.

Jerry replies, "I hold no grudges. The Bible teaches that we need to turn the other cheek. I want to put all that has happened behind me. Mamian, what I need is a gun for protection. Can you get me a pistol?"

"I can let you borrow my 38-pistol. Don't ask me where I got it and I won't tell anyone that I loaned the gun to you," says Mamian.

Jerry replies, "I feel better already. I will keep it with me all the time."

"I will give you a handful of bullets for the gun. Don't do anything stupid, Jerry. You don't want to go back to prison," warns Mamian.

CHAPTER 48 | Praise and Condemnation

The annual conference of the Georgia Association of Criminal Defense Lawyers was held at St Simons Island, Georgia. The attendees were comprised of lawyers from all over the State of Georgia. The highlight of the award's program was the recognition of those responsible for Jerry Banks' acquittal. It was a proud moment for all those who participated in the making of the incredible story.

Wade M. Crumbley, Stephen P. Harrison, and A.J. Welch were recognized for their "investigative ability, moral concern and persistent personal efforts." The speaker stressed that they defended Jerry Banks, an indigent inmate, without the benefit of compensation. "On behalf of all the lawyers in the state, we hold you in high esteem for your unselfish actions. Every young lawyer should aspire to follow your example."

Praise should also go to Det. Hart who turned over the secret police file and to all the witnesses named therein who reported their knowledge about King and Hartsfield murders to police. They provided the defense team with the information that helped free Jerry Banks.

***

Still under a black cloud after mishandling the Jerry Banks investigation, the police department's morale is at an all-time low. Henry County's deputies, officers and detectives vow to uphold the law and protect loyal citizens. Nevertheless, law enforcement's reputation in the public eye is severely tainted. A motorist stopped for speeding tells the patrolman, "Your sheriff and chief of police have been accused of drug smuggling and you have the audacity to give me a speeding ticket."

Jimmy Glass is a poor country boy who quit school in the 11th grade to farm and rose to be the most influential man in Henry County. He was always available and personally attended nearly every funeral. His popularity is unmatched in Henry County politics, but his uncanny ability to survive difficult situations finally eluded him.

It may be a small consolation that the two people in charge when Jerry Banks was arrested and incarcerated, are now held in contempt by the law enforcement community. Capt. Sugg Howard, is considered a "fugitive from justice." Mr. Howard managed to disappear in Southwest Georgia and was never required to explain the mystery of the spent shells.

The withholding of key evidence from the defense resulted in Jerry Banks' spending six prejudicial years in prison. Former Sheriff Jimmy Glass claims that he was framed, after being arrested for his participation in a drug conspiracy. Similar words were used by Jerry earlier when accused of Marvin King and Melanie Hartsfield's murders. It is quite a turn of events; Jerry is released from prison and former Sheriff Jimmy Glass is on his way in.

The Jimmy Glass era has come to an end. Gov. Georgia Busbee names Donald Chaffin to succeed him as sheriff.

CHAPTER 49 | A Pending Divorce and
Sudden Tragedy

According to Aunt Opal, after the second trial, Virginia gave
up hope that she would ever have Jerry back. She has been faithful
to her husband and promised that she would wait for his return.
With her responsibilities at work and her demands in raising the
children, she has no time to think about men. But all those years
while Jerry is at Jackson Prison, their visits become less frequent.
She tells people it is too depressing to see him suffer while sitting
on death row. She is still legally married and does not have the
courage to ask for a divorce.

Virginia tells Opal, "I have heard that many of the death row
wives file for divorce as soon as an execution date is set. They say
the appeals' process can take years, but the outcome is always the
same."

"My advice is that you forget about Jerry. He is never coming
home." Aunt Opal responds.

Virginia begins to sob and replies, "I can't do that!"

"If Jerry is any kind of a man," Aunt Opal says, "he would encourage you to find someone to help raise the young'uns. You are
still an attractive young woman. It's time that you start a new life.
Think about the young'uns. They need a father."

Virginia has mixed feelings, but she is lonely. She tells Opal,
"I will pray about it."

***

Opal Lee Phelps

Virginia has been a patient wife. She believes Jerry when he insists that he is not the murderer. When Jerry is transferred back to the Henry County Detention Center for the third trial, she resumes her visits. They are just periodic, and she seldom takes the children. She refuses to listen to Aunt Opal, who is encouraging her to divorce Jerry.

Her devotion to Jerry is challenged by her desire to find a full-time father for her children. There is a handsome man who attends her church who has recently lost his wife to an extended illness. Drawn together by similar misfortunes, a common bond ensues. He is a widower and Virginia is soon to be a widow, unless some miracle occurs at the next trial. He has two children of his own. He is respectful of her, and their conversations always end up in discussion about their children. She enjoys his company and the time with him helps fill the emptiness.

She rationalized that her prospective husband needs not to be a wealthy man. He would have to be a hard worker and aspire to better himself for his family. He should have a high school diploma and have a good job with benefits, unlike Jerry, who never managed to find anything but hourly-paid work.

Virginia envisions that one day, when everything settles down, she would seriously consider remarrying. She and the children would be much better off financially. She could buy new clothes for them instead of relying on hand-me-downs. She would not have to depend on food stamps and the children's free lunches at school. There would be no more sitting in the emergency room for hours with a sick child. With insurance coverage she could go to her family doctor without the embarrassment of not being able to pay the bill.

Then there is the stigma of being married to an ex-con. People are sympathetic toward her, but she knows that in the back of their minds what they are thinking, "How can she stay married to that man? The children need full-time parents. Lord knows, it's time."

Virginia's dreams are postponed when to everyone's surprise Jerry is granted a third trial and later released. Friends had been telling Virginia that once the U.S Supreme Court fails to overturn Jerry's death sentence, the best that Jerry could hope for is a life sentence without parole. In either case Jerry would never be home again. Then, there is a sudden change of events. Several vehicles drive up Virginia's driveway. A member of the defense team opens the rear door and out steps Jerry. Everyone is stunned and in disbelief. No one could have envisioned the drastic change in circumstances.

After sleepless nights and talking with Aunt Opal, Virginia comes to the realization that she and the children are better off without Jerry. She would grant visitation rights, but she needs to restart her life. A separation from Jerry would be difficult, but necessary. She reasons that Jerry also needs a fresh start. Their relationship had gotten off to a rough start. Like naïve kids they married while in high school. Virginia's life was changed forever. With a child to care for, she was never able to finish school or enjoy being a single woman. Her friends were dating and going out. The only man she had ever known is Jerry, her sweetheart and husband. For better or worse their marriage has not been fulfilling as Jerry spent most of his time away from her.

Now that he has been released from prison, she could not bear resuming their fractured relationship. There have been too many disappointments and unhappy moments. Virginia could not endure the sadness anymore. She calls lawyer Wade Crumbley, to discuss the possibility of a legal separation from Jerry.

"Mr. Crumbley, I have been praying over this decision for a long time," she tells him. "Jerry is my school sweetheart, husband and father of my three children. I never expected him to come home. In the meantime, I managed to survive without him. I have been able to raise our children without his support. I am considering a man that would make a good husband and be a reliable provider. He had also lost his mate, not to prison but to illness. I adore his two girls. Since Jerry was sent to prison, he is the only man that I have had any interest in. He gives my life meaning and purpose. I have a part-time job at a nursing home that I thoroughly enjoy. Jerry and I are never going to make it. I am older now and know what is right for me and my family. I am tired of being poor. I am tired of apologizing for Jerry's sins. I need a new life."

Crumbley answers, "I can understand how you feel. I suggest you file for a divorce instead of a separation. You are better off ending your marriage, rather than prolonging your relationship through a complicated separation. I can draw up the papers. It is easier if Jerry agrees and doesn't fight the divorce. A contested divorce gets ugly and takes a while to finalize."

"Jerry is not the same person that I once knew," she says. "At first, he seemed to be happy and adjusting to his newfound freedom. But, on Christmas Day his mood changed. He began acting strange. He was nervous and when the children started picking on one another, as they sometimes do, he began hollering at me and scolding the children. After I criticized his behavior, he began to cry like a baby. Jerry said he was not feeling well, and his mind was not right. He felt depressed. He appeared to be angry at everyone. He mentioned that he might kill himself. I am worried for him. He needs help."

Crumbley: "Let's hope Jerry doesn't do anything drastic," Crumbley tells her. "Virginia, I will call you next week."

***

Jerry Banks spends Christmas at Opal's house. He has no desire to go anywhere. On New Years' Eve, Perry and some neighbors come by. Virginia has picked up some chicken and sides from Kentucky Fried Chicken. Jerry has little to say and stares at the television most of the day. He is drinking from a bottle of whiskey one of the visitors had given him for Christmas.

Later in the evening Jerry complains that he is not feeling well. Virginia tells him, "Take a nap on the sofa." When she is unable to wake him and get him up, she suspects something is wrong.

In his pocket are the remains of empty bottles of cough medicine and sleeping pills. It is the same cough medicine that she had just purchased the day before. Jerry Jr. has a cold and was coughing a lot. She was giving him a teaspoon full before bedtime. It helped him to fall and stay asleep. The bottle is now nearly empty. Jerry must have drunk the rest and mixed the alcohol with the sleeping pills. He passes out and cannot be awakened.

Virginia reads the label, "Codeine, Caution for Adults, No More Than 4 Doses in 24 Hours." A good portion of the whiskey is gone too. "Jerry must have poisoned himself," she utters to herself. "I better call 911."

Perry, who is still at the house, and Virginia follow the ambulance to Henry General's emergency room. The waiting room is full. Unconscious, Jerry is immediately taken to the examining room. The attending physician, Dr. Barlow says that Jerry will recover once his stomach is pumped and its contents removed.

Jerry does awaken and is released from the hospital in the early hours of the morning. He tells Virginia that it was an accident. He said he felt a cold coming on and forgot how much cough medicine he was taking. He does not mention the sleeping pills. Virginia knows he is not telling the truth. He is distraught because she told him earlier in the day that she had met with Mr. Wade Crumbley about a divorce.

Jerry is determined to prove to Virginia that he is capable of being a worthy husband. Several people have offered him jobs. He has not done any work in long time. He has been locked in a cage and gotten lazy but knows he can be a good worker like he was before he went to prison. The man at the asphalt paving company asked Jerry to come back. He likes driving a truck. This time he wants to buy a truck. With his own truck, he thinks he can earn more money hauling rock and crush-n-run from Vulcan's granite quarry in Stockbridge.

***

The First State Bank, chartered in 1964, is owned by local shareholders. It is the only bank in north Henry County and is *supported by the businesses and residents in Stockbridge. After two years teaching at Stockbridge High School, I began employment at the bank in 1971 as its consumer lender. After Jerry Banks' arrest and conviction, I made Virginia several loans to help with her household expenses. After Jerry's release, he approaches me about financing a second-hand dump truck. The $5,000 truck would be used to haul for his new employer, the paving company. The notion of granting a loan to a recently released inmate from the Jackson Prison is contrary to the bank's lending policy. Following serious apprehension, I finally agree to lend the money on the condition his family guarantee the loan. Jerry is pleased and thankful for the opportunity. He said he would get the necessary signatures, furnish title information and return.*

***

In March, Jerry goes to Wade Crumbley's office to sign legal documents prior to the upcoming divorce hearing.

Crumbley tells him, "Jerry what I have here is a document that gives custody of the children to Virginia. She is their mother and has taken care of them for most of their lives. She is better suited to care for them than you are."

"Will I ever be able to see them again?" Jerry asks.

Crumbley says, "Under this agreement you will have visitation rights on week-ends."

"I know I have not been a good father," Jerry says, "But I love my young'uns. Losing Virginia is bad enough, but without my young'uns I have nothin'."

"You are a free man," Crumbley says, "You have the opportunity to begin a new life. Virginia wants a change. She cannot bear the thought that you might get into trouble and end up back in prison again."

Jerry, in tears, says, "I don't know what I am gonna do. I will try to convince her to give me a little time to get my feet on the ground. I just got a promising job offer from M&M Products in Forest Park. With help from you, Mr. Crumbley, I was able to renew my driver's license without any trouble. They want me to drive one of their trucks. I plan to save money and buy me my own truck. I have learned a big lesson. I am no longer that crazy fool that shot Robert Walker. I shouldn't have been accused of killing those other two people. All I want is a chance. People have always taken advantage of me. Virginia is hurting me at a time I need her help and understanding."

Crumbley consoles Jerry as he begins to sob, "Next Thursday, April 1st, is the final divorce hearing. You will have the opportunity to express your intentions and feelings to the judge. Jerry you are an ex-convict. How does that affect your children when they have to explain to their classmates where their daddy had been for the last six years. For the sake of the children, please don't contest the divorce."

***

Jerry leaves Crumbley's office very despondent. When he was sent to jail, Virginia and the children moved in with Opal. Upon Jerry's sudden release there was no room for another adult in Opal's house. Virginia asked Jerry to move in with his mother in Kelleytown, until he could find his own place. She did not feel comfortable having him hanging around the house now that their marriage is about to be legally over.

Jerry wants to talk to Virginia before the hearing. So, Sunday March 29th, he attends church knowing Virginia would be there. When the pastor notices Jerry and Virginia sitting together, he thinks that maybe his prayers for their marriage reconciliation are being answered.

After the service, following her to the car, Jerry begs Virginia, "I want you to take me back. I want you to give me another chance."

Virginia, in tears as she walks away, "I can't Jerry. I just can't. Let go of my arm. You have got to understand!"

Later that afternoon, Jerry heads to Red Oak Road. The 38-caliber pistol goes with him.

Jerry tells the children to go play next door. He says he has some business to talk over with their mother. Unlike Virginia, the family assumes that everything is going well with Jerry. They figure the divorce is probably best for the couple. Jerry and Virginia can be heard arguing and then there is a shot.

Opal tells police, "From my front window, I watched Virginia attempt to run from Jerry. In disbelief I saw Virginia staggering across the front lawn collapsing near my front steps. I ran outside and noticed that she had been shot. Jerry followed Virginia. I yelled. 'Don't shoot no more! Give me your gun!' Jerry said no and yelled back. 'Everything I have in the world has been taken away.' I ran back into house to phone for an ambulance and then I heard a second shot."

Virginia, shot in the back, was bleeding profusely. As Jerry stares at his beloved wife lying motionless on the ground, he points the pistol at his heart, pulls the trigger and fires the fatal shot. In Jerry's back pocket is a letter addressed to Mrs. Phelps. In the body of the handwritten letter is the sentence, "May all of you and God forgive me. If I can't have Virginia, then nobody can."

When the police arrive, they find Jerry and Virginia lying five feet apart. Jerry apparently died instantly. When the ambulance arrives, the EMTs discover Virginia, non-responsive but still alive. Both Jerry and Virginia are rushed to Henry General Hospital. Jerry is officially pronounced dead and taken to W.D. Lemon Funeral Home. Virginia is in critical condition with two life threatening gunshot wounds to her back.

CHAPTER 50 | Jerry Banks' Funeral

Jerry Banks died Sunday, March 29, 1981. Funeral services were held the following Saturday at Bentley Hill United Methodist Church, the church Jerry had attended as a young man. The sanctuary is filled to capacity. Seated on the front rows are the immediate family: Opal Phelps, the three children, his mother, Nannie Dodson and his brothers, Ludie, Jr., and Perry. The members of the defense team, Charlie Tomlinson and many who had grown up with Jerry in Kelleytown are in attendance. There are also strangers who had never met Jerry but came to pay their respects and want Jerry to be remembered as a martyr.

Reverend T.J. Hunter gives a rousing eulogy. Rev. Hunter is a short, corpulent man in his mid-forties. He has a drifting right eye that is very noticeable, a condition that he probably had since birth. When facing him one eye looks directly at you while the other wanders in another direction. Somewhat distracting, as one tries to focus on his sermon. But there is nothing lacking when he is behind the pulpit. Few Methodist preachers in the area can deliver a sermon better than Rev. Hunter.

Following a prayer, Rev. Hunter tells those who came to pay respects, "Jerry is not suffering any longer. The young man was tormented by the injustices bestowed on him by the legal system. It is not fair nor is it just to what happened to our brother, Jerry

Banks. He was no longer of sound mind. He was driven into illness caused by the loneliness and misery he endured while on death row. There is no excuse for what he did to Virginia, but I know that God will forgive Jerry for what he had done. Jerry may have suffered on earth, but he will find peace and happiness in Heaven."

Rev. Hunter then asks everyone to bow their heads as he says a prayer for Virginia. "Merciful God, we ask that you heal

After the release, the Banks family are pictured on their front porch: Jerry, Virginia, Jerry Jr., Elbert, and Felicia Banks

our sister, Virginia. Her time here must not come to an end. She has been faithful to you, Lord, her whole life. She needs to raise her young children. We ask this in your name. Amen."

Rev. Hunter also asks those present to pray for President Ronald Reagan who had been shot the day before in Washington, D.C. He delivers a short message, "God's Commandments forbid violence and murder. There is too much hatred and violence in the world today." There were 'amens' heard throughout his eulogy, but the entire congregation gave the Reverend a rousing 'amen' at the conclusion of his passionate remarks.

Opal Phelps asks herself, "How do I help twelve-year-old Jerry Jr., nine-year-old Elbert and eight-year-old Felicia understand why their Daddy is dead, and their Mommy is lying in a hospital bed and may never come home? The confused young'uns cannot understand, why their Daddy shot their Mommy.' She had been so good to them. Other than me, their Aunt Opal, they now have no one else to look after them.

"They were not close to their Daddy because he had been away for most of their lives. He was in prison. It was hard for them to tell their friends in school and church that their Daddy was in jail. That he was there because he killed some people. I had told the young'uns that their Daddy was never coming home. So, it was an unexpected surprise to see him arrive at the front door three days before Christmas. He was their Daddy and little ones were glad to have him home. Now, after what he has done, their longing for him may turn to hatred. I hope not." Opal ponders the thought. "If he had only stayed in jail and not come home, their Mommy would not be in the hospital."

Little Felicia asks Opal, "Why did Daddy shoot Mommy?" Opal tells her and the two boys, "Your Daddy had a messed-up head caused by being in jail so long, that he didn't know what he was doing. I pray for God to forgive him for what he had done. You young'uns should do the same."

Tragically, Virginia dies from her wounds forty-five days later and is buried next to Jerry at the Bentley Hill Methodist Church Cemetery.

Opal tells the children, "Every day the sun comes up and someone is born. Every night the sun goes down, and someone dies. That's God's plan. The angels came and took your Mommy to heaven. It is the saddest moment in my life to see your sad faces. We all cry together." Jerry Jr. asks, "What are we are going to do?" Aunt Opal says, "Don't fret, your Aunt Opal is going to take care of you."

The death of their loved ones brings Opal Phelps and Nannie Dodson closer together. They have lost Virginia and Jerry who they had raised, but they have the children to perpetuate the memories. Mrs. Dodson accompanies Opal to Bentley Hill Methodist Church cemetery.

Seldom are the victim and the victim's murderer buried in adjoining graves. They take flowers with the intention of placing them on the respective graves. But with Virginia's grave already covered with an assortment of fresh and artificial flowers, Opal opts to place her flowers on Jerry's near-empty grave. After Nannie finished securing her flower-filled vase near the head stone, Opal kneels and gently shoves her flowers into the dirt mound. She whispers under her breath, "I can't forgive you,

Jerry, but you deserve some understanding for your suffering. Twenty-nine is too young to die."

Epilogue

As one approaches the twilight of life, certain memories are indelibly etched in the mind. Certain events that occurred near home and impacted friends and neighbors are never forgotten. Such was the twelve-year period that began with the death of Robert Walker and ended with the conviction and sentencing of Jimmy Glass. Five local people were dead. All were shot between 1970 and 1981. Seven children were without their fathers, three of them without their mother. There was a wife without her husband, parents without their son and daughter. All because of the tragic circumstances that occurred in Henry County. The victims' families had their lives changed forever. For the families of Marvin King and Melanie Hartsfield, the killer or killers were never found.

Law enforcement built a convincing, circumstantial case against Banks. The district attorney and the juries determined his guilt based on his previous felony conviction and by his ill-conceived lies to police about the victim's wallet and the loan of his shotgun. The only physical evidence—the three spent shotgun shells—were probably planted at the scene of the murders. The legal system failed Jerry Banks. Several conscientious citizens stepped forward to inform investigators of what they saw or heard as it related to the murders. Had statements from these witnesses been provided to the juries, Jerry Banks might not have been sentenced twice to the electric chair. Since the information was considered irrelevant by law enforcement, Jerry Banks spent more than six years in prison for a double murder which he did not commit. With his spirit broken and his dreams shattered, he was unable to face the loss of his wife through a divorce. He chose instead to commit suicide to end his misery.

Despite the wrongful verdicts, there were those in law enforcement who investigated the crime and attorneys who tried the case, who did their jobs and attempted to find the truth. Working within a legal system in existence in the 1970s, Charles Tomlinson, Bobby Lemon, Tommy Floyd, Paul Robbins, Ed McGarity, Arch McGarity, Hal Craig, Hugh Sosebee, Sam Whitmire, Andrew Whalen and others should not be blamed for any miscarriage of justice in the Jerry Banks case.

Many of those mentioned in the story continued in their professions and had distinguished careers.

- *Judge Hugh Sosebee served as superior court judge for fifteen years and continued as senior judge. He became a charter member of the Georgia Code Revision Committee and was considered to serve on the Supreme Court of Georgia. He died in 2015 at ninety-eight years of age.*

- *Tommy Floyd, who began working for Henry County law-enforcement in 1971, first as a radio operator, jailer and then investigator, would obtain his law degree and pass the bar. He was appointed assistant district attorney and in 1988 was elected district attorney. He held the position for twenty years.*

- *Paul Robbins remained with the Henry County Police Department and would attain the rank of lieutenant before retirement.*

- *Ronnie Stewart became the director of Henry County's emergency service and taught classes to rescue workers. In 1982 he was involved in a pedestrian accident which left him partially paralyzed. Mr. Stewart spent thirty-six years as the Henry County Coroner until his death in 2005. He was probably the only elected and active coroner performing his duties from a wheelchair. He is remembered as a dedicated and caring civil servant.*

- *John Hudson Myers, Jerry Banks' first attorney, was not heard from until he resurfaced in Birmingham, Alabama years later. Myers was able to get a license to practice law in Alabama and resume his legal career.*

- *Buddy Welch, Steve Harrison and Wade Crumbley, who gathered the evidence and found the witnesses that freed Jerry Banks, continued their law practices in McDonough. Wade Crumbley later became superior court judge of the Flint Judicial Circuit following his brother, Alex. Buddy Welch became a juvenile judge and would head the largest and most prominent law firm in Henry County.*

- *Hal Craig and Arch McGarity who prosecuted Jerry Banks also became superior court judges.*

- *Byron E. Smith the district attorney, who refused to try Jerry Banks for the third time, became superior court judge in the Towaliga Judicial Circuit.*

- *Alex Crumbley, who without his efforts, this incredible story would not have occurred. Convinced that Jerry Banks did not get a fair trial, he refused to believe the State's contention that robbery was the motive. Later Alex Crumbley served in the Georgia Senate for two terms and wrote numerous guest editorials for* The Atlanta Journal-Constitution. *After retirement he received numerous accolades from the Henry Grady College of Journalism at the University of Georgia and the Georgia Bar Association. He was commended in a newspaper article as a fearless advocate for what he believed was right.*

- *Jerry Key and David Clark emerged as heroes. Risking their lives, they were instrumental in the capture of notorious serial killer, John Paul Knowles.*

- *Sandy Fawkes, British journalist, did write about her three-day affair with serial killer, John Paul Knowles. Her novel,* Killing Time, *became a best-seller.*

- *Agent Ronald Angel retired from the G.B.I. In addition to the John Paul Knowles case, he served as agent in some of the GBI's most historic cases including the Alday fam-*

ily murders in Seminole County and the Floyd Hoard assassination in Jackson County. Through his efforts, five members of the Dixie Mafia were convicted for the dynamite-slaying of Hoard.

- *Larry Ellington, an agent for the F.B.I., was instrumental in solving the Atlanta child murders by spearheading the bridge surveillance. It was at such a stakeout that Wayne Williams was captured and later convicted. Accused Atlanta child murderer, Wayne Williams sits in Georgia State Prison. After his assignment in Atlanta ended, he reported to the Chicago Bureau where he participated in a case involving a Chicago bank officer who had embezzled $615,000 and disappeared. Seven years later, he turned himself in, confessed to the crime and disclosed where he buried the stolen money. The accused banker, a bank security officer and four F.B.I. agents, flew to the locations described by the embezzler. In route to a site where the stolen money was buried, the Cessna 411 crashed on approach to Cincinnati Municipal Airport, killing all on board. Larry Ellington was one of those who died in the fiery crash on December 22, 1982.*

***

I am sure not a day passed without Jimmy Glass, Larry Tew, Herschel Childs and Bill Hinton regretting their past illegal acts. Sheriff Glass, sentenced to thirty-five years in a federal prison and fined $35,000, would serve nine years. Larry Tew, the ringleader, received a thirty-year sentence and a $10,000 fine. Herschel Childs and Bill Hinton each received a ten-year sentence and $5,000 fine. Before their arrest none had ever been convicted of a crime. Herschel never smoked a cigarette or touched a drink of liquor. Three hundred people wrote character letters on his behalf. The sentences were considered stiff for defendants who cooperated and testified for the government. Bill Hinton died in prison after serving one year.

Larry Tew did not return to Henry County. Jimmy Glass and

Herschel Childs did and were welcomed by families and accepted by the people in the community. Jimmy, who learned the barber trade while in prison, opened a small barber shop. Herschel began a one-man delivery business of "home-products."

Jerry Banks died before his counterpart Jimmy Glass was convicted for his role in a drug smuggling attempt; posthumous retribution for his imprisonment, perhaps.

On December 18, 1981, members of the defense filed a lawsuit in federal court on behalf of Jerry Banks' children. Nannie Dodson, the Administratrix for the Estate of Jerry Banks, the plaintiff, was seeking $12 million in damages. The defendants in the suit were the former Sheriff, Jimmy Glass, the former lead detective, Phillip "Shug" Howard and a host of detectives, who were involved in the investigation and testified against Jerry Banks at the two trials. The suit also named the governing body of Henry County. The complaint alleged that the intentional omissions of information caused Jerry Banks to be convicted of two counts of murder, sentenced to death, and incarcerated for a crime which he did not commit. Rather than face a long-drawn-out suit, the parties agreed to settle the $12 million suit for $150,000. The trust fund for the Banks children received the funds thanks to Henry County's insurance company.

Both victims' families were able to cope with the loss of their loved ones. The King children all attended college, received their degrees and were successful in their professions. Lee King, the son, followed in his father's footsteps. He became the music director at Smith-Barnes Middle School, the same school attended earlier by Virginia Lemon and Jerry Banks. He and his family became my neighbors when they moved to Margrit Court. Mrs. King remarried and secured a job as a teacher's aide at a local elementary school. Truett Cathy, the founder of Chick-fil-A, befriended the King family and established the WinShape Foundation in 1984, which offers ministries to families and children, who had suffered a tragedy as did the Kings. Charles and Evelyn Hartsfield and their children resumed their lives without Melanie. They later relocated to Rum Ridge Subdivision which adjoins the Broder Farm.

Opal Phelps' "young'uns," as she called them, also overcame their tragic childhoods. Jerry Jr. pursued a career in law enforcement in DeKalb County and Felicia became the first member of the Banks family to receive a college degree.

The "Old Jail" remains. Remodeled into offices and meeting rooms, it has been the home of the Sheriff Department and other Henry County agencies. The most recent occupant was the Henry County Public Defenders' Office. Today it sits empty.

The electric chair, "Old Sparky" located at the Georgia Diagnostic and Classification Prison in Jackson, was retired in 1998, but not before participating in twenty-three executions.

I often travel on Rock Quarry Road. I automatically slow down as I pass the site of the King and Hartsfield murders. No longer the secluded woody spot as it was in 1974, the old roadbed is gone. The area is now filled with offices, townhouses and apartment buildings. Many who live and work there probably have no idea of the tragedy that occurred in their backyard years ago. Perhaps someone should place a marker or a cross in memory of the victims and the grief felt by those left behind.

Jerry Banks had asked to be forgiven for his misdeeds. Forgiveness does not undo the past, but it is a beginning.

About the Author

Hans Melchior Broder, Jr. was born July 6, 1947, in Bern, Switzerland and immigrated with parents and siblings to Stockbridge, Georgia in 1951. He has dual citizenship and speaks Swiss and German. He was raised on the family's dairy farm, where he presently lives and is the oldest of eight siblings. Married to Lyndy Lynberg, they have four children and ten grandchildren. He received a bachelor's degree in Business Administration from the University of Georgia and began his working career as a Business Education teacher at Stockbridge High School in 1969, where he taught Typing I and General Business courses. In 1971 he accepted a lending position with The First State Bank and became its CEO in 1975. He was the Organizer and CEO of Enterprise Banking Company until 2011. With a partner he developed and a managed Rum Creek Golf, a driving range and a nine-hole, par-three golf course. He is a past Chairman of the Henry County Chamber of Commerce and served on several bank, civic organization and church boards, including the Henry Medical Center, Henry Medical Center Foundation, The William R. and Sara Babb Smith Foundation, Camp Fortson and St Philip Benizi Catholic Church.

He is the author of *This Too Shall Pass*, a book about the failure of community banks during the Great Recession, and the causes and consequences. Motivated by the closing of Enterprise

Banking Company in 2011, he takes the reader from his bank's creation to its takeover by the F.D.I.C. The book provides insights and details of the challenges faced by community bankers during that period.

Hans Broder has spent most of his life in Stockbridge, attended the local schools and worked in the community. Many of his neighbors, classmates and bank customers contributed to the events that occurred during the brief period of Henry County. It is these relationships that inspired him to write the book, *May All of You and God Forgive Me.*